Thinner Than
Water

SUE HAMPTON

The right of Sue Hampton to be identified as the
Author of the Work has been asserted by her in accordance
with the Copyright, Designs and Patents Act 1988.

Copyright © Sue Hampton 2015

First published in Great Britain in 2015
Cover by Bryn Lloyd & Shaun Russell

Published by
Candy Jar Books
113-116 Bute Street,
Cardiff Bay, CF10 5EQ
www.candyjarbooks.co.uk

A catalogue record of this book is available
from the British Library

ISBN: 978-0-9931191-0-1

Printed and bound in the UK by
CPI Group (UK) Ltd,
Croydon, CR0 4YY

Dedicated to
Irina Belyaeva and Anna Iskanderov

CHAPTER ONE

From the time she could kick a ball, Kim Braddock knew the score. And in the long mirror where nine-year-old Kim practised her impressions, Mourinho and Wenger soon agreed. Her father, Kris, was bottom of the league and asking for relegation. Not from her life, because he played no part in that. He deserved to be booted off planet Earth – up to some airless ball of rock where he could do less damage.

One night she looked up at a full moon, stuck her thumb on her nose and waggled her fingers.

'Have fun,' she muttered, and as she grinned at the darkness, Kim felt tough.

She told people who asked that she'd never met her dad, but this wasn't true. Even though they'd never had a conversation, Baby Kim must have recognised some kind of blob or smell. Walking Talking Kim was glad she'd forgotten. Her mum Jeanette had stories, told and retold as she grew, but Kris was only in one of them. He'd propped her up in a high chair, and tried to feed her something disgusting from a little jar without bothering to heat it first. So Kim had snatched the loaded spoon and thrown it right back.

All the other stories were about Jeanette's own childhood in Barbados, and the school friends she'd left behind. She'd never bothered to mention meeting Kris in

Southend, where he was playing guitar in a band. Kim had only learned that much from her gramps when he was drunk at a wedding, with Caribbean flowers on his head. But her Auntie Lianna had shushed him and dragged her off to dance.

Kim got the message. Jeanette didn't want to explain Kris any more than she wanted to talk about the anti-depressants she took each day. And Kim didn't want to hear. But that didn't mean she never wondered. On the team, most of the others had dads who cared – at least enough to shout from the touchlines a few matches a season – and Kim often wished she could swap. But she wouldn't wish Kris on her worst enemy, which in any case was him.

Kim collected accents, smiles and hand gestures. Her repertoire was growing. But Kris Braddock gave her nothing to work on. There wasn't a single photograph in the flat, and no footage on YouTube of the wannabe rock star; she'd checked. Kim knew she must have heard his voice (probably protesting, '*Oi! Watch my shirt!*' as pureed chicken flew his way) but that was with ears the size of butterbeans. She'd need a lot more material if her Kris Braddock impression was going to be dead-on, like her Joker, Darth Vader and Voldemort. And sometimes she wished he was just plain dead. End of.

For a while the anger settled. Like the dust under her bed, she left it alone – until the child maintenance stopped.

It was late November. Kim would be fifteen at Christmas and the timing was as terrible as the weather. There was talk of the library closing or being run by volunteers for nothing. Braided hair and jangling jewellery made Jeanette Braddock a wild kind of librarian, but they

2

didn't mean her mood was bright. Not at home, anyway.

'Jeanette!' Kim cried, but still her mum stared down into her mug. 'Fight him!'

Jeanette sat at the kitchen table, looking like she'd shatter into pieces if the phone rang or a siren blared down the street.

'It's the law,' Kim told her. 'You've got rights. Make them hunt him down.'

But by her fifteenth birthday, all the law had done was send more letters. Her mum said they were complicated. Money was getting tighter than Jeanette's tops so it wasn't likely to stretch as far as a ticket for an Orient home game. Kris Braddock might not be there in Kim's life, but now he was back to ruin her birthday by remote control.

'Sorry, hon,' said Jeanette, handing her a parcel much too DVD-shaped for the football boots she'd counted on. Now they'd shot right out of Jeanette's price range. The old pair would have to keep on kicking into another year – with a wobbly stud, a worn toe and a stink to scare off a bin lorry.

'Not the same, is it?' asked Jeanette next day at Christmas dinner, after the first mouthful of budget pudding and fake cream.

Kim's face invaded her mother's space for her own good. 'You don't be sorry,' she told her, like a Tarantino heavy, 'all right?'

Jeanette smiled softly. Kim knew the impression had been too good, without being funny. There was only one person to blame. Thanks to him it was getting harder to make the home audience laugh.

Kim supposed her father must be lying low, like a bug under rotten wood. But some mornings on her way to school, she found herself eyeing every good-looking white man who passed by. *Is it you?* And if any one of them were to shoot her a look of guilt or fear, she'd make a citizen's arrest. If he ran, she'd tackle him. He'd find out the hard way why they called her 'The Crab'.

She didn't upset her mother with the abuse she'd like to throw at Kris. Instead she worked on her impressions, letting the celebrities in her mirror deliver it. The filthiest language was a lot funnier coming from Her Majesty the Queen.

Months later, when Jeanette said she had to give a DNA sample, she used phrases like 'formality' and 'the maintenance business' but Kim guessed why. It was Kris Braddock's latest tactic and he had no idea about fair play. But she didn't want to poke about in her mother's wound and have to mop up blood. So for a couple of days she held back, until they were sitting in a hospital corridor.

'He's saying he's not my father?'

'It's a theory he's had for a while,' said Jeanette.

Jeanette was speaking to the wall when Kim would rather kick it. Was this the limit now? Could she feel any angrier?

'He's sick,' she muttered. 'Not theory. Fact.'

Jeanette gave her a sad smile, and opened a poetry book by women of the world. So they still didn't talk about why Kris had chosen this particular moment to test his stupid suspicions. As Kim checked Facebook she thought of a follow-up question, an obvious one. But she didn't ask it, because the answer was even more obvious. Jeanette was a very moral mother.

'I remember visiting you here with Auntie Lianna when I was about seven,' said Kim. 'What op did you have?'

Jeanette said she'd had a hysterectomy and explained, as if Kim was still seven, that she couldn't have any more babies with no uterus. It might be difficult without a boyfriend too, thought Kim. She couldn't remember any, but she had an idea there might have been one, long ago. She'd found a fair hair on the sofa and fag ends in the bin.

But that might be another wound. Looking at Jeanette, Kim could see she shouldn't have reminded her about losing her womb.

'Were you gutted?' asked Kim. She pulled a face. 'That wasn't meant to be a joke.'

'I was,' said her mum. 'Yes, I was. But I've got you.'

Jeanette's eyes were even cloudier now, so Kim patted her hand and looked back to her phone.

But she didn't suspect just how wrong things really were, not until the first day of the Easter holidays, when she opened the door to find Nelle, her only grandmother, with a suitcase. Her face was shiny, and beaded hair sprang out from under a purple felt hat. A pink flower hung by a thread; dangling from the hat, it looked as if it was wilting, but her gran was full of tense, determined energy. This wasn't the happy, hip-swaying gran who taught her to dribble and tackle on the sand. The line of her mouth was grim.

Normally Jeanette spent the days before Nelle arrived on a frenzied makeover for the flat. This time she hadn't said a word, hadn't cleared out the fridge, hadn't warned Kim at all.

'I got the first flight,' said her gran, kissing both Kim's cheeks but stepping past her before she'd had a chance to make room.

'What's the emergency?' asked Kim.

From upstairs Jeanette cried, 'Mother! I told you there was no need!'

When Nelle kissed them on both cheeks, she seemed braced-up, with no sign of jet lag. Kim supposed the emergency was the child support that had dried up. But unless Nelle had brought a shotgun to fire at Kris Braddock's butt, she couldn't see what she planned to do about it. Better to stay on the other island and post them what she'd saved on the flight. Kim's impression of her little, feisty gran was one of the best in her repertoire, but the real thing gave her a headache. After a week of the brass-band voice, she always wanted to pull the plug.

As soon as she could, Kim slipped away to her room and watched a movie. She felt uneasy but she didn't suspect a crisis with a capital C. Even that night, when she woke in the early hours feeling thirsty, the snatch of conversation she overheard from the kitchen seemed like a puzzle, an annoying one she couldn't work out. Not an earthquake.

'I told you, Mother! It's wrong. I should know.'

'So you say,' said Nelle. Her voice, as it carried up the stairs, was flat and crisp as the tablecloths she spread in Barbados for a family occasion. 'But you don't argue with evidence like that.'

'It's a muddle! It has to be.'

Kim stumbled in for a glass of water. 'What muddle? What evidence?'

Silence thudded down faster than the vertical drop of a theme park ride. After a long pause Nelle said she was talking about Kim's cousin in Barbados.

'He's facing a court case,' she added. No details.

'Right,' said Kim, sarcastically. She showed them her back while she filled her glass.

'It's a long story,' said Nelle, but she didn't get on with it.

Kim ignored them both when they said goodnight. In bed she put down the glass and reran the words. She did the two voices, volume down but the same tones: hurt and accusing.

There was only one explanation, wasn't there? Evidence meant DNA. The results had come back at last, and Kris Braddock's theory was right. He wasn't her dad after all. So he could be drinking coffee outside a café on a Spanish street, or sunning himself on a beach, and nobody, not the police or 'The Crab' herself, could arrest him and make him pay child support. Not if she was someone else's daughter. He'd had the test done to prove it because he didn't want her. But who cared? She didn't want him either.

Ha! Kim wanted to laugh out loud. She went to the window and winked at the moon.

That night she dreamed a different father. He was cheering her on from the touchlines. If they needed a sub, he looked fit enough to join in the game. It was Kim's fault the team lost, because her foul gave away a penalty, and she didn't want to look at her dad in case his head was down. But afterwards he put his arm round her and told her not to feel bad because the tackle was borderline – and anyway, the other girl took a dive. He was a tough dad, but not a hard one. He didn't run on the pitch and badmouth the ref. He took her out for a hot chocolate because he loved her.

When Kim woke, she was sad for a while that the dream dad wasn't downstairs. But whoever her real father really

7

was, he hadn't left her. He just didn't know she existed. So when he did, he might care – more than Kris, anyway.

Kim went to text her friends, but she soon deleted the messages, unsent. This was private and personal, and in any case she didn't know the facts. It was impossible to celebrate without them. Lying on her bed, she began to feel a sense of outrage. She had a right to know.

That lunchtime, she came downstairs to find Jeanette prodding her food as if she had a grudge against it. Nelle sat opposite her, stiff as a skewer.

'By the way,' said Kim, 'I know when two and two make four. I'm not a child. I can deal with it. Assuming my dad wasn't an axe murderer, a perv or a Tory, it's got to be an improvement. It's the best news of my entire life, whatever. Whoever.'

Jeanette looked shocked. 'That's not it, Kim! Not unless I've got dementia at thirty-seven!'

'Then what is it?' Jeanette turned to Nelle. 'See what you've done, Mother!'

Nelle said something about fifteen years being a long time, and that no one should overlook the power of alcohol, but Kim wasn't waiting for them to start again. She left the flat still hungry. Thank God for football training and a ball to kick. But however hard she ran, she couldn't get any closer to making any kind of sense out of things. She must be missing something more than a father.

She arrived home to an almost matching pair of smiles, and Nelle's reassurance that one way or another, things would soon be sorted. Kim didn't know whether to roll her eyes, go back out again or jump around all evening to the loudest hip hop she could find. But her gran offered to buy fish and chips: 'Your favourite, Kimberlie!' Soon she found herself leaning on the wall outside the chippy, eating supper out of the paper.

'It's common,' said Jeanette, who wanted to take it home.

'It's one of this country's proudest traditions!' scoffed Nelle, examining for bones.

Kim ate with her eyes on the food, until she heard a low male voice behind her.

'Are you feeding your brain or your belly?'

It was her favourite male, Brad Pandya, who lived virtually next door, except that he was at university now, most of the time.

'My brain's a healthy weight,' she told him, wiping the salt from her top lip.

Brad smiled and pushed back his super-black hair, which never encountered gel, a stylist or anything else that might tame it – even a comb. His mum was a hairdresser, but she wasn't around to cut it any more. Kim had never asked what happened because she hated being questioned about that kind of thing herself. It made her feel like the fish her gran was pulling apart with her plastic fork.

Now Brad was charming Jeanette and Nelle with a white-teethed smile. 'Ladies!' he cried.

'You not studying, Brad?' asked Jeanette, offering him a chip.

'I've just got home for Easter, Mrs Braddock,' he told her. 'But of course,' he added, deadpan, 'I'm studying hard.'

Nelle asked about his subject, which was Politics. Since he'd started the course, Kim had been watching more of the news and practising her impressions of the Cabinet. Brad was a good audience. He had a funny laugh that sounded as if it was stuck to the back of his throat and trying to pull free.

Kim's friends couldn't understand that she didn't fancy him, and wouldn't either, even if he was straight. She only wanted a brother, and he'd be a very strong candidate – the best. Partly because he was a fantastic listener, and he was proving it now, asking Nelle about Barbados, nodding, responding, posing questions she couldn't wait to answer.

'He's got studying to get home to, Gran,' Kim told her.

But Nelle was playing to her new audience, eyes bright, volume rising. There was only one way to stop her. A fat, salty chip lay stranded on the end of her gran's fork. Snatching the handle, Kim put it out of its misery with a 'Yum.'

'Hey!' said Jeanette.

Nelle raised a pointed finger and narrowed her eyes.

'See you guys, then,' said Brad.

'Suppose it can't be helped,' said Kim.

Watching Brad wave to an old white guy with a stick, Kim realised that now there was someone she could talk to about the big mystery and the DNA. The only person who really knew what she felt about Kris. Or rather, the whole range of things she'd felt, and wanted to feel, and didn't dare feel in case she had to voice them and own up. Kim believed in owning up, even though it had earned her a few detentions. She didn't lie, because it broke the connections between people.

Then she realised something else: she had nothing solid to tell Brad. She was no closer to the truth, the whole truth. And she'd waited long enough.

Jeanette went to bed early and Nelle ran a hot bath. Kim

listened until the clunking pipes told her the taps were finally off. Then she knocked once on Jeanette's bedroom door. She found her mum sitting on the side of the bed. In her long lacy nightie, with a box of tissues on her lap, she looked battered all over like the cod, but on the inside.

'Talk to me? Please?'

Kim sat down next to her. Her mother covered her mouth with both hands. Kim supposed that was a no.

'Jeanette! It's a kind of lying. It's worse!'

'Oh, Kim.' Jeanette put her hand on top of Kim's. 'There's not a lot I can say at the moment, hon, until this mess gets cleared up. But you do have faith in me, don't you?'

'Yes, course!' It was the only option, but what did it mean?

'As soon as I understand myself, I'll explain, I swear to God. I promise, hon. From the start, everything.'

Kim sighed. 'All right.'

What choice did she have?

Sliding into bed, she repeated the last word in her head, just as Jeanette had said it. 'Everything?' When was 'the start'? It was like having a flat pack without the widgets. Or widgets with nothing to join.

It was true that Jeanette always asked Kim whether she'd seen her lock the front door (as soon as they reached the bus stop or tube). But she wouldn't forget a thing like that! When it came to the lyrics of love songs, or every mean, smart-mouthed, outburst Kim had ever come out with, Jeanette's memory was amazing. In any case, even though she wasn't great at saying no, it was hard to imagine her ever being the kind of girl who didn't know how to say it to boys.

But that 'faith' Kim had claimed was a problem. If the results were really a mistake, then Kris was her father after all, and she might have to break his legs.

CHAPTER TWO

The next morning Jeanette pointed to the kitchen calendar as if Kim didn't know the date. Underneath it were the letters *TAT*. Kim just kept on chewing her toast.

'Aren't you glad to be going to Tatiana's?' Jeanette asked. 'Have you two fallen out?'

'No,' said Kim, voice swerving up as if the question was stupid.

But it wasn't. She'd liked Tatiana better at first, when they met at Drama Club on a Saturday back in the days when Jeanette could afford it. Kim had made Tat laugh, and Tat had said she was different from the girls at her school, which was private.

Kim hadn't met anyone posh before, but the novelty had quickly worn off. Six months into their friendship she was tired of *being* the novelty: the working class girl with no money, the friend Tat called 'half and half'. Once she'd been to Tat's house, packed wall-to-wall with the latest technology, she didn't need to go again. Or see any more of her still-married, loved-up parents.

Tat's actress mother picked her up at midday on her way back from an audition. Her car was long, sleek and silver even though she called it her 'runaround'. Kim couldn't face the usual giggly quiz about girls' football – 'Don't your boobs get in the way?' and 'Wouldn't you rather lock legs with boys?' So she kept her eyes on her phone. When she arrived, Tatiana lifted the remote to greet her from the sofa. The TV was so new it still had the smell of an iron turned on for the first time. It was bigger than Kim's kitchen table and thinner than a chopping board.

'Wasn't that your mum?' she asked, as Tat flicked through one image after another.

'Probably. She's such an exhibitionist.'

There seemed to be about five thousand channels, but Tat controlled the hopping. Kim would rather *do* something. In the end it was boredom that burst the lid open. Or maybe Kim just wanted to exist.

'My gran's come all the way from Barbados,' she said, 'because according to the DNA test my dad's not my dad.'

It worked – better than she'd planned. The screen blanked. Already Kim wanted to reach for the remote to bring it back.

'How many men did your mother *have*?' asked Tat, with wide, bright eyes and an excited smile.

Kim swore. 'That's not it!' she cried. 'She was brought up in the church.'

'What do you mean?' asked Tatiana. 'I mean, it's like… biology. She must have had an affair with at least one other white guy.'

'The test's wrong,' muttered Kim, dropping a cushion and kicking it across the room.

'It's never wrong in murder investigations,' Tatiana pointed out. 'You can argue with other evidence, but the DNA is like… hard-core.'

'Well it's wrong now. Mum should know.'

'Well, yeah. She should. But maybe she was like…?'

Kim stiffened. 'What?'

'If you want me to spell it out...' said Tatiana, eyes on the blank TV.

Kim was on her feet. She gave Tat the kind of look she saved for cheats who dived.

'I'm not staying here,' she told her.

'Don't let me stop you.'

Maybe Tat didn't believe her. In any case, she didn't move – except to click everything back, louder and larger than life.

Kim was in the hall and through the door. 'We're a double act,' Jeanette would say, like she did when things were tough. Now there was some kind of shambles that had to be sorted out, and they had to trust each other. Kim decided that whatever her mother said – however hard-core the evidence stacked against – she'd have to believe it. Kris or no Kris.

Kim found the bus stop, but while she waited she realised she'd left her purse at home. Angrily, she started walking – until she found herself somewhere she'd never been in her life. She swore again, at Tat, at herself. There was only one person she was prepared to call: the first name in her contacts list.

'Is that the Two Wheel Taxi Co?'

Finding a sign with a street name, she spelt it for him. Brad didn't mention sense of direction or the need for extra apps on her phone. He just told her to wait in the newsagent's she was facing.

He arrived less than ten minutes later on the old motorbike Kim called Norman the Norton. Tatiana would think the bike was sad, but if she showed her smug, snotty

15

face, she'd find Old Norm had enough revs to mow her down. Brad unstrapped the spare helmet from the back and Kim filled it with her curly hair. Climbing on behind Brad Pandya and holding on to his skinny-boy waist, she thought she'd never been more excited in her life.

The air felt cool against her face. It carried with it the London dust and smells that seemed to lift off the tarmac. Fruit outside a corner shop. Drains being plumbed by men smoking. Exhaust fumes and coffee brewing. There were bumps and swerves and turns that tilted her low, but Kim felt completely safe. Soon Brad was slowing outside the flats.

When he helped her untie her helmet, she realised she'd been smiling all the way.

'Thanks,' said Kim.

'I'll have to call you Damsel,' he said.

'I fly and buzz round ponds?'

'In distress,' he added. 'You all right now?'

She nodded, hoping he'd suggest a cup of tea.

'Your mum will be worried,' he said instead.

Kim couldn't argue with that. But she was in no hurry.

'Send me an email if you like,' Brad added.

'OK.'

Kim noticed the police car parked outside the flats but thought nothing of it. Probably some ten-year-old caught shoplifting again. As she turned her key in the door, she heard a male voice, an official one. She didn't call out. Instead she moved quietly along the hall to the lounge door – but not silently enough. The conversation stopped.

Standing in the doorway, she could see a scene that looked frozen, like a photo in a theatre programme. As well as her mother and her gran, and four mugs on the coffee table, there were two uniformed police officers. One solid, with a Tudor-type beard and moustache. One young and curvy, with a pony tail under her hat. What had Nelle done? Slapped some lads for spitting in the street?

Stepping in, she saw a woman in a business suit and court shoes with little heels. Not her head teacher but the kind of woman with her name on a door. She tucked in her red lips. What didn't she want to say?

Nelle was leaning forward, her ankles crossed, her bare brown feet curling up on the carpet. One hand was on Jeanette's arm.

Jeanette's other hand, the one with three rings on it, was across her mouth. Kim could see the tear-stained skin under her eyes.

'Kimberlie,' said Nelle.

The policeman stood up. Jeanette's hand moved as far as her necklace. She fingered a bead, then another.

'She has to know,' she said, quietly.

'Is it Kris?' asked Kim. 'Is he in prison or something?'

Jeanette looked helplessly at the police officers. 'I don't know how to start,' she said, and began to cry.

'Jeanette?' she asked. 'Mum?'

Her mother tried to swallow a sob but she didn't quite force it down. 'It's hard. There isn't a way…'

'Honey,' said Nelle, 'the police are here because Kris Braddock stopped paying child maintenance and demanded a paternity test.'

Kim didn't say 'You're kidding!' She just waited, but Jeanette didn't seem to want to look her in the eyes. Or couldn't. Her body and breath were shaking.

'Kim, darling…' she began, one hand reaching out

across the room.

'Is he dead?' guessed Kim. She looked at Nelle, half-expecting to see a cop clip a pair of handcuffs round her wrists.

'Sit down, Kimberlie,' said the policeman. 'I'm Sergeant Fry and this is Constable Dubrisky. We need to talk to you about circumstances that are very difficult and distressing – and very unusual indeed.'

'Very rare,' said Constable Dubrisky.

'We've brought the manager of the hospital trust,' the sergeant continued, 'because there's been a mistake.'

'With the DNA test?' asked Kim. She smiled quickly at her mum as if to show that she believed her when no one else seemed to.

The police officers both looked at the suited manager, who tucked the edge of her bob behind one ear. Then Jeanette took one hand in the other and dragged tightly across it, as if she was trying to remove all three rings at once.

'At the hospital, Kimberlie,' she said, quickly, 'when you were born.'

'When I was born?' murmured Kim, her echo faint. This was making no sense.

'The test showed Kris Braddock isn't your father,' Sergeant Fry told her, 'but it also showed that in fact Mrs Braddock isn't your mother after all.'

Nelle reached a hand towards Kim. But she didn't take it. Jeanette's mouth had broken so wide apart that it tore her face open, reshaped it. For a moment Kim hardly knew her.

'Kim,' said Jeanette. 'Kim, come here, love.'

Rising from the sofa, she reached out her arms, and Kim let herself be wrapped. But still the words hung, neither contradicted nor explained. Still Kim couldn't decode them. Not her mother. But she was. Of course she was. Kim clung to Jeanette, but not as tightly as Jeanette clung back. Kim knew these smells, the scent and contours and textures. These were ears she used to pull. This was the head she used to tuck hers under, where it fitted. The hands that tugged her back when a car was coming, or stroked her out of a nightmare.

For a moment she remembered films where someone peeled off a mask that only seemed made of skin. She drew away.

'I don't understand.'

'We believe there was a mix-up in the maternity ward,' said the hospital manager, her throat dry and almost sucking in the words. She coughed. Her eyes watered. 'Two babies born within minutes of each other, and taken to be weighed, and tested, and labelled with their mothers' names, were – we presume – returned to the wrong mothers. Two babies almost the same size, their skin and hair the same colour. Nights can be busy and well, Christmas Eve... We guess the ward was understaffed.'

Kim looked at Jeanette. Shouldn't she have known her own baby? Where was her mother's intuition? If she was too weak and exhausted, wasn't it up to the father to keep his eye on the ball? Where was Kris – having a Christmas drink at the nearest pub?

Then she realised. Still the wrong bed. Wrong mother. Wrong dad. All her life she'd had two other parents in the world, two strangers who would want her back. But who were they? How could she love them?

She looked at Jeanette holding herself together with both arms on the sofa. Did she want her own daughter now, instead of her? Because she, Kim Braddock, was an impostor. Not Kim Braddock at all. Any mother would want the real thing, wouldn't she?

She looked at Nelle, who was telling her to sit down. She wasn't her gran any more – just a woman with crazy clothes, no volume control and a way of walking that pushed the air right out of the way. Nelle's life was no more connected with hers than President Obama's or Rihanna's.

She glanced from Nelle to Jeanette – one stiff with guts and one more of a sponge. But they had the same brown eyes and high cheekbones, because they still belonged to each other. She was the outsider.

All her organs, the ones she'd had to label in Biology, felt contracted or squashed inside her. Her breathing was shallow.

From all sides voices told her to sit down. As if it changed or helped anything. Someone would offer her tea soon.

Where should she be? Did her parents want her? Or were they happy with the other girl, Jeanette's real daughter, who should have been a Kimberlie all along?

The policeman and the hospital manager both had more to say, but Kim found it hard to listen. It was as if the other words were circling, playing again and again. No room for any more.

'So,' finished the manager, 'investigations have been thorough and conclusive. I'm afraid we're satisfied now that there's no doubt.'

'Kim,' said Jeanette, wiping her nose and patting the sofa beside her. 'Sit here, sweetheart.'

'I'm not Kim, though,' she murmured. 'I should be something else. What should I be?'

'But of course you're Kim,' Jeanette cut across. 'And it makes no difference, any of it, because I love you.'

If the last three words were newborn, Kim thought they'd be in little incubators. Hanging on. If she was the director she'd make Jeanette say that line again.

Now the woman who used to be her mother pressed her tightly against her chest. 'It's all right,' she said, almost a whisper. 'It's all right.'

'Yeah,' said Kim, 'I can see that.'

'You're still who you are, honey, and that's yourself,' declared Nelle.

'I don't want a different family,' said Kim.

But she couldn't help picturing the father she'd missed all her life. Did she have brothers or sisters? Both? Maybe she had a mother who was happy – or had been. That would change, like everything else. Any mother would be in shock, even the kind who didn't replay deathbed scenes in movies so she could keep on crying. Were the jokes and impressions ever going to be funny again?

'I need to be on my own,' she said. 'You can carry on without me now.'

'Kim,' said Jeanette, 'sweetheart...' and Kim waited, but what was there to say?

'Love you too,' she told her, and went to her room.

CHAPTER THREE

It was Damon Duvall's ninth birthday, his first in the big new house. That meant another chance to tease his big sister, Fizzy, who had been born on Christmas Eve. Last Christmas he'd counted her present total and pointed out that it wasn't double his, but she shrugged and said that wasn't what maths was for. Fizzy hated being centre-stage anyway. Sometimes he called her 'Angel' because she was such a goody-goody, but it was hard to wind her up. Fizzy was fifteen and had been baptised in a white dress, but he knew angels in pictures didn't have a tummy.

Damon was in his pyjamas, enjoying birthday cake for breakfast. Fizzy always managed to get dressed before him. She was wearing a pink denim skirt and polka dot top, and smelt flowery.

'Want some?' he asked her, mouth full.

'No, thanks,' she said.

So as she spooned her muesli he said, 'Angel!' and stuck out a sticky brown tongue.

Fizzy rolled her eyes.

'Put it away, Damon,' said Laura. 'I keep telling you, darling. In the Bible angels are men.'

'You'd better stop trying, then!' Damon told his sister. 'You'll never *be* one! You could forget your homework – and stick your tongue out!'

'No she couldn't, darling,' said Laura. 'One visible

tongue per household is quite enough, thank you.'

Fizzy smiled. Even with the tongue back in, Damon looked stickier than usual. Chocolate butter icing coated his top lip and clogged the gap between his front teeth when he smiled. Barry had the same gap but Fizzy didn't. She didn't feel like his sister at all. Because it was the Easter holidays, his wild friends were all skiing or on safari, so she didn't have to dread the party until the new term started. But she told him to save some room for The Tandoori Madras early that evening.

'Is Auntie Ro coming?' he asked.

Laura said of course Ro would be there. Fizzy smiled. She loved her white auntie – and she knew the sisters loved each other, even though they disagreed about God.

'With her boyfriend?' she asked.

Fizzy was happy that her aunt had one, even though she was forty-five, but Damon pulled a face, just like he did when there was a kiss on TV.

'I'm glad you haven't got a boyfriend,' he told Fizzy, through a mouthful of cake.

'I don't think Auntie Ro will be bringing Mike,' said Laura. 'We didn't actually invite him. We don't really know him yet.'

Fizzy's parents didn't approve of Mike because he was a humanist, so Fizzy thought that couldn't be as good as it sounded. Barry also said he looked like an off-duty pirate.

'And Fizzy,' added Laura, 'is too young for boyfriends.'

But Fizzy knew lots of girls in her year were 'in a relationship'. Sometimes she thought she was the only one who'd never been on a date. She realised that even if anyone asked – and she wished Michael Conradi would – she wouldn't be allowed.

'The Queen fell in love at fifteen,' she pointed out, 'with Prince Philip.'

Damon laughed.

'Really,' said Fizzy. 'They said so on *The One Show*.'

She remembered Laura telling her not long ago that she was too romantic for her own good, but she loved it when her parents held hands along the High Street. Laura said church couples didn't split up like other people's parents. Fizzy was glad, but it didn't stop the bad dreams.

She knew Barry wanted her to trust the Lord and stop waking up in the night, crying out and sweating. Jesus was perfect, and some of the stories were sad and beautiful, but God felt harder to love properly because He wasn't really a character. She hadn't mentioned that to her parents but she knew Ro would understand.

Once, Fizzy had prayed real, urgent prayers all through a Monday at school. Her Grandma Floella in Jamaica had been rushed into hospital after a brain haemorrhage. But God didn't stop her dying, or even keep her alive until they could fly over to say goodbye. After the phone call to say she'd gone, Barry had stayed in his room without food for all of Tuesday. 'Our faith is so puny,' he said once he came out, as if it was their fault and they'd failed God as well as Floella. But Fizzy couldn't see how her prayers could be weak and useless when she'd prayed so hard, with hundreds of tears.

At church once, as they sang, 'He's Got the Whole World in His Hands', Michael Conradi muttered, 'He shouldn't keep dropping the ball, then.' It wasn't a joke. War, hunger and poverty weren't funny, and Michael was the only one in her Sunday school class who asked questions and didn't seem satisfied with the answers. Once she'd dreamed about him kissing her, even though she didn't know what a kiss felt or tasted like. She'd like to have that dream again.

'Do you feel different now you're baptised?' he'd asked her outside church, after the photos.

'I want to,' she said.

Fizzy wondered when Damon would be old enough to be baptised and whether he'd wear white too. He might like the idea, because of the Michael Jackson moves he showed Fizzy in secret. Barry and Laura didn't let him watch *Thriller* at home, so every time he played with Billy Walsh they put it on repeat until they knew every step. But Fizzy couldn't learn them when he tried to teach her, and she didn't like his ghoul face. Could Barry really have been the same kind of boy?

Damon had finished his cake. He washed his hands and mouth at the sink while Laura scolded, 'Bathroom!'

'Now I'm nine can I play cricket on Sunday mornings?' he asked.

Laura said she couldn't see what difference it made being nine. They went to church on Sundays.

'Granpop was ace at cricket,' said Damon, 'in Jamaica.'

'Not on Sunday mornings he wasn't,' said Laura. 'There are six other days of the week.'

Fizzy smiled but wondered how Laura knew what their Jamaican grandfather did. She grew up with Ro in Harrow.

'I'll read the Bible every night!' he cried.

'You should be doing that already,' Laura told him, giving Fizzy a smile.

Then the post arrived with a thump and Damon ran to collect his pile of cards. He weeded out an official-looking letter for his mother and put it on the end of the table. One of the envelopes in his pile was fat enough to contain a small present. Fizzy watched him grunting as he tore it apart.

'Who's it from?' asked Fizzy, wondering whether it was their Harrow grandparents, who were on a cruise.

But Laura answered, reading the letter: 'The hospital. I don't understand.'

Something about the strangeness of her mother's voice made Fizzy look up to her face. Laura was standing with one hand on the letter and one holding the edge of the table.

'What is it?' asked Fizzy.

'It's just a gift token,' said Damon, tossing aside a shredded envelope, 'for a Christian shop.'

'*Mum*?' Fizzy persisted, ignoring him.

Laura folded the letter back into the envelope.

'Oh, nothing to worry about,' she said, moving to the sink. 'They've made a mistake about something, sent the letter to the wrong person. I'll have to give them a call and sort it out.'

Fizzy watched her mother's back as she bent to wipe the draining board and all around the taps, again and again. Fizzy felt a stirring of doubt that was like panic. If she could see the face Laura had turned away, would it scare her? Was she ill? Should she be *in* the hospital? Laura wouldn't want them to know that, not on Damon's birthday. But Fizzy knew she often worried about things she only imagined. She told herself God wouldn't allow Laura to get sick.

'Do you want your present now, then?' she asked Damon. He'd finished with the cards.

Fizzy fetched the cricket ball, which had taken ages to wrap. She thought better of throwing it across the table and telling him to catch, because of all the china and glass in the house.

'Cool!' he cried. 'Thanks, Fizzy.'

'No googlies indoors!' she told him, proud of her cricket knowledge.

As he scrambled for his trainers, Laura didn't say a word about noise, broken windows, neighbours or his pyjamas. Soon he was banging on the back door and shouting, 'Come and play!'

Fizzy couldn't make excuses on his birthday. They stood at the furthest ends of the garden and practised long throws. Then he insisted that she throw a high ball – 'So I can go after it, and cup my hands like this, and take a catch, the kind that gets replayed on the highlights and goes down in *history*!'

So Izzy threw.

'Noooo!' cried Damon. 'Fizz-zeeee!'

The brand new ball soared over the hedge.

'We've got tennis balls,' said Fizzy, 'somewhere.'

Damon said he didn't see how he could train properly without the right ball. He wanted Fizzy to go next door for the new one, but she said it was probably at the bottom of the neighbours' pond.

'Take a net then,' said Damon. 'Please?'

'Later,' said Fizzy. 'It's early.'

More than once Fizzy had seen Mrs Vince-Jones looking out of her window, examining every inch of her. Their dad said she couldn't work out whether Fizzy was black or white. Damon was darker, his hair really black and crinkly.

No one would know he was mixed-race.

Damon wasn't happy as they went inside. But then the doorbell rang and there was their Auntie Ro. She wasn't wearing her minister's dog collar but a spotty shirt tucked into her jeans. Her hair, which was darker than her sister's but white in places, was fluffier and freer than usual.

'Happy Birthday, Damon,' she said.

She gave him a kiss on the forehead, along with a collection from the joke shop. She said he'd better tuck it away in a secret place and 'use it with discretion'.

'That means be careful who you trick,' said Fizzy.

Ro told Damon she didn't mind being a guinea pig.

'Fizzy's the right shape!' he said.

'Thanks a lot!' said Fizzy.

Ro told him to watch it or she might have to do some magic on him. Then he said it was a cool present. 'I've hardly had *any*.'

'And it's only nine twenty-four,' said Fizzy.

But before nine thirty Laura was leaving with three quick hugs, apologising that she had to pop out 'for a second'. For Fizzy it was hard to feel quite normal inside. What was so urgent that Ro had been called out in a kind of emergency response?

Ro proposed the Common, and as soon as Damon raced ahead on his bike, Fizzy asked her what was going on.

'I really don't know, Fizzy. It might be work, but your mum didn't say.'

'Are you still on your break?' asked Fizzy.

'Sabbatical? Yes, I've got a few months left,' she said, 'but I'm at the prison twice a week now, and I'm still studying. The old brain seems to have developed some holes since I last did any, and anything a bit clever drops straight out again.'

'I know what you mean,' said Fizzy.

'You have to test knowledge, you know, Fizzy, probe and weigh it. Examine it from different angles and feel your way through it. Measure it against the heart.'

Fizzy didn't say so, but she generally put hers on cards with different coloured pens and learned it in time for exams.

A stray football shot towards Ro, who trapped it with one foot. Her arms made for perfect balance as she kicked it back to some boys. Fizzy clapped but Damon was too busy to be impressed. Doing what he called 'stunts' on his bike, he shouted, 'Look!' every few minutes.

It was nice to chat to Ro but not the right time to ask about the deep, mysterious things Fizzy cared about most. She'd been wondering whether souls ever changed, like minds and weight. Now she just wondered where her mother was and how much longer she'd be. After a while Laura called Ro's phone to say she'd been delayed. Fizzy could hear her saying the meeting was taking longer than expected. Then they were both saying, 'Bye.'

'What meeting?' Fizzy asked.

Ro told Fizzy she was none the wiser, but Laura would explain when she got home. Fizzy remembered what Ro had said about her brain. Was she pretending the information about the meeting had dropped out through one of those holes?

No, thought Fizzy, because Ro believed in honesty. In Year Four, Fizzy had asked her about Santa, to get a proper answer. Ro had told her that it was just a fairy tale. But she'd added that she shouldn't let this spoil the magic, because stories helped people to understand what was real. Then Laura had walked back into the room and said some people ducked truth by 'imagining it was fiction'. It was one of her favourite phrases. The sisters had long debates about the Bible, and Fizzy could see they'd never agree.

Now Ro linked arms with her again and they talked about milkshakes. But for Fizzy the morning was in shadow. She had to do some pretending of her own, because there was a question mark she didn't want Damon to notice. Luckily he was far too excited about the big presents ahead. All he kept asking was, 'What's the time?'

But when the answer was 'Just after one' and their mother still wasn't home, he wanted to know why. Ro had no answer, and looked relieved when at last there was the sound of the front door. In the hall Fizzy was surprised to find both her parents arriving together. Even on her Christmas Eve birthdays, Barrington Earl Duvall – as it said on his business card, with all kinds of qualifications afterwards – sometimes worked till five-thirty. And now he was taking the afternoon off! Had he been at the meeting, too? Was it at the hospital?

Whatever had brought his father home, Damon was wild with joy.

'Now it's the best birthday ever!' he said, even before a long package with a handle settled the question of what he would do with Barry that afternoon. 'Or it would be,' he added, 'if Fizzy dared to get the ball from the dragon's lair.'

Fizzy decided that Mrs Vince-Jones didn't scare her half as much as the secret her parents wouldn't share. Maybe they were just waiting for the birthday to end, once Damon had gone to bed.

'All right,' she said. 'I'm going.'

'I'll be off too,' said Ro, kissing everyone and telling Laura to call her.

So Fizzy slipped out with Ro, who started to strap on her helmet. Fizzy waved back, crunched down the drive and knocked on the door that said 'Alhambra'.

Making sure she kept a good posture to help her look confident, Fizzy waited on the doorstep until Mrs Vince-Jones appeared.

When she did, she was squeezing her eyes small. 'Yes?' she asked suspiciously.

Fizzy explained politely, speaking as nicely as her parents wanted her to when she was on the phone to her friends.

'No,' said Mrs Vince-Jones. Her mouth was slack but her eyes felt hard. She folded her arms across her narrow chest. 'I'm afraid not.'

Her lipstick was tangerine. Some of it had stuck to her teeth, which Damon said were false. Fizzy couldn't help but stare for a moment, before Mrs Vince-Jones stepped back, her hand firmly on the edge of the door.

No? *Why*? It felt like a slap. Fizzy didn't know what to say next. Not 'thank you' but not 'sorry' either. She made a sound that wasn't quite 'oh', and as she ran back to her front garden, her eyes began to feel hot and full.

Still astride the bike, Ro was talking on her phone by the gate. She frowned at Fizzy's face.

'She said no?'

Fizzy nodded.

'Wait there,' said Ro.

Two minutes later, she returned with the ball, kissed her

31

cheek again and rode away. Fizzy wished she knew what Ro had said to Mrs Vince-Jones. Then she wished she'd said it herself, whatever it was.

'Hero!' said Damon, when he saw the ball in Fizzy's hand. But he might have been making fun; Fizzy couldn't always tell.

Barry was changing out of his business clothes. Fizzy wondered what he would say if he knew the truth about Mrs Vince-Jones, who hadn't welcomed them when they'd moved in. Maybe there was a racist next-door. Fizzy felt shaken, but she decided not to tell what really happened. It wasn't the same as lying, and it made things nicer, especially on a birthday.

Barry was their Sunday dad now: on show, louder and bigger and more playful than everyone else. Fizzy hoped it wasn't just an act, a way of covering up the secret.

But through the cricket and the phone calls from Jamaica and the cruise ship, she almost stopped worrying. Perhaps it wasn't serious after all. At the Tandoori Madras, Barry seemed to be enjoying his wine and his jokes, laughing a lot with the Harrow cousins and winking at Damon and his best friend, Billy.

'It's *inflated*!' cried Damon around eight o'clock.

He was pointing to his stomach, which was filled to nearly bursting with popadoms, chapatti and biryani, a long tall Coke and pistachio ice cream. Fizzy had to wait until he was in bed and Ro and the Harrow cousins had gone home. Then she took her opportunity.

It was a short question, but the answer was longer than the Creation story. There were vague parts that were hard to understand, but the message was just as clear in the end.

When she was born she had gone home with the wrong parents, and another baby girl had grown up with the life that should have been hers.

CHAPTER FOUR

Brad Pandya hadn't heard from Kim since he'd rescued her on his motorbike – and seen the police leaving the flat. His father claimed to know nothing, even though Brad suspected he was sweet on Jeanette.

'I suppose we'll be told if they want us to know,' he told Brad. 'Aren't you changing?'

They were having lunch with Brad's uncles, aunts and cousins in a smart hotel. He hadn't thought about alternatives to old jeans and a hoodie.

'I washed my hair,' he said.

'Comb it too,' said his father. 'Smart trousers. And a shirt, an ironed one.'

Upstairs Brad delayed the hunt for clothes to meet his father's specifications. Instead, thinking of his mother, he turned on his laptop. For Muslims too, it was a time for family, regardless of crosses, bunnies or chicks. A time when a mother might think of her son.

But the message in his Inbox wasn't from his mum in Birmingham. It was from Kim, and it was the longest email he'd ever sent. It was called 'mega foul up', and it was full of emoticons, none of them smiley.

Brad paused to breathe a few times as he read it but it was the last part that made him saddest, the part with no decorations and no 'noooooos'.

Jeanette says she's still my mum and always will be. But that's not exactly true because she's dying to meet her real daughter (who may not know yet what a rubbish so-called dad she has). My real parents want to meet me. Any ideas what to say to them? Apart from hi.

I've been wondering. You know people love babies the moment they're born, or before, even when they're the size of a comma, just because they're theirs? Does it work when they're five foot eight with a face that looks sulky if there's nothing to smile about? I don't think so.

Hope you're OK.

From the girl who was meant to be Felicity Duvall.
X

Brad breathed out hard and deleted the message. His father was in the doorway behind him.

'Dad, I'll join you later on the bike,' he said. 'I've got to...'

'Whatever it is,' called his dad, 'you shouldn't put it before family, Brad.'

'Family can be a complicated thing,' Brad told him. Sometimes he wanted to shout the word 'Mum' round the house like a swear word, because it might as well have been banned.

'I hope this isn't,' began his father, pausing to give Brad his serious look, 'to do with Kimberlie Braddock?'

'We had that talk, Dad, remember?'

Brad could see from his father's face in the hallway that

35

he hadn't forgotten. His look was sad, a kind of appeal. Then he stepped back from the door. It was where they'd been, a year or more ago, after Brad had bought Kim a coffee and come home to be questioned about 'age difference' and charged with behaviour that was 'inappropriate'.

'You've no worries about me and Kim, Dad,' Brad had told him. 'I'm gay.'

Now, just as then, Brad left with his keys in his back pocket.

'I'll explain later,' he said, conscious that the last time he never had. Mission impossible.

Arriving outside the flat a minute later, Brad heard Jeanette call out from inside. 'Who is it?'

'It's Brad,' he said, 'to see Kim.'

He heard the gran, who wasn't really Kim's, barking the same question like an accusation. He supposed they'd had a lot of official visitors, and not one of them could have been welcome.

The door opened and Jeanette Braddock stepped back to let him in. He'd never seen her without make-up before. It was after eleven but she was still in a bath robe. Normally Jeanette had a full smile; he sometimes thought she kept it on a shelf by the door. But this time she didn't bother to put it on, any more than she'd bothered with daytime clothes or lipstick.

'She'd rather talk to you than a counsellor,' she said. She spoke quietly, but he felt the intensity. 'You're like a big brother to her.'

Jeanette broke off. Brad realised how powerful the words were. Ordinary words with new definitions.

'Take her out for a walk, Brad,' Nelle told him.

Her accent was even stronger and deeper than Brad remembered. She stood at the bottom of the stairs, in a bright green top and a full print skirt busy with parrots.

'*Kimberlie*!' she yelled. With one hand on the banister, she put the other on his arm, shaking her head with big, concerned eyes. 'She's not answering to that name,' she confided. Rather a stage whisper. 'Melodrama doesn't help any of us.'

Kim appeared at the top of the stairs. She was dressed, but carelessly, Brad thought. That was his style, not hers.

'Hey,' she said, quietly.

'Brad's come to take you out for some air,' Nelle said.

Without a word or smile, Kim came down slowly.

'Keep in touch, hon,' said Jeanette, moving into the background, half-way between the door and kitchen.

Kim held up her phone before slipping it into her pocket. Brad could see the strain in her face, replacing the spark. She couldn't have slept. Shock had washed away the familiar things he counted on: light, humour, and enough front when she needed it.

'Come back for lunch,' said Nelle, as Kim trod her way impatiently into old trainers.

'Only when you're hungry, hon,' came from Jeanette. 'Take your time.'

Kim left it to Brad to say goodbye. The door closed and she breathed out, closing her eyes a moment.

'Thanks for coming,' she told him. 'Bit of drama. Not the usual.'

'Yeah,' he said, remembering a few fall-outs with mates and beefs against Jeanette. He picked up a crushed and dirty beer can. There was a recycling bin a few yards further on.

'Not my fault this time,' she said. 'I'm innocent as in blameless, right? But not a victim. I won't be a victim.'

'No way.'

He dropped the can in the hole. It seemed to him that everyone else was blameless too – with the possible exception of the muddled nurse, but she was only human and bound to make a mistake once in a while.

'Can't even blame Kris Braddock,' she said half-heartedly. 'I've tried.'

'Park?' he asked. 'I've got enough cash,' he added, feeling the coins in his pocket, 'for two coffees somewhere.'

'Park's fine,' she said, which wasn't her usual verdict. 'No one to earwig there. Except the earwigs.'

'The beetles are nosier. And the woodlice love a bit of gossip.'

Nothing, not even a smile. It was an attempt at third-rate humour with no bite, safe but lame. This time she was prepared to let it go, but it wasn't much of a tactic. He had no training for this.

They went in through what he called the back entrance, past a smattering of graffiti on toilet doors locked up with rusting chains. The bins, one for rubbish and one for dog owners, were both spilling over. A gust of wind tugged a cider bottle and sent it rolling until Brad picked it up.

'Eco warrior,' she said.

'Someone's got to be.'

'I hate litter,' said Kim. 'It needs a kicking.'

He felt the passion as her voice shook and her mouth tightened around two rows of clenched teeth. Was that what they called transference?

They made their way to the nearest seat. A bent red structure of perforated metal, it was out of place among the trees. Birds and vandals had both targeted it, so it was a job to tell the graffiti from the guano. He wiped away the wetness from overnight rain.

'This place would be all right if people respected it,' he said, looking ahead at the trees and flower beds along the path.

'People don't respect each other,' she said, 'not enough. They've got none to spare for nature – even though trees and flowers do a lot less harm. They're the blameless ones.' She blew out through her nose. 'I'm babbling.'

'Babble away.'

'My blood parents are still married. They might even love each other. That would be a lucky strike.'

Brad smiled. He remembered that counsellors didn't say a lot. The important thing was to be encouraging so that she felt free to talk. Bent over, she crossed her legs at the ankles, her fingers knitting loosely between her knees. She rocked, just once. Then she straightened and looked ahead as if she was daring someone or something to come near.

'The other girl gets a crappy flat and an absentee father who doesn't give a toss. She's the one I feel sorry for – Felicity Duvall.'

'You're allowed to think of yourself too,' he told her. 'And Jeanette.'

'I do,' she said. 'Don't worry. But we're not joined any more, me and her. You know, like that cord that comes from your tummy button. It gets the chop but you know it was there. Well, it wasn't. No connection.'

Brad shook his head. He thought about his mother in

Birmingham, in a home he'd never visited, and wondered what the connection was, really, and why it was so hard to sever. For him, anyway. His mum had cut her own cords, all of them. Except the thin, virtual line that wasn't a vein or an artery, just a tiny thread in the worldwide web. He'd never known why and there must be a reason.

Another story, he reminded himself. It was Kim's he was meant to be helping her narrate, with silences and prompts, and smiles that weren't too big and crass. A car radio threw out the kind of pap Brad thought anyone should be too ashamed to air. Kim's head nodded to its predictable rhythm. Then the driver roared on, leaving no trace.

'That can't be right about you and Jeanette,' said Brad. 'We're not related, but we have a connection.'

'Yeah.'

'Maybe what you think and feel – and live,' Brad suggested, 'counts for more than blood. It's like the practice being more powerful than the theory.'

Kim nodded. 'Pigeons aren't pretty, are they?' she said, as one investigated a greasy red food spill near her feet. 'But maybe we'd like them more if they had a pretty name. Like 'sweetpeach' or 'silvermoon'. People wouldn't eat them then.'

'They'd be in pop songs,' said Brad, 'and Shakespeare.'

'Alas, poor silvermoon,' she said, arms out, 'they cooked thee well.'

They watched the pigeon, which seemed to sense there would be no crumbs and strutted off.

'I know you can't take away fifteen years,' she said. 'Highlight and delete and they're gone. But they're wobbly now. They've got dotted edges, like they're fraying.'

Brad understood. What people had lost, or always lacked, could seem so much bigger than anything they had. Big as a black hole. But the lives they could have had, if circumstances had been different, might only *look* better. They could have been worse. Did these blood parents know how to love like Jeanette?

They both lifted their heads at the caw of a crow bullying a squirrel along the brick rim of a flower border. It pecked at the bushy grey tail, trying to pin it.

'Park rage,' said Kim. Making a fist, she saw them both off with something like a war cry.

Brad grinned. She had something to prove.

'I saw some programme,' she told him. 'There was a painting under the one you could see, and it was there all the time. Better than the one on the surface that covered it. All you had to do was clean off the top layer.'

'Yeah?' Brad waited like a counsellor should, but Kim only breathed deeply. 'I suppose with a painting,' he said finally, thinking better of a reference to the other girls' grass being greener, 'you can't have both pictures. You have to wipe away one to see the other. But you – you and Felicity – you don't have to choose.'

'What do you mean?'

He thought her tone was sharp. She must feel powerless.

'One life or another. Wipe one home and family in order to find the other set...'

His voice trailed away. He had a suspicion that he'd broken the rules, crossed the line. He gave her an apologetic look.

'You mean I can have both?' she asked him. 'But how does that work? It doesn't for you.' She stopped and looked anxious. 'Not the same.'

'No,' he said. For a moment he missed his mother more than usual, almost as if he was eight again and her smells were still lingering around the house.

'I'm glad to get out,' she told him. 'Jeanette can hardly speak in case she blubs. And Nelle's charging around with superglue but everything's still broken.'

Then Kim stood and he could see it was time to move on. Usually she approached walks like fitness training. Today as she ambled, he remembered his old school librarian at chucking-out time, asking, "Have you got no home to go to?"

'People say there's no pressure on me to do anything,' said Kim, eyes ahead, 'but at the same time THEY – my real parents – are entitled to what's theirs, aren't they? I can't refuse to meet them. It's not as if they binned me.' She grimaced. 'But they might want to, once they've seen me.'

Brad scrunched up his nose. 'No way.'

'I might want rid of them,' she said. 'And I might hate Felicity. She might be more spoilt and stupid than Tat and look right down her nose at me.'

Brad knew it sounded as if the two girls didn't have much in common. He supposed it would be like a blind date. If they didn't hit it off, they didn't have to commit to a shared future, did they? He supposed that in practice it would depend on what the adults wanted. Like it always did. Brad was an adult now, although he sometimes forgot.

'I guess there's no handbook,' he said, 'No self-help tips on the Internet.'

Two dogs were barking on the other side of the park, out of sight. Brad pictured them straining on their leads.

One sounded big enough to eat the other. One owner sounded aggressive enough to cheer it on if it tried.

'There's no escape either,' said Kim. 'But I'm enjoying this one while it lasts. Buy me an ice cream?'

'Sure.'

She looked back at the sky, and Brad followed her gaze. It was pale, with light blue patches which the wind was breaking up, marbling and blotting with fast-moving cloud. Everything changed, he thought, every second. The sky, the soundtrack, and the thoughts people didn't always form into words.

'Do you remember when you used to babysit,' she asked, 'and we acted out stories with my bears? Didn't that gravelly Scottish accent you gave Big Ted hurt your throat?'

He nodded, pinning his chin to his chest the way he used to do. 'Och aye.'

Even when she was five, her voices were better than his. They entertained each other for hours, and then he would have to make sure to remember to bundle her up to bed before Jeanette came home. Otherwise she'd find at least one of them bouncing on the sofa.

'I wouldn't like you any better if you were my brother,' she told him as they watched the traffic. 'So that proves something.'

He supposed she meant blood was really thinner than water, not thicker. She wanted all that life she'd lived to count for more than birth. It made sense. But his mother was still his mother wherever she was, always would be.

There was a chance to cross and Kim ran ahead. She was first into the café and lifted the lid on the freezer cabinet.

CHAPTER FIVE

Fizzy had been working on breathing. It let God in deep, where the panic was. She couldn't read anything but it helped to do things quietly. She had drawn up a chart on her laptop, a blank one for the two of them to fill in, headed 'Felicity and Kimberlie'. The rows were a getting-to-know-you idea, like the games Barry and Laura played at parties and church meetings. Of course, if Barry and Laura would let her have a Facebook account, she could ask to be Kim Braddock's friend and look at her wall. In a way, if they weren't her parents, they couldn't ban anything anymore.

Fizzy felt the shock all over again, and it freed more tears. Of course they were her parents. She loved and would always love them, even with a new birth certificate and a new surname.

She felt, though she couldn't say why, that she must focus on Kim Braddock. But maybe Barry and Laura had done that already. They'd switched their attention. That was why they were giving her the space she'd asked them for.

'What's she like?' Fizzy had asked them – stupidly, as if they knew.

They'd thought she meant her birth mother, but she didn't need a new mum. She'd like a kind of sister – as long as this girl didn't hate her for stealing her identity.

She'd seen a picture: a photo from the summer before, of Kim Braddock on a pebbly beach. The sea was as grey as the sky so the resort must have been British. In cut-off jeans, bare feet and a jacket zipped up, Kim wasn't posing or smiling. In fact her mouth was open as if she was objecting.

Damon had suggested she was asking, 'Why couldn't we go to Florida?' and Barry had said they didn't have 'that kind of money'. Then Laura gave him a reproachful look.

Fizzy took another look at the image, which she'd tucked under the Bible beside her bed. She guessed Kim Braddock was probably telling Jeanette to put the camera away. Fizzy always wished she could tell Barry the same. But she wouldn't like it if Kim looked at her that way.

Underneath the picture was another: of Jeanette Braddock, printed onto cheap A4 paper with a cartridge that was running out. According to the note, it was the one from her profile on Facebook, and Fizzy supposed it was the most flattering portrait she had. With her shiny lipstick, long earrings and a bead necklace looping above a scoop neckline, she looked as if she was going to a party. Or, since she had a wine glass in her hand, was partying already. Younger and curvier than Laura, she wasn't pretty exactly, but glamorous.

A Facebook account would let her look, thought Fizzy, help her understand who her mother was. But how could she open one now? She had no name and no life!

Jesus knew her, whoever she was. He was the way and the life. All she could do now was lift it all to the Lord.

Fizzy turned back to the first box in her chart: 'Religion'. Barry and Laura didn't think the word 'Christian' was enough, because not all churchgoers believed the same. Should she put 'Born-again'? It went back to truth and stories, way beyond anything Fizzy understood. But she knew Ro – who gave knowledge a prod and tested it against the heart – had a different way of believing. And that even though Ro was the kindest person Fizzy knew, Barry didn't think her way was right.

Fizzy looked back at the photos. Maybe at this very minute Kim and Jeanette would be looking at her picture too, finding words to fit her face and shape. Why had Laura chosen the annual school photograph? Fizzy didn't think Kim was likely to be impressed by how smart she looked in her blazer, white shirt and tie. Fizzy hadn't asked which picture of themselves Laura and Barry had sent as a way of making the introductions. Maybe the one from the company Christmas party, with Barry in a tuxedo and Laura in the kind of dress you called a gown. But would that be tactless if her blood family didn't have 'that kind of money'?

'She looks more like Mum than you do,' Damon had commented. 'She's skinny.'

'Thanks,' she'd told him.

Laura had said that was nonsense and she mustn't take any notice. Fizzy wasn't sure which part she disagreed with.

It was all right for Damon. He was still his parents' son. He could carry on the same life, using the same names, but for her the labels had been torn away. She watched his face for signs of understanding. Damon was much quicker than her with computer games, but he could be slow at working out consequences. She didn't think he'd seen where things could lead.

Barry thought things could end up in court. She'd heard him the night before telling Laura that the hospital must be held to account. She'd heard the anger in his voice. When he raised his volume, it was usually in church, where he was an elder and sometimes spoke in tongues or made a prophecy. The voice had to be a big one because it was really God talking. Fizzy always tried not to giggle because it seemed so strange that the Lord was speaking through her dad and saying things like 'my people' and 'my beloved children'.

Barry had never called her his beloved child, and now that they both knew she wasn't his child, she wished he would.

Fizzy couldn't ever remember seeing Laura angry. She said that the Lord never gave them anything to deal with in life that they couldn't handle with His help. But Fizzy didn't know what handling this particular thing involved, and she didn't think Laura did either. 'We must keep praying, darling,' she kept saying, each morning and each night.

Fizzy had tried but she didn't know what to pray.

Please, Father, let the mistake be wrong. Make me the right daughter after all. She tried to imagine the DNA swapping over. She had no idea what DNA looked like, but she pictured it whizzing up test tubes like mercury when you put a thermometer in the jam pan, pushing off the stoppers and then pouring into other tubes, the right ones.

No other prayer seemed good enough, but she made do with *Lord, help me not to cry.* Kim Braddock didn't look like the kind of girl who cried. Or the kind of girl who kept a heart-shaped cutting of a boy, not much bigger than a raindrop, in an envelope in her Bible.

Fizzy tore up the profile forms. Kim would think her childish. Some of the other teenagers had stopped coming to church, like Michael Conradi. Fizzy missed his difficult, interesting questions. She could still hear his voice, deeper than other boys', and see his hand next to hers on the table in the hall. A gentle hand. The only other faithful attender over thirteen was Suranne Washington, the most Christian girl Fizzy knew and the one she admired most. They were friends because they had God in common, and silence and dreaminess – even though Suranne's hands sometimes lifted in the joy of the Spirit and Fizzy's wouldn't. Kim wouldn't understand about church. Maybe she wouldn't understand anything about her.

Now Laura was at her door, her shoulder-length hair pinned up to show her long neck. She was wearing Fizzy's favourite perfume.

'Ready?'

'Is it time?'

'Best be off. We're not sure how long it will take.'

'Why can't they come here?' asked Damon, as he trudged across the landing.

'Neutral territory's best, this time,' said Laura.

Fizzy knew that in the First World War, the one with trenches, they called that No Man's Land. It couldn't have been much like Trafalgar Square. But she supposed that even though they weren't armies, or even on different sides, they were meeting to make a kind of treaty.

'All right, darling?' asked Laura.

'Nervous,' admitted Fizzy.

'So am I. That's natural. But keep trusting in the Lord and He'll help us through. It'll be harder for them – for Jeanette and Kimberlie – without faith. We need to pray for them.'

Fizzy didn't answer but followed Laura downstairs.

48

Kimberlie Braddock had grown up with no dad, no faith and not their 'kind of money'. So if there was a swap, not of DNA but daughters, it seemed to Fizzy that her own life would shrink, while Kim's grew bigger. Kim would have – already did have – a new auntie too, the best.

Maybe that was why Barry and Laura had said there was no need for Ro to come along today, although she'd said she'd like to, if it would help. Barry had explained that there were more of them than there were Braddocks as it was, and it might be quite overwhelming for Jeanette and Kim if a whole crowd turned up.

'But I'm a Braddock,' Fizzy had thought. Then she'd realised it made no difference. There were more Duvalls than Braddocks whichever daughter you slotted in to whichever category.

Of course, Laura and Barry had promised that it wasn't like returning a purchase to the shop and exchanging it. But what, thought Fizzy, if that was what Kim wanted to do?

It was time to go but Fizzy lingered a while in the doorway. She looked back into the hallway at the abstract painting of the Resurrection, the South African flowers spiking out like a sculpture from a painted vase, and the rug Barry bought in Peru that was too expensive to walk on. She didn't see what would stop Kim Braddock standing right there and claiming it all: 'This is *my* house and you're *my* parents. This is where I belong.'

Barry reached in to set the burglar alarm, closed the front door behind her and locked it.

The Duvalls had further to go, because they'd just moved into a quieter and greener part of London. Fizzy knew which line Jeanette and Kim would take and how many stops they'd have to Trafalgar Square. Not many. She'd gone online to find out about the area where she would have grown up, and discovered a stringy little park and a Mosque, a secondary school named after St Ignatius, and of course, the hospital that must be held to account. But no church like theirs, not in walking distance.

No one talked much on the way to the tube station, not even Damon. On the platform Barry looked crossly at the sign that told them how long their train would be:

'Seven minutes!'

Laura said that wasn't long but Fizzy could see he didn't agree.

'I'd like to get there first,' he said, and Fizzy didn't like to ask why.

After another long pause, Damon pulled at the hem of Barry's jacket. 'Dad, are you going to tell the Braddocks what God wants?' he asked.

Barry looked as if he was about to answer but didn't in the end. Fizzy saw a small, brief smile on Laura's face.

'Your father doesn't *always* know,' she said quietly. Barry didn't reply to that either.

'Why?' asked Damon.

'All any of us can do is seek His wisdom,' said Barry quickly, looking at his watch.

Damon didn't seem interested in seeking wisdom. He looked around the station.

'Hey, I want to see that film!' he said suddenly, pointing excitedly to a poster, one with an explosion behind a man with a gun. The blonde in the background was wearing shorts and even less on top.

'It's not suitable,' Barry told him wearily. 'Fifteen

certificate.'

Damon's mouth drooped sulkily, but Fizzy could see he didn't really mind. He'd known the campaign was a non-starter. But he was carrying on as normal. Everyone seemed to be ignoring the question of what *she* wanted.

Maybe Kim was like her, she thought, and didn't know what she wanted at all. So far Fizzy hadn't been able to tell anyone, although all the official visitors had asked how she felt and what she'd like to happen. Mostly she'd let her shoulders do the talking, because when she opened her mouth, the words came out cracked.

'Can I call Ro?' she'd asked, as soon as all the visitors had gone, but Laura had said she was at the prison.

'You need to think for yourself, darling,' Barry had told her.

But how could she, until she knew who her parents were and how they lived? Just one thought was clear and didn't shift. Even before she started the chart on her computer, Fizzy had realised how much she wanted Kim to like her, and begun to hope they could be friends. After all, even if they were in the wrong families, they were also in the same boat.

Kim hadn't been to Trafalgar Square for years. The lions seemed so much smaller now. She wouldn't mind sitting on one, like Lucy riding Aslan, except that she wouldn't want to be caught by Felicity Duvall. In her room Kim had looked in the mirror and said that name aloud, like a caption for what she saw. It was the kind of name you expected to read in the credits of a Hollywood movie, and if swapping labels was all that was involved, she'd do it. She already did it every time she became Beckham or Russell Brand, and this time she wasn't changing colour or sex. The rest was like dog shit on a trainer with tread – too messy to handle. Except that she couldn't leave it to either of the mums to make things clean and sweet.

White water gushed from the fountain. Where it thinned cool and clear, the sun shone through. There were lots of tourists taking pictures on their phones. Kim listened, echoing American and Chinese accents under her breath, while pigeons trotted around in their hundreds. Jeanette pointed out a fat one up on Nelson's head.

'No wonder he's blind in one eye,' said Kim. She pretended to be the targeted Admiral staggering as he tried to wipe away pigeon shit.

Jeanette didn't laugh. Nelle's chortle attracted glances. Kim didn't think her grandmother should be there at all, but Nelle had said she'd stand in for Kris in his absence. No one had said whether Kris knew about the meeting, and Kim hadn't asked.

'We're early,' said Kim. 'I said we would be.'

'They'll be here in a minute,' said Nelle. 'No one's late for this kind of appointment.'

'How do you know?' asked Kim. 'Been checking the data, have you?'

She didn't suppose there had ever been a meeting exactly like this in the whole history of the world.

Nelle wasn't wrong, though, because as Kim looked away from the fountain towards the National Gallery, she saw a girl her age with a black man, a white woman and a boy. Heading towards the square, they weren't talking or making eye contact but gazing intently ahead. No smiles.

Kim could almost see their stress zigzagging out like electric current in cartoons. It made her wonder whether the three of them had given themselves away just the same. But what fizzed and hissed out of Nelle was more like hostility.

Kim's hands were in her pockets. As she chewed her gum, she did an impression of a presenter about to go live but way too cool to sweat.

The other girl was shorter than her but wider, and wearing clothes Kim considered too young and too cute for anyone over ten. Those floral Doc Martens didn't come cheap but Kim would choose full-length and black. Behind her, Laura Duvall was taller than Kim had expected, with fairer skin, and sculpted hair the colour of caramel. Elegant. Not an ounce of fat on her. So different from Jeanette that Kim could almost have laughed at the idea that this was her mum.

But it was her father she found herself staring at. Leading the pack in his sharp, polished shoes, Barrington Duvall was as glossy as his name, with smooth skin and hair that gleamed. Kim could tell even before they crossed to the square that he smelt good. But *was* he good, a good man – the kind Jeanette had never found and wasn't sure existed?

She watched him take Felicity's hand. Laura held the boy's, but Kim could see he wanted to pull away. Kim decided he was annoying. That was one thing she could be sure about: she didn't need a nine-year-old brother.

'You're all right, girl,' she heard, and saw Nelle grip Jeanette's arm as if she needed steadying.

'Jeanette,' Kim muttered, wishing her voice didn't sound cross when it was meant to be a prop. 'Mum,' she added, softly.

Jeanette squeezed her hand. 'I'm fine,' she said, and straightened.

The others were close now. Jeanette took a couple of steps towards them. In spite of trying, Kim couldn't see anything on her white mother's face that she could read. Barry started to stride. The girl could hardly keep up. Then he stopped, at arm's length. A pigeon landed in the space between them, so Kim growled and kicked one foot towards it until it hopped off.

Kim looked at Felicity, who was looking back at her with eyes that were bright and a mouth that began a smile. But it wavered and couldn't hold. She stared down at her flowery boots.

'Good morning,' said Barrington Earl Duvall, like an actor stepping on stage and making sure that even the back row could hear.

He held out a hand, and for a moment Jeanette didn't seem to know what to do with it until Nelle nudged her. Kim watched as the adults greeted each other first. 'Hi,' Jeanette was saying, and 'Morning.' Then, when she took Damon's hand, she asked, 'All right?'

Not the best idea, thought Kim, when any of them could have shouted, '*NO!*' She would have liked to yell it herself, because it wasn't Christmas and they weren't family. They weren't even Facebook friends.

Damon Duvall was announcing his own name, one that no one could dispute. But no one took any notice either, even though his middle name was Moses.

Nelle had ended up between Kim and Felicity. 'Say hello, Kimberlie,' she said.

Kim's eyes narrowed slightly as she glanced back. She

wasn't going to take orders from her ex-gran, especially not now. Instead she just looked.

Felicity Duvall opened her mouth and let it hang a moment. 'Hello, Kimberlie,' she said.

A kind of laugh broke out through Kim's nose. The wrong girl was obeying instructions, and maybe all their words had two meanings now.

'All right?' said Kim.

CHAPTER SIX

For a moment Fizzy thought Kim Braddock was laughing at her. But she wasn't. It was the situation. The confusion. She didn't exactly smile, but her look wasn't scary. Not like the mean girls at her school, who liked to hang around in huddles, waiting for people like her. They sneered when she went past, leaving her wondering what was so funny or so 'sad'.

This was a straight, full-on gaze, and it made Fizzy want to avert her eyes again. But this time she didn't.

'I like your...' she began mentally, but remembered being teased in Year Five for comments like that, made to a teacher she loved. Kim Braddock's clothes weren't pretty like Miss Taylor's, but she was slim enough to make tight jeans look cool. Fizzy thought she had street style. In any case, it made her feel as if she had no style at all.

The adults were talking about the tube, how long their journeys had taken, the delays and the bad service.

'Weather next,' murmured Kim, her thumb towards them.

Nelle announced that London Transport was a disgrace – as if she was a speaker on a stage at one of those rallies they held in Trafalgar Square. Fizzy was astonished by her new grandmother. So small but so vivid! She made her English grandma in Harrow look like a sketch or a ghost. Her accent was different from the one Fizzy had heard in

Jamaica: slower and more American, but rounder, firmer and fruitier.

'She only uses the tube ten times a decade,' Kim said. 'You'd think she was adviser to Boris.'

This time Nelle heard. She shot a look at Kim then turned to Laura. 'I live in Barbados,' she said, pronouncing the word proudly.

'That sounds very glamorous,' said Laura.

Fizzy watched Kim's reaction: critical but not as fierce as the grandmother. *Her* grandmother.

'Not so glamorous for the locals who mop the tourists' floors,' said Nelle, tartly.

'Of course,' said Laura. 'I meant beautiful really.'

'I was born in Jamaica,' said Barry, 'but I came to England when I was about Damon's age.'

'That's why he's not a sprinter,' said Damon.

'Who says?' cried Barry, his arms pumping in a running movement. Fizzy fired off a quick prayer that he wouldn't do Usain Bolt's lightning strike, not there, not now, in his Sunday suit.

As a conversation began about how the capital had changed, Kim asked her, 'Comedian, is he?'

Fizzy pictured Barry deadly serious on Sundays and serious on work days, but crazy on holiday, with clown faces and sillier voices. Then he'd chase and tease and whisk Damon up into a kind of frenzy.

'Sometimes,' she said.

'I do impressions,' said Kim, but added quickly, 'I'm not offering just at the minute. Enough of us already.'

Fizzy wished she could think of a talent she could claim that was half as much fun. She drew quite well and could play the piano and the violin, but if she said so it might sound competitive. Which she wasn't, not at all.

'I can run quite fast as it happens,' Kim told Barry. 'I'm in the football team.'

'Is that right?' he asked.

'Yeah,' said Kim, 'it is. I'm a defender.'

Fizzy thought that sounded sci-fi and heroic, but she couldn't think what to say. She wished Barry and Laura would try harder to look impressed. Her new granny nodded forcefully.

'I know we have to get to know each other,' said Kim, 'but we need to sort things out too, you know?'

Fizzy murmured, 'Yes.' Kim had a confidence she never felt. Even when she read in church, one leg shook, and Damon always noticed and asked her why. Kim made her feel like a child.

'As much as they can be sorted,' added Jeanette.

Fizzy realised that her birth mother's eyes were sad now. Not party eyes at all, in spite of the make-up. The smile she gave her was tender. It made Fizzy feel sorry for not loving her instantly and automatically – the way she'd hoped (and feared too) that she might.

'I think getting to know each other may be the biggest part of sorting things out,' said Laura.

'Or at least the first step,' said Barry.

'You can't rush things,' said Nelle.

'Of course,' agreed Laura. 'It will take time.'

Fine rain began to fall, even though the sun still shone and the sky was more blue than grey. Kim didn't seem to notice but Laura said she'd forgotten her umbrella.

Barry turned towards The National Gallery. 'Shall we

relocate?' he asked. 'It's free.'

Remembering that the Braddocks didn't have much money, Fizzy hoped they wouldn't be offended. Kim was looking at the gallery so it was hard to tell.

'There's a café,' said Laura. 'Although I'm afraid it's rather fancy,' she added, her voice trailing away.

'We'll try to remember our manners,' said Nelle, linking arms with Jeanette Braddock.

Fizzy could see her new gran was taking everything wrong.

As they made their way across to the creamy building, which was one of Fizzy's favourite West End places, Damon pointed to the sky. A faint rainbow had formed behind them, fading away at one end of an incomplete arc. There was no perfect symmetry, but it was beautiful all the same.

Surely, thought Fizzy, it was a sign. She expected Barry to proclaim that God was with them, but he didn't say a word. She hurried to catch up with Kim.

'I love rainbows,' she said, and smiled.

But Kim didn't smile back. 'They'd be better without the rain,' she said, leaving Fizzy to work out whether that was a joke she didn't get.

As the stiff glass door to the gallery closed behind her, Fizzy glanced back at the sky. At once the light dimmed and the colours washed away.

The café was full and Damon wanted to go in the shop.

'He has some money left from his birthday,' explained Laura.

'Two hundred and twenty pounds,' announced Damon.

Fizzy gave him a look. He had no tact at all.

'Lucky boy,' said Jeanette, and Fizzy could tell she liked children.

'Indeed!' cried Nelle, disapprovingly. She meant they were spoilt, and Fizzy thought perhaps they were.

Laura asked Kim whether she minded Damon having a quick look around. Even though she answered, 'Why would I?' Fizzy thought she minded everything the adults said. They wandered around with Damon, who picked up all the puzzles and games.

'I don't know much about art,' said Kim.

'I like the umbrellas with paintings on,' Fizzy told her.

'No point,' said Kim. 'You wouldn't see the picture. You'd be buying it for random tall guys who might be passing by. You'd be entertaining basketball players!'

Fizzy smiled. 'I'd like to,' she said, shyly. 'It might help them enjoy the rain.'

Kim grinned. 'Don't let me stop you,' she told Fizzy. 'I'm skint anyway.'

They both watched Damon making his way to the counter with an art kit and an excited smile on his face. Then Fizzy looked around and saw the adults standing a few feet away. Not talking. Not even looking at each other. They were all together, staring at the two of them.

Barry stepped forward. 'Is there anything you'd like, Kimberlie, as a souvenir of a special meeting? Is there something you fancy here?' he asked.

Fizzy could see Jeanette was shocked. Nelle frowned. But Barry might not realise because he was pointing towards the silk scarves and T-shirts.

'That's not necessary, thank you,' said Jeanette.

'We'd prefer it if you didn't throw your cash around,'

said Nelle, 'and try to *buy* Kimberlie.'

Kim turned. 'Kimberlie's not for sale – whoever she is!'

'No,' murmured Fizzy, but it was hardly more than a whisper. And she didn't know who it was for.

'No one's trying to...' began Laura.

'I didn't mean to give offence,' said Barry, his voice smoother than usual, but Fizzy could tell he was shaken.

'Kim has everything she needs,' said Jeanette. 'She hasn't gone short.'

'She's taller than Fizzy,' remarked Damon, pocketing his change.

Fizzy smiled at him, suddenly afraid he was going to add, 'and thinner'.

Kim grinned too. 'You're right,' she told him. 'I am.' She looked at Fizzy. 'We're quite alike, though, I suppose. Hair and eyes. Your nose is nicer.'

'Oh, no,' said Fizzy. Then she smiled. 'Yes, I think we are.'

'It'll take more than a slight resemblance to excuse what happened fifteen years ago,' said Barry.

'People make mistakes,' said Jeanette, and both girls turned, surprised. 'Everyone does. I do!'

Kim put her arm around Jeanette, just for a moment. 'Nah,' she told her, 'only one.'

Fizzy wondered whether Kris Braddock, who didn't pay child support, was the mistake she meant – the big mistake. *Her* father, who wasn't here and who no one mentioned. It hurt to think that she might never see him, and never know whether she might have loved him. He'd made a mistake too, the same kind as the Prodigal Son, and the woman who wasn't stoned to death because Jesus wouldn't throw the first rock. But maybe Kris was sorry and would undo it if he could, like the hospital.

Fizzy watched Jeanette smiling at Laura, a kind smile. Her real mother wore a kind of leopard skin print under her jacket, the kind Laura called *flashy*. It made Laura look drained.

'Of course,' Laura was saying, 'I make plenty – of mistakes, I mean.'

'I do too,' Fizzy said, and smiled shyly at her blood mother. It came out so weakly that it might have been lost if the shop hadn't been in silence. The other customers were as quiet as an audience at a show.

'Yeah, especially on the violin,' said Damon, covering his ears.

'Damon!' said Barry sternly. 'Felicity is making good progress. Grade Three now.'

Jeanette gave Fizzy an encouraging smile and said she'd love to hear her play.

'I wish I could play an instrument,' said Kim. 'I fancy the drums!'

Her drumstick mime seemed to Fizzy quick and right, not overdone.

'Not in our little flat!' said Jeanette. Then her expression changed. 'Our flat's just fine. I didn't mean that the way… No one's asking for anything,' she added. 'Just to be heard. We all need to be heard.'

'And to listen,' said Fizzy.

The silence started to fill with murmurs of agreement.

'Yes, indeed,' declared Nelle. 'Smart girl!'

'It would be easier to talk and listen if we split up,' said Kim. 'Shall me and Fizzy wander off for a bit, find a few paintings?'

Fizzy waited. She wondered whose permission she was asking. Of course if she had asked that question herself, her English would have been corrected: 'Fizzy and I, darling.' But then she saw Kim wasn't really asking at all, but telling. She was moving away, looking at her, as if she expected her to follow.

'I don't see why not, if you...' said Laura, checking with Jeanette, who was nodding, but not quite happy either.

'As long as you stay together and in the galleries,' said Barry. 'Let's say we'll meet you here in half an hour? That's quarter to twelve, no later. You absolutely must be on time because we're not supposed to use phones in here.'

Kim made a playful gesture like a small salute, which Fizzy knew he wouldn't like.

'Quarter to twelve,' Fizzy told him. 'Here.'

She realised she felt almost excited, and relieved too.

'You sure you're happy about that, Felicity?' asked Jeanette.

Fizzy thought it was nice of Jeanette to check how she felt. 'Yes,' she assured her, hoping her smile was as kind as hers.

'Don't be railroaded,' said Nelle.

'I don't railroad!' Kim objected.

Fizzy knew she would have been told off if she'd used that tone herself with Barry or Laura – who stood giving each other anxious glances.

'I think it's a great idea,' Fizzy said, wishing it had been hers. She heard her voice sound firmer now.

'Cool,' said Kim.

They went at once. Turning out of the shop, they hurried

63

towards the escalator, and Fizzy found herself leading, with Kim speeding up to follow.

CHAPTER SEVEN

At the top of the escalator, Kim offered Fizzy some gum, but Laura didn't like to see girls chewing.

'This is so weird,' said Kim. 'They'd put us on the front page of the papers if they knew. Interview us on the TV news.'

'I'd hate that,' said Fizzy. 'They'd ask us how we feel.'

Kim thought she sounded like a softer version of Princess Kate.

'Yeah, and want a soundbite. Don't worry, we're not telling anyone. And the hospital isn't likely to broadcast it.'

As she spoke Kim had a sudden doubt. What if *Hello* magazine offered Jeanette half a million? What if Kris sold his soul (if he had one) for a beer and some crisps?

'Where shall we go? Have you got a favourite school?' asked Fizzy.

'No? What school where?'

'Like the Impressionists? They're my favourites – I like colour.'

'I got that,' said Kim, looking at the floral boots. 'I think it might be in the genes.'

It took a moment to work out what Kim meant, but Fizzy smiled at the idea of three generations all sharing a love of colour: Nelle, Jeanette and herself. Then she felt sorry for Kim, who didn't belong. But at least she seemed more cheerful now that they'd left the adults behind.

'Impressionists then,' said Kim. 'That's me.'

Before Fizzy could say she knew roughly where to go, Kim had targeted a guide in uniform and asked for directions in quite a different voice, very upper-class. The man, who was old enough to be their grandfather, was happy to help.

'Cheers,' said Kim.

'Thank you,' said Fizzy, remembering how Barry hated 'cheers' because life, he said, wasn't a bar.

'Sisters, are you?' asked the man. 'Or twins?'

'Twins,' said Fizzy. She didn't know why she had said it, and was immediately overcome with embarrassment as she wondered what Kim would think. She dared not look at her, half-expecting her to explain the truth to the guide.

In fact, Kim was trying to avoid a giveaway smile. She'd thought Fizzy wouldn't say boo to a goose and now she was telling a barefaced lie!

'Thought so,' said the guide. 'Enjoy the Impressionists.'

As they walked away Kim said, 'Come on, then, twin. This way.'

'I didn't mean to,' said Fizzy, 'but I kind of see us... you know? We've got the same parents after all, in a way, and we were born at more or less exactly the same time.'

Kim wanted to ask what the Duvalls were like – whether her father was really controlling and sexist, and her mother met friends for coffee while someone from Eastern Europe cleaned her house. But it wouldn't be fair to put Fizzy on the spot, and anyway, after the twin thing she wasn't sure she could rely on the answers. Could Fizzy Duvall be a secret nutter underneath all that good behaviour?

She grinned. 'I feel more related to you than *them*,' she

told Fizzy. Kim could see from her tentative smile that she didn't need to explain who *they* were.

'Jeanette seems really nice,' said Fizzy. 'She's more upset than my... than Barry and Laura.' Suddenly she knew why. 'Probably because there's only one of her,' she added. 'Jeanette must be very brave underneath.'

'She hides it well!' said Kim. Then she felt bad. 'She's had it tough.'

Fizzy supposed she'd had an easier life than Kim and Jeanette – so far, anyway. It made her feel guilty.

They were walking without taking much notice of the walls, which seemed to Fizzy disrespectful of the great artists whose work was on display. But it felt good, somehow, to put rooms between the two of them and the adults, and she could tell Kim thought so too.

'Not far now,' said Kim, checking the number under the next doorway. 'No one talks much in here, do they? There's more chat at a funeral.'

Kim remembered when Nelle's brother, Uncle Des, died in Barbados. She began to tell Fizzy the story because it was her family after all.

'I'd just started school and we didn't fly over, but Nelle rang from the party. I could hear the music, and voices in layers, like 3D, so I threw a massive sulk about missing all the fun.' She grinned. 'I can still do that now and then. The coffin was open so people could see and talk to Uncle Des right up to the end, even though he couldn't answer.'

Fizzy grimaced.

'I know!' said Kim. 'They're used to it out there.' She hesitated. Uncle Des was just one of many relatives Fizzy would never be able to catch up on now. And how many aunts and uncles and grandparents had she missed herself?

Kim guessed from Fizzy's wistful expression that she might be drawing the same kind of conclusion, so she didn't add that she also had a grandad buried in Barbados. And she suddenly realised she had no idea who Kris Braddock's parents were, dead or alive. It was a downer. It made her wonder what she could talk about that wouldn't lead in the same direction.

Fizzy had enjoyed the way Kim told the story, with voices, but she didn't like to think about funerals. One of her regular nightmares was about Barry or Laura dying – sometimes both at once. She loved the idea of Heaven, but it was hard to believe it was as real as the skeletons in graves.

'Auntie Ro told us a story,' Fizzy began. 'Oh, I mean, your Aunt Ro!'

'Yeah, yeah, go on,' Kim told her.

'It was the story of an old lady whose husband had just died. A robin came right up close to her when she was in her garden, and seemed to give her such a beady look that she said, "Harry?" and he chirped. The old lady asked Ro if Harry's spirit could be in that bird, before it flew to Heaven.'

Laura had told Ro she should have put the old lady straight, because it was 'quite simply wrong'. And she'd warned Fizzy not to mention the story to Barry. But Fizzy didn't tell Kim that.

'Yeah?' said Kim, narrowing her eyes and nodding, waiting for some kind of punchline. Was this a joke?

'Ro said if something's loving, it can't be bad,' said Fizzy, 'even if it isn't true.'

'Seems wacko to me,' said Kim, grinning. 'I thought you were dead straight, but you're crazy on the quiet, aren't you?'

'I don't mean… I just think…' Fizzy's voice trailed away.

'No, I like it! It's cool.'

Fizzy smiled. She liked the idea of being crazy if it made her interesting to Kim Braddock.

Moving on, they looked at some snowy landscapes dotted with hundreds of Dutch people, and talked about the white winter. Fizzy said she'd been sledging, and skating on the Hampton Court ice rink. Kim started to complain that she hadn't had much winter wonderland fun because Jeanette was moody about getting to work. Then she stopped. She mustn't make Jeanette sound miserable, even though Fizzy would find out about the anti-depressants sometime. And she didn't want Fizzy to think that just because they didn't have a big garden to fill with snowmen, they were what the media called disadvantaged.

Kim had a thought. With Fizzy for a daughter all along, would Jeanette have *been* depressed? The two of them could have been soft and squidgy together and watched weepy movies, eating chocolates.

'Avercamp,' said Fizzy, pointing. 'I remember the artist's name because when Damon saw it he said, 'Can I, Dad – in the back garden, with tents and all my mates and a fire?' but it would spoil the lawn.'

Kim grinned. 'He might not be your real brother, but he's nuts too. Maybe we all are, in different ways.' She looked at the scene, with its huge but tiny cast. 'It's a bit like *Where's Wally*.'

Fizzy laughed.

'Without the Wally,' added Kim. 'Although she looks kind of stupid,' she said, pointing to a flashily dressed girl holding on to a poser of a boyfriend. 'Walking on ice in those shoes. She's a fashionista, no sense. Must be a WAG.'

Kim had to explain that one. She couldn't believe that Fizzy didn't know about footballers' wives and girlfriends.

'I suppose,' she said, 'the space in your head that most girls fill with celebrities is taken up with saints and prophets.'

Fizzy opened her mouth. For a moment she thought Kim's raised finger might tap that head. Now she had no idea what was filling it.

'I'm not making fun, not of you, I swear!' cried Kim. 'They might be dead men with long beards, but people still remember them. Some people anyway. The WAGs get forgotten after fifteen minutes.'

Fizzy recognised where they were now, and led Kim away from the landscapes. As they walked she remembered the conversation about death. Something told her to front the big things – the things that brought them together, and separated them too. Their time was running out and this was their chance without the adults.

But before she could speak, Kim did it for her, as if they were thinking the same thoughts.

'I used to think Kris must be dead,' she said, 'or else he'd want to know me. But he isn't. He's just …' She paused. 'I was going to say a low-life, only he's your dad now. But I suppose you'd better know. Otherwise you might imagine something else.'

In fact, Kim thought 'low-life' was way too generous. Even so, she tried to check Fizzy's face, expecting her to look like she'd just had her legs taken out because that was quite a bad tackle from The Crab. But Fizzy was glancing away, her eyes on a portrait of a woman in lacy black.

Fizzy remembered Ro telling her Jesus loved losers. 'I suppose I don't need a father, really. Not another one anyway,' she said, 'on top of Barry and...' She stopped but knew she must say it, own it. 'Father God.'

She kept walking, perhaps faster, but Kim was keeping up.

'Really?' Kim asked. She hadn't heard anyone talk like this. 'You believe that?'

'Yes,' said Fizzy, with her church voice – not as big as Barry's but stronger than she could make it in school.

Kim tried to keep her mouth from sliding diagonally, like the emoticon. She wasn't sure what to say. *Why not Mother God?* She supposed that if she visited, the Duvalls would want to save her. They'd take her to church the first chance they got, to confess her sins and clap and praise the Lord. Best make sure visits were on Saturdays. But Kim wasn't going to spend time with people who disapproved of her. She hoped Fizzy wouldn't disapprove too.

They'd reached the room they wanted, which was more crowded than the others. Kim might not know much about art, but she recognised some of the paintings around her now. Sunflowers. The Monet bridge that curved. Waterlilies.

'You can go to his garden in France,' said Fizzy. 'I'd like to. It must have been awful when his eyes were too blind to see the light.'

'That'll be what Barry wants *me* to do,' said Kim, and grinned. 'See the light! There's too much darkness, though. It gets in the way.'

Then they looked towards the old chair with the pipe on it.

'Where's Vincent?' Kim joked. Then she considered. 'He's not there, but he's there anyway.'

'What do you mean?' asked Fizzy.

'The chair shows you what he was like,' said Kim. 'Scruffy, lonely and poor.'

Fizzy thought Kim must be clever. She didn't know the facts but she guessed things in a feeling way.

Kim felt quite pleased with herself. Pointing at the sunflowers, she said he'd painted that on a better day. 'When he was trying to get his mojo back,' she added. 'Do you have up days and down days?' she asked Fizzy, guessing they weren't allowed. 'I do.'

'Not really,' said Fizzy.

She'd grown up dedicating each new day to God and thanking Him, whatever had happened, at the end of it. 'Down' would be ungrateful for all His good gifts. But then she realised she wasn't quite being truthful. Valentine's Day, not so many weeks ago: that was an up and down day, too down to tell.

Was she flushed? Kim was giving her a look. She wondered what the Braddocks did on Sunday mornings, and whether Barry and Laura would let her stay with Jeanette if she wasn't a proper Christian.

But did they have any right to stop her doing anything now? And what about their rights – hers and Kim's?

'Van Gogh shot himself,' she said. She wasn't sure why she'd said it, except that maybe she hadn't really forgotten the robin.

'You're kidding.'

'In a cornfield,' said Fizzy. 'It's so sad.'

Kim put an imaginary gun to her head. Wincing, Fizzy

hoped her real father wasn't depressed. Nobody understood Van Gogh when he was alive. She realised that what she'd said about not needing to meet Kris Braddock wasn't true.

'Must have been a really bad day,' said Kim. 'Too much darkness, see? I have those. But don't worry, I wouldn't top myself. I'd rather fight than give up on anything.'

Like identity, thought Kim, but she didn't say it. Fizzy Duvall was innocent and a victim too. She didn't want her crying like her mum.

So Kim talked about a girl at her school, the older sister of someone in her class, who'd dated a guy in a gang, until he was stabbed. Kim kept it simple, no embroidery. It was an old story but telling it to Fizzy she felt it recharge, all its power rushing back. *My world's not as pretty as yours,* was the message, *less pink.*

Fizzy grimaced, and then wished she hadn't.

'Nothing like that at your posh school?' asked Kim.

'No.'

'I keep well clear of the psychos, but most of the boys in my year are all right. I probably scare them.' Kim made a quick Gruffalo face. 'I like the ones who can talk a bit – not just grunt and swear, or strut about like rappers.'

'My school's just for girls,' Fizzy told her. 'Laura says girls work harder with no boys around.'

'Don't learn as much about life, though,' said Kim.

Fizzy thought she might be right and wished she didn't feel embarrassed around boys. Even Michael. Especially Michael.

'I know girls who obsess about their so-called love lives,' continued Kim. 'It's sad. Boys can mess you up if you let them.'

She thought Fizzy looked surprised, probably because she expected to fall in love with a nice Christian boy, have babies and live happily ever after.

'I'm not arm candy, and I'm not doormat material. I don't need a guy to make me feel good about myself. It's still my life, whatever it says on my birth certificate, and I can take charge of it. No one can stop me.' She paused. 'Talk, Fizzy. What about you?'

For a moment Fizzy warmed at the thought of talking about boys. Perhaps she would mention the picture of Michael Conradi at her baptism. He was wearing a sort of blazer and his hair looked glossy.

She was suddenly aware Kim was staring at her. Waiting for an answer. 'I'd like to be a lawyer,' she blurted.

As soon as she'd said it, she realised she didn't exactly know why, except that it was a profession, an important job, the sort that required smart suits and good exam results. Suddenly she didn't think she would fit it at all. She'd rather be a nurse and look after babies – being really careful with the names on their hospital bands.

'I might get into stand-up. With the gang, obviously,' said Kim. She grinned at Fizzy's alarm. 'Not that kind of gang!' she explained. 'Becks, Lenny, Usain and Darcey. I've got forty-two. My repertoire.'

Fizzy smiled. Kim Braddock was someone she could never have imagined.

'I think we should head back,' she said, looking at her watch, 'or we'll be late.'

Kim, who supposed Fizzy was probably grounded for less, asked whether Barry was really strict. Fizzy's shoulders lifted and her mouth pursed. Kim took that as a yes.

'Let's go then,' she said, and looked at her watch. 'If we're fifteen seconds late, I'll say it was my fault. Which it will be.'

Suddenly Kim jerked forward with a big comedy stride. Fizzy followed, giggling quietly. Kim couldn't believe she hadn't heard of Basil Fawlty, Silly Walks or Monty Python. She told her about Jeanette laughing so much she gasped for breath and almost rolled off the sofa.

'I knew we must have something in common after fifteen years of *not* being mother and daughter. Same mad sense of humour!'

Fizzy was glad to know her birth mother wasn't always sad.

Realising she knew the quick route back, she showed Kim the way. Fizzy always followed Barry on the underground blindly, without a glance at maps or signs. This felt different, good.

Her phone rippled a text which she stopped to read – even though it came from 'Mum and Dad' so she could have passed it to Kimberlie.

'In trouble?' asked Kim.

'Yes,' said Fizzy. The message was an order. She felt her stomach drop when she read the word 'now' at the end.

Kim frowned. Jeanette would never be so unreasonable. Once, when Kim had called her 'Squidgy' in a text, her friends had thought it was a mean joke about Jeanette's figure. But she'd meant her softness. That seemed like a quality now.

Kim couldn't imagine how to like the Duvalls, and it was obvious that Fizzy didn't know how to stand up to them. She looked anxious, as if the fun had drained away.

Her Majesty the Queen could have given Barry a royal telling off, but Kim saved it for another time.

Fizzy wanted to tell Kim as they walked that Barry was a good father and love had to be tough sometimes. But she wished he hadn't spoilt things.

'We haven't talked about what we want to happen,' she said.

'Because we didn't want to,' said Kim, 'but you're right. We can't duck it. They'll want to know.'

Fizzy knew, suddenly, and very clearly, and dared to say it.

'I want us to be friends.'

Kim grinned. 'We are,' she said.

CHAPTER EIGHT

From the escalator Fizzy saw Barry outside the shop, looking up at them. She realised how Kim must see him: big and solid, like a polished pillar. Why couldn't he smile? Waving, she willed him to give them a friendly wave back, but he only looked, mouth straight, eyes holding hers.

Then Nelle stepped out of the doorway behind him.

Kim thought Fizzy must register the message in her grandmother's shoulders, lifted and stiff. She looked like a scrum-half ready to take Barry out. But Jeanette, who followed her, wore that pummelled, caved-in look that meant she couldn't speak.

'Excuse me!' barked Nelle, like an accusation, starting to barge past.

He made way first, then said, 'Wait – please.'

His was such a thick, dark voice that Kim thought he might have been a President or a movie star, but Nelle didn't take the slightest notice.

'Kim!' she called, and waved her down off the escalator, which felt as if it had gone into slow-motion.

'What?' Kim asked, looking at Jeanette. 'What's happened?'

'We're going,' said Nelle, as if the gallery staff needed to know. 'We're not staying here to be insulted.' She beckoned again. 'And patronised.'

No, Fizzy thought, looking around, wishing Laura

would appear and smooth everything over. They mustn't let the Braddocks just leave. Couldn't they all get a cup of tea?

Fizzy looked at Kim, who only scowled at Nelle. The two girls stood at the bottom of the escalator and didn't move until someone arriving behind them needed to pass.

'I apologise sincerely for any offence taken,' said Barry, turning towards Jeanette. 'It was kindly meant, in the best interest of both girls.'

'What was?' asked Kim. Looking at Fizzy, she saw her face had frozen with panic.

'There's nothing to talk about,' announced Nelle. 'Come on, Kimberlie. We're leaving.'

'Does Kimberlie have a voice?' called Barry.

Seeing the wide, wet wildness in Jeanette's eyes, Kim had no choice. She linked her arm in hers. Then she looked up at Barry, determined not to feel young or small.

'Yeah, I do. And I want you to back off and stop upsetting my mother.'

She knew Fizzy never spoke to him that way, and it was obvious he didn't like it one bit. Then she heard him from behind.

'Your mother is with Damon.'

The words were so quiet that Kim wondered whether they'd just squeezed themselves out like toothpaste from a crack in the tube. So quiet but cruel that she hoped Jeanette hadn't heard them. She held her arm tightly.

'Bye, Fizzy,' said Kim, and winked back at her. 'Keep in touch.'

'Don't go,' Fizzy cried, and looked to Barry. His gaze shifted and his mouth didn't seem to know what shape to make. 'Dad?' she began. 'Please.'

'Mrs Braddock,' said Barry, forceful again, 'Jeanette, will you give it some thought when you're calmer? You might see it differently. I hope you'll understand.'

Jeanette wrenched round so wildly Kim had to turn too. 'You can't have both of them,' she cried, her voice weak but thickening with feeling, 'just because you've already got everything!'

'What do you mean? Mum?' asked Kim. She thought she did understand. She just didn't believe it. It was too outrageous.

'No deal, Mr Duvall,' said Jeanette.

'Pay your fancy lawyers all the cash you like!' cried Nelle. 'No deal!'

'Mother, enough,' Jeanette told her.

'Talk to Kimberlie, Jeanette,' called Barry.

Kim glanced back. Way behind them, he seemed shorter. Not so much the headmaster now.

Fizzy watched miserably as Jeanette and Nelle walked away. Kim was between them, no longer looking back or winking. Fizzy wanted to call her name, but she didn't dare, in case she didn't even turn.

'Come on,' Barry said.

He sighed and shook his head. But Fizzy could see he was upset too, too upset to speak. They marched on past a queue to the café, found Laura and Damon and sat down. The café was busy, and smelled good, but Fizzy didn't understand how anyone could consider eating now.

Damon's top lip was already shiny, with flakes of pastry attached. 'What?' he asked.

Everything seemed so normal that Fizzy could have

thought the rest had been a dream or a story. For a second she almost wished that it had been. Except then she wouldn't have met Kim Braddock.

Laura said the lemon and poppy seed cake was excellent. 'What would you like, Fizzy? Cappuccino?'

Fizzy said an automatic 'yes'. Damon wanted to know where the others were, but nobody answered at first.

'They had to go,' Barry told him.

'Why?'

Yes, why? Why exactly? Fizzy waited but there was no answer. Laura told him not to eat with his mouth full and asked her whether she'd seen any interesting paintings, any she recognised.

'Yes,' she said. 'Kim's really clever. And funny.'

She could feel the power of Barry's silence beside her.

'I'm glad you and Kimberlie got on well,' said Laura, after a moment's silence.

'Funny how?' asked Damon.

Fizzy ignored him, even though it was something she tried not to do. He used a licked forefinger to attract pastry shavings like a magnet.

'How could the deal be in our interests,' asked Fizzy, her voice not big but growing as she spoke, 'Kim's and mine?'

'We'll talk later, darling,' said Laura. She raised a hand to attract the attention of the nearest waitress.

Barry loosened suddenly, all smiles. They ordered, and Fizzy found herself persuaded to have soup, which her mother called a healthier option than the chocolate brownie.

When the waitress had gone, Barry and Laura talked about whether she was Spanish or Italian, and guessed that the tiny, gold cross round her neck was only a fashion statement, like the beads that tangled it up. Fizzy didn't know how they thought they could see into people's hearts. Hers felt tight and no one seemed to know or care.

'Can't you explain now?' she asked.

'What?' asked Damon.

'You didn't really mean that? You didn't try to buy anyone...' began Fizzy, but Barry cut in.

'I made Jeanette an offer – an offer to put before Kimberlie. We're in a position to take care of her and provide the opportunities she wouldn't otherwise have.'

'Not in your place, darling,' Laura told Fizzy. 'With us, all of us. No one's proposing a swap.'

'She's coming to live with us?' asked Damon, looking horrified.

'You did propose exactly what we agreed?' Laura asked Barry. 'Damon, please, I'm talking to your father.'

'I called it a kind of compensation. They didn't like the word; I suppose it is a bad one. The grandmother hit the roof.'

'You offered to pay Jeanette money to give Kim up?' asked Fizzy, scarcely believing the words – or the way her voice sounded, using them.

'Not at all. Not like that. It was meant to be an offer of help. She's facing redundancy.'

'What's redundancy?' Damon wanted to know.

The waitress arrived with their order. Fizzy waited for the polite smiles to clear again once she'd gone.

'But you did make it clear,' said Laura, 'that she could see Kimberlie whenever she wanted? And Fizzy too? That they could both visit and stay over?'

'Of course!' Barry sounded angry. 'What do you think?

But Nelle didn't let me finish.'

'I'm not surprised,' said Fizzy, and for a second or two she wasn't sure anyone had heard her. Then she saw the adult faces turn to her. She picked up the menu.

'You don't understand, Felicity,' said Barry, 'so it's best not to comment until you know all the facts.'

'But I understand how Jeanette must feel,' said Fizzy.

'Yes, of course,' said Laura quietly. 'So do I.'

'We'll talk properly at home,' said Barry, firmly, and looked for the waitress, then at his watch.

'With me?' said Fizzy.

'Of course,' said Laura, looking at Fizzy's soup. 'That looks lovely, doesn't it, Fizzy?'

Fizzy looked at it through the steam.

'I don't like the smell,' she said.

Kim was angry herself, but Nelle's outbursts on the walk to the tube were so OTT they were almost funny, like Basil Fawlty kicking his car. Scattergun insults sprayed complete strangers around them.

'The sheer arrogance!' she cried.

'They should be ashamed!' came soon afterwards. 'Who do they think they are?'

Kim tried pretending she was nothing to do with the madwoman half a step ahead. Then she realised she didn't have to pretend – she wasn't anything to do with her. No relation at all!

But on the tube Nelle continued, no drop in volume, treating the whole carriage to her opinion of 'Mr High-and-Mighty' 'Mr Flash' and 'Mr Moneybags' and her thoughts about just where he could stick his offer. Jeanette kept shhhh-ing her, and Kim muttered, 'Doesn't her battery ever run out?'

Jeanette was the one with the power cut. Kim glared at Nelle, who was set on making things worse, and realised that what she heard was history repeating itself. Having badmouthed Kris all through Kim's life – in phone calls she wasn't meant to overhear and stage whispers that probably reached Brad's flat – Nelle had transferred all her scorn and fury to the other father in the space of an hour.

'Out of order' didn't begin to cover Barrington Duvall's behaviour. Kim had made it clear what she thought of him. But she didn't want a father she'd only just met to be rubbished and cleared out of her life before she'd had the chance to find out who he really was. He wasn't Nelle's to trash, or Jeanette's either. Why couldn't they let her make up her own mind?

So in the end, just as they stood to make their way off the tube and Nelle declared, 'Thinks he's God Almighty!' as if everyone in the carriage needed to know, Kim muttered, 'Do you mind? That's my dad you're talking about.'

It must have hit the target because Nelle was too angry to reply for a whole second before she said, 'You should be a gymnast, girl, with a flip like that.'

Kim ignored her, stepped off first, and walked on ahead. Not the time or place for a cartwheel.

Once they'd arrived home, Kim offered to get some shopping, just to be alone. But as she walked the same old street and passed the same old faces she'd been seeing all her life but still couldn't name, she wondered whether she really belonged in this place after all. It was her world but only by accident. Only by mistake.

Never had she imagined she could be living on a road lined with trees, where the gardens were bigger than supermarkets and the cars cost more than her mother earned in a year. And no one lurched around in the early afternoon with a cider bottle, or smoked outside the betting shop in baggy joggers that hadn't been washed for a fortnight. The kind of area where people exercised their dogs on Hampstead Heath and knew what pooper scoopers were for.

When she saw Brad come out of the library, she felt guilty. This was his neighbourhood too and it wasn't so bad. People rubbed along all right, people of different colours and faiths. As she watched, Brad looked across to the bus stop opposite, greeting an old black man leaning on a hospital crutch. Or maybe it was the white woman he knew, the one who'd been laughing as the old man made funny faces for her child. A cute-looking mixed-race toddler just like she'd been, Fizzy too.

Kim supposed the Duvalls fitted in where they lived. They had the right jobs, clothes and voices. She'd stand out like a Goth at a garden party.

Brad saw her then and smiled, waving his paperback. He hurried across the road to see her, and offered to carry her bag.

'I'm not a weakling,' she said.

'I know *that*, Atlas!'

Pulling the bag away from him as if he was a mugger, she swung it back and it hit his legs harder than she meant. He hopped and hobbled, gasped and groaned.

'Talk about taking a dive! You're more embarrassing

than Nelle.'

She realised it had been hours since she'd even thought about being funny. Remembering Atlas, she asked who he was. She never felt ignorant with Brad; he taught her things.

'Greek, held up the world,' he said now. 'Muscle man.'

'Muscle girl,' Kim told him, her biceps up and fists tight. It made her wonder whether Fizzy Duvall even *had* fists. Did her throat come with a growl option? Had she ever said 'innit'?

Kim started to tell Brad about the gallery episode, beginning at the end of it with the fight.

'That's terrible,' said Brad, blowing out a puff of air as he shook his head, 'but he must have meant well, I guess.'

They'd been walking as they talked but now Kim stopped. '*What*?'

'People can have good intentions and be rubbish at handling them. Like in Shakespeare.'

'So we'll all be dead by the end.' Kim grabbed her throat.

They'd reached the library and the door slid open with a hiss.

'Should have saved the money and let everyone keep their jobs,' she remarked as they walked through. She gave the librarians smiles as automatic as the doors, and felt a fake – because if anyone got laid off, she hoped it would be them, any of them.

Apart from the spaceship doors, it was a shabby old place, but Kim liked the smell of books and wood. When she was small she'd spent hours on the Story Carpet. Elmer the elephant's colours weren't so bright now and might be soaked through with drool and worse. At the foot end of the rug, some kids were grouped with their mums. Kim looked around but there wasn't one dad in the place – not with a child, anyway. A few men were on the computers and at least one of them had been drinking. One of them wasn't clean. She recognised the Special Needs guy who memorised timetables and sometimes stood at the bus stop reciting them.

'I don't like Barrington,' she told Brad, sitting down on Elmer's trunk. 'I've got two fathers and I wouldn't want to spend time with either of them.'

'You don't know the Duvalls yet,' said Brad. 'First impressions can be wrong. I thought *you* were dead hard.'

'I *am* hard,' said Kim, making a fist of her face. 'Bit obvious, innit? That I'm with the wrong mother?'

He smiled. 'No comment.'

She told Brad she remembered Jeanette being happier when she was small. 'You know she got depression after the hysterectomy?'

Brad nodded.

'But before that she was more fun, wasn't she? I mean, not all soggy,' continued Kim. 'I was remembering staying with you for weekends so she could go away.'

'When my mum was around, yeah,' he said.

'And I spent a whole summer in Barbados without her once. Why was that? She wasn't ill then.'

Brad shrugged. He wasn't sure he'd ever known.

'I like Fizzy, though,' Kim told him. 'She's got promise. She's way too nice, but maybe this mess will put a stop to that.'

Kim's bag of shopping tried to fall and spill, but she caught it between her legs. One of the toddlers watched her intently. She gave him a crazy, silent movie wave, noticing that a string of dribble connected him to the board book he clutched. For a moment she thought he was going to howl. But then he laughed, waddled over and presented her with the book. At which point his mum whisked him up – as if she had been about to bundle him into a sack and run for the nearest exit.

Kim might have shown her the finger, but the child was still waving at her over his mother's shoulder.

'I'm who I am, Brad, even if that's not who I'm meant to be.'

'They don't have to change you.'

'They'd want to. They'd try.'

'Good luck to them!'

Brad always took the sting out of things. Inside her head it all felt cooler now. She asked him if he could take care of the whole case like a hotshot lawyer but he told her she had to, Fizzy too.

'That's what any court would say. Like in custody battles. I was wrong before about the adults deciding. It's what the kids want that counts.'

Across the library Dribble Boy seemed to want something his mum wouldn't give him. The noise was bigger than tomato-sized lungs should be able to make.

'We'd better work out what that is, then, the two of us,' said Kim. 'Barry can't stop us. And if he learns some manners, I might even cut him a little bit of slack. Yeah?'

She presented her knuckles for Brad's to meet.

'Yeah.'

Over the next couple of days, Fizzy found herself praying a lot. She wanted the Lord to help her fiery grandmother not to be so angry. She asked Him to be with Kimberlie Braddock and make sure she felt loved. And for herself she prayed for patience and understanding. She'd never felt so distant from Barry, who didn't seem to know how to listen any more than she knew how to speak.

It was hopeless trying to talk to Laura because Laura only said, 'Trust him, Fizzy. He's a good man.' As if good men couldn't make mistakes because God wouldn't let them.

She knew there were plenty of other prayers being said, at church and in the homes of all the faithful, and it felt strange to be at the centre of them. Her name, repeated in other houses, lifted to God. Hers and Kim's – but how would Kim react to that? Might she call it cheek and claim hers back, asking what gave them the right? In any case, since the whole story was meant to be top secret and she wasn't supposed to talk to anyone, even Suranne, how did the faithful know what to pray?

'Lots of love', said Suranne's card with a photo of a snowdrop. She wrote in lilac pen and curled her letters, as if they were trying to lift off and praise the Holy Spirit. Fizzy had no idea what Suranne would say if she knew why the Duvalls needed extra love and prayer. But she didn't see the point of meeting up with her, texting or phoning. Not now that the silence they both liked was full of something too big to mention.

Fizzy kept hoping Ro would drop by, but when she rang the landline no one gave Fizzy the chance to speak. And she wasn't sure what she could have said anyway, with Barry in the next room.

So Fizzy did what she wouldn't have dared to do before. When Laura was in the bathroom and Barry was at Bible

Study, she found Ro's number and left a whispered message on her answerphone. She knew that she must have sounded strange, as if she was scared of something or someone, but Ro would understand. She needed to talk to her, just her. When she saw Laura a few minutes later, just from behind as she loaded the dishwasher, she felt alarmed by her sneakiness. What was the word? Subterfuge. The awkwardness of it drove her out of the kitchen and kept her in her room. But when she went to bed, nothing had happened, and she realised she was glad Barry wasn't back in time to say goodnight.

It was next morning, still early, when Ro turned up unannounced. Fizzy heard her say she thought her favourite niece might like to check out the new vegan café.

Fizzy hurried through to intercept, to sidestep any problems Laura might throw in the way. She didn't need to. To her surprise she found the sisters hugging – which always looked funny because Ro was so much shorter and rounder. And all her surfaces were a lot less smooth.

Fizzy wasn't sure what Barry would say about Ro stepping in, but Laura seemed glad to see her, almost grateful. She gave Ro a letter which she seemed to be expecting.

As they left, Ro angled her elbow for Fizzy to slip her arm in hers.

'Lots to talk about?'

Fizzy tasted the outdoor air. She felt as if she'd escaped or got away with something. She told Ro about meeting Kim, Jeanette and Nelle, then paused. 'And Dad – I still call him Dad...'

'He'd want you to keep calling him that,' said Ro.

'Yes,' said Fizzy. 'He offended them.'

Ro nodded. 'Mum told me.' She patted her handbag, the crazy recycled one made of old crisp packets. 'There's a letter in here, a peace offering. Mum wants me to deliver it later.'

Fizzy stared at the bag. Could Laura have written without consulting Barry, who insisted that the Braddocks had been 'impossible'? Whoever wrote it, Fizzy hoped it was short and careful.

'What did you think of your dad's offer, Fizzy – to bring up Kim Braddock too?' Ro asked her. It wasn't her quick, jokey voice, but her gentle one, very calm. Fizzy thought nuns must talk like that, as if they knew words had power to hurt. 'Did you understand why he made it?'

Fizzy shook her head. 'I thought it was... thick,' she said, shocking herself. 'I know he's clever, but it's a bit dim. Not to imagine how Jeanette would feel, I mean. The sort of mother who would like the idea would have to care more about money than people.'

They had reached the Hindu temple Ro had visited more than once, even though Barry and Laura wouldn't approve. Fizzy tried to smell it as they passed. Ro had described the incense, the fruit and sweets.

'Do you think that's the only reason a mum could have for agreeing to it?' Ro asked.

Fizzy frowned. 'If she had a daughter who gave her a hard time and she couldn't control her, I suppose,' she suggested, 'but Kim's not like that.'

'No,' said Ro. 'But maybe a mum might agree because she loved her daughters, both of them, more than herself.' She smiled. 'Do you remember the story of Solomon and the baby? The real mother would rather give up her child than see it harmed.'

Fizzy knew the story well enough. Damon tried to act it out after church when he was six, with a real saw from Barry's shed and one of her old dolls. He wouldn't listen to her insisting that the king never actually used the saw.

'It's not the same, though,' she said. 'Nobody's harming Kim.'

'I agree with you,' said Ro.

But Fizzy saw what Barry believed: that Kim was in danger, at risk, open to bad influences like hoodies and gangs. She thought he might add Hindu temples to that list. And Muslims like Brad, the friend Kim had told her about. He wanted to rescue and protect her. But he was wrong and she was sure Ro thought so too, even though she didn't say.

'I'm sure Jeanette's a lovely woman, Fizz. But I'm trying to understand – reasons to make the offer and reasons to accept it. Because I believe that when it comes to the crunch, the big things, people are basically good.'

Fizzy wasn't sure Barry agreed, because of the Devil. He thought there was one, an active, undercover one who wore a nice smile. Ro didn't. Fizzy didn't want to believe in that either. Otherwise she wouldn't sleep at night, ever.

'And I believe that if the two families are going to connect,' said Ro, 'and build together, it'll be through listening and respecting and trusting. Not judging.'

She gave Fizzy's arm a squeeze. Fizzy didn't think, in that case, that they'd got off to a very good start on either side. So if the grown-ups couldn't manage, the girls would have to, starting with her.

No judging Barry, decided Fizzy, even though it was

hard not to mind the way he judged the Braddocks. No judging Kris. That was easy for her but she wasn't sure Kim would agree.

'Will you help us, me and Kim?' she asked Ro.

'I will if I can,' said Ro.

'You can measure it against the heart,' said Fizzy.

Her ex-auntie smiled. The lines that curved under her eyes and up from her mouth made her even less smooth but Fizzy liked them.

'Tell me how,' Ro said.

It took a while, and a shared slice of chocolate and beetroot cake, to be sure what Fizzy wanted to happen next, but Ro made notes in a ring binder. She asked Fizzy to check the list of proposals before she took them to the Braddocks:

Communication with Kim by email and/or phone, in private.

A date for Fizzy to spend a day with Kim and Jeanette.

A date for Kim to spend the day with Fizzy and the Duvalls.

No pressure to decide anything because that would take time.

But the guidelines only worked if Kim Braddock wanted the same. So Ro would ask her.

Fizzy was worried that Barry would be angry. He might not let Ro be what she called a 'mediator', even though she'd done a course. But Ro said it would be fine.

'Mediators can't express their own opinions. He'll love the idea!' she laughed, pretending to zip up her mouth.

Laughing too, Fizzy realised that Kim might love Ro as much as she did, and Ro might love her too. Which felt strange, even though Ro was really Kim's aunt, not hers at all. For the first time it struck her that there was a lot of sharing to be done. Lives. People. And the things that were so private and personal, only God knew. It felt thrilling and scary at the same time. In a way, she and Kim were like plants that had been pulled up out of the earth with their roots dangling. But because there were two of them, together in the air, it didn't feel quite so helpless.

She wondered, as Ro paid at the till, what happened if their feelings were as different as the worlds they'd grown up in.

CHAPTER NINE

Sitting at the old computer in the lounge, Kim wished she could write privately in her bedroom on a stylish laptop like Tat's. The shared PC was all right when she was doing homework and Jeanette was around to help. Now Kim kept casting backward glances in case she sneaked in barefoot without her usual giveaway bangles. Facebook was for messing but emailing felt important.

Hi Fizzy, she wrote, and paused, looking around the room. Jeanette and Nelle were washing up in the kitchen with the door shut, but she could hear the two of them chewing over the same subject like a pair of cows regurgitating the same old stuff. Kim couldn't understand why 'cow' was an insult. They were harmless animals that only terrorised grass and more people should follow their example. But not Jeanette. She was way too harmless already.

'Intimidate!' she said, Dalek-style, pointing both arms towards the kitchen and thinking of the two fathers as the deadly Jeanette's first victims. 'Or in Kris's case, exterminate,' she added quietly.

The flowers Nelle had bought the day after she arrived were smelly now, the water browning around slimy stems in the vase on the coffee table. Nothing cow-like about Nelle really. She was more of a rhino on the rampage.

Kim stared back at the two words she'd typed so far.

Fizzy would be a perfect speller, and besides Kim wasn't sure about words on screen. You couldn't hear the expression in the writer's voice or see it on her face. And even if you sent the messages to Trash, they hung around under your reply and you couldn't delete them from the other person's Inbox. Ghost words haunting people. She didn't want hers to hover around like that, feeling wrong, being mistakes she couldn't put right. Like Barrington Duvall's.

I like Auntie Ro. That was the obvious opening. But she couldn't say she'd never imagined such a cool aunt because that was like pointing out that Ro was hers now, not Fizzy's. I don't know any other vicars but she's not like the ones on TV. Kim had an impression of a sitcom vicar in her repertoire, with a slow nasal voice that went up and down in a two-note tune. It was boring, snobby and ridiculous – all the things Ro wasn't. Kim remembered her smiling on the doorstep like a child at Santa's grotto.

Jeanette says the letter is a kind of apology and she accepts it. The word 'sorry' wasn't there – as Nelle had pointed out – but Jeanette said that it had been between the lines, like the meaning in poems. Your blood mother is clever but she doesn't know it, wrote Kim. Nelle can be nice and fun, like she was when I stayed with her all summer. She only does her rhino thing when she thinks someone's attacking the herd. You might not believe it but she's got a mushy side.

Kim didn't think she had any news, but then it had only been forty-eight hours since the gallery. I'm looking forward to you coming over next Saturday. I might even tidy my room. Would it be half the size of Fizzy's, she wondered, or a quarter? Maybe we can go to a film. If there was anything on at the multiplex that Barry would approve of, apart from cartoons drowned out by toddlers.

What happened wasn't your fault. I hope you haven't felt bad or been told off. Maybe the parents can get on in the end like we do. I know my first impressions (not that kind!) are sometimes wrong. Kim had a thought that seemed horrifying. Did she get that quickness to react and judge from Big Barry? Just like Fizzy got her softness from Jeanette?

They could use us like lab rats. See how much genes count and how much is down to upbringing. But what could Fizzy have inherited from Kris? And how long before Nelle told her exactly what kind of father she'd got? I'm not really hard, just tough.

Kim wondered how tough Fizzy would be now if she'd lived her life. She couldn't imagine her surviving in it. I've only talked properly to Brad. I don't mind you talking to Ro. Otherwise let's just talk to each other, because people outside won't understand, even friends.

Since the Big Shock, all she'd sent Danielle, May and the rest was jokes on Facebook, and texts with smileys about football.

With no warning, Nelle stepped into the room. Quickly Kim signed her name with a kiss and pressed Send – without reading the message through.

'Supper's ready, hon.'

Kim closed the Internet.

'I'll need that to look up flights,' Nelle told her. Then, raising her voice and looking back towards Jeanette in the kitchen, she added, 'Your mother wants me to go home.'

'That's not what I said!' called Jeanette.

Kim sighed. It was going to be a long meal. But it would

be easier if there were just two of them to welcome Fizzy on Saturday.

'If you want to lie down,' Nelle yelled back into the kitchen, 'and let the Duvalls walk all over you, don't let me stop you!'

'No one's going to walk over anyone,' said Kim, pushing open the kitchen door. Sometimes it helped to be in role, and she was a Hollywood hero now. Following, Nelle gave her a look as they sat down at the table and Jeanette placed a hot pan on a mat in the middle. 'Right, Mum?'

With Kim's eyes willing her on, Jeanette raised herself a little. 'Certainly not.' It was a good effort.

'I'm glad to hear you say so,' Nelle said, laying cutlery with a rattle.

Kim had a sudden thought that deleted the relief quicker than the backspace key. What about Fizzy, who was losing her grandmother days after meeting her for the first time? She'd have to send another email before she helped Nelle book a flight, one that said: P.S. Do you mind if we get rid of Nelle?!

Kim told herself that the Duvalls were rich enough to fly Fizzy out to Barbados every Half Term of the year. Not that Nelle seemed exactly desperate to get to know her blood granddaughter. Everyone always talked about big news taking time to sink in, and maybe for Nelle it hadn't started yet. Anger must have flooded the brain cells.

Kim rushed her food a bit because there might be a reply, and there was.

Dear Kim,

Thank you for your email. I'm in the car going home from my violin lesson but I was watching out for it on my Blackberry. I'm glad you like Ro. She likes you and Jeanette and Nelle too but she said Nelle is going back to Barbados soon so if I send her an email in a minute would you show her?

I don't think you're hard and I haven't been told off. The atmosphere is strange sometimes but Damon is being his normal self when the rest of us are being very careful and that kind of helps. Ro says it's all right to feel whatever we feel. I don't feel like crying now that I've met you. I trust the Lord, and Barry, Laura and Jeanette. Ro says all the parents want what's best for us and we have to help them work out what that is.

Will you do some of your impressions for me on Saturday?

Fizzy X

Kim smiled and deleted it, without scrolling down to read the message that began Dear Grandma.

'Nelle!' she shouted, leaving her to read the email, while she helped Jeanette wash up. How long could the message be? They heard Nelle sniff over it a few times before she blew her nose loudly.

'She means well, Kim,' Jeanette whispered, handing her a soapy plate.

When she came back to the lounge, Nelle looked like Jeanette did when she'd watched a weepie movie, had a bath and a hot chocolate and remembered that no one had really died. Her smile was shiny.

'She's a good girl, that's obvious. Jeanette's been telling me I'm a very lucky gran to have two gorgeous granddaughters,' she said, her eyes shiny, 'and she's dead right. I lost my focus but I've got it back now. So tomorrow morning I'm booking a proper studio portrait of both of you together, to put by my bed.'

'What? I hate photographs. And you hated my team photo!'

'I did not. I've shown everybody with pride.' Nelle smiled, almost cheekily. 'My granddaughter, The Crab.'

Kim stared. Had she been drinking?

'Don't worry, hon, I won't ask you to wear matching cardigans. Even though,' she said as she held the door, 'you'd look pretty in strawberry or peach, with a nice lacy collar and scalloped edges.'

Nelle winked. Kim almost gave her crazy ex-gran a hug for understanding – a bit late – that it wasn't a competition, that the two of them were individuals and that was all right. So was Nelle, underneath the bravado that made everything about her oversized. But Kim was still glad she'd be gone by Saturday.

CHAPTER TEN

On Good Friday Fizzy sent Kim a text: Off 2 church. C U 2moro. Waking late to find it, Kim pictured her in a dress that Barry thought suitable. She wondered whether everyone would be crying in the pews because of Jesus dying on a cross. It was worse than a horror movie, but Fizzy would get the whole bloody story uncensored: nails, whips and a crown of thorns. And Barry had banned Harry Potter!

Kim wasn't sure she'd ever understand the Duvalls. Except for Fizzy, of course, who was really a Braddock.

But at least they were doing something with their Good Friday. Now that Nelle had gone, Jeanette was sleeping like a patient after an operation. Nelle had been a bit like her surgeon, cutting her open for her own good. But then she'd switched treatment to hug therapy. On their last night, they'd watched *Dirty Dancing* with red wine, and Kim had put a cushion in front of her eyes whenever Nelle did some of her own.

It was quiet without her. Tat was skiing somewhere, and in any case Kim hadn't forgiven her yet. Danielle was staying with her grandparents. And Brad had gone away to cousins in Birmingham. Kim had made excuses not to go shopping with Suri and May, who wanted to know what was up, because they were the biggest blabbers in the class. If she sent one of them a message that her real father was one of the Rolling Stones, it'd be all of five minutes before people started singing 'Brown Sugar' as they passed her on the street.

Kim wasn't curious when the doorbell rang. Jeanette had been shopping online to replace the old kitchen things Nelle had found fault with, from the greasy filter in the cooker hood to the black old frying pan.

So Kim had expected parcels. But what she got was a man-shaped blur.

The guy wasn't carrying anything, but bulking out behind him was a backpack big enough to hold a whole set of pans for a school kitchen. As Kim began to open the door, she smelt smoke mixed with spicy aftershave. Wearing a leather jacket and skinny-fit jeans, he was short and tanned.

'Uh, morning,' he said, almost like a question, with minty but acid breath. His eyes were a maximum kind of blue. 'Is Jeanette Braddock there?'

He let the backpack clump to the ground. Then he ran one hand through his hair, which was layered and fair with highlights. He gave her a wide, boyish smile. The blue eyes looked right at her, full on. If this was a teacher, girls would be leaving love notes under his windscreen wipers. But he didn't look like a teacher.

'Mum!' yelled Kim.

She half-expected him to push against the door if she shut it, but before she had the chance, he took a step inside.

'MUM!' she shouted.

He stopped and put up both his hands, palms facing her, his shoulders lifted. Like a joke.

'Call the police!' she cried into the flat.

'I'm Kris Braddock, Kimberlie,' he said, quietly, eyes still smiling.

'I know who you are,' she said.

All that staring and breathing him in when she could have slammed the door tight-shut even before the backpack hit the ground!

It was only then, as he looked back at her, amused, that she remembered.

'But you're not my father!' she said.

And she could almost have laughed out loud, because there was nothing he could do or be that mattered to her now. For years she had imagined him on the doorstep and wondered what she'd say, how she'd feel. Whether Jeanette would swoon like a Victorian with her bodice laced up too tight. But now it was different. He was nothing to her.

Except that he was someone else's father. Fizzy wasn't going to like the way he smelt or smiled, and she shouldn't have to try. Why couldn't he disappear permanently and leave them all alone? After all, the Duvalls didn't need the child support cheques he didn't send.

'No one asked you to come,' she told him. 'We can sort this without your help.'

Kim smelt vanilla and turned. Jeanette joined her on the stairs, not in a rush but shocked into slow motion. Her towelling robe clung to damp skin. She pulled the belt tight but that was all she did. As she looked grief-stricken at Kim she found nothing to say!

Kim willed her to remember she really was Nelle's daughter. Somewhere in the jelly there was rhino blood.

'We needed warning,' she said.

'You've made it hard to communicate.'

His voice was flat, but at the end of the sentence his mouth lifted again. He looked younger than he could be. In

Kim's head she heard Tat call him 'fit'. But Jeanette had warned her often enough not to judge a book by its cover. Maybe she'd had someone in mind?

'It's not convenient, Kris,' Jeanette told him.

He was still just the warmer side of the doorway, but the hall was narrow enough for the two of them to block any progress he tried to make.

'No one wants to communicate,' Kim told him, 'not with you.'

Kim saw him look from her unwashed face to her grubby old slippers, thin and bendy as sheets of lasagne. Some of the lads Kim knew would steal his so-cool shoes if they could.

'I never thought you were mine,' he said.

'I never wanted to be.'

It wasn't true, because of all the stories and films with dads – kind, brave ones – who put an arm round their girls and made them feel good. There had been a few dreams about him coming back and making everything the way it was meant to be. But she'd woken up.

'Do I get five minutes and a coffee, J? To catch up?'

Now he was looking straight past Kim. *J?* One letter, but it jolted. It was intimate, warm – and a shock, because it didn't only shut Kim out, it upended the past, Kim's version anyway. There'd been too much of that already.

Jeanette nodded and stood aside. Kim couldn't stay there any longer. She had to warn Fizzy. But the Duvalls would be praying in their pews by now, phones off, with no idea what they should have asked their Lord for if they'd only known. To have Kris Braddock struck by a thunderbolt before he reached the door?

Listening from her room above, she wondered whether it had been the pet name that had done the trick, like a code you tapped in, or an Oyster card you swiped at a barrier. How easy could Jeanette be?

Kim heard her saying something but her voice was low and quiet. 'J' should be threatening him with the cops. She could call them herself, but what would she say that they didn't hear every day of the week? This waste-of-space father wasn't even guilty of child maintenance evasion – not for her.

Kim heard footsteps below. Two sets, into the kitchen now. Phone in hand, she thumbed down to another new name on her list. 'Ro', who might not be in church because she was taking a year off but hung out with prisoners when she wasn't busy studying. She could handle Kris Braddock, couldn't she?

Kim waited through the rings, her chest sinking as she expected the voice message. There it was, not a vicar-ish drone but airy with lifts. Kim managed something faltering, a bit breathier than she'd meant. A news item in a way, live from the scene, but also an appeal. Ending the call, she told herself there was nothing more she could do.

But maybe she should give Jeanette some support, in case the wrong memories were making her mushy as third-day raspberries. Not so long ago Kim had tried to teach her to growl, because some woman at the library was picking on her, but she'd flunked Grade One. Kim had no idea whether Kris had a temper. How nasty could he be?

Kim edged into the kitchen, where Kris was sitting with his back to the door. He didn't turn round as she walked in and past him. She stopped to stand beside Jeanette, who was searching the cupboards.

'Have we got any sugar, Kim?'

'I told you we were out of it,' said Kim, but now wasn't the time to blame Jeanette for anything – even letting Kris Braddock touch her in the first place.

Kris pushed the mug away. Around his wrist Kim noticed a band that looked like twisted leather, and on his middle finger was a snaky knot of a black ring. It could do plenty of damage in a fight. Pretty boy or hard man? She wouldn't trust him to feed her hamster, if she still had one.

'Can't drink it without sugar, sorry. I like things sweet, you know that.'

'You should learn,' said Kim. 'Give up smoking too.'

'Old habits are hard to break,' he said. 'Aren't they, J?'

'Don't call her that,' muttered Kim.

Jeanette was looking for biscuits now, murmuring to herself that she thought there were some custard creams somewhere. Kim couldn't read her. Did everything she'd said about him count for nothing now that he was calling her 'J' and smiling up at her like that?

'It's not your business what I call her,' he sneered, but he looked at Jeanette, not her.

'Leave her alone, Kris,' said Jeanette, quietly. 'She's trying to protect me.'

'Protect you?!' he cried. 'What have you told her? I'm as harmless as...' He looked around the kitchen, everything loosening in his tone and his frame. 'A butterfly,' he finished, and grinned.

More like a bee, thought Kim. And he wasn't stinging anyone if she could help it. Sitting down opposite him, she leaned her elbows on the table and fixed him with a stare that was was as blank and off-putting as she could manage. Her top and bottom teeth were closed inside her jaw.

Unfazed, he played the same game at first, his eyes glinting as if part of him enjoyed it. Kim knew she could outface him. It was like arm wrestling and she could beat him at that too. It wasn't long before he ducked the challenge, leaned back and looked away.

Jeanette had found some biscuits and torn the packet open, but they spilt. At once she began clearing away the mess.

'Chill, J,' he told her. 'Leave one crumb alive.'

Kim needed a strategy. Was she trying to get rid of him or detain him until Ro arrived? She realised she didn't know what she expected Ro to say or do, but that was the point. She didn't know, but Ro would.

The biscuits, most of which were broken and powdery, slid and jittered around the plate as Jeanette put it down. Kim tried to tell her with her eyes to get a grip. Kris chose a whole biscuit and tapped it on the edge of the plate before he bit into it.

'So... how can I find my daughter?'

'She might not want to be found,' said Kim.

'That's beside the point,' he retorted quickly. 'I have a legal right to access.'

'You weren't so keen on 'J's' legal right to financial support.'

Kim looked to Jeanette, who took the cue.

'You let us down badly,' she told him quietly, her eyes on her tea, 'so don't start making demands.'

'Yeah,' said Kim. 'You're lucky to get a biscuit.'

He stood, close to Jeanette but tall beside her. 'Can we

talk in private, J? I'm here because I want to meet my daughter.'

If there was ever a time to growl, thought Kim, and advance, and make him back away!

'Look, Kris, we're taking things step by step right now. It's a lot to get used to and the girls don't want things to change overnight. You'll have to wait.'

'Go, girl!' murmured Kim.

Jeanette looked up at him. 'Like you made me wait.'

The words crumbled at the edges like the biscuits. 'J' mustn't soften now.

'I was wrong, J, I know, believe me.' He looked back, trying his own soft focus now. 'But that's another story.' He took a sip of tea and grimaced. 'Mistakes have to be corrected. Simple as that.'

'But it's not up to you to say,' said Jeanette. Kim touched her hand proudly. 'Or decide anything.'

'No one can prevent me talking to her.'

'Fizzy can,' said Kim.

'Are *you* still here?' he asked. 'Haven't you got some balls to kick?'

'I'd like to kick yours,' she said, and rose from the table.

'Nice,' she heard him tell Jeanette as she pulled the door shut behind her. 'Quite a little lady. You've done a good job of raising that one, J.'

Maybe Jeanette would tell him not to say one word against her. Kim would like to think so, but who cared? It was Fizzy he could mash up, not her. In the lounge she typed a text warning her, but she had to highlight and delete. It was no good calling him names. He was Fizzy's dad and she might not want to hate him too. I used to want to love

107

him, she wrote, but it looked so sad. Pathetic. She made it disappear.

Would the ex-couple in the kitchen have anything to say? She supposed it depended whether he'd only come for Fizzy, or thought he could sweet-talk Jeanette into wanting him back. But he couldn't, could he, even if he tried?

Kim looked at the blank screen on her phone. She didn't know what to do. Glancing back into the kitchen, she saw Kris try to put his arm around Jeanette. Kim stared, appalled. What gave him the right?

Without a word, Jeanette moved away and stood, watching her hands hugging each other tightly. Kim realised 'J' was finding this hard to bear. She took a deep breath, trying to clear all the feelings from her face as she returned to the kitchen.

'Do you want to know about Fizzy then?'

That made him turn. She sat down, facing her suspect, working him. He looked up from his mug and his eyes looked different… moist? What had Jeanette said to upset him – mentioned his split ends?

Maybe it was just the steam from the tea, or a hard night on the booze.

'Yes, Kim, tell him,' said Jeanette. 'Tell us both.'

'Tell me straight,' he said.

'Kim's dead straight,' Jeanette cut in. 'She's not like you.'

So Kim sat at the table and told him straight, ignoring his interruptions and answering his questions only when she chose. It was a detailed portrait, with only the looniest bits missed out. She presented the facts, but with deeper stuff to read between the lines, like Jeanette did with her poems.

And as she spoke, Kim realised that she knew Fizzy Duvall already. Or thought she did.

She pictured Fizzy protesting that no, she wasn't that nice, not really patient, not clever at all. But Kris didn't interrupt once, and a rapt Jeanette gave Kim a series of watery smiles and a few squeezes of the hand.

'We're friends already,' finished Kim. 'So don't think you can shove a wedge between us.'

'What Kim isn't telling you,' said Jeanette, 'is how smart she is herself.'

'He's not interested in me.'

'Nothing personal, Kimberlie,' Kris said. 'It's just DNA.'

Kim didn't want his DNA but she knew she couldn't be that smart, because she had nothing left now, no reflexes, no slap-downs. Instead she visualised the impression she'd do. She heard herself mimicking the laddish bounce and challenge of the voice. He was telling Jeanette he planned to go back to Southend.

'All the old haunts,' he said. 'Good times, eh?'

'Things change,' said Jeanette.

Kim watched the way he sat, one leg crossed high, leaning back in the chair. Like a boy in bottom-set Maths. Kim copied it. He was easy, a gift.

'Some things don't,' he said. 'You haven't, not much.'

How did a scumbag like him get to smile like that? Fizzy would be putty in his hands!

The ring tone on Kim's phone broke in. Ro! She hurried to pick it up and heard what she'd hoped for.

'OK,' she said. 'I'll hand you over.' Holding the phone out towards Kris, she told him, 'It's my new aunt. She's a mediator. She wants to talk to you.'

Kris took the phone. Kim thought he'd soon be wrong-footed and wary, eyes all over the place. But his surprise soon relaxed to a smile. As he listened, Kim looked at Jeanette. She hoped she knew it was a good development. Kim could hear Ro's voice, but not the words, and it didn't allow him to cut in even once. All he managed was an 'All right. Yeah,' before mouthing at Jeanette for a pen and paper.

He wrote something down, an address. The street name meant nothing to Kim. Then he'd ended the call with one last 'OK.'

He was smiling as he gave back her phone. 'What?' Kim asked, suspiciously.

'I've got a place to stay,' he said. 'Thanks for the tea and biscuits, J. I'll be in touch. It's really good to see you. Swear to God.'

'We'd say the same,' said Kim, 'but we're not good at lying.'

She told herself Ro must know what she was doing, but even tough love would be more than he deserved. The two of them waited in the kitchen while he went upstairs for what he called a 'Jimmy Riddle', and Kim turned on the radio. She found some rap with the right vibe. 'Don't mess with us', it said, in words Jeanette didn't like. Kim tried to teach her some popping. It would have been funny another time.

Then he strolled down again, and they escorted him to the door. He looked back at Kim, who stood behind Jeanette, arms crossed.

'Glad to see J's got a minder to look out for her,' he said. 'Better than I did, eh?'

'You said it!' she muttered, but it was a surprise. Did he really care? How could they be sure what he really wanted?

As he stepped outside, Jeanette closed the door, and all at once her shoulders fell.

'You did all right,' Kim told her. 'You can cry now if you need to.'

'No,' she said. 'I'm not crying over him, not anymore.'

Kim's teeth set and her thumbs jerked up. She probably looked like Damon Duvall when he got his seven times tables right in a test, but she felt more like his teacher.

Jeanette clenched her fists and joined her teeth. The growl was more lion cub than werewolf, but it was a start.

'Replay that next time he shows his face,' Kim told her, 'volume up, all right?'

She used to wonder what J would do without her, but she was coming on.

CHAPTER ELEVEN

The next morning Fizzy woke feeling odd. It wasn't quite like a birthday or Christmas feeling, but it wasn't the kind of tightness that happened inside if there was a test at school. More like going on holiday to a brand new destination when she'd never seen the brochure.

Looking at the clock, she saw that it was still before seven. She wasn't expected until half past ten. Hearing voices, she imagined Barry and Laura asking the Lord to keep her safe.

Was Kim's world really dangerous? Would her body be in danger, or her soul? Fizzy gathered that setting up this visit had taken quite a lot of negotiation. She knew that if there was ever going to be a second day at the Braddock flat, she'd have to be very careful what she said when she came back.

'Lord,' she murmured, not quite in a whisper, 'let it be a *good* time for everyone.'

Then she felt stupid, as if she still hadn't got the hang of prayer, because why wouldn't God want them all to be happy? It seemed ridiculous to have to ask.

But what about Kris? Didn't God want him to be happy too? Jesus forgave sinners. Fizzy wondered whether if she met her father, she'd be able to tell from the outside what his heart was really like. Whatever the sins were, he wouldn't wear them like badges.

It took her a while to dress. Nothing too girly or expensive, she told herself. The closest she could get to Kim's darker style was a grey tunic that clung with static, low over black jeans. There was a bump where too much denim (and skin) stuck out at the zip and button. She wasn't sure she'd ever spent so much time in front of the mirror, and it occurred to her that it was probably a sin. So she gave her hair one last finger tweak, and applied caramel lip gloss that tasted sweet.

Damon greeted her on the landing: 'Lipstick!'

'Laura wears a plum colour sometimes,' she muttered. 'It's not banned in the Bible.'

'Bet it is,' said Damon, yawning. 'Can I come?' he asked. 'I could watch DVDs.'

'No good asking me,' said Fizzy.

He meant the kind of DVDs his parents didn't allow. *His* parents, not hers. She still hadn't got used to that. Should she greet Jeanette with 'Hullo, Mum'? And if she did, would she cry?

Damon yawned, shrugged and left again, pyjama bottoms trailing.

Jeanette's kitchen smelt clean and lemony. Even the cupboard handles had been wiped to a shine, and the front of the cooker gleamed like a black mirror. Kim realised she could smell carpet cleaner too, foaming on the stains in the lounge. Not a good sign.

Jeanette had been telling her for months to tidy her room, but this time 'I'll do it in a minute' didn't seem to cut it.

'Be quick,' said Jeanette, looking up at the clock.

'Have you *seen* my room lately?'

'Not the carpet, no.'

'Funny,' said Kim. She told Jeanette there was no knowing what she'd find under the bed but she'd leave nothing alive.

'We need to go shopping,' Jeanette said anxiously. 'And there's ironing to do.'

She had the flat, faded look she wore when she hadn't slept well. She'd certainly lost faith in the magic of make-up. But Kim thought it was her shelves and movie collections she should be cleaning up. *Dirty Dancing*! A comic in women's clothes! A collection of chakra crystals! She wouldn't be surprised if Barry sent an exorcist on ahead.

As soon as Kim had cut herself some toast, Jeanette knelt on the kitchen floor, chasing the crumbs. Her brushing was frantic. What was wrong with her? Why did she believe that being single and facing unemployment made her a bad mum? Where was her pride?

'Jeanette! Stop, all right? No one's ever going to do this to me.'

Do what? She couldn't have said, exactly. Jeanette's bottom lip hung down, as if some hinge had broken.

For a moment Kim felt more cross than sorry, so cross that she said, 'I wouldn't let Kris Braddock touch me. And if you take him back I'll go and live with the Duvalls.'

Jeanette stood up slowly, pulling in both lips. Without a word, she turned the radio on. The DJ's voice sounded so upbeat Kim thought he was asking for a slap but Jeanette didn't seem to hear. She just placed the honey in front of Kim and said, 'We're both bound to be nervous.'

Kim could have said she didn't *do* nervous, but checked

herself. Instead as some old rock and roll began she turned up the radio, and told Jeanette over it, 'Don't worry, Fizzy's way, way nicer than me. Like mother, like daughter.'

Jeanette didn't protest. Kim wondered how she'd feel if the two of them bonded so tightly that she wanted to pull them apart.

'I'll give the bedroom five minutes,' she said, picking up the bin liner. 'Then I'm baking us a cake.'

Fizzy was glad Ro whisked her off before Barry or Laura could remind her of all the things she must remember to do – and not to do. She was also relieved that on the tube they sat too far apart to talk. Then on the bus they only chatted about the sunshine and the people enjoying it on the streets. Fizzy thought it must be easier to watch them out shopping and talking in cafés if you didn't think they were damned and going to Hell.

The only question Fizzy was tempted to ask was about her father Kris, who was staying in Ro's boyfriend's spare room. She trusted Ro, who'd said it was a case of one step at a time and called this a big day, adding that big days weren't always easy.

'I lied about what I was doing today,' Fizzy told her. 'To Suranne, when she asked me round. I've never done that before.'

'If Suranne's really a good friend, and you trust her, maybe you should explain to Barry and Laura that you need to share all this with her...'

Fizzy had never interrupted Ro before. 'But I don't want to. I can't.' Fizzy could picture Suranne's blue eyes looking big and full with sympathy.

'You can talk to Kim,' Ro told her.

'Yes,' said Fizzy. 'I do.'

The walk from the bus stop felt strangely different from walks down streets Fizzy knew. Maybe it was the polystyrene burger cartons with ketchup drying like old blood. Or maybe it was the empty vodka bottle that rolled across the pavement before Ro picked it up and put it into her enormous bag.

'For recycling. I hope Jeanette and Kim won't get the wrong idea!'

Fizzy remembered Barry saying there was no real poverty in Britain, but she wondered whether he'd be so sure if he was walking beside her now. One man wore baggy jogging trousers that drooped as low as Damon's pyjama bottoms. They were caked hard with dirt at the hems. Old dirt, not Corn Flakes.

A plastic bag tied at the handles lay in their path. It looked as if it was full of clay until Fizzy smelt its stench. As they walked on and the smell seemed to surround her, she had to tell herself not to be sick.

Not long ago Damon had been in disgrace for using a dirty word for dog's mess – but not nearly as bad as the words being hurled from the doorstep of a nearby house by a boy who wasn't quite a man. Or the words thrown back at him from the pavement by a girl who must still be at school – so fast that they all joined together, like 'supercalifragilisticexpialidocious' from Laura's favourite film.

'Not what you'd call a good area,' Barry had said, looking at the A – Z. He'd tried to make Fizzy promise not to go out without an adult.

'Fizzy will be sensible,' Laura had assured him.

Damon said Ro would scare off the gangs with 'Chai tea', and Fizzy had told him, 'T'ai chi!'

But now Fizzy wished they hadn't highlighted the bad things. She looked at the flowers rising up behind the low walls, blooming just as beautifully as they did in Kew. Behind the bins and their overspill, the neat, bright japonica still reminded her of girls in silk kimonos with ornate combs in their hair. And the camellias seemed as English as the cushions and curtains in 'her' Harrow grandmother's lounge, where the tea was always Lady Grey and poured from a silver pot.

'Here we are,' said Ro, as they reached a block of flats. It wasn't high-rise like Barry had said it would be, but boxy.

Laura had said all flats in 'areas like that' had entry phone buzzers for security. In fact, all Ro had to do, once they'd turned off the road and taken a path across a rectangle of grass, was ring a doorbell. The flats seemed to be built in groups of three, with doors so close together that two of them shared the same doormat. Fizzy could see that Kim and Jeanette's door had been wiped over recently, because it was much cleaner than numbers nineteen and twenty-one.

Through the clouded panel in the door, she could just about see both of them, Kim in front but Jeanette on the stairs behind her. As the door opened, she hoped they were excited too. Jeanette's fragrance smelt familiar already and made Fizzy think of butter icing.

Fizzy hadn't expected the two women to embrace like old friends who'd missed each other. Tucked into white jeans, Jeanette wore a dark red satin top. Looking at the matching varnish on her mother's fingernails and toes, Fizzy imagined Kim painting them for her.

Ro told Jeanette she liked her earrings, which were zebra-striped.

'They're like mints!' said Fizzy.

'Don't say that. She's like a mole without her glasses,' said Kim, doing an impression with slit eyes and scrabbling front paws. 'If she swallows one, I'll have to turn her upside down and rattle her.'

'I'm too vain to wear them,' said Jeanette, rather sheepishly. 'My glasses, I mean.'

Fizzy thought she'd look more like a librarian if she did. Had she put on her three fat rings, red, blue and purple, because it was a special day? Or did she put them on each morning and wear them, like her make-up, for cleaning and cooking?

The four of them almost joined up on the narrow stairs, which suddenly turned at the top into a little hall. A couple more steps and they were in the kitchen. Jeanette put the kettle on and stood in front of the window.

'I hate net curtains,' she told Ro, rubbing them wistfully between her fingers. 'They go grey in five minutes. But we don't want to be on view.'

'We've got some nice neighbours,' Kim said. 'One's the closest I've got to a big brother. He's at university. Not in prison or a gang.' She said she'd introduce him and his dad, maybe later.

'They're Muslims, though,' said Jeanette, pouring boiling water onto teabags. She looked round at Ro. 'Will that be a problem?'

'What do you mean?' cried Kim. 'I might not be your daughter, but this is your house and you can invite round whoever you want.'

Fizzy felt a stab of panic. Ro told Jeanette she agreed with Kim, *absolutely*.

'They're not extreme,' said Jeanette, as she removed a lid to reveal a sponge cake. 'Kim made it,' she said proudly.

'It looks lovely,' said Fizzy quickly, hoping to change the subject.

'It's not only Islam that has extremists,' said Kim, giving her a quick smile. 'All religions do.'

'Absolutely,' said Ro again.

'Anyone particular in mind?' asked Kim.

'Kim,' said Jeanette, 'come on.'

'I only asked,' added Kim. She wiped her grin. She didn't think Fizzy had understood the reference to Big Barrington Duvall, and now she hoped she wouldn't.

'I'll cut the cake then,' she said.

Ro made humming noises in the back of her throat. Kim thought it sounded as if there was a mouth organ tucked down there and playing itself. Fizzy saw Kim watching and wondered whether she was studying her new aunt for her next impression.

As soon as they'd eaten their cake, Kim said she'd take Fizzy on a tour of the flat.

'A two minute tour,' she added.

It began with the only bathroom, which had the lavatory in it, and no window. Fizzy noticed that the fan was clogged with furry dust and made a noise like an engine that needed scrapping.

Kim's room was smaller than Laura's office. Fizzy couldn't help thinking that the worn purple carpet clashed with the chocolate brown and yellow curtains. She said it was cosy, but when Kim said she'd tidied it specially, she almost laughed before she realised it wasn't a joke.

'Don't look under the bed,' said Kim. She mimed shoving and back-kicking things into hiding.

Fizzy supposed there was just enough room for a sleeping bag between Kim's bed and the window. There were no cuddly toys and no photos, but lots of CDs leaning and poking out from the shelf at different angles. Some of the books were old and tall with pictures, and balanced in jagged piles.

It was hard to know what to say about the football trophies except: 'Player of the season! Wow!'

'Yeah, twice,' said Kim.

Fizzy couldn't tell whether Kim was proud, or sorry there hadn't been more.

'I don't know much about football,' she admitted.

'Yeah, well I don't know much about God!'

Kim punched a torn silky cushion and said she might start boxing. Glancing at the TV, she was sure Fizzy must think it was tiny. She could imagine the huge brand-new model in Fizzy's living room, half its weight and twenty times its value.

'Jeanette's a technophobe,' she told Fizzy, proving it by leading her to the next bedroom. 'See?'

Fizzy smiled because this room was neater, more co-ordinated and full of textures. There were paperbacks propped up on the window sill and more stacked on two bookcases, but no screen, big or small. A fluffy pair of heeled slippers pointed their toes from under the bed, towards a black and white spotted rug.

'No lives were lost,' said Kim. 'She doesn't skin

Dalmatians.' It was a cue for Cruella De Vil: 'I LOVE fur!' But Kim wished she hadn't bothered. Fizzy looked a bit scared.

On the bedside unit, next to a lamp that looked like an origami hat, Fizzy saw a diary, three novels and a ring binder with lined paper and pens. The double bed had a teddy propped against the silky pillow, its head leaning down, as if it was too old to stay awake and kept nodding off. Its fur was scrubby, with patches that were just mesh.

'Basil's a bear with alopecia,' said Kim. 'Nelle wore him out with cuddles in Barbados and then passed him on. The charities wouldn't take him.'

She threw Basil to Fizzy, who caught him and wondered why she felt sorry for him when it was love that had worn him away.

'Jeanette would save him first in a fire,' Kim told her, 'even before Maya Angelou.'

Fizzy, who had seen the photo of Baby Kim in a knitted yellow bonnet, on the window sill along with the books, was sure Jeanette would rescue that. She wondered whether to say so, but she only sat Basil carefully down again and then picked up a book of poems by Sylvia Plath. Fizzy didn't know much about poetry. She didn't think Barry read anything except the Bible, study notes and books about God.

'Only a head and shoulders mirror,' whispered Kim, pointing, 'so she doesn't have to see her stomach.'

Fizzy frowned. 'But Jeanette's a nice shape,' she said, and then felt conscious of her own, which was less of the same and definitely not as nice as Kim's.

'You tell her,' said Kim. 'I've been trying for years.'

She led back down the stairs to the only other room in

the flat, which she called the lounge. Nodding to the overweight computer and the chunky TV with a video slot, Kim asked if Fizzy watched *Flog It!* or *The Antiques Roadshow* and cried, 'Do I hear 17p for the two?'

Fizzy could only smile.

'When I was a toddler,' said Kim, rising and taking the edge of one dark red velvet curtain, 'I used to pretend I was on stage and open these up just to bow for some applause.'

Fizzy supposed it was an audience of one. She asked whether Kim had star parts in plays at school.

'Stand-up's better,' she said. Then she straightened herself tall, only to fall over in a joke way that she'd copied from silent movies, the jerky kind.

Fizzy laughed. Kim told her to sit down on the sofa, and they positioned themselves at each end, Kim grinning at its windy squelches. Fizzy realised it was what Damon would do. They were both performers.

'Is it harder being on stage in a big hall, though?' asked Fizzy, because she couldn't imagine finding the confidence in front of a crowd.

'No,' said Kim. 'You don't look at the people.'

Fizzy told Kim about her music exams and how she felt so sick and shaky beforehand that Laura took a bucket with them, even though Barry said she only had to pray.

'Isn't that cheating?' asked Kim. 'I always think that, whenever athletes pray on the track at the start of a race. Praying to win can't be fair. And it's selfish.'

Fizzy knew she must have looked dumbstruck, because Kim added, 'No offence.'

'You couldn't offend me,' Fizzy told her, and then felt self-conscious even though it was true.

It was hard to be put on the spot about prayer, but she heard Barry's voice in her head, telling her to stand up and be counted.

'I don't pray for a distinction,' she said, although she remembered thanking God for the one she'd had, for Grade Three piano. 'I pray for calm so I can do my best.' She realised she was looking round the room and not at Kim. Fizzy made eye contact like Barry told her she must. 'It doesn't always work, but that's because I don't have enough faith.'

'I bet you do!' said Kim.

Fizzy wasn't sure what to make of that. 'Ask Ro about prayer,' she said, 'if you like.'

'I'd pray for Kris to change before you meet him,' said Kim, 'if I thought it would work. You could try it.'

Then she apologised and said she'd promised not to knock Kris. Maybe, she told herself, Ro and her boyfriend could bring out the best in him. If there was any such thing.

'Let's talk about something else,' said Fizzy, astonishing herself. It was just what Kim would do.

'Yeah,' said Kim. 'Def. Any subject's better...' She didn't want to spend half of today dissing them both: the ex-father Fizzy loved and the new father she wanted to love.

Ro appeared with Jeanette to tell them she was going, and gave Fizzy a hug. Kim accepted hers without a word but Fizzy noticed that she stayed quite stiff. Then the women held each other much longer. Ro put a hand on Jeanette's shoulder, whispering something Fizzy couldn't hear before she told them she'd see herself out.

Kim told herself to trust Ro but part of her wanted to make her say whatever it was out loud.

With the sound of the front door clicking shut, Jeanette turned to Fizzy. 'Can I have a hug too?' she asked, as if she thought the answer might be no.

Fizzy smiled. Amongst the warmth and all the flesh squashed tight and the fragrance up close, she could feel that Jeanette was brimful of feelings. Fizzy thought her shoulder might be left damp with tears. But her mother was trying hard to hold them back, even though they kept on shining in her eyes.

'It must feel very strange for you, hon,' she said, smoothing her denim thighs. 'I don't want to butt in too much when you two are... y'know, hanging. But I do want us to get to know each other.'

'I've seen your room,' said Fizzy, and then felt awkward because it sounded as if she'd been snooping for clues like Sherlock Holmes.

'Is it a bit of a giveaway?' asked Jeanette, pulling a face.

'No. I mean...'

Kim said they had to be who they were and keep it real. Jeanette made some more tea for herself and cut large slices of cake for the two girls. They sat at the kitchen table, and Fizzy realised there was no dining room. It made her wonder what all the space she was used to, the space that surrounded the Duvalls each day and night, was actually for.

'I have a few pictures to show you,' said Jeanette. Fizzy thought she sounded as if she'd rehearsed it in her head a few times first. 'But they dry up once Kim's about eight.'

'I started pulling faces,' said Kim. 'And I never stopped. She proved it with a few, one morphing into the next so fluidly that it was hard for Fizzy to count. Then she was herself again, her face frozen and so serious that it was the funniest of all.

'You're a good audience, Fizzy,' said Jeanette when she laughed.

'Course she is,' said Kim. 'She's good at everything.'

Fizzy smiled but shook her head. 'No, I'm not, honestly.'

Jeanette was producing some pictures from a stiff, flowery box that had once held a perfume gift set. The first few she passed over were of her, small in the Barbados sunshine. As she showed them, she filled in ages and place names.

Fizzy liked them all: her mother cradling a doll as if it needed comforting; up to her knees in seawater and shyly adjusting the cling of her swimming costume around her bottom; reading to a teddy with so much concentration that she hadn't seen the camera.

'It's Basil!' cried Fizzy, remembering the teddy upstairs.

Jeanette seemed pleased and surprised.

'Oh yeah!' said Kim. She hadn't been bothering to look. 'He's lost a load of weight since then.'

Jeanette paused over a small picture from a booth, with her mouth open a little. After a moment's hesitation, she handed it across the table to Fizzy, who felt Kim's curiosity change to something else.

In the small, gloss photo with a badly cut white rim, Jeanette was a much older girl, and her laugh looked big and wild and very happy. She was on the lap of a young, blond man leaning out to one side, arm outstretched. Kris Braddock.

In her head Fizzy heard the word 'Daddy', but she knew other words would be in Kim's mind. She placed the photo on the table, where Kim could see it too. Jeanette took a long breath but offered no commentary now. Instead she got up to straighten a pile of cookery books like a pack of cards. Kim picked up the picture and held it up like evidence in a trial.

'Why have you never shown me this?'

It was an accusation. Hearing the hurt, Fizzy felt panic. Couldn't they rewind and try this again?

Kim stared in disbelief at Jeanette's back. Why was she doing this to her now?

'J?' she asked.

'I didn't want to see it,' said Jeanette, but still she didn't turn. The only eyes she met were Jamie Oliver's.

Kim pushed the book back on the table. 'I don't understand.'

'I suppose I'm not afraid of looking at it anymore,' said Jeanette.

Fizzy looked at Kim, hoping they might all understand each other. Was Kim angry because Jeanette should have shown her years ago or because she was showing her now?

Jeanette picked up the photo, dropped it in the box and closed the lid.

'Are there any more you've never shown me?' demanded Kim. It was hard to think but she needed to know. 'It was my past too – as far as you knew. But you kept it from me!'

'I'm sorry, hon,' said Jeanette, lifting the lid again. 'I am. I didn't know what to do for the best. I'm sure Fizzy would like to see some of you.'

Fizzy agreed.

Kim was silent now, and although she watched Jeanette,

she wasn't making eye contact with Fizzy anymore. Betrayal: that was what secrets were.

Fizzy wished Ro was still there. There were a few baby photos of Kim in a frilly hat, and one from her first days of walking wide-legged, a nappy bulking out her waist under a denim skirt.

'That could be me,' Fizzy murmured, avoiding eye contact in case it was the wrong thing.

'Yeah?' asked Kim. 'Let's see, then,' she told Jeanette, who was holding another picture as if she wasn't quite ready to show it.

Then she breathed out and held it up for them both to see: little Kim in candy striped dungarees, sitting on Kris Braddock's lap like Jeanette in the booth. Fizzy thought Kris looked just as young, but more grown-up somehow. He was on the sofa in the lounge, and Kim, who might have only been a year old, was facing him, her hands up in the air as if to play pat-a-cake. He was looking at her and his mouth was open, perhaps saying the rhyme.

'He looks nice,' said Fizzy.

The comment slipped out without testing because she felt such surprise and relief, just the way she did when a big, bounding, barking dog ran straight past her. Sometimes when that happened on a Sunday walk she said a silent thank you. But now she glanced at Kim and saw her anger.

Kim reached for the photo and pulled her mouth tight, as if she might be closing her teeth together inside. She didn't say anything, but she kept looking. Then she gave the photo back to Fizzy, sprang up and hurried upstairs. Fizzy looked at Jeanette, who called Kim's name after her, rather helplessly. Then she heard a door close, but she couldn't be sure whether it was the bathroom or her bedroom.

Jeanette sighed and looked back at the kitchen door.

'It's hard for her,' she said. 'She's been doing so well and keeping me propped up. I don't know what to tell you about your father, but I thought you should see that we loved each other once. She'll be back when she's ready.'

She spread out a few pictures of Kim in action, aged five or six, one with a football at her bare feet and one looking determined on a bike with stabilisers.

'At least, I was in love with him. I kept on loving him for years after he left us. He'd come back from wherever he'd been working – playing sometimes, in some band or other – and we'd have weekends together. A whole summer once. We were going to start over.' She had been holding the same picture all the while, stroking one corner with a thumb. 'It didn't work out. That's what they say, isn't it? Anyway, Fizzy, I can't speak for Kris. And I think you should find out for yourself who he is.'

'Yes,' said Fizzy, listening for sounds from upstairs, where it seemed quiet. She couldn't imagine Kim crying even one tear. 'I'll go up, shall I?' she asked.

'She's best left alone when she's like this,' said Jeanette. 'She comes round in her own time.'

Fizzy must have looked unconvinced, because Jeanette warned her that she might not get the friendliest reception if she went up now.

'Oh,' said Fizzy. Could that be true?

There was quite a lot of noise from above. What was Kim doing? Pulling out drawers like the burglars at the old house? Fizzy agreed to more tea, though she didn't really want any, and offered short answers to questions about her own memories of being small. It was hard to relive a happy past when the present felt so difficult.

The footsteps on the stairs were rapid. Kim stood in the kitchen doorway.

'Hope you haven't scoffed all my cake.'

Jeanette gave her a smile, but Kim didn't go close enough for a hug.

'Sorry, sweetheart. I got it all wrong. I didn't mean to upset you.'

'Yeah, well,' said Kim. 'We're like the TV news. The upset's built in.'

Fizzy willed her to look right back at her, eye to eye, but she didn't. She wasn't really right. She hadn't really come round at all.

'I said I wanted it real,' Kim said, looking round the kitchen. 'Shall we go out, then, before we get real rain?'

CHAPTER TWELVE

Kicking a Coke can, Kim felt like a spare part as Jeanette pointed out the library to Fizzy. The photos in the box were bad enough, but now something important was missing, and thinking about it, she felt cross. Where could it be? The photo of Fizzy, the only one she had, in her school uniform, had disappeared. And if Jeanette had taken it, because this was her daughter and nothing to do with *her*, then it was out of order. But she wouldn't do that, would she? Kim had looked for it in the drawer by her bed. Not there. She'd looked under her knickers, where she'd buried the flash one of Barry and Laura. Not there either.

Now, listening in to the conversation outside the library, Kim could hear Jeanette telling Fizzy a lot more than any daughter would need to know about her job – and losing it. Then she laughed and cried, 'Who cares now!' although Fizzy clearly did.

Some hip hop burst out of a gangster car full of lads, jolting her towards the obvious explanation. Sad old rocker Kris! He'd been to the loo before he left. He'd been into her room and nicked the picture while she tried to get Jeanette popping. Of course he had. That was him: a sneak thief who happened to have a smile that could fool good people.

She realised she was scowling when she saw herself in a shop front. But Jeanette had torn herself away from the library now. Kim tried to look casual.

'Brick Lane, then,' she said. 'Come on.'

On the bus Kim took a seat way back and let the two of them sit together. Jeanette seemed to be asking school questions; Fizzy didn't say a lot. Kim couldn't stop thinking about photos: all of them, the secret ones, but most of all the one Kris had stolen.

Fizzy had to know how low he'd stoop. But would she think it only proved how much he wanted to love his new daughter?

As the bus stopped and they queued to get off, Kim checked, 'You haven't got a ton of spending money in there, have you?'

Fizzy said no, but placed her palm firmly on the bulge of her flowery bag while the other gripped the strap. When Jeanette said, 'It's an experience, Fizzy. You'll need all your senses!' Kim didn't add that not all the substances she'd smell were legal.

They joined the crowd, keeping Fizzy in the middle of what Kim called a bodyguard sandwich. Here people brushed up closer to strangers than their own families. Yet Princess Kate could be anonymous if she wanted somewhere to go AWOL. It was a place to feel small, but part of something big – like a grain of salt in a steaming pan. And a place to walk tough – in Kim's case, tough enough for three. Along with the roast meats, spices, incense and coffee, smoke and hot fat in the air there were so many languages that mime might work better than shouting, 'Someone's nicked my phone!'

Kris Braddock had nicked her photo, hers and Jeanette's. But would it be fair to give the Duvalls a reason to stop Fizzy seeing the dad she longed to meet? Kris

Braddock should carry a health warning but people felt free to ignore those. And Fizzy would.

Glancing at her, Kim could see her anxiety fading and excitement taking its place. This was the London Kim celebrated. With Fizzy's ears she heard the sound mix alter as they walked: drum and bass, reggae, Bollywood. Some sort of piper making reedy notes, and brand new electronic rhythms playing through old speakers. But it wasn't easy to stay together, so Jeanette told them both to link one arm in hers. They joined like a cops' riot barrier, but zigzagging around people and stalls.

You couldn't call the cops, Kim told herself, if a father stole a photo of his daughter.

In the covered-in market area they stood for a few minutes to watch a group of Balinese dancers. The women were wrapped mainly in gold satin and as they moved, their painted faces stayed dead still and their hair rock-steady. Watching their bodies bending and angling like coat hangers, Kim thought she might copy their moves. But she couldn't do the blankness or the beauty of their faces.

Fizzy seemed spellbound. As they moved away she said she liked the soundtrack.

'It sounds so light and thin,' she added. 'It's like water on stones in an ornamental garden.'

'Of course!' cried Jeanette. 'That's exactly it!'

They were a pair of dreamers, thought Kim. That was why Kris could get round them. He didn't care about the basic rules – for husbands, fathers or visitors. She'd have to tell Ro too, so Mike could lock stuff away. But Ro wouldn't want to believe it. Without proof, she'd tell Kim she couldn't be sure.

As they walked away from the stage towards the street, Kim stopped. In front of her was a head of hair the right length and colour. Someone the same size and build, in a denim jacket, walked past the gap ahead. Had Jeanette mentioned to Ro where they were going? Would Ro have been dumb enough to tell Kris Braddock?

It was him. Kim grabbed Fizzy's arm.

'Jeanette!' she cried. 'He's here! Kris, tailing us! We've got to stop him!'

'Kim, no. Let go. You're hurting Fizzy!'

'We can catch him. Come on, all three of us.' She turned to Fizzy, who was wide-eyed with distress. Kim didn't want to tug her; she'd probably tear in two. 'He might listen to you!'

'Kim, stop!' cried Jeanette, trying to grab her arm. 'Think! You're not thinking!

'All *right*! I'll go myself!' snapped Kim.

She ran, not through the crowd but along one side of it, out of the covered market and to the right, in the direction he'd been walking. Shouldering past one person, slipping between others, ignoring the angry faces and shouts, she barged her way forward. She found the fair head, bobbing and then lost again. His sort of walk: fancy-free and taking his time, smoke drifting behind.

When she reached a corner she stopped. Not ahead. Not right, unless he'd gone into a sari shop. Kim turned left. There! The blond head looked straight towards her.

'Enough, all right! Leave her alone!' she yelled. 'Or you'll wish you had, I swear!'

He took off his sunglasses and pushed them back onto his head. Not Kris. This guy was younger, with thicker eyebrows and eyes that were hardly blue. He gave her a grin that was also a protest, hands outstretched.

Not a lot of English, then. Luckily. Kim raised a hand, like a driver who'd pulled into the lane in front of him and wanted to duck the road rage. She left him greeting a Rasta who strolled from behind her in dungarees. Breathing out, she looked back the way she'd run.

She heard her name. Avoiding two concerned pairs of eyes, she headed towards them.

'Are you all right, Kim?' asked Fizzy.

'It wasn't him,' said Jeanette flatly.

'It could have been. You didn't know.'

Jeanette sighed, and tried to link arms, but Kim kept hers straight.

'I didn't see, not this time, but I used to glimpse him all over London,' said Jeanette. 'Or thought I did. It was never him. I just wanted it to be.'

'I didn't! I wanted to knee him where it hurts!' Kim looked at Fizzy. 'Figure of speech, Fizzy. I avoid red cards.'

'What's got into you, Kimberlie?' asked Jeanette.

Kim huffed. She wasn't a five-year-old caught scrapping in the playground. 'I'm all right,' she said. 'Wrong guy. So, just the spit of him, then.'

Spitting was what he deserved. Who sneaked around and stole his ex-wife's only photo of her real daughter?

'Come on, Kim,' Jeanette told her. 'It's all right.' She looked at Fizzy. 'Of course your dad wouldn't tail us, Felicity. You mustn't be afraid. Kim's not herself, and it's my fault...'

'It's not, it's his!' cried Kim. 'You have no idea! While we were rapping in the kitchen he sneaked in to my room and found the school picture of Fizzy. He must have shoved it into his jacket pocket.'

'No, Kim.'

'Don't defend him! It's gone. I looked. He's running rings round you! I don't want him running rings round Fizzy!'

Against all her advice, Jeanette was opening her bag. What was she doing, inviting muggers in for tea? Did she need an anti-depressant right now? Kim saw how distressed Fizzy looked. Of course she did. She wouldn't want to believe it.

'This photo?'

In Jeanette's hand, through a plastic wallet, she saw Fizzy in her uniform.

'You took it!' Kim's face twisted as her chest sank. She breathed out hard.

'You left it on the bed, half-hidden under the duster. You were making the cake but you hadn't exactly finished tidying your room. I thought as we were going to the photographer's I'd take it with us and find the right frame.'

Kim felt her hands make fists. 'Why don't people just communicate? For God's sake! Isn't it hard enough?'

Kim could see Jeanette was working overtime at being calm and quiet, for Fizzy. She didn't seem to understand what she'd done, interfering and not bothering to mention it. All that stress on the bus for nothing. She'd never have imagined Kris in the crowd if she hadn't been obsessing about the best thing to do – not for herself but the two of them!

'It's all right, hon. I can see why… but you mustn't make Fizzy think he's some kind of Bogey Man. *You* mustn't think so. He's just... weak.'

'Well I'm not,' said Kim. 'I won't be.'

She could see Fizzy felt sorry for her now. They were the weak ones, the mother and daughter who had no idea how to stand up against a bully. But how come Jeanette was so steady all of a sudden, making her look crazed?

She started walking off. 'Let's go, all right?'

'Yes,' said Jeannette, following arm in arm with Fizzy. 'Look at the time. There's a photographer in a studio waiting for you two.'

Blocked by a woman with a buggy, Kim couldn't get ahead. She needed space to cool off, like the ice hockey players, but it was hard to find. Jeanette and Fizzy didn't seem to want to be left again. As they caught her up, she swore.

Jeanette told her to apologise to Fizzy. For swearing? For the chase scene that should be cut from the movie, so the heroine wouldn't look like a jerk?

Mainly for slandering her dad. She had to stop for Fizzy's sake.

'You need to apologise, hon, you really do.'

Kim pulled a face at Fizzy. She wasn't sure what it looked like.

'It's fine,' Fizzy said. She put her arm round Kim, just for a moment.

'I'm a lunatic,' Kim told her. 'How to look stupid!'

'You don't,' said Fizzy. 'Honestly. It was just a mistake. I'm always worrying for nothing. Don't feel bad, please. You're both giving me such a lovely day.'

'I hate photos,' said Kim. 'I can't pose. I don't know what face to make.'

136

Fizzy agreed and Jeanette told them they must be themselves.

'Yeah, right!' said Kim. 'That's what they call a topical joke. Or gaffe.'

They were only ten minutes late in the end, and the photographer was friendly but business-like. When Kim told him she did impressions he suggested Oprah, ready to go on air.

'Sharp, foxy, relaxed and warm, right?'

Kim considered. Maybe.

'You're about to interview Felicity,' he suggested, 'who is feeling glad of the chance to talk on TV about...' He looked at Fizzy, who was smoothing her hair.

'God,' said Fizzy. 'My faith.'

Kim nearly laughed because the photographer looked so appalled. 'Don't panic,' she told him. 'She won't actually do it.'

She winked at Fizzy so she wouldn't mind. There was a lot of positioning but Kim told Fizzy that was tactical and then made her smile with a few *Match of the Day* pundits before she switched to Oprah in time for the first shot.

'Lovely,' said Jeanette, and blew her nose.

After the kind of meal Kim said Jeanette only cooked for VIP guests, they slumped on the sofa, listening to favourite tracks. An old song from their fifth year reminded them both of starting school.

'I cried all that first day,' said Fizzy. 'I said my blazer was heavy.'

'I came home and did an impression of the teacher shouting,' said Kim. 'Jeanette never did, so I'd never heard anything like it, not in real life. I was traumatised.'

Another track prompted Kim to tell a story of a holiday in Barbados and Jeanette singing karaoke after too much beer.

'Roxanne!' she sang, badly, waving her arms around and making her hips swerve more slinkily than Jeanette had managed at the time. 'You don't have to put on that red light! Purrout the red light!'

Jeanette came into the lounge and tried to tell her, 'Stop, Kim! That's not fair!' But she found it hard to link the words together through her laughter. Fizzy took her phone out and caught her on camera.

'I must look a sight!' cried Jeanette.

'A welcome sight,' said Kim, which meant it was way better than blubbing.

In the last part of the day before Ro was due to collect Fizzy again, the girls decided they hadn't found out, or shared, enough.

'Best ever day?' asked Kim. 'When and where?'

Thinking hers might be the day in Year Eight when the Hawston Girls won the Cup, she started the story. 'What won the match wasn't a goal or a save,' she said. 'It was a tackle, mine. Strategic. Precise. Like keyhole surgery!'

Footwork was hard to do out of context. Even though she enjoyed Fizzy's smile, Kim thought the first idea wasn't always the best. She looked back at Fizzy, handing her a mic.

'My baptism,' said Fizzy, after a few seconds' thought. 'I'll show you the photos when you come to me.'

Kim hoped she didn't look as puzzled or incredulous as she felt. She'd been thinking she should have said Barbados sun but now it bleached pale.

'Maybe I haven't lived it yet,' she said, 'my best day.'

She hoped Fizzy didn't think she'd had a sad life because it had felt fine, most of the time.

Fizzy looked to her phone as a text came through. 'Ro,' she said, then looked surprised.

'What?' asked Kim.

'There's been a change of plan. She's caught up so I'm supposed to get the bus and meet her.' Fizzy reached for her bag. 'I'd better go.'

Kim objected that it was too early but Fizzy just said there must be a reason. So then Kim offered to go with her but she said she could manage. Even though Felicity Duvall wasn't exactly streetwise, Kim didn't want to make out she was helpless.

'But we haven't been round to see Brad,' she said, disappointed.

Then she suspected that really she'd been putting it off – not because Barrington Duvall would object (although he would) but because Brad was someone she didn't really want to share. Not completely.

Fizzy thanked them so many times Kim had to tell her it wasn't the Oscars – even though she couldn't think of anyone less actressy. Jeanette became calm and quiet again but Kim knew she was emotional underneath. Waiting at the bus stop, they talked about the highlights but left out the dramas, and promised they'd keep in touch. Then Fizzy got on, smiling and waving.

As the bus drew away, Kim saw her still smiling. Still waving.

In her head, Kim swore. She hadn't said sorry, but

Jeanette knew. Even though they were on a street, with people on all sides, Kim let herself be held.

CHAPTER THIRTEEN

On her her way to meet Ro, Fizzy remembered the photos of her father: such a surprise, and so handsome. Picturing his smile, she looked at herself in the dark glass of the underground carriage, but she didn't think she'd inherited it. Hers was dimmer, even on the baptism day she'd chosen as the best of her life – a day that seemed ordinary now, as well as beautiful. No troubles, tears or confusion, just flowers and sunlight and a bright white dress. This was a different kind of day, best and worst.

Like Valentine's Day, when Michael must have found a red envelope on his doormat. And when, around the same time, Damon had called, 'There's a card for you, Fizzy, a Valentine!' It was just a hand-made notecard from Harrow, signed 'Grandma'. No reason (just 'I thought you'd like it') and bad timing. A whole minute of breathless, shaky joy and then tears she couldn't cry. She'd worked out then that people could believe anything, if they wanted to enough.

Misunderstandings could be painful and the Braddocks and Duvalls were part of an enormous one that just kept on hurting. Fizzy hoped Kim wasn't feeling bad, and ran through the wording of some texts she could send to help. In between, she focused on the map and the moving screen messages about which station was next. Fizzy felt independent, travelling alone like Kim was allowed to do, but just slightly abandoned.

Checking Ro's text on her way up from the platform, she thought she must have typed it without her glasses, or been in such a hurry that she didn't bother with punctuation. Laura would be horrified by the inaccuracy. But she'd be even more appalled by the idea of Fizzy travelling all this way alone – which was why Fizzy had already decided not to tell her.

When she arrived at the exit mentioned in the text, it was some minutes after the time Ro had said. Fizzy felt uneasy. Ro was never late. Even though Fizzy was pretty sure she could find her own way home from there, she knew that if she tried there would be trouble, for her and for Ro.

She was about to text Where r u? when a man stepped out of the newsagent's opposite, tucking a packet of cigarettes into the pocket of his leather jacket. Even before he smiled at her, she knew who it was. He hadn't changed so much from the pat-a-cake picture but now his hand was in the air, not quite waving.

He didn't hurry, but crossed the road towards her, his smile growing.

'Hey!' he said. 'Felicity?'

'Yes.'

'Do you know who I am?'

'Yes,' she said. 'You're my father.'

His smile was even wider and brighter now, as if she'd made him happy. But how did he know? Why was he here? Fizzy wanted to feel happy too but it was all so hard to understand.

He looked her up and down, from the gauzy flowers stitched onto her hair band to the floral Doc Martens.

'You look nice,' he said, 'like a girl should.'

'I'm meant to be meeting Auntie Ro,' she told him.

'Ro's been delayed,' said Kris. 'She's not your aunt, remember? She'll see us back at Mike's place.'

Fizzy knew she must be staring. She'd never seen such a large ring on a man, or so much fair chest hair bubbling up like toffee in a pan where his shirt buttoned down low. But it wasn't really her father who surprised her. It was what he said. Ro wouldn't let her down. And would she ask Kris to meet her like that? It must be a mistake.

She didn't move, even when he said, 'Come on, then. Mike's out for the day, but you probably know I'm staying there a while. Have you been to Mike's?'

'No,' said Fizzy, but she knew it was somewhere between Ro's manse and the Duvall house that wasn't really home.

'I'll call her when we get there and let her know where you are,' said Kris.

Hadn't he said she knew? Fizzy still didn't move, but then he started to cross the road, holding out a hand for her, and she took it. It felt unfamiliar but warm, and led her between the traffic to the other side. Then he let go, turned to her and smiled.

'Dad...' she began, the sound of it shocking and strange.

'Yes, Fizzy?'

She could see he enjoyed both the names, the one she gave him and the one he used for her. He offered her gum, which she accepted. She couldn't see that chewing in the street was so bad, whatever Laura said.

He told her she talked nicely. 'Like a Royal,' he added. 'Princess Felicity.'

'Is it far to Mike's?' she asked.

'Not to worry,' he said. 'Nearly there.'

They turned a corner into an unfamiliar street. Fizzy was worried now, even before her phone rang. She saw 'Auntie Ro'. For a moment she saw an expression she couldn't quite name cross her father's face as she answered the call. It made her uneasier.

'Fizzy? Where are you?' asked Ro. 'I'm with Jeanette and Kim.'

'I'm with...' began Fizzy, registering an unfamiliar anxiety in Ro's voice, 'Dad.'

'Barry?' asked Ro.

'No,' said Fizzy. 'Kris. We're on our way to Mike's.'

'Put Kris on the phone, Fizzy,' said Ro, and she sounded strangely firm, as if she was holding back feelings that might break free. Fizzy didn't want to know what they were.

Kris was already reaching out for it, smiling at Ro through the screen.

'Rowena!' he cried. 'Not to worry – everything's fine here. You said my Fizzy was lovely but you didn't tell me she was a princess!'

Fizzy couldn't hear what she said in reply but Kris kept smiling while he talked, telling her they'd see her soon and it was a shame she'd had a wasted journey but they were getting along great.

Wrapping the gum in a tissue, Fizzy heard Ro's volume rise a little but Kris just talked over it.

'Initiative, I'd call it. How else was I going to meet my daughter?' he asked, and then, seconds later, countered with, 'I'm not what you'd call patient, Ro, and I've had to wait fifteen years.'

He told her he was handing the phone back to Fizzy,

who heard Ro say, 'Kris?' as if she hadn't finished.

'Has there been a mix-up, Ro?' asked Fizzy.

'You could call it that! A kind of fraud, really.' Ro sounded tense, more like Laura! Then she paused and her voice loosened. 'All right, Fizzy, don't worry. You're fine and that's what matters most. I'll be there as soon as I can.'

Fizzy looked up at Kris as she clicked off. What exactly had he done to be told off by Ro? Was he going to tell her? He didn't look sorry, or ashamed, or even very serious.

'What kind of fraud?' she asked.

'You have to take your chances in life, Felicity,' he said, 'if you don't have many opportunities come your way. Rev Rowena left her phone on the table while she went for a pee. Put the idea in my head, in fact. On a plate! I hope she's not so trusting when she's dealing with cons at the prison.'

Fizzy remembered the text with no punctuation – the text he'd sent, from Ro's phone! She imagined how worried all three of them must have been at the flat when Ro turned up to collect her, only to be told she'd gone – and because of a text she hadn't actually sent! It was hard to believe that anyone could be so sneaky. But fraud was criminal and Kris wasn't that. He hadn't gone into Kim's bedroom and stolen her photo. He hadn't followed them to Brick Lane like a stalker. He just wanted to see his daughter.

'I wanted to see you too,' she told him. 'But Dad, you shouldn't.'

His smile reminded her of Damon's face after he'd played a trick on her. Long before Valentine's Day he told her it was Michael Conradi on the phone, when it was really someone from the church calling for Barry. And the worst bit was feeling stupid afterwards, because no boy would ring to speak to her, least of all the boy she wanted to call. Or stroke her cheek the way Michael had done in the dream, before he kissed her.

Fizzy could see her dad was enjoying himself. Just like Damon had enjoyed the fear and thrill she'd had to try to suppress when she took the receiver and said a timid, 'Yes?'

Now her father hung his head like a dog that had been naughty and still hoped for a bone. She saw the shades in his sundried hair, and how lovely it could be with conditioner and care. She'd love to wash and dry it for him, if he'd let her.

'Have I been bad – for a good reason?'

'Yes,' said Fizzy. 'No. Not good enough.' More confusion! How could she tell?

'All right, maybe not. But you are, though, aren't you? You're good enough.'

He nodded as he smiled, and looked straight into her eyes. As they walked he chatted about Mike and how good he was too.

'In a weird, hairy way. Green as a Martian, Mike. He'd recycle my cigarette butts if he could knit them into socks!'

A minute or two later he led her up to the front door of an old terraced house, with a narrow front that stretched back deep. Fizzy stood watching awkwardly, feeling like an intruder as he produced a key from his back pocket. The hallway was long, with a bike leaning against the stairs and a wooden umbrella stand with African carvings around its curves. Kris wrinkled up his nose at a pair of trainers that looked as sweaty as they smelt. He picked them up and dropped them outside the door.

'Mike's sound,' he said, 'but he's an exercise freak. I

146

don't get it myself.'

He showed her into a lounge that Laura would say needed decorating, the plants dwarfing the furniture. Kris said he was supposed to be watering them, but opened a cabinet and poured himself a drink instead. The smell of the golden liquid that filled the glass was stronger than anything the trainers could manage. Fizzy wasn't sure it was much nicer, but Kris seemed to like it.

'Good stuff,' he said. 'Mike's a generous man. He'd do anything for that vicar of his. But then, it's in the Bible, isn't it – hospitality to strangers?' He drank, and ran his tongue around his front teeth. 'You'd know better than me.'

He told her they could watch TV if she liked. Fizzy didn't answer. She just wanted him to explain, so she could believe his reasons really were good.

He told her to sit down and make herself at home.

'All right,' he began, when she made no move towards the remote control. 'Let's talk, shall we? Something tells me may I need to correct a few wrong impressions you might have got, thanks to Kimberlie and that mouth of hers.'

She waited. He sat down in the armchair opposite, holding his glass in front of his face, smelling and smiling before he drank again.

'Never liked that name! I never bonded with the baby that came home from the hospital either. Instinct, you see? Something deep down didn't gel.'

He took out a cigarette and left it between his fingers as he waved them. Hoping he wouldn't light it indoors, Fizzy practised telling him he'd have to smoke outside.

'Of course it didn't occur to me that some nurse had fouled up big time.' He shook his head. 'I didn't want any baby, not then. I was just too young to be a dad, too much living still to do, places to go. J got so moody – post-natal depression, they call it – and I couldn't handle her. It wore me out trying.'

Fizzy pictured Jeanette crying, and worn out too. The scene was so sad.

'So I went,' he continued, 'to give myself some space. I came back, though. Your mum and me, we had a good thing going, as the song said. We nearly turned it round.' He looked up at the ceiling and sighed. 'I wish we had, I really do.'

Fizzy saw how forlorn he looked. He was full of regret and that was sad too.

'But now I know why I never felt that connection with my child. She wasn't my daughter. If she had been, I wouldn't have wanted J to myself those weekends. We'd have been a proper family.'

Without the smile his face looked older. He looked at her as if he wanted her to understand.

'If it had been you,' he told her, 'everything would've been different.'

His eyes travelled to the window where the evening light was grey. The room was dim, because he hadn't turned on the lights. The brightest thing in it was the drink in her father's glass. But his eyes shone too. Was he crying – almost crying?

'I can see you're a good girl. You don't backchat and snipe like her. You don't judge and condemn, any more than Ro and Mike. Church people don't, do they? They give the benefit of the doubt.'

Fizzy realised there had been nothing at all, so far, that

she could think to say. But she imagined Kim having plenty. It must be possible, she supposed, for two people to have different versions of the same story without lying. She remembered the smile in the pat-a-cake photo. He hadn't been ready fifteen years ago, but he'd come back again now and he seemed sorry. How bad could he be, if he made Jeanette so happy at the start? He'd made her love him – and maybe she hadn't stopped.

'You don't judge me, do you, Felicity?'

She shook her head. He said she was shivering so he'd better put the heating on. When he came back he said, 'Tell me you don't judge me.'

'I don't,' she said.

'Maybe you can save me. I think you're an angel.'

Fizzy smiled shyly and shook her head. She'd been right. He wanted to be saved.

'Tell me about Mr and Mrs Duvall,' he told her, 'and where you live. Smart, is it?'

She told him a little, and answered his questions about holidays and cars. When he wanted to know how many rooms were in the house, it took a while for her to count and then she missed one. So when he said, 'Oh, just the twelve?' she had to say, 'Thirteen.'

He wanted to know about the garden. She thought he was enjoying listening to her. Did she really sound posh?

'I love flowers,' he said. 'Men can, you know – even hard nuts. Flowers and their mums.'

So Fizzy asked about her grandmother, the white one she hadn't met, and he told her she was dead.

'I was abroad when she died. We lost touch before you were born. She was a talented woman, though. I got my music from her. She had a beautiful voice – did the pubs now and then. I bet you sing, don't you?'

'Not really,' she said, 'only in church.' She told him about all her music certificates, pointing out that some of them were just passes and she always felt sick with nerves before an exam.

'I'll take you to the next one,' he said. 'Then you'll walk in, head high, and get another distinction. You'll see.'

He emptied his glass.

'Listen, sweetheart,' he said, 'I'm just going outside for a smoke, all right? You watch TV for five minutes.'

Fizzy wished he wouldn't but she didn't argue. As he unlocked the patio door he looked back.

'No talking about me on the phone, eh?'

She didn't answer. Watching him slide the patio door to a close and light up with his back to her, she wondered what Kim would have done differently in her place and realised the answer was just about everything.

Kris wandered down the garden, smoke clouding around his fair head. To one side of the path sat a Buddha with a large belly, a bigger smile and a garland of flowers round his neck. He stretched up chubby arms as if life was for celebrating. Fizzy felt sure Kim would like it as much as she did. Then she realised that Barry and Laura would want the ornament thrown on a skip – even though it couldn't be demonic or even heathen, could it, if Buddha meant peace and love?

Kris didn't seem to notice it anyway. Just as she was thinking of defying his instructions and ringing Kim, he took a call of his own, pausing by the vegetable patch near the upturned wheelbarrow.

A text drew her back to the phone. Kim: This is kidnap. Don't let him play you. Can you run for it? X

Fizzy breathed out, shocked. No! Why did it have to be like this? First fraud, now kidnap. He was handling it all wrong and now everyone was going to gang up on him, and stop her seeing him again.

'Please, Lord,' she murmured. This was worse than the Valentine's card, the photos in the box, Brick Lane. Worse than she could have imagined.

Looking down the garden, she hoped he would turn and smile, but he was engrossed in his call and his cigarette. For a moment he felt like a stranger again, and even church girls didn't talk to those, not alone.

She made herself think through what he'd done. Even Ro was cross, and Ro thought the best of everyone. Kidnap and fraud: the labels fitted if people wanted them to. Kim must think she was right this time.

Maybe she could find her way home from here, like Kim told her to. But how would that help now, and what would her dad feel, opening the patio door and finding her gone? He'd trusted her to wait for him. She would be telling him, by running away, that she didn't trust him, didn't want him for a father, didn't believe a word he said. That when she said she didn't judge him, she'd been a liar.

Fizzy looked at the lounge door and the hallway through it. Perhaps she could write a note explaining that she did want to meet again, but with Ro and Mike there, without tricks. In her head she heard the word 'Angel'. Angels were guardians. They stuck by people, there at their shoulders, keeping them safe and giving them strength. Angels didn't give up on anyone.

Another text came through: R U all right? X.

She realised Kim must be worried, and trying to calm down. Yes fine. X

As she pressed 'Send', Kris finished his call and headed back towards the house, drawing deep on his cigarette. Smiling at the Buddha, he stubbed it out in the bare belly button on the brown tummy.

Fizzy breathed out shakily and realised that if anyone spoke to her she would cry. She saw the key in the inside lock of the patio door he was approaching, and in her head Kim told her to turn it, now! But he was pulling another naughty boy face, his hand over his mouth. He picked up the butt he'd thrown on the path and made a show of putting it in his top pocket. Bending over the Buddha, he sniffed the flower garland and made a face that meant dreamy. He lifted it over the round brown head and carried it in, ringing his arm.

'Here,' he said, stepping in from the patio, and placed it on top of her curls. 'A halo for you.'

The flowers were silk, so they didn't really smell. He dropped the cigarette butt into a saucer that had turned into an ash tray.

'Another contribution towards those socks,' he said.

Fizzy smiled. He was funny and kind. The Buddha and his belly button were unharmed so why did it matter? It wasn't a crime or even a sin.

'You're a good girl. Better than I deserve. But I'm going to make it up to you from now on.'

Fizzy smiled. She was glad she'd stayed. He went to the cabinet and picked up the bottle but screwed the lid back on the moment he'd wound it off.

'Don't want to be found drunk in charge of an angel,' he said, and suggested coffee. 'You can tell me all about a week in the life of Felicity Braddock.'

Checking his face, she knew the name wasn't a mistake. But even if he was making a point she couldn't blame him for that. The surname should have been hers and it wasn't his fault that she'd been given a different one. It was a solid name even if it wasn't pretty.

The kitchen was old-fashioned and narrow. Fizzy picked up a cloth to wash out with eco-cleaner while he spooned coffee from a jar and fetched milk from the fridge.

'You're like your mother,' he said, when he turned with a milk bottle in his hand to find her wiping surfaces.

It didn't feel as if he was making fun, or criticising. It seemed to Fizzy softer than that. She remembered Ro saying that a lot of the prisoners just needed to feel loved.

'Yes,' she agreed. 'I'd like to be, anyway. She's lovely.'

'I know. That's what I mean,' said her father. 'Two sugars for me. I'm trying to be a lot sweeter, you know?'

Fizzy stirred them in.

CHAPTER FOURTEEN

When Ro said the blossom was lovely on the walk home, her voice didn't match, as if she really meant it was dying.

'Mavericks,' she said, nodding to some straggly bluebells by the roadside. 'They've got a stranded look. Sad, really.' She sounded as if she blamed someone for that. 'They should be in a wood, part of something amazing.'

Fizzy couldn't bear the stiffness in Ro's face and voice, in the brisk arm close to hers as they walked. She'd never felt it before, ever.

Finally, after practising in her head, she spoke: 'We had a good talk.'

'I'm glad,' said Ro. 'But I can't help being angry with him, Fizzy. I don't want to be, but what he did is inexcusable.'

'Is it?' asked Fizzy. 'No one's hurt. He just wanted time with me.'

Ro shook her head. 'I've got to know him a bit in the last few days and he can be very charming but that's not enough. He'll have to be totally straight from now on if he wants anyone to give him the benefit of the doubt.'

'He said Christians do that,' Fizzy told her.

'Did he?' Ro sighed. 'He's not stupid, is he?'

'Are we going to tell Barry and Laura?' asked Fizzy, imagining a different kind of anger, Old Testament-style.

'I think we'll have to, but a short version. Let me.'

That was it. No more talk, just more flowers to name as if the words were carved on gravestones. Even Ro had changed now!

Then Laura was at the window. There was something on her face as it broke open in an anxious smile that made Fizzy feel strange. It was as if she'd been reading a story that took her to the other side of the world and made her forget everything that was most familiar, and now she was herself again. Except that part of her had been left behind in the life of the book and wanted to return.

When Laura opened the door her face was even paler than Fizzy remembered, and her eyes looked tired.

'I've been praying so hard,' she said, quietly. 'Did you have a good day?'

'Yes,' said Fizzy. 'Can I tell you tomorrow? I'm really tired.'

She knew her voice sounded weak and she couldn't really control the smile she needed, to show that everything was fine.

Barry came out of his study in his soft cream cardigan and linen trousers, taller than anyone she'd seen all day, much more solid to hug. Only he didn't hug her, and she couldn't bear it if he did.

'I need to go to bed,' she told him, and hurried away.

From the upstairs landing she heard him ask Ro whether she was all right and imagined for a moment shouting down, 'YES! YES! Just leave me alone!' the way she heard it in her head.

She hoped God would understand and call it a prayer. Five minutes later she was in bed and about to turn off her phone when a text came through from Suranne asking whether she'd enjoyed Kew Gardens. Fizzy clicked off.

In bed, she asked God to help Ro smooth things over, and to bless all four of her parents, and Kim, and Damon and all the old and new relatives in Barbados and Jamaica and Harrow too. She rolled onto her side. The moment she closed her eyes she was back in Mike's garden and the Buddha's navel was specked with ash. What if it had been a statue of Jesus?

She turned to face the door and tried to bring back the smell of Jeanette and the craziness of Kim, joking.

Damon knocked and whispered loudly, 'Fizzy, can I come in?'

She lay absolutely still with her eyes shut, even when he tapped again and asked, 'Are you awake?' It seemed a long time before she heard him pad away in his pyjamas and call out, on his way down the stairs, 'Fizzy's asleep!'

She knew what to do. She'd take the blame for Kris, and say she asked him to find a way to get together. Barry would be furious but she didn't care because it would be the right thing for the right reasons.

By the time Kim sent an email to Fizzy next day, Jeanette had censored it. She'd deleted 'abduction', 'schemer' and 'fake', and all references to Kris Braddock.

'It's hardly worth sending now,' objected Kim, looking at the three lines that told Fizzy things she already knew about how good it was to have time together.

'He's her father. We have to let her make up her own mind,' said Jeanette.

'You never let me!'

'I wanted to, but no...' murmured Jeanette. 'We all do things we regret.'

'Like meeting Kris Braddock in the first place,' muttered Kim.

'Let's put that aside and look at the positives, hon, shall we? Like you and Fizzy getting on so well?'

Since when, thought Kim, had Jeanette been looking on the bright side? But she censored that too.

No reply came until Sunday lunchtime because of course the Duvalls would be at church.

Dear Kim,

How is your day so far? Thank you for making me so welcome yesterday. The cake was delicious. I'll try to do some muffins when you come. I think I may be getting a cold so I hope you haven't caught it. I might go back to bed. Laura's sneezing a lot too and her eyes are red and watery.

Ro told Barry and Laura I met Kris, but she missed out the bit about using her phone when she was upstairs. She's given him what she calls more ground rules. Laura is looking forward to meeting you, though. They both are but they don't always show their feelings like Jeanette does. Well, only about Jesus usually.

See you next weekend. Give my love to Jeanette.

Fizzy XXXXX

Kim wondered whether there were other words and

sentences that had been edited out at Fizzy's end. But it was a giveaway, wasn't it? It meant Big Barrington was being hard and dark, Laura wasn't on-side and Fizzy just wanted to be loved as much as Jesus.

Barry and Laura could do with some ground rules too and Kim was sure she could think of a few by Saturday.

Although Fizzy was still on holiday, Kim wasn't. Usually it was good to see her friends again but things were different now, including her – even though she worked hard on her Kim Braddock impression, to fool them.

'Great,' she said when Jeanette asked on Monday how the day had been. 'I've got a detention tomorrow for some History homework I never did, and Danielle's gone all moody on me. Nobody told me turning off my phone was some kind of hostile act.'

'So,' she said on Tuesday, 'Tomorrow's match has been postponed. The girlies at St Michael's don't like the nasty mud.' Kim could have done with a ball to kick.

On Wednesday she could see Jeanette didn't like to ask how the after-school shopping trip with May (and her birthday money) had gone.

'She asks me along for an honest opinion about whether jeans are flattering, and then blames me when they're not. Not her belly, backside or doughnut habit. Me.'

But Fizzy shouldn't worry about her figure, Kim thought. She was just right. People were so stupid about being thin.

'Kim,' said Jeanette, putting supper in front of her, 'what we're dealing with is very stressful.'

Kim had a mouthful so she didn't say, 'No kidding.'

On Thursday after school Lola Hedges nagged her to go

to the park. Normally Kim tried to be nice to Lola because most people weren't, and it wasn't her fault she had bird legs, spots and a weedy voice. But Lola only wanted to sit on damp grass and smoke, and pester Kim to do the same when she'd already said no a million times to a hundred people. Lola never knew when to leave things alone – including the ball, when she was in goal. One more dozy game and she'd be dropped from the team.

This time Lola had decided Kim had been off the radar because she had a boyfriend. She kept needling until Kim ran out of patience and sympathy. The shove didn't turn out playful and Lola blew smoke in her face. Kim walked, calling her things under her breath that Fizzy wouldn't understand.

'Who needs fake friends like you?' she heard as she hurried away.

Kim kept on walking – like Will Smith, Men in Black.

'That's it with Lola Hedges,' Kim told Jeanette on the doormat. 'End of.'

Fake! That was Kris pretty-boy Braddock with his blue-eyed smile. It was one thing Kim would have sworn she wasn't, and would never be. Lying down with a headache, she wished Brad wasn't away for a few days with some mates from uni because he'd understand. He'd make her feel tough again.

Then Fizzy sent a text to say she wasn't well and sleeping a lot.

Get well by Saturday, Kim told her, and changed the sad face to a smiley. Kim thought how funny it was that Lola wanted to be a bad girl, when she'd rather be good, like the girl who'd lived all her life in her place. But then she decided that if Fizzy was really going to let Kris Braddock trample all over her, goodness could go over the limit.

The next day she never dressed, drank the juice of two oranges and sat leaning over a pan of hot water with a towel over her head. Jeanette didn't even suggest giving school a go.

At lunchtime Jeanette came home as promised to check she was OK. No shout. Maybe she thought she might be asleep. Hearing her padding around, Kim decided to put on her dressing gown and stagger downstairs to the kitchen. Jeanette was standing looking at the steaming, squeaking kettle as if she might have to draw it from memory. What was she thinking about, Kim wondered? Probably everything!

'I'll tell you everything.' That was what Jeanette promised not so long ago, at the start. But now she'd forgotten – or hoped Kim had.

'Tea, lovey? Toast?'

'I'll have everything,' said Kim, sitting down at the kitchen table and looking at the empty chair opposite. 'Like you swore to God you'd give me. When Nelle was here, remember? The truth?'

Jeanette nodded, then sighed much too long. No words. As she poked teabags in mugs, Kim watched her. Even from the back she could see her breathing deeply, her shoulders rising just a centimetre. Was she panicking? Shaping the narrative?

'I've only got till ten to one,' she told Kim, looking at the clock.

Kim swore. How long *was* this story?

'It may not be the best time, when I'm rushed and you're

not well. How *are* you, love?'

'Jeanette! I'm big enough and fit enough to take it, all right? How much worse can it be?'

Jeanette sat, but then said she must eat, and put two slices of bread in the toaster. Kim was wishing she hadn't asked. She sneezed, a wet one. Jeanette fetched her kitchen roll but it was rough on her nose.

'I don't know where to start, Kim.'

'All right,' said Kim, 'skip the sorry for not telling me whatever it is before. You must have had good reasons.'

Kim could see Jeanette was struggling already but she had to be Jeremy Kyle now. 'Tell me why I've never seen a wedding photo. Where you were when I went to Brad's for weekends, or your friend Lynne's.' Kim had just remembered Lynne who used to work at the library and her annoying son who didn't like her being better at football than he was. 'And why you sent me off to Barbados for weeks one summer holiday.'

The toaster popped. Jeanette fetched the marg and cheese from the fridge but Kim told her to start talking while she produced jars and tubs. Kim wasn't hungry, but she broke a corner off the dry, crisp toast, and looked up expectantly.

'All right,' said Jeanette. 'There's no wedding photo. We married when you were in Barbados. It was at a registry office. No one took pictures. But I was happy.'

'What? But I must have been seven, eight? He left when I was a baby. I never saw him after that, not until the other day.'

'No. But he turned up again, on and off, between countries, gigs and jobs on building sites in Germany.

Evenings, sometimes, when you were in bed, and he'd leave before you woke up – but he'd creep in and have a look at you sleeping. "I don't believe how fast she's growing, J," he'd say. "You'd better go easy on the fertiliser."'

Even though Jeanette was smiling, Kim wasn't stealing that one for her act. What kind of father sneaked around like that? Why couldn't he have read her a bedtime story and given her a hug? Was he scared she'd beat him up with her little fists for being such a useless drop-in dad?

'Months would go by, best part of a year even, but then I'd get a call and he'd want to come for the weekend.'

'So instead of telling him where to go, you got rid of me? You farmed me out. I was in the way?'

Kim had never imagined this. She watched Jeanette with the knife in her hand, marg hanging on. Shaking her head.

'Kim, no. It was more my idea than his. Yes, we needed time together if we were going to sort out something that would stick – for your sake as well as ours. But I didn't want you crying when he'd gone, asking when your daddy would be back, and thinking he didn't want you.'

'He didn't want me!' Kim cried. 'He wasn't giving you trouble then, about me not being his?'

'Not really, only joking. Once you were at school, and I showed him the class photo, he said something: nothing of him in you. But he didn't know you. I didn't let him. I never knew when I'd ever see him again.'

Jeanette seemed lost in some sad dream now and Kim took the knife that was still swaying around in her hand. She started to spread the marg for her.

'Why did you marry him when all he'd done was mess you about and drop by for...' Kim stopped. She wasn't Nelle

162

and she wouldn't say it. She must listen.

'I was pregnant.'

'What? Don't tell me…' Kim stopped, because if there was a secret brother or sister somewhere it wasn't hers. Then she replayed the word the way Jeanette had said it, not emotional but flat and empty. Kim understood. There was no baby.

'I believed him when he said this was it; he was ready now. He wanted a son. He told me he loved me and I supposed he must, because he could never stay away.'

From free B and B, thought Kim. Had she no self-respect? How could she have been so easy?

'Because you couldn't stop loving him,' she said, quietly – not a question but an answer.

'I tried. I wanted to. Everyone told me, especially Nelle – you can imagine! She wouldn't have anything to do with the wedding.'

'But she took me off your hands so I didn't spoil the honeymoon.'

'No honeymoon. So I could rest. He looked after me, Kim, he really did.'

Kim imagined what that meant – staying in bed all day to save her washing? Tearing himself away from *Match of the Day* to hold out an empty mug?

'It started with spotting – blood in my knickers, not much. Then stomach pains. I was sixteen weeks.'

'Mum!'

Kim hadn't used the word for so long but there wasn't another. She reached out both her hands. Jeanette didn't seem to see them at first.

'Nelle said you could stay on. You were having a fine

163

time. Football on the sand! I stayed in bed for a few days, and he took care of me. I thought: *He loves me. He does.* Then… end of.'

'End of?' Kim hoped she was gentle.

'Baby first, then marriage.'

Kim sat silently, and not very upright, while Jeanette talked cramps, blood and hospital. And how she'd had to smile everything away on the phone to her in Barbados.

'I'm right out of tears now,' she told Kim, 'at last!'

Kim pushed her plate away.

'Are you telling me,' she said, trying to link the words slowly, without the anger breaking things up, 'that as soon as you'd lost the baby he was out the door!'

Jeanette stood and faced the sink. Kim guessed the tears were making a comeback, but if they were, they were quiet. Kim's sniffs were louder. But not as loud as the doorbell, pressed long and hard.

'I'll go,' said Kim.

She was running. The postwoman had a firm, flat package with both their names on it: 'Jeanette and Kimberlie'. No Barbados stamp. The writing was so perfect it looked a bit like one of those manuscripts monks used to write out in ink.

Not heavy. Poetry, probably. Whatever it was, it was an interruption. The drama might not have an end but she didn't want any ad breaks now. But Jeanette came out of the kitchen and took it, turning it over.

'It's from Laura.'

'What!'

Jeanette was tearing so Kim supplied scissors. Inside was some sort of herbal tea for colds that probably cost a tenner a sachet. And a programme for a dance show. Pulling a puzzled face, Jeanette passed it to Kim.

A bookmark made her turn to a page of cast photos. There was Laura – even thinner, but red-lipped, her hair auburn and falling in thick curls onto one shoulder.

'She looks so…' began Jeanette, and stopped.

'She's showing off!' cried Kim. 'She wants us to know she used to be a ballerina! I'm supposed to be impressed.'

She could tell Jeanette *was* impressed. She started to read the bio by the photo.

'Hey!' cried Kim. 'Don't let her butt in. You were saying, remember? I think we'd got to the bit where Kris walked.'

Jeanette pushed the programme away, but held on to the corner.

'Not straight away. He was heartbroken. I'd never seen him cry before.'

'Oh, poor Kris!'

'He was wonderful at first. But I couldn't hold it together. I drove him off, in the end.'

'No!' Kim told her. 'You didn't. It's him, not you. You were grieving.'

'And things weren't right inside. You lose a lot of blood, but it never quite stopped. I wasn't a lot of fun.' Jeanette didn't seem to notice Kim shaking her head. 'A job came up and he took it.'

'Then I came home and you had to go back to hospital for the op.'

'Mm.'

Kim told her to sit down. Jeanette dried her cheek and picked up a half-eaten piece of toast, took a bite and dropped it again.

'End of, end of, end of.'

'Don't you hate him?' asked Kim. 'I do! More than ever!'

But Jeanette covered her ears with both hands, and shook her head. Kim reached for both hands and brought them both down, so she could hold them.

'Tell me he brought you grapes.'

'He called from Dusseldorf. It wasn't what he said. He sounded so alive. I could hear music and voices. I could almost hear the beer bubbling! "You take care, J. You look after yourself and the Bruiser."' Jeanette swilled her tea around. 'It was what he didn't say. He never came back again.'

'So you divorced him.'

'In the end.'

'You could have told me.'

'I didn't want you to know who he was or what he did. Better to hate a shadow for not being there.' She placed both hands over her mouth a moment. 'Please understand.'

'I understand!' cried Kim. 'So would a jury! If you'd killed him a good defence team could have got you off scot-free!'

Jeanette laughed but it was wild and wailing. If she'd laughed like that in court they'd have locked her up.

'Have I answered everything?' She looked at the clock, and drank her cold tea quickly. 'You haven't eaten, Kim.'

'I'm not hungry. Funnily enough. I'll drink Laura's tea.' She pretended to read a sachet. 'Orchid and asparagus. Yum! You don't have to worry about me,' Kim told her. 'I'm a bruiser, remember? He got that right!'

The hug was a long one. Then Jeanette was gone, back

166

to her books and her regulars.

Kim cleared the lunch things away and sneezed over most of them. She was tucking Laura's programme on the shelf with the cookery books when a postcard fell out. It was a bluebell wood, with the same fancy writing on the back.

'I don't talk about this because it's over now but I thought you'd like to see who I was.'

Kim frowned, trying to translate. Laura didn't want ballet mentioned on Saturday? Because Barry didn't talk about it, or because he didn't know what she was posting behind his back?

The present was hard enough without adults dragging the past in all over the place. What made Laura think she cared? Even if she'd broken her leg in the middle of Swan Lake, she'd had life easy compared with Jeanette.

Never mind Laura the ballerina. Kim realised she'd asked Jeanette for everything and learned too much. How much was anyone going to tell Fizzy? What a dad to land! What a prize!

Where was the photo, the pat-a-cake one? She had to find it! It took a while, but when she pulled it out of the scented box she ripped it in two, four, eight.

'Like you destroyed her,' she muttered, her throat sore. 'But you're not destroying Fizzy, all right?'

On Saturday Kim woke with a headache and a temperature. Jeanette appeared with a cup of hot lemon and honey, and the news that Fizzy was much better.

'I'm worse,' said Kim, thickly. 'My nose is trying to explode.'

Jeanette laid a hand on her forehead and pronounced it

167

hot.

'Do you think...' she began, but stopped.

'Yes,' said Kim as firmly as she could, her throat burning.

'But maybe you need to feel... your best?'

'It makes no difference,' said Kim. 'Even my record-breaking best wouldn't be good enough for them.'

She wished it was Barry coughing and sneezing in his deluxe bedroom, so the voice of God could take a break. Picturing him made her think she'd take the next fag anyone offered her, and fast-track a habit just to put his nose out of joint.

When Ro arrived to escort her, Kim thought she looked older than she'd remembered. Was she losing weight, or just sleep?

'It's crazy, Ro, you having to do all this to-ing and fro-ing,' Jeanette told her after an XL hug. 'What's wrong with me taking her?'

'What's wrong with *her* taking herself?' asked Kim.

Jeanette asked whether Kris was behaving himself at Mike's.

'I think he's doing his best,' said Ro, heading for the door. 'He really is.'

'Ha!' said Kim, but it turned into a cough.

On the journey, Ro told her to save her voice so Kim just watched the people on the bus and tube, and wondered whether any one of them had a life as tangled as hers. Looking at the map of the underground, Kim imagined all the coloured lines crossing and fusing, knotting and bending off in different directions, like a badly-wired fuse box. Fizzy would want the pink line, the Metropolitan. Ro would choose the District because it was green. And Barry, with his hotline to heaven, might have to settle for silver with the Jubilee.

Kim sucked tarry lozenges between sneezes. The heat inside her kept coming in waves. She'd been determined to probe for details of what happened with Kris and Fizzy but when Ro said that would have to be a case of no comment she didn't feel up to pushing.

Ro never said, 'Nearly there,' but Kim guessed. The road they'd turned into seemed to have more trees than houses, and driveways big enough for whole blocks of flats to be lowered down into the space.

Ro pointed out that some old rock star from a hairy Seventies band lived behind a long, high wall greened by even bigger bushes. And threw in a rumour that some of the Pope's team stayed at the large, pale grey house with a fountain the two of them could hear behind bank-vault gates. Then, a few mansions later, she stopped. A thicker and sweatier feeling surged inside Kim's head.

Ro told her in a gentle voice that some of her blood parents' ideas might seem strange to her but she must always remember that Barry and Laura had good hearts.

Kim said, 'Yeah. OK.' But she thought the only Duvall with a really good heart wasn't technically a Duvall.

CHAPTER FIFTEEN

This was it, then: a new-looking house with a dark green door and light green trims. It was set back from the road, at the end of a drive that curved round cricket-pitch grass and designer borders.

'Must be worth a couple of million at least,' Kim said darkly, and sneezed.

Ro touched her arm and told her, 'Real value's not about money. You're worth more to them than bricks and mortar.'

Kim didn't see how she could be. Not just because the value of everything she was wearing added up to a grand total of twenty-five quid, but because they didn't like her. They were stuck with her and she was stuck with them.

As they approached the front door, they heard a purr from behind. Turning, they watched a sleek, black BMW glide up the drive and lie low a moment, soaking up the sunshine. Then the garage door opened automatically, like in American movies, and Barry Duvall drove it in, parking beside another car that was chunkier but equally shiny. Apart from a ladder and a wall unit storing DIY bits and pieces in labelled sections, the garage looked as neat and clean as a showroom.

'Kimberlie,' cried Barry, unfolding himself from the car and projecting across the garden. 'Welcome!'

'Hi,' she said, as if she could take it or leave it, all of it – and him.

He greeted Ro with a quick pair of kisses. Hoping he wasn't going to try for her own cheeks, Kim kept her distance. But his arms were long. He reached for both her hands, pressing them together in his, which felt huge and very warm.

His eyes locked on hers. But what was he trying to tell her? Kim tugged. He loosened his grip. Explaining that he'd been to the gym, Barry was about to put his keys in the door when it swung open.

Fizzy stood there smiling.

'A dress would have been nice,' Barry told her.

'Hey. Like the necklace,' said Kim, because she couldn't believe the grated edge in his voice. Was he angry with Fizzy? What had she done? Got a B for an essay?

'A baptism present,' said Barry, removing his shoes on the mat.

Ro almost tumbled over trying to climb out of her desert boots. Fizzy tried to tell Kim not to worry about taking her shoes off, but Barry jumped in to point out how pale the carpet was.

Kim glanced around the hallway, thinking it might as well have a sign that read 'Beware of Living'.

'Whiter than snow,' she said, disapprovingly.

'I'd call it cream,' said Barry, 'like cherry blossom. Come on in. I don't know where your mother's got to.'

Kim glanced at Fizzy. No wonder she looked tense. Did he not consider anyone's feelings?

Laura emerged soundlessly in soft pumps. She was crease-free in a grey jersey dress down to her knees.

'Lovely to see you, Kimberlie,' she said, her voice low but cool. No hand clasping or kiss – not for her, anyway.

Ro gave her sister a squeeze.

Holding her shoulders straight and extending her neck, Laura Duvall still moved like a ballet dancer. Kim suspected her parents of making their first mental notes: slumps and shuffles, posture needs work. She began a gangsta swagger down the hall but no one reacted.

'Damon's gone to a friend's house for the day,' Laura explained as they entered the kitchen. 'Billy.'

'The name's Kim,' she said.

Laura gave her a soft, sad look.

'We know your name,' said Barry.

'I thought *I* did,' said Kim. She knew why Damon had been sent away – to escape contagion.

Looking around the kitchen – which took a while – Kim thought Jeanette would love it. So much cupboard space. So many bare surfaces to keep shining, all of them marbled black. Laura made coffee the slow way, with glinting beans and an aroma powerful enough to filter through Kim's blocked nose.

Kim breathed deep and a sneeze caught her by surprise, dragging out an involuntary 'Achoo!' The snot had flown somewhere. Barry's expensive creams? She told herself to try harder next time.

'Bless you,' said Laura.

Kim followed the sneeze with a grating cough.

'Poor you.' Laura produced a box of tissues in a decorated case seemingly out of nowhere. 'Should you be in bed?'

'It's just a cold,' Kim said gruffly.

She walked across the room to look out of the large window. How far did the back garden go? Laura talked about the problem of managing it, even though it turned out that someone was paid to do that, twice a week.

But the coffee tasted as fantastic as it smelt, so when Laura asked, Kim said it was the best she'd ever had.

'Thank you, Kimberlie,' said Laura. 'That's sweet of you.'

Kim certainly hoped not. 'I'm just honest,' she said. 'Someone's got to be.'

But she didn't mean Ro wasn't, and she didn't want Fizzy to think she meant her.

'Show me round, Fizzy?' she asked, but Laura asked her not to carry the mug upstairs.

'Why?' Kim knew the answer. This was a house with rules and they expected her to break them just like she intended to.

'In case you have an accident, Kim,' said Laura.

'I'm toilet-trained,' said Kim.

Fizzy blew her nose. Kim stood, making a point of finishing her coffee in gulps, one eye on the kitchen clock. She could feel Laura tensing with each mouthful. She took one long slurp and Laura told her not to rush. Then before Kim could put her mug on the table, Laura had intercepted with a glass coaster.

Following Fizzy back out into the hallway, Kim heard Barry say something that ended with 'Smart Alec remarks'. She felt like calling behind her, 'Smartass, Bazza! Who's Alec when he's at home?' Then she heard the word fun in Ro's reply and wished her aunt was staying to keep him in order. Kim pictured the three of them in the enormous kitchen, talking about her. Barry was even more massive than she remembered, but Laura might be scarier still underneath. She was like a robot wife, ready to short-circuit over a spill.

They stopped in a doorway, and she realised they were looking into Barry's study. Above the desk was a cross fixed to the wall. She noticed a Bible within reach of the keyboard. If they'd prayed for her to be easy, it wasn't working. If they wanted easy, she thought, they should stick with the daughter they'd got.

There was her parents' wedding photo. The soft focus, flowers and heart shape didn't mean they were happy, she thought, now or then. She grinned at a painted clay fish Fizzy had made in Year Four. It was droopy and lop-sided, with a wonky grin.

'Good job they got you, not me,' Kim told her. 'My fish would have been binned. I'm rubbish with clay.' She did a quick impression of the fish's hanging mouth and fat cheeks. 'It'll be an antique when we're eighty-seven and we've forgotten all this.'

Kim couldn't care about the expensive things – whether they'd been bartered for at a Bangkok market or bought in the kind of auction she'd seen on TV, where rich white people talked like Tories.

If Barry and Laura had to bid for her, how high would they go? Or how low?

From down the hall Ro called goodbye, and suddenly Barry appeared, pointing at various furnishings and dropping place-names like Cairo and Santiago. It made Kim like all the bowls and hangings, candlesticks and rugs a whole lot less.

'What about your room?' asked Kim, following Fizzy upstairs without a glance at Barry.

'Make it a quick tour,' he called after them.

'How quick can it be,' muttered Kim, 'with thirty-four rooms?'

'Thirteen,' murmured Fizzy. 'They're not special – I mean, interesting.'

As Fizzy named them all in passing, Kim was inclined to agree. Everything was outsize. She could have started her own multiplex with all the huge widescreen HD TVs. And the bath was more of a pool.

'I'll bring the girls here after the next game, shall I?'

Didn't Jesus say something about giving your money away? Kim thought she must ask Barry if he'd read those bits. But Fizzy wasn't showing off. It was the views of the garden she seemed to like best, and Kim couldn't blame the flowers and trees for being beautiful.

There was only one closed door: Barry and Laura's room. She tried to imagine the luxury hidden inside. Was there a bed size past 'king'? But when Kim asked what they didn't want her to see in there, Fizzy only hurried on with the tour.

By the time they reached Fizzy's own bedroom, Kim was worried that she might have made her feel uncomfortable. But as they stopped in the doorway, her mouth dropped.

'I love it!' she said.

Fizzy glowed at once. Guiltily, Kim realised how dim her light had been so far, and that wasn't all Barry's fault.

The room was neat and romantic, just like Fizzy, and all the colours were shy, egg-shell pastels. Even the photo frames were lemon or lime, lilac or peach, decorated with suns, flowers and super-cute bumble bees. On one white, dust-free shelf they showcased grandparents and a crowd of cousins dressed for weddings or christenings, none of them hers anymore.

All these years, thought Kim, she'd had a pocket-sized family when she should have been part of a clan.

Beside the bed was a Bible with a white leather cover, a Kindle, and a diary with a lock and a decorated pen. Fizzy looked furtively towards the door, then reached under her pillow and pulled out something tiny.

'It's a worry doll,' she explained.

She passed Kim the wiry figure. Its stamp-sized scrap of fabric was pinched in with one stitch to fake clothes. Kim smiled.

'Ro gave it to me, but Barry says I only need to trust the Lord. I was meant to take it back to the Oxfam shop, but I really like it.'

Kim supposed it had been clutched a lot recently.

'Cool,' she said. She imagined it holding the heat from Fizzy's closed palm, or the warmth of her worry soaking through the pillow as she tried to sleep.

Fizzy slipped it back into hiding and patted the pillow as if it needed soothing as well as smoothing.

'What else do you worry about?' asked Kim. 'Apart from us and the mix-up.'

'Too many things. It's a sin, really.'

Kim frowned. 'Must be way down the list,' she said with a head shake, trying to get the timing right. 'I wouldn't worry about it.'

Fizzy was slow to smile, but then she let out a little, secretive laugh, which was interrupted with a shout from below.

'Come on downstairs, girls.'

Barry wasn't counting down from five, but Kim could tell he meant at once. In the living room, they found him filling a wide armchair, facing the sofa where Laura sat. He gestured to the space around her. Room for two. Fizzy sat where the white hand suggested, but Kim chose the floor with its deep-pile carpet, faced them and crossed her legs.

'It feels right to give thanks that we're here together,' said Barry, bright-eyed but solemn. He linked his hands and closed his eyes.

Laura and Fizzy closed theirs. Kim watched. Her cough wasn't intentional. Barry leaned forward.

'Thank you, Jesus, for these your daughters.' He breathed deeply. 'For Kimberlie and Felicity. Lord, be with them in the sunshine and the shadows.' He joined his fingertips together in a gappy pyramid that peaked under his chin. 'We praise and thank you, Lord, now and always, for these your gifts. Amen.'

Laura and Fizzy echoed the Amen. Kim watched the other eyes open.

'Can I ask a question?' she asked, and didn't wait for permission. 'If me and Fizzy are like gifts with the wrong tags on, what's to be grateful for?'

Barry's look was absolutely straight and blank. Laura opened her mouth but nothing came out. She looked a bit like the fish, but prettier and a lot smoother.

'Because God couldn't have meant it to be a muddle,' Kim continued. 'You wouldn't be grateful if Laura got the Y-fronts and you got frilly thongs.'

Laura stood and left the room, eyes ahead. She moved like a fish too, gliding.

'Something I said?' asked Kim. 'Grammar wrong?' She wasn't going to apologise, because what she'd said wasn't just clever. It made a point, an important one.

'There's no need for vulgarity, Kimberlie,' Barry told her, his whisper thick and prickly.

'I'm being serious,' she said. She suddenly realised any couple would just exchange the wrong present for the right one – and that would mean she stayed with the Duvalls. 'I'm trying to understand.'

'I'd like to think that's true.'

'It is true,' said Fizzy quietly from the sofa.

Kim thought Fizzy might be braver than she looked. But Barry's glance was meant to silence her, and it made Kim angry.

'I can do serious,' Kim continued, uncrossing her legs and stretching them out in front of her. 'I'm not all impressions and smart remarks. I'm sunshine and shadows – I liked that bit, even if we're in the shadows now.'

Kim had never talked like this before, but she was starting to feel as if she was getting the hang of a new vocabulary, even though the words were oddly emotional and came out big and mysterious and the tone all wrong.

Barry gave her a long look: no smile, but no frown either. The phrase 'continuous assessment' came to mind. It made her sit up and straighten a little. He had no right to measure her.

'God,' he said slowly, 'is always with us, wherever we go.'

'He must've been off duty at the hospital. He could've sent an angel to watch over the nurses. All it needed was a tap on the shoulder and a pointed finger.'

As she acted it out, Barry breathed out through his nose, and Fizzy played with her necklace. Kim hoped she wasn't upset – at least not with her. Everything came out overloaded with attitude. It was a bit like singers who got autotuned in the studio, but in reverse.

'I'm not being funny,' she said.

'No one's laughing,' Barry pointed out, hands outstretched, smiling. 'Your mother and I are very sad that you have no faith. But we have prayed for you every day since you came into our lives, and we will pray for you every day, always.'

There was a sudden resonance in his voice, but still his face was clear. Kim thought Fizzy looked upset, but startled too. Was she was thinking about the Duvalls dying, or sending up her own prayer about her heathen ways?

With no warning footfall on the super-soft carpet, Laura was back. So was her poise. She announced that lunch was ready and the girls could eat theirs in the garden if they wished.

'Not the best idea given Kimberlie's cold,' said Barry. 'It's not August.'

'Whatever,' Kim said, wondering whether Laura ever challenged him on anything.

The table was set in the large, blue and white dining room which felt cool as Kim entered it. All the glass arranged in the cabinet – some of it crystal, some of it dark – caught the light through the window and seemed to thin it.

The meal began with another prayer, thanking God for lunch. After that it became very quiet, apart from the tapping of cutlery on thick, octagonal plates.

'How are your hands?' Laura asked Barry.

Kim looked up, puzzled.

'They'll heal,' he said. Turning to her, he explained that at Easter he'd carried a huge cross which was harder and heavier than he expected, so his hands had been sore since Good Friday.

'You got off lightly,' said Kim. 'Didn't Jesus have nails through his?'

'His wrists,' said Fizzy, 'and feet. And a spear in his side.'

Kim looked, but she didn't think that had scored Fizzy any points with Barry. He had the nicest girl in London living in his house – by mistake – and he didn't seem to see it.

'Have you ever been to church, Kimberlie?' asked Laura.

Kim had expected the question and had an answer ready, dead straight and as true as possible for Fizzy's sake:

'I was christened if that counts. I went with Nelle once in Barbados when I was little. She says I stood on the pew but I couldn't clap in time. Why don't you all go to Ro's church?'

Laura looked at Barry, waiting with her fork loaded.

'Ours is a different kind of commitment,' Barry said, 'and relationship.'

'Ro's brilliant at relationships,' said Kim. 'And she's committed to this. To us.'

'I'd like to go there,' murmured Fizzy.

Kim might have supposed she was the only one who heard, because Laura offered her more juice and Barry looked back to his plate. He was acting as if it didn't matter what Fizzy would like. He was behaving as if she didn't exist.

'I'm not sure you're really inviting a theological discussion, Kimberlie,' he said.

Then he wanted to know what she did on Sunday mornings, and made no comment when she said she slept, mostly, or watched repeats of *Friends*. That was a cue for silence thicker than the carpets.

After lunch Kim hoped to be left alone to find the Fizzy she'd got to know a week ago. But no sooner had they escaped to her bedroom and chosen some music to play than Laura appeared at the door.

'Time to go,' she said. 'It's a lovely day out there.'

But not in here, thought Kim. 'Where?' she asked, realising there was no question of her getting to choose.

'I think you'll like it,' said Fizzy, lifting the sentence into a question.

Barry appeared in a Burbery jacket that was meant to be casual, like he was trying to be. 'We've been meaning to go for ages. I've booked in advance.'

'I haven't brought much money,' Kim told him, as if she had more, in some bank, money box or secret hiding place, but she'd chosen to leave it behind.

Barry smiled. 'On the house.'

As the Duvalls led the way into the hall, Kim told him, 'Jeanette said she didn't want you splashing the cash.'

'No second mortgage needed,' Barry said, over his shoulder. 'More of a ripple than a splash.'

On the doormat a backpack waited, tough enough for a rainforest expedition. Kim noticed a First Aid Kit protruding from one of the pockets. How wild could SW19 be?

'He likes secrets,' Fizzy told her once they set off walking.

The two girls were a few steps behind the adults. Kim didn't suppose her shoes were as comfortable as Fizzy's, but then they'd only cost four ninety-nine. Hardly a plop.

They'd only turned a couple of corners when he turned to ask if she'd guessed yet. He was Mr Jolly now, hand in hand with Laura, casually swaying his other arm. When he smiled, Kim saw how good his teeth were. She'd like to think she'd got his skin, too – not as dark, of course, but smooth as butter. But why wasn't he nicer to Fizzy? Why did she love him if he treated her like this?

The Duvalls – her parents, she corrected herself mentally with a shudder – talked all the time, and although Kim couldn't hear Laura's part, she could see that she'd relaxed a bit. She wished Fizzy would do the same, because something seemed wedged between them now. Maybe it was the *vulgarity*. Or maybe it was money. Or Kris and the story Fizzy wouldn't tell about what happened at Mike's house a week ago – and what had happened since to put her in Big Barry's Bad Books.

'Give me a clue,' Kim said. 'It's not church, is it?'

But as she asked they rounded a corner, and the secret spread out before her. Wimbledon! As in the tennis championships! Kim didn't want Barry to think she was excited, even though she watched, highlight by highlight, every summer. Instead she told Fizzy that Jeanette was the one with the addiction.

Kim found herself grinning at the space age entrance, with its beam-me-up tube and the rackets arranged like the petals of a giant flower. But the Centre Court tour seemed to leave Fizzy a bit cold, at least until Kim made her smile with her Andy Murray impression. She threw in extra scratching and ear pulling, and it came out better with a sore throat. Barry didn't manage a twitch of a smile.

'The likeness is uncanny,' he said, like a serve with a slice.

Arriving at the changing room with the 'ghost' of John McEnroe, Kim did the famous, 'You cannot be serious!' with a throw of an invisible racket. Fizzy smiled, but unlike the Seventies crowds, Barry and Laura didn't seem to find it entertaining. If he couldn't be bothered to appreciate anything she did, Kim didn't see why she should jump about bright-eyed, like a kid on a Bouncy Castle.

Two hours later her cheap shoes were hurting her more than any muscle Nadal had ever pulled on court. Kim was quite glad that a sneezing fit cut the wandering short in the end. Her last tissue had shrunk and felt soggy as she wiped her sore nose. And when Barry offered her a perfectly folded handkerchief, a real one with BD in one corner, she couldn't help but stare at it for a moment before she took it.

Barry ordered four cream teas in the café.

'I hope you enjoyed it, Kimberlie,' he said, as she sat down and slipped off her shoes under the table, hoping they didn't stink.

'Yeah, it was all right,' she answered, with a lift of the voice at the end, so it didn't sound too rude. Not to Fizzy, anyway.

'We hoped you'd find it more than all right,' he said, crisply.

'All right's all right,' she said, like an EastEnder. Barry wasn't getting a thank you until he was nicer to the daughter

183

who did behave.

While Laura was in the ladies, the Wimbledon tea arrived. It was good enough to stop them talking for a while, with cream in a little pot, real butter and fruity jam. The strawberries were so big that just one filled Kim's entire mouth. She told Fizzy she felt like her old hamster, Lurgy – who was always sick – when she tried to eat it whole.

Then Laura returned.

'Tea for ballet dancers,' Kim said, in her best Darcey Bussell impression. She looked at Laura but there was no reaction.

'Tell Kim about ballet,' Fizzy prompted.

'Oh,' said Laura. 'Nothing much to tell. I had big dreams, as a girl. I took it as far as I could. I was very serious about it at the time.' She smiled. 'Have you ever had dance lessons yourself, Kimberlie?'

'Mum couldn't afford it,' said Kim. She didn't feel bad about the M word. Laura wasn't her idea of a mum. She looked like she'd break – or scream – in a hug. 'But I copy the moves from pop videos sometimes.'

'I'm not sure I'd call that dancing,' said Barry.

'What would you call it?' asked Kim, her mouth still quite full.

'Oh,' he said, 'cavorting perhaps? Certainly titillation.'

'Is that a rude word?' asked Kim, hoping she wasn't sniggering.

'It's not the word, in fact, that's rude,' said Barry.

'I'm sure Kimberlie's dancing isn't like that,' said Laura, and quickly offered to pour more tea.

'Like what?' asked Kim, tempted to do a few moves right there.

Laura asked, 'What else do you enjoy, Kimberlie?'

'Apart from *vulgar* dancing? Cream tea,' said Kim, chewing and swallowing as best she could. 'Dogs. TV that makes me laugh. Messing about on Facebook. Proper conversation with Brad – that's my Muslim friend. One of them. My best Muslim friend.'

The silence was thicker than the cream, with no sweetness.

'I think,' said Barry, 'that Kimberlie enjoys being provocative.'

The words were followed by a brief, knowing smile. Kim might have protested that she was on best behaviour: no texting at the table, swearing, elbows or licking her fingers. But it wouldn't be true.

It was like a reflex; they provoked each other. But she wasn't like him, so she'd better stop now.

For most of the walk back to the Duvalls' house, it was the sneezing she couldn't stop, and then, just as she thought it was safe to put Barry's hanky back in her pocket, she found herself coughing.

'I'm going to ask Ro to come early,' said Laura.

'That might be best,' said Barry.

'I'm not arguing,' said Kim.

Barry disappeared into his study. A few minutes later he asked them to come and see what he'd found.

'Deep breath, Kimberlie,' he said. 'Knee-jerk reactions can be unhelpful.'

Keep your knees under control then, Barrington, she told him privately. On the screen of his new-looking PC, she could see a photo of an apartment block – new, smart and expensive – overlooking the river.

'I've already emailed the link to Jeanette, and she likes it. She's prepared to consider the advantages of a place near here – fifteen minutes door to door. And a room with a view, as you see.'

Kim could see. But she couldn't quite believe where it was leading.

'You could keep your current flat for as long as you wanted and just use this over long weekends, school holidays, whatever you wished. You and Jeanette would be my tenants, part-time at first perhaps, for a nominal rent. Felicity could stay with you there, of course, by arrangement.'

He was skimming through shots of the rooms and the view of the Thames. It wasn't just smart; it was flash. Victoria Beckham might have designed the décor. The plants were so lush the rainforest would be green with envy.

Kim looked at Fizzy. She was looking right back at her, and if she had her worry doll to hand, she'd be strangling it. But he had to be told or he'd never learn.

'We've got a home,' she told Barry. 'No one needs two. That's greedy. Didn't Jesus say you have to give stuff to the poor? Or is that what you're doing?'

Barry's sigh went deep. 'Sit down, Kimberlie, and have a proper look, both of you. I'll leave you to it.'

He rose from the leather swivel chair, but Kim was in his way. She pulled a big-kid excited face with jazz hands.

'We'll share it, me and Fizz,' she said, 'when we're sixteen. Not long to wait! What do you think, Fizzy? Nominal rent? Rooms with a view?'

'Now you're teasing, Kimberlie.'

She gave him a puzzled look. 'Not at all,' she said, just

186

like him, each word full and firm. 'We'll be old enough. I can cook. I'm good with money – I've had to be. People get married at sixteen. I'm accepting your offer – if Fizzy feels the same.'

She could see that Barry wasn't quite sure for a moment. He looked at Fizzy, and Kim realised she'd put her in the eye of the hurricane.

'No need to answer,' she told her. 'Think about it. We're not sixteen for eight months.'

Fizzy smiled, but Kim didn't expect her to say a word.

'I'd love that,' Fizzy said.

It was quiet but clear. Kim grinned at Fizzy, astonished but very proud of her. Barry leaned back to the screen and clicked off the images.

'That wasn't the offer on the table, and you both know it. It's out of the question.'

As he tried to sit down, his leg knocked the chair flying. Kim stepped back. His shoulders were huge. He could be a wrestler. She'd like to throw him to the floor and put a foot on his chest.

'Of course,' said Laura, behind them in the hallway. 'Let's forget it for now. You barely know each other, so it's far too soon. Let's not spoil the time that's left. Ro won't be very long.'

'Why is it out of the question?' asked Kim, turning back to Barry. 'We're not children. We're coping better than any of you so-called parents.'

'The subject is closed for now,' said Barry, following the deepest of breaths with the faintest of smiles.

'I know why,' said Kim. She waited. '*Dad.*'

If he knew what she meant, he didn't deny it. He just

walked away, leaving them in his study.

Looking out of the window from behind his desk, Kim saw where he'd gone. But she could hardly believe what happened next. Barry sat down on the swing. She looked back at Fizzy and by the time she turned back to the garden he wasn't just sitting still – he was really putting some force into it, gathering some serious height. Kim bet Damon was never allowed to swing that high or fast. She couldn't help but laugh, and turned again to share her grin with Fizzy.

But the smile vanished. 'He thinks I'd corrupt you.'

'You wouldn't.'

'I know. I couldn't if I tried.'

As she watched him, she pictured him punctured all over like a Voodoo doll. After all she'd been needling him all day, no breaks. Kim felt tired now.

Laura appeared again, with knitting in her hands.

'Do you know how, Kimberlie? I've been teaching Fizzy.'

'Nelle knits for Barbados. It's meant to be therapeutic, right?' said Kim.

'Oh, very.'

Laura looked relaxed and the wool looked fabulous: thick and soft and changing colour all over the place like a mallard's head in the sun.

Kim sneezed. 'Go on then.'

When Ro arrived, Kim's first scarf was growing fast and looking gorgeous. Fizzy was in the bathroom and Kim wandered upstairs too, declaring she needed to go herself. Really she wanted to sneak a look at the master bedroom. But creeping along the corridor, she was surprised to see

Fizzy was already there, exactly where she'd been heading herself. Kim smiled. Fizzy was full of surprises but she had no idea she was there. She was just about to hiss '*Psst*' when she saw how still and stiff Fizzy stood. It looked like she was listening to something on the other side of the door. But what?

Then she saw Fizzy's hands lift to the space on each side of her head, as if she wanted to shield her ears without touching. What could she hear? Whatever it was, it was getting through. As Kim watched, Fizzy's shoulders sank and she covered her head.

A floorboard creaked under Kim's foot. Fizzy turned, shocked to see her there. Whatever she'd heard had pulled her face out of shape, and though Kim could see her trying, she couldn't quite mend it. Her eyes looked dark and full.

'What?' Kim asked. 'Fizzy?'

'I don't feel well. I think I've caught your cold,' Fizzy dashed towards the nearest bathroom, as if she might be sick.

Kim stared, disbelieving, at her back.

'Talk to me!' she cried. 'I'll wait.'

But when Fizzy came out, she only repeated that she felt ill.

Why are you lying? Kim's eyes asked her. *Don't. Tell me the truth.*

'Kim!' called Ro.

It was time to go home.

CHAPTER SIXTEEN

'That girl has some apologising to do,' Barry said, before Kim was half-way down the drive.

Fizzy didn't answer. How could it be Kim's fault she was different? It felt mean, like a set-up by journalists to catch people out and make them look bad. When Fizzy thought about how kind Kim was and how hard the visit must have been for her, it seemed so unfair. It was like scowling at a carrot and asking God to forgive it for not being a mango.

But now Kim didn't like her anymore, not the way she had. She might not be as angry as Barry and she might not be praying about it, but they were both disappointed in her.

'Are you all right, darling?' Laura asked her. 'You look very tired.'

'I am. I've got a headache. I'm going to lie down.'

No sooner had Fizzy curled up on her bed than she heard the door slam. She jumped up in time to see Barry from the landing window, in his tracksuit and running shoes, sprinting out of the drive.

Closing her bedroom door behind her this time, Fizzy studied herself in the mirror and wondered who she was, really. Her face was so flat, with no smile and no brightness. She remembered the voice in the master bedroom, not talking to Laura but the Lord. Not in his church voice or his holiday voice, or even the cold tone he used with Kim.

This one was new, shaky and off-key. Even before she'd digested the words, the sound of them had made it hard for Fizzy to breathe.

'Lord, forgive Kimberlie and bring her from darkness of unbelief into your light.'

Were those the words? Perhaps she was remembering wrong. Or maybe she'd misheard. Fizzy could imagine Kim laughing at that, but not at the prayer.

'Calm the storm of my anger, Lord.' Was that really it? His voice had lowered, scratchy with breath that would roar into a shout if he let it. She knew that scratch. But it was hard to be sure of the words even then, and now she didn't want to bring back the rest. 'Give me the patience to guide Felicity back from her waywardness, and protect her from the sin that draws her from your path.'

Kim was right, thought Fizzy. Barry thought she was being corrupted already. But if he knew Kim, he'd understand how wrong he was. 'You're wrong about both of us,' she murmured, tears filling the words, even though Barry would be miles out of sight by now.

Why did he have to cry out to the Lord like that, about her? Didn't he care that she might overhear? And why did Kim have to find her there outside the door and know she was lying? She couldn't tell her the truth, not without making sure she hated her own father more than ever.

Fizzy understood that Barry was finding it hard to forgive her for plotting with Kris. But how could it be a sin if you measured it against the heart, like Ro said? And how could he blame Kim for darkness when he'd been the stormy one?

Now Fizzy understood something else, something new

but obvious. Barry had always wanted a daughter like Suranne, who closed her eyes when she sang 'Shine, Jesus, shine', and smiled as if the light was inside her. But now things were different – she was different. He'd loved her anyway, when he had to, but he didn't love her now. She wasn't his; he wasn't hers.

Fizzy gave the worry doll a stroke and picked up her phone. From her Bible she took a piece of paper with a number on it. The smell of cigarettes was faint now. She should have added the number to her contacts, but putting her real dad next to all the other names and numbers would be like adding him to the rest of her life and that was much too full already. She imagined Barry checking through her messages for a 'Dad' that wasn't by him, and using it as watertight evidence of how far she'd strayed.

The little note kept Kris separate and special – but not safe, unless she was really careful. She could picture Laura too, checking her pockets before a wash and holding the note as if to say, 'Fizzy, how could you?' But this scrap of paper was the first thing her father had ever given her. It was a secret, and a kind of escape.

Fizzy looked at the scribbled digits. What would she say in a text? She'd rather hear his voice; maybe he'd be happy to hear hers too. Nervously she tapped in the numbers and hoped he'd be free to answer.

She could barely hear his answering 'Yeah?' for all the noise around him: voices, the dance beat of some song she couldn't place. He wasn't at Mike's house.

'Daddy?' she asked, and something wobbled. She sounded like a six-year-old, and felt like one, too.

'Sorry?' he shouted. 'Speak up.'

'Dad,' she said, and it came out flatter this time. 'It's Felicity. I can't shout.'

'Hang on, sweetheart,' he said, his voice different now, and she heard the background noises thin until they were replaced with running water.

'That's better,' he said. 'Are you all right, sweetheart?'

It was true that he cared about her; she could hear it now.

'I don't know why I've rung,' she said.

'To speak to me?' he suggested. She pictured his grin.

'Yes,' she said, smiling.

'Missing your old dad, eh?'

'Yes,' she said.

'You don't have to miss me,' he told her, and she heard him moving around. His voice was low but urgent. 'We could meet. If you want to, that is. If they haven't poisoned you against me?'

'No,' she said, weakly. She told herself there was no need to be afraid. Why shouldn't she spend time with her father? He was just as good to her as Barry was to Kim, but without the money. He was much kinder.

'Leave it to me,' he said. 'I'll sort something. I'll text you tomorrow morning, all right?'

'Yes,' she said.

'Bye, sweetness,' he said. 'Thanks for calling, yeah? You sleep tight.'

'Bye,' she said, because the word 'Daddy' broke up in her head.

As Kim approached the flat, the sharp evening air made her nose run. Wiping it, she told Ro that giving her the hanky was the nicest thing Barry did all day.

'I couldn't help saying stuff I knew they wouldn't like,' Kim told her. 'Pushing their buttons, the red ones.' She mimed electrocution and pictured Barry with a few volts fizzing through him. 'But I felt like they were doing the same to me. And Barry was horrible to Fizzy.'

Ro was nodding but she looked surprised too. 'He's a good father, Kim. He tries to be.'

'He wasn't trying today.'

Ro talked about challenging situations, but Kim couldn't see any excuse.

'Jeanette gave Fizzy space, you know? She didn't put her through some sort of test so she could fail.'

A cat mooched up to them, mewing its interest. 'Don't even think about it,' she told it. She wasn't a fan of cats that tried to get familiar, even on a good day. But she didn't expect the animal to understand, turn kamikaze and shoot out across the traffic as if the road was empty. And though steering wheels must have swung in a James Bond kind of way, and at least one brake squeaked, the traffic moved right on. Like a chain that had twisted but straightened up, no links broken. The stupid cat hadn't killed anyone, but was it mashed under someone's wheels?

Gripping Ro's arm, Kim breathed out with relief at the sight of its tail and backside on the opposite pavement. It disappeared round the side of a hedge, but only after it had turned back towards them, eyes glaring fiercely in the twilight.

'Do you think it knows how close it came?' Ro asked. 'There could have been a pile-up.'

'I hate that,' said Kim, suddenly angry. 'Lives just end.'

She used a throat-cutting forefinger. 'Or get squished out of shape but people have to limp off and get on with it. Nothing anyone can do. Not even Barry and his sidekick up there!'

She pointed up to the sky, which looked full of rain.

'Oh, Kim,' said Ro. 'The cat's alive. You have so much living and loving to do, so much to give.'

'I can't love them and they'll never love me!'

'Love isn't always an arrow strike. Sometimes it's a slow burner. But you and Fizzy fit, don't you? That's obvious. You connected right away.'

'I thought so, yeah, but not anymore.'

'Trust me,' said Ro, one hand light on Kim's shoulder. 'She does. She doesn't blame people or hold grudges.'

'I do,' said Kim. Hate could be a slow burner too.

A bird landed on the top of an old, leaning fence with jagged holes and graffiti. Kim thought of Laura and the strange biological fact that Ro really was her sister.

'Why can't Laura talk about ballet? Anyone would think she was a lap dancer in some seedy club!'

Ro stopped. Kim saw her shoulders fall. What did it mean?

'We've all got histories, Kim. Sometimes we'd rather rewrite them. She'll tell you what she wants to tell, if and when it feels right. She was a lovely dancer, but things don't always go the way we plan.'

'Tell me about it!' joked Kim. But she wished Ro would, because Laura gave nothing. Tea and programmes in the post didn't count.

She'd have to do some investigating of her own.

Damon waved goodbye to Billy and his stepdad. When he

started to tell Laura about his day with Billy, he could tell she wasn't really interested.

'What?' he asked.

But she only said that wasn't a very polite kind of question and told him to run a shower.

'Where's Fizzy?' he tried, but he was told she wasn't well and probably asleep by now even though it wasn't even eight o'clock.

'I hate it when people are in moods,' Damon said, heading upstairs. 'I bet Jesus doesn't like it either.'

He guessed it was his new sister's fault. Kim Braddock must have been rude. His dad thought she was an unbeliever and hadn't been brought up properly. So now she got more prayers than anyone else.

Damon turned on his laptop, but his mum soon appeared to make him shut it down.

'Bedtime,' she said. 'It's been a long day.'

'I like long days,' he said, 'as long as they don't start too early.'

He asked her what they'd done when Kim Braddock came, but his mother didn't look at him when she talked. And when he heard about Wimbledon, he couldn't believe they'd gone without him.

Under the shower, he remembered telling Billy things he wasn't supposed to mention – about babies going home from hospital with the wrong parents. It made him feel cross with Billy, who'd made a big deal of it all over again. But Barry and Laura would make a ginormous deal of him telling, if they ever found out, because it was such a big secret and he'd promised.

'Don't tell *anyone*,' he'd told Billy.

Damon noticed in the mirror that he was frowning in a way his dad called a pout. Things were all right before. Now he was supposed to get used to a new sister, a hard one who probably swore and might be in a gang. And nobody thought about him, even Fizzy because he wasn't her brother. She liked her new dad more than him, even though he was mean and probably a criminal too.

Damon wondered what would happen if he prayed for Kim and Kris to go away again. How did it work when two people prayed for opposite things? He wouldn't waste one unless he was sure it would stick.

'Please Lord, make Billy forget,' he muttered as he turned off the water. That wasn't a big job for God. It'd be a bit like wiping away the wrong answer on his whiteboard before the teacher saw, and he was getting good at that himself.

Jeanette greeted Kim with an uneasy smile that looked like a question.

'I'm ill,' she said. 'But I don't need a Mother Hen. I just want my bed.'

Jeanette said the photos were back from the studio and absolutely lovely of both of them. Kim only grunted, but when she'd cleaned her teeth, she found them in their plastic wallet on her bed.

Kim looked at herself in her blacks and greys, silver hoops and Converses, her hair gelled and blocky. Next to her, Fizzy looked soft, like blossom by a stone wall. A bit heavier but much less solid all the same. Her eyes were big with everything Kim kept out of hers. It was her baptism look, with the light on inside. But why? Was she glad to be there, with Kim and her new mum? And if she was, if that was some kind of happiness, where had it gone? Had Barry snatched it away? Or was that her fault, going for the tackle at every glimpse of leg, with or without the ball?

Kim didn't know what had happened between the flat-share smile and the bathroom, but it must have been big. She had seen right through Fizzy's wobbly little smile in the Duvall doorway – seen through it and read something desperate: the need to head for her room and shut the door, just like Kim was going to do now.

Kim turned on the TV, volume up.

CHAPTER SEVENTEEN

Fizzy woke hot and damp. Her throat was pricking and the air felt hard to breathe. She cried out, 'No!'

Maybe it was more of a whimper than a shout. What had made the dream so bad that the fear hadn't stopped even now she was awake? Through her curtains she could tell that Sunday morning was beautiful and dewy. But she was lying with the sound of feet pounding and voices clashing in the dark. The room was bright but the darkness of the dream clung like a shroud, and made her shiver all the more. Was she trapped or hiding? Was she lost or couldn't they find her? Why was it so hard to breathe?

The worst dreams were very nearly real.

But it was over now. She thanked the Lord for sunshine and hoped He'd helped Kim to sleep peacefully.

A text showed she was already up. Asking Fizzy if she was all right, it ended with a kiss. I'm fine, she answered. Hope you are too. It's a new day. X

Remembering 'sunshine and shadows', Fizzy took her phone to the window, where she saw both in the garden below. There was another message, sent late. Kris. He would see her at the same newsagent's at nine-thirty if she could get away to buy a paper or a loaf of bread.

Her chest tightened. How? She never went out alone on a Sunday morning. Her parents didn't buy a paper because church meant there was no time to read it, and anyway it was the Sabbath. Laura was far too organised to run out of anything. It was impossible!

She sent a reply: Will try but not sure how. There was no response to that. Fizzy realised she couldn't really ask the Lord to help her plan a way of meeting Kris in secret, which might include lying and would definitely mean disobedience. Excitement made her breathy. More waywardness! 'Every sin,' Barry had said once, 'makes the next sin easier and bigger than the last.'

But Barry didn't see her heart like God did. Although she couldn't imagine how, Fizzy knew she must go. Everyone else was angry with Kris, but it would show she still believed in him. She'd give him another chance to prove them wrong. Wouldn't Jesus do the same?

Fizzy heard footsteps, a tap and a kettle filling. Barry and Laura were already up, washed and dressed. But when she walked towards the dining room, she felt the silence between them, louder and thicker than water or steam. It broke into a gasp, and from the doorway she saw that one of them had just spilt coffee on the linen tablecloth. There was panic in the way Laura soaked it up with paper towel, cleared it away and dabbed at the polished table underneath.

'It'll stain,' said Laura.

'Take it easy,' Barry told her, in a voice that was hard.

He turned. 'Good morning, Felicity. I hope you're feeling better.'

Fizzy could tell he hadn't forgiven her. He reminded her of a manager at an expensive hotel, greeting people he barely knew.

'Not really,' she mumbled, and was allowed to eat breakfast on a tray in the living room as long as she watched the Christian TV channel.

Looking out of the front window towards the road, she felt helpless. Soon her dad would be waiting for her, and she still had no clue how to get away. Kim would have ideas, but then Kim would say, 'For God's sake, are you mad! Keep away from him. He's scum.' Fizzy couldn't help knowing some worse words, but she didn't like to imagine Kim using them. And whatever words she used, she was wrong, because people could change. Look at Saint Paul.

Fizzy could tell from the conversation, or lack of it, that Barry and Laura were still upset or angry with Kim – and maybe with each other too. It made her long for Damon to wake up and be his loud and tiring self.

Fizzy spent so long in the bath that by the time she climbed out she was wrinkly. And Barry had already left early for church because he was on steward duty, but she knew she had to write him a letter. She could be careful about her words and make him see that Kim wasn't a bad girl at all. In her room she began, only to screw up the best blue writing paper.

By nine o'clock she still couldn't get it right. Maybe she should write to Laura instead, even though she was downstairs? But it was impossible to defend Kim without criticising Barry, and Laura wouldn't go with her usual theory – 'six of one and half a dozen of the other' – when he was the one and Kim was the other.

As for the rest, what could she say? That she'd lied about lying? That she'd done it for Kris?

She put down her pen. The clock was ticking; Kris would be on his way already. She didn't know how she was going to get out of the house but did it matter? She was already guilty of so many sins. Even if she was found out, how much worse could it make anything?

Downstairs she glimpsed Laura through the dining room doorway, cloth and polish in rubber-gloved hands. Fizzy opened the door to the under-stairs cupboard and took her softest sneakers off the rack. She crept to the door and slipped them on. Opening the door as quietly as she could, she called, 'I'm just going to get some air. I've still got a headache.'

She wasn't lying. Waiting a moment, to be quite certain Laura had heard, she stood on the doormat.

'Fizzy? Aren't you well?' came faintly from the dining room.

At once Fizzy shut the door and ran. She had to make sure that by the time Laura opened it again, she was out of range. Laura wouldn't shout; she never had.

Still running, she couldn't believe how soon her phone rang in her back pocket. 'Mum and Dad'. Of course! She was no good at this. She couldn't switch off, so she'd have to answer. 'Hello?'

'Ten minutes, Fizzy,' said Laura. 'Don't go further than the end of the road.'

'Ten minutes,' she said, as brightly as she could. 'I haven't got much battery.' It was probably true, because she hadn't thought to charge it for ages.

Outside it was colder than it looked, and she hadn't brought a coat. Her bare feet soon stiffened inside her shoes. The road was so quiet that when a squirrel aimed a sharp, angry cry at a rival a branch below, she almost jumped too. The pair of them scampered along the rock star's wall, disappearing behind the security fence of trees.

A jogger passed her by, a serious one with a full kit and no flab. Otherwise the people were mainly dog walkers heading to or from the Common. No one spoke. The bus that stopped to let someone off had more faces on the film poster along its side than at its windows. The emptiness made her feel even more furtive.

'Lord,' she murmured, 'Let it be all right.'

Then she could see the newsagent's and customers passing in or out, some with newspapers and one with a loaf of sliced bread, the cheap sort Laura said had no goodness.

Kris had goodness. She was sure of it. He hadn't said whether he'd be inside or out, but there was no sign of him yet. She crossed the road carefully and tried to look through the windows, decorated with 'Deals of the Week' like a classroom with the best work on display. A man stared back. It wasn't Kris and she didn't like his stubble or his belly. She looked away. Wandering towards the post box, she told herself there was no need to be afraid. The Lord was with her.

Fizzy pretended to be texting until the man had passed. Hearing footsteps, she turned round to find a stick-like old woman with piled-up pink hair and smudged coral lipstick. She was taking small steps with a short, fluffy dog shuffling from side to side as if it had no legs. Neither of them noticed her as they headed into the shop.

Fizzy checked the time on her phone. Her father was late now and her ten minutes were up. No message. How long before Laura called again?

She clicked on 'Kimberlie'. As she heard the ring, she realised what she was doing. Tactics. Making herself unavailable, using Kim. *Lord, forgive me,* she thought, as Kim said her name.

'I'm sorry about yesterday,' Fizzy told her.

'Don't you think that's my line?'

'No. You were being real.' It struck Fizzy that Barry had been too, and that being real had its drawbacks.

'A real badass?' Kim laughed. 'Sorry. At least I didn't swear.'

'We're still friends, aren't we?' Fizzy asked, hoping Kim couldn't tell she was starting to feel sad again.

'Yea-ahh!'

Fizzy wanted something to seal it, to show Kim she trusted her. 'There's something I haven't told you,' she blurted, unplanned. 'There's a boy I really like, called Michael. There's a baptism photo of everyone who came to the church and he's in it. I scanned it and cut out his face in a heart shape.'

'Fizzy Duvall!'

'It's in my Bible. I might show you one day.' Fizzy realised she was smiling stupidly.

'Only if you want. I won't tease if you do. Swear!' Kim laughed. 'It's all right, don't panic – that's not an instruction!'

Ending the call, Fizzy felt her smile straighten. How friendly Kim would have been if she'd known where she was and why? The little woman with the white dog was back now, a Sunday Times under her arm. She watched them edge away as if they were low on battery too. The time on the phone had moved on another minute. He wasn't coming. It was all for nothing.

She tapped in a text: Waited but had to go. Sorry Dad'. Then she turned off her phone and started to hurry home, running and then slowing and taking deep breaths.

Remembering the short cut through a new estate, she took it, feeling the quietness away from the road. She mustn't cry. There would be a reason. He'd be really sorry and explain.

On a bench at the foot of a cherry tree some way ahead, a boy and a girl were kissing. So romantic! There was blossom around their feet. But Fizzy felt like an intruder. She'd have to go right past. Perhaps, she thought, they wouldn't even notice or hear. Their legs were touching and the boy's arm was round the girl's waist.

As Fizzy drew closer, trying not to look at the couple on the seat, she stopped. She heard herself breathe in. She knew the peach folds of asymmetric cardigan hanging down. She knew the long white neck and the small, silver cross around it. Suranne, dressed for church in a full, new skirt. Suranne, mouth to mouth with Michael Conradi.

All she could do was run straight past them, looking ahead like Barry when he ran, focused and strong. As if she ran every day and was good at it. As if she hadn't noticed them, any more than the man washing his car on the drive or the boy taking aim at a basketball net next door. The faster she could be, the greater her chance of disappearing out of the cut-through before they saw her.

If Barry could see the speed she managed, he'd be astonished! With no idea how, she kept on running. Her eyes were dry, but the tears were deeper down inside her, blocked up, hard and jagged like shards of ice. But what had she seen? The back of a boy's head, that was all. Michael Conradi wasn't the only boy in Wimbledon with beautiful hair. She might be jumping to conclusions, fearing the worst the way Laura told her not to do.

Fizzy couldn't run any more. There was so much air to breathe out; she was full of it, too full. Her heart felt huge and hot.

She turned out onto the road. Bending, holding her knees on the pavement, she kept her eyes down. She didn't dare look back into the estate. They were Michael's legs. They were Michael's hands touching Suranne.

He might have turned and seen her, smiled and said, 'Hi, Fizzy.' But it was hard to be thankful that the Lord had spared her that. Of all the boys Suranne could have chosen, why hers? Why now, when her new dad had let her down and it was already hard enough to think and be?

Looking at her watch, she told herself there was time. She must walk calmly to her front door, as if nothing had happened at all.

But when she saw that door, it was open and Laura was holding it, shoulders falling.

'I said ten minutes,' she said, crisply. 'I tried to call you back. You must make sure you keep your phone charged. How's your headache?'

'Bad,' Fizzy told her. Her eyes filled. She was afraid her lying was improving fast. 'Can I stay home?'

Laura looked horrified. 'Oh, darling, no! Take a couple of painkillers, quickly. We're having late lunch at Ro's, all of us. Not that Barry knows yet.' Laura put on her velvet jacket and picked up her handbag. 'By all of us I mean Jeanette and Kim too. Both families, complete. Well, nearly.'

At first Fizzy was too busy wondering how this had been arranged so quickly to process all the meaning. For a moment she was glad, but then she understood.

'You mean my father won't be there,' she said. She

wiped a tear away with the back of her hand. 'Nobody invited him, not even Ro.'

Laura put down her bag and took Fizzy's shoulders in both hands.

'No, Fizzy, that's not it. Ro wanted him there. That was the point, or part of it. Barry would have other ideas, of course, but I said yes, because it can't go on. Kris Braddock has to be told.'

Fizzy saw now. They wanted to gang up on him. She pictured him at the table, outnumbered like Robin Hood in the old film Barry and Damon liked – but with no sword, and no outlaws standing by in case he needed them.

'Has to be told?' she repeated, following Laura into the kitchen.

She watched her running the cold tap, and tried to keep her breathing under control. The indoor warmth was too thick and too much. Laura didn't answer. She just handed her the glass of water and the tablets.

'Told what?'

'Nothing, in fact, darling,' said Laura. 'He's gone. Ro rang Mike to say lunch was on, but when Mike went to wake Kris, he wasn't there. He'd left a note saying he'd outstayed his welcome and was moving on.'

Fizzy clenched so she wouldn't sob.

'It's for the best, Fizzy. You'll see. I'm sure of it. Take the painkillers.'

The tablets sat in the palm of Laura's white hand. An impatient hand, fingers pulled tight. Fizzy took and swallowed them. She followed her out again into the hall.

'Damon!' called Laura. 'We're going to be late!'

'Where's he gone?' asked Fizzy. She needed control

now. 'Tell me, please.'

'What? Who?' cried Damon, bounding downstairs. 'What now?'

'Later,' Laura told him. 'We're going to lunch with Ro.'

'Not with them!' cried Damon. 'Not Kim Braddock!'

'You don't know her,' protested Fizzy thickly, 'so don't judge! You just have to give people a chance and let them be who they are.'

Her nose was running but she had no tissue. Laura handed her a crisp, clean one from her bag.

'Where's he gone?' Fizzy asked, so quietly she barely heard the words herself, but slowly, with pauses between them because they mattered. 'My dad – where's he gone?'

Laura put an arm round her, but it felt stiff. Fizzy wished Jeanette was there to hold her and let her cry.

'I don't think the note said, Fizzy. I'm sorry.'

'I'm not going to lunch,' said Damon, pouting. He held on to the end of the banister as if the hall was flooded. 'Not if she's coming. Why can't they all go away, not just him?'

'Stop it!' cried Fizzy. 'Please! Just shut up!'

He pulled a face. 'See? She's ruining everything. She's ruining Fizzy!'

'Damon,' said Laura, his name suddenly sharp at the edges, 'your father's expecting us. We'll talk about lunch later. So please be sensible, or it might be my turn to throw a wobbly!' She picked up her pumps. 'Or a shoe!'

Damon's eyes rounded at Fizzy. Laura opened the door and said, 'After you, both of you.'

They stepped outside and watched Laura lock the door. It seemed to take longer than usual, and she was very impatient with the keys that wouldn't turn.

'You haven't set the burglar alarm!' said Damon.

Laura stiffenened. 'As far as I'm concerned,' she said, testing the door with a vigorous shake, 'the burglars can take everything we've got.'

'Not my cricket bat!'

'Burglars don't care about cricket bats,' Fizzy told him.

'Everything's going to be all right,' Laura said, turning towards them and sounding smooth again, almost furry, 'from now on. Really it is.' She gave Fizzy a brave smile. 'Your head'll clear soon, you'll see.'

For hours Kim's Sunday morning was weirdly dull. Then the phone rang and she could tell Jeanette was talking to Laura. What did she want? Would one of those strawberry bracelets Kim had refused arrive by courier any minute?

Remembering that some secrets were easier to find out than others, she turned on the computer. She tapped Laura's name, the one on the ballet programme, into the search engine. Not an American psychotherapist... not a chick lit author. There she was! There was a Wikipedia entry on her mother!

No photo, and not much text either. But enough. 'Considered one of the most promising dancers of her generation, Laura Glendenning won acclaim in a daring production of Stravinksy's Firebird. She abandoned classical ballet soon afterwards to set up her own modern dance company, Jagged Edge, but the enterprise ended in bankruptcy.'

Kim had already seen the key words in the final sentence but she wasn't sure she was reading them properly.

'Glendenning had a breakdown and was admitted to

The Priory with addiction problems. She no longer dances.'

'Kim!' called Jeanette.

Kim clicked off the screen.

'We're going to lunch at Ro's,' Jeanette told her. 'Don't argue. It's overdue.'

But Kim wasn't arguing.

Fizzy had never been late for church before. She felt awkward as they crept in and slipped into the empty seats near the back. Suranne was sitting a few pews ahead, glowing. Fizzy tried not to look at the hair Michael had fingered, now coiled up in a spiral held by a wooden comb, or the white neck his lips had touched. There was a big wooden cross on the wall above Suranne's blonde head, and Fizzy kept her eyes firmly on it. But Suranne was hard to overlook. Through all the songs she clapped and swayed, calling out more than usual, 'Praise Jesus!' and 'Yes, Lord!' with her hands up high.

When it was time to leave the service for their class upstairs, Fizzy had no choice but to follow the others out, but she kept at the back of the group. At the bottom of the stairs was the toilet. As the others walked up chatting, she went inside and locked the door.

Holding the basin, she wished she could be sick. Wished she could stay there, or run all the way home. She stuck her fingers in her mouth but only spluttered. It was no use. Emerging quietly, she smoothed her cheeks and her top and went slowly upstairs. They would have begun by now, with a prayer. She'd sit behind Suranne so she couldn't see her face, and too far away for her to talk to her.

Pushing the door, she found everyone still talking while

the leaders stood beside a laptop, checking loose connections. The drop-down screen was blank. The chairs were arranged in a circle, one waiting for her, next to Suranne. With no choice, she sat.

'Fizzy,' whispered Suranne. 'Are you all right? I didn't know you could run so fast. I nearly had to run myself. We lost track of the time.'

Fizzy tried to smile, but she didn't think it was working. So she *had* been spotted. Had Michael seen her too? She didn't want to imagine how she looked running, her breasts and bottom swaying.

'I was going to tell you about Michael, but your phone's always off. Dad says he's lost because he doesn't come to church but he's got a good heart.'

'I know.' She knew better than anyone. She didn't need to be told.

'You're not upset, are you, Fizz? I was a bit worried, you know?'

Suranne didn't look worried. Fizzy wished she could do Oprah. Beyoncé. Anyone but herself.

'Of course not.'

'I thought maybe you fancied him?'

Fizzy frowned with her forehead and tried to make her mouth smile. 'No,' she whispered – truthfully.

She didn't fancy him. She liked his hands and his dark hair that would be soft to touch. Most of all she liked his thoughtfulness, but now he'd be thinking of Suranne.

Fizzy looked up at Eve and Winston, who were leading their class today. It was time to pray, but when she closed her eyes, she saw Michael Conradi smiling – not at her, dumpy and shy in her white baptism dress, but at Suranne

211

Washington, tall and slim with Rapunzel hair. Mouth to mouth.

Michael would never love her. Maybe she was hard to love.

Eve was praying aloud: 'We lift into your hands, Father, all those we love who are blind to you, and ask your help to bring them out of the darkness into your light.'

Inside, Fizzy felt her breath snatched away as heat filled her. The prayer was hers. Picturing Kris, she surrounded him with that light. Once he believed in it, he would love her the way she loved him.

Then she tightened her own grip on her hand. The prayer could be about her! Barry could have told Eve and Winston about her – her lies, her deception, her wandering from the path. But how could she keep walking it when she couldn't see for darkness? She didn't make the darkness, and it felt so thick, as if the dreams had reached out into daylight and wrapped around her.

Fizzy opened her eyes. The other eyes were closed, heads bowed. She looked at the door. She could do it. She didn't have to stay. And before she knew it, she was running down the stairs. She felt a rush of shock at her own behaviour but she wasn't going back now. Outside the church she drank in the air until her eyes ran. She listened but no voice called after her. No footsteps on the stairs. So she wandered around the back to the old graveyard where no one was buried any more.

'ELLEN LOOSESTRIFE, beloved wife and mother, GONE TO GLORY', said the carving on the nearest gravestone.

A corner had broken off, lying a centimetre from the

slab with dandelions sprouting in the space. She pulled up the stone corner and felt the rough edge where it had torn away. Holding it in her right hand, she scraped her left wrist where the vein rose, and wondered how far down the blood flowed. 'Glory'. 'Heaven'. 'Paradise'. The words were so beautiful. Even the dandelion was beautiful, but it wouldn't live long.

Footsteps at last. His?

'Fizzy?'

They'd sent Suranne. Of course. Who else?

'I just needed air,' she said, and walked back inside.

Kim knew Ro's house would be easy to find because the home went with the job. The church next door wasn't ancient, with a needle of a spire, but a modern, red building with angles. Kim thought it looked as if the oversized 3D shapes from primary school maths had been fitted together by a drunk. Jeanette said Ro had told her it was a 'down-to-earth kind of church – eccentric too'.

'Like Ro,' said Kim, just before the Rev herself opened the door with a cry of 'Welcome!'

Stepping inside, Kim noticed a thin cross that wasn't made of paper, wood or plastic, stuck with a blue blob to the wall.

'What's that about?' she asked, as the women greeted and hugged.

'A palm cross,' Ro said. 'Every year we give them out to the kids from the primary school down the road, so the boys can hold them at the wrong end and have sword fights.' She grinned. 'Bless 'em.'

Kim could hear the others. She saw Fizzy's flowery

boots neatly pointing towards the wall. Rising from a spread bin liner opposite was a small tumble of shoes that must be Ro's, with a shopping bag, a bicycle pump, an umbrella and a net for pond dipping. It was all a bit like landfill, without the seagulls and flies.

The dining room had a long table with rows of chairs down each side. Enough room for all the disciples, Kim thought – all apart from Judas. Because Judas couldn't come.

Mike jumped up to introduce himself. He reminded Kim of the hairy bikers on TV, and she found herself talking like them when she spoke to him. The adults all stood up, and there was some hand-shaking across the table. Fizzy stayed sitting. Kim tried a wink to help her feel less awkward.

Fizzy smiled, grateful, wishing she could wink back. It was so good to see her. But she shouldn't have told her about Michael, because now sooner or later she'd have to know the rest.

With a forefinger Ro counted people and then places. There was one plate too many. Watching her clear it it away without comment, Kim kept her thoughts to herself. She was glad to sit next to Fizzy and hoped that Jeanette, being opposite, would kick her under the table if Barry set her off.

Fizzy was glad too. Ever since church finished, Barry had been treating her like a glass ornament that sat on the edge of a shelf and had to be watched and checked and kept safe. Now he seemed to forget her. He reached over the table to squeeze Laura's hand, before she glided into the kitchen to help Ro. Then he talked to Mike as if being a humanist wasn't so sinful after all.

Fizzy looked at the chair opposite hers, where Kris

would have sat. She imagined him smiling, and blinked him away. Then she glanced at Kim, but she didn't know what to say.

'Bad dreams?' Kim asked. 'That worry doll must be pea-sized by now.'

Fizzy nodded.

'Don't let any of them push you under,' murmured Kim.

When Laura and Ro brought all the dishes through, Damon sat up like a dog hoping for a bone, and Kim copied with paws and a tongue. She thought he might be growing on her. Ro joined her hands and everyone else closed their eyes.

Kim knew Jeanette would be willing her to shut hers too, but Barry couldn't check on her without breaking the rules. She could throw a tomato at his forehead and he couldn't prove a thing.

'Healing God,' said Ro, 'help us to love.' Then silence, a long one that continued until Ro tossed the salad leaves in the wooden bowl and said, 'That's all. Tuck in.'

Silently Kim added her first prayer for about ten years: *God, if you're there, keep Kris away from Fizzy. For ever and ever, amen.*

After lunch, when Fizzy asked whether she and Kim could go and sit in the garden at the back of the church, Barry surprised them both by saying that would be fine. They left most of the adults clearing away, while Damon had a chess lesson from Mike.

'He can't even name the pieces,' said Fizzy, 'and he still thinks he can win.'

Kim did an impression of Geordie Mike trying to teach

Damon that the knights didn't actually pour boiling oil out of the castle turrets onto the poor attacking pawns. Fizzy didn't quite laugh, but it was good to see her smile. Kim didn't say she wondered where Damon got his cockiness from. It was Barry's and she supposed she'd inherited her fair share.

As they walked down the path that led to the church, they could see the garden behind, tucked away from the road by bushes. There was a seat at the bottom of a gentle slope, and they sat and looked up to Ro's bungalow on the other side of a low wall where flowering plants climbed and blossomed. Fizzy named them.

'They can see us,' Kim realised, 'if they look.' Seeing Fizzy look puzzled, she added, 'Not the flowers – well, only in your world. The parents.'

'But they can't hear us unless they open the window,' said Fizzy.

Kim nodded. 'So, the summit meeting? Verdict so far?' She left the rest to Craig from *Strictly*. 'Not a total disaster, daaahling. I'll give it 6 so far.'

'Jeanette's lovely,' said Fizzy, thinking her mum deserved a nine for being so nice to everyone, even Damon. 'When she talks about Barbados, she goes all sunny.'

Kim let that go. Fizzy was such a romantic. But maybe Jeanette would be sunnier if she lived with Fizzy instead. Kim thought living with Barry and Laura would bring out the tornado in her.

'*Our Father* can't stop you meeting Brad next time you come,' she told Fizzy, 'whether he likes it or not.' She hadn't mentioned that Brad was gay as well as Muslim but imagined Barry's reaction to the second blow while still staggering and fizzing under the electric shock of the first.

Fizzy wasn't sure about that. Barry didn't like to be stopped. She leaned down to pick some daisies and started to thread them into a chain. Kim watched her using her perfectly arced thumb nail to slit a hole in each stem.

'Last time I did that I was eight,' she told her, and Fizzy stopped. 'No, go ahead. Adults should do it. You should teach Barry. It's more therapeutic than knitting.'

'He's all right,' Fizzy told her. 'He's kind really.'

'Yeah,' she said, 'but you think Kris is kind, don't you?'

For just a moment Fizzy felt found out. Could Kim know about the secret meeting?

'Yes,' she said, knowing how weak the word sounded and keeping her eyes on the daisies in her lap. 'I do.'

Kim could have laughed. That was just what Jeanette had said at the registry office wedding. Same trust, same blindness. When was someone going to let Fizzy in on the whole story? She supposed it didn't matter so much now that Kris had gone, and was a shadow again.

It was all very well Ro saying relationships took time to build, but secrets got in the way, and Kim was carrying too many around. She didn't suppose Fizzy knew her born-again mother had once been some sort of addict, before God and Barry saved her.

So many things poor Fizzy was too nice to be told.

'Kim,' said Fizzy, 'I need to tell you something. I saw Suranne kissing Michael Conradi this morning.'

'No!'

Fizzy looked up towards the road. 'Since then I've been feeling a bit... mad.'

'Whoah, mad-angry?' asked Kim, feeling quite angry

herself. Suranne Washington sounded two-faced to her.

'No, I mean mad-weird. Insane?' Fizzy smiled suddenly. It had felt true in the graveyard, but now, with Kim, the clematis and japonica, it seemed ridiculous.

Kim grinned. She couldn't help it. Fizzy grinned back, and when Kim laughed, Fizzy laughed too, only with a lot less noise. Kim thought a laugh like that must tickle. If it was hers, she'd want to force it out and let it go, like everything else Fizzy was bottling up.

'Michael's the mad one, must be!' she told Fizzy. 'He needs a hammer to knock some sense into him.'

Fizzy went to pick more daisies with her back to Kim, so she missed the hammer mime. Kim wasn't sure she was getting this right. She'd have to try again.

'You'll have all the nicest boys after you. Trust me.'

Fizzy sat down again, a handful of daisies in her lap. Kim was glad she hadn't mentioned Kris. Another blow and poor Fizzy would be on the ropes, counted out.

'Have I been behaving?' she asked. 'Better anyway.' She threaded a couple of daisies. 'I won't say better than who.' She became Prince Charles again. 'I say, Felicity, should that be 'whom'?'

'Yeah, kind of,' said Fizzy – just the way Kim would. At least, that was the idea. 'That's to the first question. And yeah, it should, so get it right!'

Kim fell back on the seat in overacted shock. She couldn't believe it! 'Cheek! I'm the impressionist!' Then sitting up, she put the daisies round Fizzy's neck. 'Gold medal,' she said.

When Fizzy said she liked Mike, Kim asked whether he and Ro were going to get married.

Fizzy smiled. 'I hope so,' she said. 'We can both be bridesmaids.'

'You can,' said Kim, grimacing. 'Pink satin wouldn't suit me.'

Suddenly Fizzy wondered how she would feel if Kris married again – a stepmum to add to the two mothers she already had. Then Kim took a text, smiled and said it was Brad making sure she was OK.

Fizzy turned on her own phone while Kim was replying, and found Suranne's message: Are you all right? Remember I'm here for you. X.

Before this morning, Fizzy would have believed in the kindness. Now she wondered whether it was just a tactic to stop her telling. She turned it off quickly. Such a risk! So stupid! She flushed imagining Kris calling. Kim was amazing, but she wouldn't understand, and all this was just pretend, really. The secrets were so big and heavy they'd smash the bench in two if they landed between them.

'Maybe we should do some match-making with Jeanette and Brad's dad,' said Kim. 'That way we'd both have Brad for a stepbrother.' She turned to Fizzy with an open-mouthed grin. 'And we'd be step-sisters. Kind of.'

'Cool,' murmured Fizzy, although she thought they already were.

'Can you get God working on it?' asked Kim. 'No disrespect. I don't really understand prayer. I could ask Brad, because he does it, set times a day. On a mat, I think. If there's a God, it must be the same one.'

Fizzy smiled but she wasn't sure.

'You can say what you think,' Kim told her. 'Big Barry hasn't got the japonica bugged.'

A bird hopped across the ragged grass on the slope. It had a long tail that tipped and bobbed as it hopped along, and a yellow backside.

Kim caught Fizzy watching it, and smiled remembering her story about the old lady and the dead man's soul. 'I don't know much about birds but that's definitely not Harry.' She could see Fizzy was pleased she hadn't forgotten. 'Look at him! That's Napoleon. Better salute.'

Fizzy laughed as Kim raised her upper body stiff to attention and the bird eyed her before flying off. She told her it was a grey wagtail.

'When I get a dog, that's what I'll call it,' said Kim, 'Wagtail.' She thought she could ask Laura for a puppy for Christmas. Why not? Maybe she should start pulling a few strings herself.

She looked at Fizzy in her daisy chain necklace and felt her face grow serious. 'No repeating what we say together. Both ways, I mean. I can keep it zipped. It's between us two, yeah, whatever?'

The chain broke and a few daisies fell to the ground.

'Oh no!' cried Fizzy, leaning to pick them up. Another couple fell. It was like the Buddha and the cigarette butt but worse. It had to be mended.

'It's all right, we don't need them,' Kim told her, 'just each other, right?'

Fizzy stopped scrambling. 'Yes,' she said, too weakly, and wished. 'About what happened before you left the house – it's hard to explain. It wasn't you.'

'OK,' said Kim. 'Cool. Tell me when you can. I've got things to tell you too.'

Fizzy smiled but she was glad not to hear them. Not

today.

'Between us – a pact. Promise, right?' persisted Kim, because there was a faraway look in Fizzy's eyes and she thought they might be clouding.

'Promise,' said Fizzy, giving Kim a smile that she wished was real.

At the window Ro was waving them in.

The game of 'Crounderten' on the Common was Damon's idea and Damon's word. So the rules were his too. Fizzy didn't like games with bats, balls or scoring, but she could see Kim enjoyed it nearly as much as Barry and Damon. They were the three who struck every ball and scored every time – three peas who couldn't see they belonged in the same pod. No room for her.

Fizzy wished she could be more like Jeanette, who wiggled as she waited with the bat, mistimed, laughed and ran anyway, not caring when Damon yelled 'Out!' at first post. When it was Fizzy's turn to bat, Ro bowled a gentle ball, but she still missed it completely. Barry muttered, 'Bad luck,' but it was a kind of lie. He'd always been ashamed of her uselessness, and now he could just feel sorry for her instead.

Kim was hoping Fizzy would knock the next ball right to the river – or into rubber pieces exploding like Bonfire Night around their heads. It might help. But she missed all three and wouldn't take an extra chance.

Barry was more predictable than a boy-band song. Tense as a predator, he waited for the ball as if he needed to rip it apart to survive. Then he swung his bat and whacked it half way to Putney Bridge, sprinting chest first like an Olympic finalist in a photo finish. Kim supposed he must win the Fathers' race at Fizzy's posh Sports Day every year, probably in a straw hat and white trousers with a cocktail in his hand. Because he needed to.

At the end, when Ro announced that he was today's champion, he took a showy bow and looked straight at Kim, eyes bright. Did he need to impress her as well as beat her? *You could*, she thought, looking back, *if you looked at Fizzy and used your heart.*

'Second!' cried Damon. 'Silver medal!'

'Joint silver with Kim,' said Ro.

'Hey, bro!' Kim offered a high five.

He paused, then slapped his hand against hers. It was only when she looked at Fizzy clapping half-heartedly that she realised she hadn't had much fun. Kim's own day had gone from a six to a seven somehow, with balls to hit and sweat cooling on her forehead and her father – very briefly – almost awesome as well as needy. But poor Fizzy's was probably a minus one.

A soft, clean Barry kissed Fizzy's cheek when she said goodnight.

'Why couldn't I stay at Ro's?'

In the bath she'd replayed the invitation, and her own role was different. 'I *need* to!' was what she should have said.

'You were looking so tired,' said Laura, joining him in the hallway. 'Sleep well, darling. Lift it all to the Lord.'

But that was the point. At Ro's she might have slept without the dreams. She might have woken to a different kind of morning, where secrets could breathe. It was too late now. Her own bed was waiting to take her to the dark places that kept pressing in.

Wearing an auto-smile, she started up the stairs.

Then Barry called from behind her, 'Is something going on between Suranne and Michael Conradi?'

She stopped just a moment, turned and asked, 'Why?'

'Graham Washington asked. He thought you'd know.'

'I don't know why!' When Damon spoke like that they called him sullen, but the word didn't even begin to cover the way Fizzy sounded to herself. Barry's questions were making her see them all over again again, on the seat with blossom around them. 'He could ask his precious daughter,' she said.

'I'm asking *you*, Fizzy.' His voice was quiet, but she knew it didn't let go. 'Do *you* know?'

Laura laid a hand on Barry's arm. 'Never mind…' she began.

Barry looked from Fizzy to Laura. 'I suppose it'll keep until the morning,' he said, turning away. Fizzy knew he was disappointed again. He was mourning her and it wasn't fair because she wasn't the one who'd stopped loving.

'They're dating,' Fizzy said. She hadn't planned on telling anyone, certainly not Barry. But it was the truth, and she couldn't lie awake all night making and remaking the sentence, thinking what all the different versions would mean and do. 'But he's not wayward. He just thinks for himself.'

Without waiting for Barry to disagree, she hurried upstairs.

'Shall I come up, darling, and pray with you?' called Laura.

Fizzy shook her head. From the top of the landing, she

told them, without turning round, 'I just want to sleep. God knows that already.'

'Of course He does,' she heard Laura say as she closed her bedroom door.

CHAPTER EIGHTEEN

Kim couldn't believe Fizzy's term still hadn't quite started. She told Brad by text that she might want to go to the posh girls' school after all. But nothing was getting any clearer except Fizzy and the pact. It was hard to concentrate on Geography or Science, and at the start of the first game since Easter, she felt even more charged-up than her phone.

The other team had a reputation for being hard to beat, and their freckled striker had scored twenty-eight goals since September. She was the one to stop. But Kim was aiming for a pincer-like grip on the ball – not a savage kick at the girl's long right leg that sent her screaming to the ground.

'Sorry,' muttered Kim, one hand raised as her coach ran on. Guilty as charged.

The sandy girl was quickly surrounded by teammates. Heads turned to glare at Kim as the ref beckoned her. She walked slowly, heart tight, and the red card sent her to the touchlines. No smiles from her teammates there. Just heads turning the other way.

'What's the matter with you, Kim?'

Hodge stopped shaking his head, but only to hold out his hands. Kim shrugged.

'You saw red before the card,' he said. 'What's up?'

Kim shrugged again. Her eyes were on the pitch, willing the number ten to her feet. She'd heard all the words before, but this time she deserved them. The foul was bad. Terrible. No excuse.

'Shame on you.'

It was a defender, her opposite number, who'd run half-way down the pitch to say it. Her eyes were narrowed and her cheeks were a fraying kind of red. Kim pretended not to hear, half-expecting a discreet spit. Instead she watched the injured girl lean on her coach and wince as she limped off.

The number eleven scowled at Kim before she took the penalty.

It was way too sharp for Lola in goal. She threw a scornful stare towards Kim, further than she'd ever managed to lob the ball.

Trust Lola to kick the guy in the gutter, she thought. Then she remembered the kick that counted was hers, and it stank.

More tank than crab, she told Jeanette by text on the bench, then wished she hadn't sent it, because the last thing she wanted was sympathy.

Kim walked home fast and alone. Thanks, Barry, she thought, heart rate increasing. But when she spoke to Fizzy that night, she only said the match had been a nightmare and that she'd tell her later.

Tell her what, exactly? That some girl she didn't know might not walk for months because of Barry and Kris? *Yeah, Kim*, she told herself. *Not your fault. Fizzy will be packing a knife in her lunchbox. The first teacher she meets will get stabbed through the gown. There'll be blood in the corridors.*

She didn't sleep that night, but at ten to nine the next morning, when Hodge sent for her, it was to tell her the girl was OK. There were details but Kim couldn't process them.

No thanx to me, she told Brad by text.

Don't beat yourself up, he told her. Mistakes are how we learn.

Prof, she answered. Be my dad. Or at least come and meet Fizzy on Sat. Kim started to add that her blood mother might have had a breakdown, but she wasn't planning to have one herself.

Some things didn't need to be said.

That day Fizzy took up knitting again, for the twentieth time, in case it really was soothing like Laura said. It didn't work. She still kept dropping stitches. One for Michael? Another for Suranne? Not much chance of surprising Kris with a Christmas jumper when every time she thought of him she got into another knot or lump. She probably couldn't even manage a scarf. Not that he'd need one in Brazil or Argentina.

She didn't really believe he'd gone far. In the dreams, when he called for her, he had no suitcase, even though he was dancing with Jeanette on a white beach, with flowers around his neck. One time he changed into a yellow bird and flew into a storm. The feathers fell down like daisies into the grey waves while lightning fired through dark clouds. But he wouldn't leave the country without saying goodbye, would he?

After lunch she went to an art exhibition with Laura while Damon was at Gym Club. One of Laura's friends had painted some of the flower pictures, but they were trying to be brighter and bigger than life and Fizzy preferred the real thing in the border outside. So much pretending. It never stopped.

While Laura was talking, with a 'splash' of champagne in her glass, Fizzy checked her phone. It was on silent, but there was a text waiting.

Not Kris.

Suranne: I can't believe you. Judas.

Fizzy breathed out shakily. No. She imagined herself back on the stairs with Barry at the bottom. Why did she never think, pray, predict or just wait? Words came out and no one could unsay them. Now Michael would blame her too. There was another message, sent a couple of minutes later: Will never trust you again. Told Michael U R jealous. Jesus may forgive you but I can't.

The top part of Fizzy's body was rattling, as if it was packed with ice. There was no way to reply. What did people call an anti-Cupid who fired the arrow to break the lovers apart? If there was such an evil spirit it would be hated by everyone.

She turned off her phone. She'd told the truth but why? Because really she'd wanted Graham Washington to come between Michael and Suranne? Now she'd lost the only one of her friends who really knew bodies had souls inside. And Michael would think hers was twisted.

She wondered whether she could sneak out of the art exhibition without Laura noticing. But soon Laura said they were leaving anyway. In the car Fizzy put on the radio and managed not to speak because Laura was only chatty in public now.

As soon as they were home Fizzy ran up to her room. Opening her drawer, she took out the heart-shaped head with the shiny hair. It was already shred-sized. She couldn't destroy it.

And she couldn't keep waiting for Kris to contact her. One day soon, when she was alone and strong, she would call him.

That evening she sent Kim an email, telling her everything she'd ever felt and thought about Michael Conradi and Suranne, individually and together. When she'd finished, she didn't read it through. She just pressed Send. Then she went for a shower, feeling looser inside. She found a reply waiting.

> Hi, Fizz. Things will get better. Thanx for telling me and I don't think you're stupid. Or mean! Yeah right - Ro might be meaner. I'm like a bank vault. Barry couldn't break me open or guess the code. Don't worry about Suranne. She's blowing off. If she thinks for a second, she'll see who's the stupid one.
>
> While we're truth telling I nearly took some girl out on the pitch. Worst tackle of my life. If her team-mates clubbed together to hire a hitman I'd put my hands up and say fair enough.
>
> C U soon. Baking an immense cake for Sat. Jeanette says she thinks it's time the rules changed so she could text you herself and she's going to talk to Barry and Laura but she can't wait to give you a hug.
>
> X

Smiling, Fizzy sent back a Thanx xx.

In bed she remembered the worry doll, but left it under her Bible. Maybe the daisy chains were more powerful. The words wouldn't line up in any kind of order for a prayer, especially 'Kris', 'Barry', 'Michael' and 'Suranne'. But Kim believed in her, and as she closed her eyes, she felt her mother's flesh and smelt the vanilla.

It was a good night's sleep until the blossom streaked with blood. When Fizzy woke, it was there: red splashes on her hands, staining when she tried to rub them away. A scream broke silently inside. But as she tugged her eyelids open wider, she saw her hands were clean and her room was real. The dawn was pale outside. Fizzy opened the window and tried to let in the light with the sharp morning air.

Looking at the two girls the next Saturday afternoon, Brad could see reasons for them to be friends, and great gaps between them that they'd either overlooked or found ways to join up. He could see Fizzy was innocent, too shy to make eye contact. Not like Kim, who looked right at him, mostly with a grin hanging ready to spread.

'I'm going back to uni in a couple of days,' he told them, 'so I'm glad to catch you before I go.'

'You're kidding yourself,' said Kim, 'if you think you're quick enough to catch me.'

'How's it going, then?' he asked, realising the question was so oblique that they might not see what he was asking. This, he meant. The two of them and the two sets of parents. The adjustment.

'We're going to each other's schools for the day,' said Kim, 'Big Barrington's sorting it with the Heads.'

'Cool,' he said, when Kim explained that it wouldn't be a swap. She'd show Fizzy round hers, and Fizzy would be her escort at what she called the 'Young Ladies' Academy'.

'I'm learning to e-nun-ciate,' she said, with a long, slow stretch and her nose lifted high.

Fizzy's frown wasn't cross but amused. She kept her eyes on Kim or the doorway and still hadn't looked at him. When he asked her about school, she said, 'It's OK. I don't mind.'

'We're way ahead of the parents,' said Kim.

'I suppose you've got less life to ...' he paused. 'Rejig?'

'Is that the kind of technical vocabulary they teach you at uni?' teased Kim, and he told her not to be cheeky. A sharp whiff of smoke tickled his nostrils.

'Whatever's in the oven smells well done.'

Kim roared, scrambling for the oven gloves. She opened the oven door and let out some smoke, but it was hardly billowing.

'I don't believe it!' cried Kim. 'I never do this, never!' A hand thrust the tray at them.

'It's only black at the edges,' said Brad. 'It's not like it's ablaze.'

Fizzy said it looked great, but Brad could see Kim wasn't going to believe that either. With its dark crust, the cake looked even harder than Kim tried to be.

'I know you love ginger,' she told him. 'I've baked this recipe ten times. It never does this.'

She sounded angry, but he didn't expect her to open the bin and drop the cake in whole. It landed with quite a thud and probably ripped right through the bin liner. Fizzy looked shocked and dumbstruck.

'Bit OTT, Kim,' Brad said. 'I was looking forward to that.'

She didn't smile or turn into Ainsley Harriot or

231

Raymond Blanc. Her glower was almost as dark as the cake. Without speaking, she went upstairs. Fizzy looked worried. He heard Jeanette follow her.

Brad told Fizzy she'd be fine and got her to show him a few photos. He had to ask for the information she didn't offer about who he was looking at, when and where. Even on a Jamaican beach, with a crowd of a family, her smile was cautious, as if she wasn't quite sure about something.

'Where's your... Barrington?' he asked.

Brad could see the white 'mother', and the 'brother' with a grin that might have been a laugh, and grandparents, and cousins too, but no big, black man lording it over everyone the way Kim had told him Barry Duvall liked to do.

'He's taking the picture,' she explained. Brad knew that meant the happy face she showed was for him.

In the flesh Brad thought Fizzy looked uncomfortable, turning to look round for Jeanette more than once. Was something against the rules? Was it him? According to Kim, there was a long list of rules in the Duvall house that mustn't be broken. Brad knew about rules, but he didn't know how many were on both lists: the ones from the Qu'ran that his own father sometimes forgot, and the one drawn up from the Bible by Kim's new dad. As far as he could see, Christians chose the bits that suited. Maybe Muslims did the same. He reckoned there were as many kinds of Christian, and Muslim, as there were books on Amazon.

'I'm glad I live in London,' he told her. 'It's a mix. The world is here. We can be who we are – mostly, most places.'

What could he ask her without prying? What did she need to say? She locked her fingers together on her lap, straight as the wicker in his dad's old chair.

'I don't know who I am any more,' she said.

Brad gave her a kind of nodding smile. She needed a counsellor. Couldn't the Duvalls see that?

'You've got the same heart and soul. That's who you are. We don't choose our names or our families.'

'I don't trust my heart any more. Other people don't. Some people anyway, people I love.'

Brad looked to the doorway as Jeanette filled it. 'Well, Brad, this is my Fizzy,' she said. 'Our Fizzy. Didn't we get lucky?'

She hugged her then, and whether or not she'd overheard, he thought it was a pretty great kind of counselling. But he didn't get a chance to find out more about Fizzy or her father's rules, because Kim appeared too.

'Have you two been chatting, then?'

Fizzy made a kind of 'mm' noise.

'No one's going to tell Big Barrington unless you do,' said Kim. 'Chill! It's all right. It's more than all right. They've brought you up wrong. He's not the enemy because he's got a different religion.'

Brad realised Fizzy wasn't really scared of the Big Bad Muslim, but what the Big Bad Christian would think or say.

He found himself smiling at Kim because he was proud of her. She had authority.

'Dead on,' he said. 'I'm harmless, me.'

'Harmless, brainless and tasteless,' said Kim. He tried to point out that in fact his long, full shirt was *ahead* of fashion.

'You could hire it out to the primary school for the next nativity play,' said Kim, 'for a shepherd.'

'Yeah, might do that.' Brad stood. 'Gotta get on,' he

said. 'Essays. Deadlines.'

As he strolled across to his own door, he hoped he wouldn't mean trouble for Fizzy Duvall back 'home'. Brad knew about prejudice.

There had been the badly-spelt chalk message outside the front door: 'DERTY PAKIES GO HOME'. Even though Brad's grandfather had moved from India to Uganda – until the fat dictator Amin had given them all a few months to leave.

And years before that, after 9/11, a couple of white kids at primary school had thought it was funny to call him 'Bomber' and point finger guns in his back.

He didn't keep a log book of incidents like headteachers had to, but that didn't mean he'd forgotten. Sometimes he thought it was the neighbours – the Nigerian woman above and the white family below– who'd driven his mother away. Hate mail, his dad had said.

Would she have gone if he'd known then that he was gay? Maybe, he thought, she knew before he did, and another kind of fear drove her away.

In any case it made no difference. She had another life, and he'd have to find one of his own. It was quieter now, on the terrorist front. In fact, the last taunt he'd had in the street was about cricket cheats. *Water*, he'd thought, feeling the rain drip from his hood onto the tip of his nose, *off a duck's back.*

It wasn't about him, he reminded himself. Kim might have refused counselling, but those two girls needed to say the things they hadn't let out yet.

He was better now at letting things go, like balls that were heading for the boundary whether he moved or not.

Better at keeping up the swing of his shoulders and the casual purpose of his stride.

CHAPTER NINETEEN

Kim recognised the voice at the door as soon as the first deep Pavarotti note sounded below. Had he tied Ro up in the boot of the BMW? Who said he could pick Fizzy up? Wasn't he the one who thought arrangements had to be carved in stone?

'Barry's here,' Jeanette announced, letting him in. Kim gave her an accusing look from the top of the stairs. 'There's something he wanted to run by us.'

'You can run by any time,' Kim told him, 'but don't feel you need to stop.'

She thumped downstairs with Fizzy following behind and doing a good impression of her worry doll. Kim was sure she was praying madly that she'd back off and give Barry a chance. But whatever he was planning, Kim could see Fizzy knew nothing about it.

'Felicity,' said Barry. He was smiling, but not at either of them. It reminded Kim of the advice teachers gave when she was on stage, to stare at some point on the wall instead of faces. And it made Kim want to lock eyes with him until he couldn't hold. 'Kimberlie.'

Jeanette bustled them into the kitchen. Barry accepted Jeanette's offer of a chair and said, 'Yes, tea would be lovely, thank you.'

He cleared his throat.

'It's all right,' Kim told him, 'Brad's just gone. But he's

left some leaflets about Islam if you'd like to borrow them.'

Shut it, Kim, she told herself. *Stop pulling the petals off the daisies.*

'You're very kind,' said Barry, as Jeanette placed a mug in front of him.

'Don't keep us in suspense, Barry,' Kim told him. 'Sugar?'

He covered his mug as if Kim might tip some in against his will. 'No thank you.' Then he cleared his throat and tapped five fingers very lightly on the table. 'I know you promised to think about the idea of a place nearer to us. I also know that you will hear on Monday about the future of the library, and my offer of a job still stands – until the end of the week.'

'Thank you,' said Jeanette. 'I appreciate it.'

'But something happened this morning. I met an old friend from school, a Christian friend who went into the world of drama...'

'Like us!' interrupted Kim. 'Big drama. *Les Mis* ain't got nothing on us.'

'...And we had a chat about what he's doing these days.'

He placed a glossy flyer on the table. Kim had never heard of the theatre company it advertised but she couldn't help looking.

'Kimberlie,' he said. 'You think I don't appreciate your impressions and the sharpness of your wit. But I do.'

Kim bowed.

'I think you have a gift, and none of us should waste the talent God gives us.'

'I don't intend to.' Kim guessed what was coming, but she needed to hear the words he chose. They made a difference.

'You're determined, and I respect that too. I've made a lot of mistakes in good faith, and I don't want to make another, but I believe the Lord meant me to meet Gavin today. It's clear to me that the best way I could show you how genuinely I want to reach out and support you where you are – who you are – is to show you a place where you can grow, learn, flourish, develop.'

Kim stared as the words rolled – like a head for a snowman, smoothed and firmed. Had he learned this speech by heart? Any minute he'd be flashing his cheque book again.

'My friend, Gavin Marshall-Brown, OBE, is the director of this teen theatre company, which tours schools around the country. They do all sorts of plays, secular things from Shakespeare to West Side Story and Annie.' He cleared his throat. It was such a big, volcanic noise that Kim almost laughed. 'He's been auditioning for a new musical based on Passion Week – the last days of Jesus. He's got most of the big parts filled but he hasn't found the right Mary Magdalene.'

Kim opened her mouth even though she wasn't sure what might come out. She glanced at Fizzy, who gaped, her eyes round – but not filling with tears. She looked excited.

'I love Mary Magdalene,' Fizzy said.

'Mary M, apparently, in this production,' said Barry.

Glancing at Jeanette, Kim saw she looked uncertain. Did she know something, or just a lot less than she wanted to show Barry?

'It's a rap musical,' he added. 'I admit I can't quite imagine it myself, but then I'm forty-one. I told my friend I knew someone who could be what he's looking for, someone who can dance as well as act, and really hold the stage. I have his phone number. He'll audition you as and when it suits. If it suits. No money involved.'

'You'd be amazing, Kim!' cried Fizzy. 'I can just see it!'

'I can too,' said Jeanette, hesitantly.

The only Mary Kim could think of was the saintly virgin mother, and that wouldn't exactly be obvious casting. In any case, wouldn't it be Christian propaganda? There was no way she was going into schools to try to convert Muslims or Hindus or dead-set atheists, however good the part might be. But secular meant normal, didn't it?

'There's really no need,' Barry said, his hand in the air above the table between them, 'to answer now. Just let the seed settle, and see if it takes root. Matthew 13: 3–23.'

He smiled as if he wanted house points – and was awarding them to himself. Jeanette thanked him and Kim knew she was meant to join in.

'Give it time and thought,' he finished, and sipped his tea.

All of a sudden Kim felt cross with him again. He'd put her on the spot, a spot in a place she didn't know, where it was hard to even guess what, who and why. It was a bit like waving a rubber carrot in front of a hungry donkey.

'Kim,' said Jeanette. 'Please take a breath.'

'Can I go now please?'

'It's only a red rag if you want to be a bull,' said Barry, smiling, first at her, then Jeanette.

Kim stood. She hoped he wasn't trying to prove she got her humour from him. 'Me and Fizzy are in the middle of a movie,' she said. '*Demons of Hell 2.*'

He smiled so widely she thought he might laugh. 'Of

course. Finish your movie.'

Nothing could wind him up. But Kim herself felt wound as tightly as anyone could be expected to bear without shooting up to the ceiling. The two of them left Jeanette asking more about the job and Barry opening up the latest all-singing, all-dancing tablet to show her everything she could want to know.

In the lounge, watching *Happy Feet*, Kim told Fizzy she didn't mind Jeanette taking a job. How could she? It was Jeanette's choice, and even though she'd made some bad ones, no one else could make them for her. No, she explained, it wasn't Jeanette she was angry with.

'He thinks he knows what I want most,' she said, smacking a cushion on top of her stomach. 'But I'm not like algebra. X plus Y equals Happy Ever After.'

That was all. Fizzy smiled as if she understood.

'I'll tell you about Mary Magdalene if you want – sometime – when you feel like it. If you do.'

Fizzy was being so careful she could be tiptoeing barefoot! It made Kim sorry if she came across as fierce and difficult with her too. She must try to let things go. Barry was trying to help in his great big, heavy-footed way.

'Yeah, all right,' she said. 'Next time.'

But Barry appeared. The visit was over.

Later, unable to concentrate on anything she tried to do, Kim heard Jeanette singing on the landing. She shook her head in disbelief. Next time they met they'd be hugging. What if Barry left Laura for Jeanette – that'd change the mix! And Laura could hook up with Kris for a bit of rough! What had she been like in the old days on stage? Had her dancing been *dirtier*?

'Kim?' she heard.

'I'm a fighter,' Kim called down. 'I don't do silver spoons. Handouts. I can earn money soon. I'll get three jobs, work twenty hours a day – if I want, when I want.'

'I know. But don't pull the seed out just yet, eh?'

Now he'd got Jeanette using his lines. Her Master's Voice. If God ever needed a sabbatical like Ro, Barrington Duvall would be jumping up and filling the heavenly role while the golden throne was still warm.

Did he know what he was doing? Did he even see Fizzy, right there in that kitchen, probably thinking how generous he was? What did he do to help her with her dreams? He just gave her nightmares!

Kim punched her duvet, one fist, the other, alternately and together.

He thought he'd worked out where her strings were, but the other boys knew she wasn't for pulling.

From her bedroom window Fizzy noticed a bird flitting across her lawn, and even in the twilight she recognised its quick, light bob, as if it was skimming the tips of invisible waves. Only the second green woodpecker of her life! Looking around for Laura, who would want to see, she heard her on the phone. To Ro? Fizzy sighed. It didn't matter. Whatever it was they were saying she didn't want to hear it.

Where Kim lived there were no woodpeckers of any kind, and the only gardens Fizzy had seen were hardly big enough for a wicket. She didn't really like the traffic or the mess, and the people made her feel invisible. Even though

Barry was talking about accompanying her to Kim's school, she felt nervous already. The students there would think she was posh and call her Goody Two Shoes, like Damon did sometimes. Except that they might add a swear word or two somewhere between the others.

She felt tired. She would have liked to record the day in her journal, but it still felt unsafe. And there were thoughts she could write that even she didn't want to read. The last entry said, 'Things are better now. People are calmer, mostly. I can bear it with the Lord's help – and the daisy chain pact.'

But were they better? Did Barry even like her? Or care who she was now, never mind who she could be? Even Laura only pretended to trust in the Lord, when really she wanted to throw shoes. And Michael and Suranne were sweethearts, bound together by hatred of the enemy who'd tried to keep them apart. Out of spite? No, that wasn't it. She wouldn't. She wasn't wayward, or corrupted – was she?

Not better, then. Worse. Nothing went right, even when Barry offered Kim something that was perfect. Perfect in his eyes – and in hers too – but not in Kim's. You could keep refilling the vase with clean water, but the flowers still died.

'Father, help me!'

Then it came rippling through. Yes. She realised how much she'd hoped it would, at the right time. Because it had to be a secret, even from Kim in spite of the promise. There was no choice.

Need to C U sweetheart. Same place 2moro at 9:30. Will be there. Promise. XX

Fizzy rose and quietly closed the bedroom door. Kris wasn't in South America. He was near enough to meet her at the newsagent's, and she would go. It did no harm, and no one need know but the two of them. And the Lord. He mixed with tax-gatherers and prostitutes, and on the cross He forgave a murderer. He didn't judge Mary M! So how could her father, who'd only made mistakes, be beyond forgiveness? It made no sense.

Jeanette emerged from the bathroom. It was only half past eight, but she'd removed her make-up and was hanging loose in her silk pyjamas. The skin under her eyes looked sore. Kim thought Fizzy would be shocked to see her mother now, drab and lifeless, as if all the shine and patterns had been wiped away. Why could nobody find a solution, like the trellis in Nelle's Barbados garden, to stop the mothers flopping?

Hadn't Barry rescued this particular wilting plant? He'd saved her from redundancy before it struck. So what happened to the singing? Kim supposed she'd been the one to put a stop to that – beating duvets and staying in her room with loud music, refusing tea and cocoa. But she wasn't Fizzy, and she couldn't just smile nicely and ask Jesus to make people to love each other.

'You should've asked Fizzy to *pray* for your job,' Kim told her, with a little puff of air from her nose at the end.

Jeanette stopped on the landing. Her face had changed now. Kim thought she looked ready to growl – lion-style.

'Don't mock her faith.'

The words were almost fierce. Kim's shoulders fell. Her mouth opened.

'I'm not!' she protested. 'I wouldn't mock anything about her! She's perfect, isn't she? But I'm not, and the

243

Duvalls won't have me. But they won't let go of her, either! Of course not! Who would? You'll have to fight over her.'

'Kim, please, you're upset. You know that's not what I'm saying.'

The bathroom fan still rattled furrily. Jeanette's mouth chewed, as if she was keeping back other words she might have said.

'Why don't you just take his job, and a flashy flat too, if that's what you want? If it'll stop you drooping and sagging around the place, like you've got no muscle? Like some great jellyfish without the sting! Don't let me stop you. I'll live with Brad or my Auntie Ro! I don't need him to give me a leg up, and I don't need you to bring me down.'

Kim hated this, being like this, turning on Jeanette who had no defences. Where was her sympathy now? Barry took everything. She leant against the wall. She felt like a jellyfish herself, loaded and ready to fire.

'Honey,' said Jeanette slowly, 'why can't you let anyone help you? He's your father. An offer like this, it's your dream!'

'Wrong girl!' snapped Kim as the fan whirred to a stop. 'I'm not the dreamer. That's your daughter.'

'Kim, please! When are you going to believe me? You ARE my daughter. Of course you are!'

'I think you'll find,' she told her, 'that biologically and legally I'm not.' Kim felt her chest rise tightly as she saw Jeanette slump from inside. 'That makes you the lucky one. No one would choose me if I was on special offer, free for two!'

Kim headed for her room, ignoring the name Jeanette kept using as if it was really hers. Why was she still here in the wrong house? At the top of the stairs, she turned.

'I can't, I just can't. Forget it, all right? It's not you, or Fizzy. It's me. I'm having trouble being me.'

Jeanette gave her the tenderest smile she had, just like Fizzy's at Brick Lane. 'It was a nice day, wasn't it?'

'Yeah,' Kim murmured.

But the nice days felt like a thin kind of scab, new and flaky. Things were still raw and bloody underneath. Kim felt so tired, as she lay down on her bed, that she closed her eyes until she heard the slippered footsteps pad away.

CHAPTER TWENTY

It was an obvious idea. But the great thing about it, thought Fizzy, was that she didn't have to lie about what she was doing or why: going running, to get fit and slim. She could actually run – as much of the way to the newsagent's as possible.

Laura smiled at her well-ironed pedal pushers and the long-sleeved top with appliqué on the neckline.

'Joggers don't normally look so chic.'

'I've got my oldest trainers!' Fizzy pointed out. She was sure Laura was smiling because she expected her to get as far as the end of the road before she turned back.

'I don't like you going out on your own,' she added, as Fizzy reached for the door handle. 'I'm sure Suranne would jog with you.'

Fizzy couldn't let the word shake her now. Barry was in the shower, so she had to go quickly.

'I'm fifteen, not twelve!' she said. 'I'm only going... you know, round the block.'

'I wouldn't call it a block,' said Laura. 'Isn't that a New York term, for areas like the Bronx?'

'I'll be fine. It's not like...'

She stopped, but Laura probably knew what she meant. Not like Kim's neighbourhood.

'You want me to lose weight,' she tried.

Laura's hip bones jutted out through her flimsiest

clothes, and Fizzy had seen the way she looked at everything she used to call her 'puppy fat'. That wasn't what Kris saw when he looked at her. He saw her heart.

'No, darling, I never said so, really!'

This was hopeless. In her place, Kim wouldn't be stalled; she'd be through the door. Fizzy finished tying her laces and stepped outside.

And it worked. Fizzy didn't look back, but she didn't hear the door close, so Laura must be standing there watching her go. As simple as that! Then footsteps hurrying after her. No! Laura called her name.

'If you go near the shops, will you buy a pint of milk?' she heard from behind her on the drive. 'Damon drowned his cereal again.'

She went back so Laura could give her a two pound coin for her pocket. Fizzy couldn't believe it: they never ran out of anything. It was almost a sign!

At the end of the drive she waved and began running. It was no problem for the first hundred metres, but soon after that her tight chest gave her an excuse to stop. She checked the top of her head for dampness. She didn't want Kris to see her sweaty or breathless. *If he turns up,* whispered a voice insider her head, *he's let you down before*. It was the voice of Kim, but it shook everything out of place where she'd arranged it inside. It threw furniture around. It smashed things and knocked down the walls. Because if he didn't come, it was over. It would mean he was only pretending too, and she'd have to stop believing in him and his love – just liked she'd stopped believing in Barry's. The love wouldn't be an idea any more, like the idea that Michael might love her. It would be dead.

But he'd be there this time. He'd explain.

The same old lady with the dog was back again, wearing coordinated shades of draping lilac over white trousers with a sharp crease. She was stepping gingerly because everywhere was wet from last night's rain, but the dog frisked around her ankles and refused to be jerked into line by a tug of the lead, until it scuttled through a large black puddle. Dirty water sprayed her immaculate white legs. Her face, which was stiff with foundation and blusher, cracked open in a grimace that showed her old brown teeth. As she disappeared into the shop, she was the one who did the yapping, with some sharp words for the dog.

Fizzy looked around in both directions, for more Sunday regulars she'd recognise from the same time a week before. But only the dog lady seemed to be running to timetable. She checked her watch as she emerged from the shop with her newspaper, followed by the dog, its tail drooping. Stopping, she fed him a doggy treat from her hand and fluffed the white coat behind the short neck with a smile that was girlish, murmuring, 'Good girl, really, aren't you, Fliss?'

Fliss! It was what her Harrow gran used to call her. The dog was a girl, and the woman loved her after all. The world was full of mistakes, but Fliss was a good girl, really. It was another sign and it meant she was loved.

One minute after half-past. He mustn't be late, because they didn't have long. Nobody was going to believe she could jog for more than twenty minutes without calling the paramedics.

A car approached and pulled up on the corner, crossing over onto the kerb. It was dirty, rusty white and boxy, and looked past its sell-by date, but she didn't take much notice at first. Then, when the door opened on the pavement side, she saw a leather arm and a hand that beckoned her over: a hand bulked out with rings, with a plaited kind of bracelet made of leather at the wrist.

She didn't know he had a car! But it made her feel sorry for him, because Damon would jeer at this one. The passenger seat was ripped as if a knife had slashed it through, but he passed her a thin old cushion. Taking her phone out of her back pocket before she sat down, Fizzy felt something like her heart jumping – not with fear, but excitement. Joy. He was here.

'All right, princess?' he asked with a wide smile, pulling out before she could answer. 'Is that thing on or off?'

'Off,' she said, putting it in the glove compartment. 'How are you?' She could feel a smile growing on her face, but she wished the car didn't smell so damp and smoky.

He turned, his grin delighted now. 'Thank you for asking! No one else does – or cares, either. I'm not so bad.' He looked across at her a moment. 'Not as bad as they say anyway.'

Then he indicated right.

'Where are we going?' Fizzy didn't want to panic, not now.

'Aha,' he said.

'Have you got a new place to stay? I haven't got long – it's church.'

He didn't answer at first, but turned and sped down a road she didn't know. Watching the dial, Fizzy saw his speed hover near forty. The engine ground noisily.

'I thought we'd have a coffee,' he said vaguely, his eyes

on the road.

'That'd be nice,' she said, hoping she sounded more enthusiastic and less worried than she felt. Kim wouldn't be impressed by her acting.

'Sound as if you mean it then.'

At the traffic lights he lit a cigarette, and she wound down the window, hoping he wouldn't take offence. She couldn't go home smelling of tobacco.

'Where have you been, Dad?' she asked, as he inhaled.

'I'll tell you all about it over coffee,' he said.

He looked so happy. He was excited too – she could see it in the way he sat and held the wheel, like Damon pretending to drive a Ferrari. But he wasn't pretending, because he really did love her.

'Which café are we going to?' she asked.

She realised they were so far from home now that she had no idea how to get back. Tension snatched the smile away. But she mustn't spoil their time together fretting.

'You'll see,' he said, and turned on some rock music. 'Who was it who said the Devil has all the best tunes?' He grinned again. 'You'll have to ask Barry.'

'He'll be angry,' she said nervously. There was a tight cord running down from her throat to her stomach and it just wouldn't slacken. 'If I'm late back.'

'Don't worry,' he said, as they passed an industrial estate. 'You can give him a call later.'

Fizzy stared at the face that looked ahead, and the mouth that blew out smoke as it joined in with the chorus about 'rocking all over the world'.

'Dad,' she said, 'there'll be so much trouble if I don't get home – in time for church. Soon.'

'I told you not to worry, didn't I?' he said. 'We're entitled to a little bit of quality time, just the two of us. Anyone can see the fairness in that. You have time with J and the Duvalls. No one seems to understand that you want time with your dad too. So you'll tell them, simple as that.'

'Yes, but you have to make an arrangement,' she said, imagining the raised voices and the blame.

'They won't let me. I'm barred from the negotiating table! I don't have a voice, princess! You know that. What else can I do?'

Fizzy didn't answer. She didn't know. Maybe Ro would make it all right if she rang her. But when she suggested it, Kris said to wait a bit. He didn't seem to understand how hard it was before, how angry everyone was and how wayward Barry already thought she'd become. Her face couldn't hold a smile any more.

He smiled at her, a teasing sort of smile that changed to disappointment.

'Come on!' he said. 'I want us to have a happy time, a great time, the best day of your year. Of my life, maybe. Not so difficult, that!' He was glancing up at her in the mirror. 'So make an effort. Don't be a wet blanket like your mother.'

She wished he wouldn't talk about Jeanette, who couldn't help being sensitive and emotional. She'd be emotional now if she knew what was happening. And Kim would steam and call him a kidnapper. It made it hard to look forward to the fun he promised when she knew it was going to end in the kind of scenes she wasn't allowed to watch on TV. Why did he handle everything wrong?

Her phone was still off, but her watch told her Laura would already be looking out of the window, wondering

251

what could have happened. Barry would be cross with Laura for allowing her to go, and they'd both be angry with her for letting them down. They'd all say she'd proved she couldn't be trusted after all. And that was just the start. She reached for the phone as discreetly as she could, while he looked the other way at a junction.

'No need to phone anyone yet. I'll call Ro in a bit.' He glanced at her with a smile. 'Let me take the flack, eh? My fault, not yours.'

He threw his cigarette out of the window, turned down the music and asked her for the news.

Fizzy couldn't think of anything that mattered.

'Come on then. I bet you get A-stars for everything.'

Her grades had slumped lately, but she wasn't sleeping much. So she told him she'd started designing a clock in Tech, with a shape like a fried egg. It was going to be made out of dark pink Perspex with purple hands that actually moved. As she talked, she tried to care about the clock and forget about the difficult things, but it didn't work. Kris was breaking the rules again, and she was his sidekick, like a magician's assistant who set the tricks up. They'd all blame her too, even Kim. By the time she finished talking, she couldn't see the clock any more – only angry faces pulled out of shape.

'Cool!' he said. 'Can I have it for Christmas? Show it off? I can tell everyone my clever girl made it.'

Fizzy smiled. 'Yes!' she cried, as brightly as she could. 'Of course you can.'

'I wish I'd behaved myself at school. It might have helped if I'd done some work now and then. I'm not as thick as I seem. Just lazy.'

'I know you're not thick,' said Fizzy, picturing him as a boy with a cheeky smile. She bet the teachers couldn't have helped enjoying him even when he messed about at the back. She remembered how he'd met Jeanette as a teenager, and told herself it was important to keep hold of the good things. 'You can't start a band if you're lazy.'

Kris said it wasn't the starting that took effort but the carrying on and not losing heart. 'I give up,' he said. 'That's my trouble. But I'm not giving up on you.'

It was hard not to love him when he said things like that. But still he hadn't told her when and where they were going to stop for coffee. As soon as he'd finished a story about getting the car cheap from an old mate (who'd put him up because he was starting to overstay his welcome at Mike's place), she asked again.

'When we get there. Another couple of hours, or sooner if I push it. Lunch first, then coffee.'

Fizzy's mouth must be hanging. She started to repeat, 'A couple of hours...' but it tailed away. Something snatched at the tightness and tugged with clammy fingers. 'Where are we going?'

'Surprise,' he said. 'You'll love it, like I used to at your age.'

'But we need to ring,' she said, 'before they call the police.'

He looked behind in the mirror.

'No cops on our tail – not yet, anyway.'

'Dad! It's not funny!' She could hear the tears starting to break out.

'All right, all right! I'll stop first chance I get. It's not even ten o'clock yet. The police would tell them not to waste

253

their time.'

But Laura would be whiter than the carpet by now. Barry would be charging off like St George with a dragon to slay. He had no idea! But here she was, looking out of the car window as if all this, the whole thing, might disappear like the shops and restaurants they left behind, gone as if they'd never existed.

Kris tried to get her talking about her favourite singers, but he didn't like it when she said she couldn't remember, like Damon often did when Laura asked him what his homework was. How could she chat as if everything was fine when really it was getting bigger and more out of control than ever? Only by letting go, drifting and bobbing on the surface when it was deep and dark underneath.

In the end, about half an hour after she should have been home, they pulled over onto a layby lined with bins and strewn with litter. Stepping out of the car, Fizzy saw giant dandelions straggling all over, making midgets of the cowslips Laura liked.

'Cramp!' said Kris, stretching his legs in a dance that would have been funny if Kim had done it. But Fizzy felt that if she laughed the sound would scare her, like the kind Mr Rochester's mad wife let loose in her attic.

Her phone showed four texts and two missed calls. Kris must have been watching, because he reached for it before she could read or listen.

'The important thing is to call Ro, right?' he said. 'Or Mike. Yeah, even better. He's a good lad, Mike. It was Barrington Duvall who was bothered about the whisky, not him.'

He found the number in his pocket, on a creased scrap

of paper which he unfolded. He gestured to Fizzy to come closer to hear better against the cars whishing past.

She wasn't sure she wanted to hear, but as he started to speak – 'Hiya, Mike!' –she moved in and he put an arm round her waist. 'Kris here. Just calling to let you know I've got Fizzy with me and we're off on a bit of a day trip. Ro's not answering her phone, and we don't want anyone to worry because everything's fine here. Isn't it, princess?'

'Yes,' she said, and at Kris's volume-up hand signal she repeated it, louder this time. 'The trip was my idea!'

Kris's mouth opened as if he might laugh, and his free thumb went up. He held the phone away from her and his ear. Fizzy's mouth opened too. She didn't know what had happened! But she'd had no choice. It was the only way.

Kris said, 'Sorry, mate, bad reception. Can you make sure Barry and Laura know there's nothing to worry about and Fizzy'll text them later. See ya!'

He clicked off and passed it back to Fizzy.

'You told a porky pie,' he said, quietly, but as if it amused him.

'So did you,' she said.

'Just to oil the wheels and stop the thing breaking down,' he said. 'Yours was a good lie, though. Whiter than white! A Jesus lie – a sacrifice!'

She frowned and he apologised if he'd offended her. Even though he had, she hoped her face didn't show it. Her heart had known what to say. It was better if they blamed her more than him. Like Suranne and Michael blamed her, just her. If she told the truth, they'd never let her see him again.

'Thank you, sweetheart,' he said. 'You did it for me.'

255

'Will it be all right?' she asked him.

'It'll be brilliant!' he said. 'But I'd keep your phone off just for a while, or I don't think we'll get any peace at all.'

He told her to look away while he had a pee (which he called a 'Jimmy Riddle') a few steps out into the dandelions. Fizzy sat in the car, her phone on her lap, discreetly checking who'd sent the texts. One from Ro, one from Kim and two from Laura. Both calls in her voice box were from Barry's mobile.

Kris was back. She saw him looking at the phone and turned it off. He smiled and started the engine. As the car grumbled into action, he started singing with one-handed disco moves in her direction. '*Ain't no stopping us now – we're on the move!*'

Fizzy's smile was slow to start and quick to end. The song only made her think of the people who'd want to stop them if they could, which made her sad, and anxious too.

He asked her to guess where they were going; she said she couldn't.

'Somewhere I loved as a boy,' he said. 'I haven't been there for years. Of course, it's changed and probably not for the better. Like me.'

Although he'd told her he was an East End kid, Fizzy had the feeling they were leaving London behind. But she couldn't be sure. On busy roads, whatever their letter or number, she tended to look out for red kites and name the flowers on the banks. So she just made an agreement sound when he said that the M25 was 'underrated'.

'And maligned,' he said, grinning. 'Again, like me.'

Fizzy remembered her English teacher saying Thomas Cromwell was a 'malign influence' on Henry the Eighth. It was what they'd all think about Kris and his influence on her, even Kim.

'Where are we going?' she asked again. She still had no way of working it out, and she wanted it to be wonderful and worth it, a day she'd never forget.

'Somewhere we went on hot days,' he said, 'and not-so-hot days too. Trains didn't cost an arm and a leg in those days. And it was easier to dodge the fare. Mum was a looker with a kid; she had her sob stories and they worked a treat.'

Fizzy asked if he had a photo of this pretty singing grandma, who was a young mum then, and apparently a not-very-honest one. But maybe they were poor, she told herself. She didn't like to ask him about her grandfather, but Kris must have known she was wondering.

'My dad came and went. Mum used to say he probably had another family or two in other places. They never married, so you know what that makes me?' Kris grinned. 'It's all right. You don't have to say it, princess. Mum used to say that word suited Dad better, but maybe I was meant to end up like him, eh? A wanderer – not as responsible as I should be? Maybe it's in the genes.'

He patted his faded denim legs as if that was a joke. For a few minutes he talked about going to Upton Park with his father to see the Hammers and their 'glory days long gone', but she wasn't thinking about football. Just the daisy chain, and the messages she couldn't face, and 'Judas'. It made no difference that she'd deleted words from conversations when they were still there on the screen in her head.

'Shall I tell you about my travels?' he suggested, and began before she could answer.

Fizzy wasn't sure she could have placed them all in the

right continent, but she tried to learn what she could about Morocco, Algeria, Bolivia, Sardinia and the rest. When she asked him whether he was in particular places before or after she was born, he said it was hard to be sure.

'I always knew Kimberlie wasn't mine, deep down,' he said. 'She's got a big mouth, that girl. Too much lip.'

'Don't say that,' said Fizzy. 'You don't know her like I do. I think she's amazing.' Even though Kim would think that right now *she* was crazy, stupid, a mug.

'That's more to your credit than hers,' he said. 'You think well of people.' He pointed his thumb at his chest. 'She's hard-nosed, thinks I'm trash. Hasn't got your soft heart. Yeah, I got a better deal than Barry and he knows it!'

Fizzy frowned. She'd been feeling brave and hopeful because it was the love that mattered, but she loved Kim too. 'Please don't talk like that,' she said.

'Sensitive flower, aren't you?' Kris smiled. 'OK. I'll be on best behaviour for my nice, kind daughter. Least I can do.'

Fizzy was smiling back, but still he looked expectant, waiting for a reply.

'You don't think I can keep it up – best behaviour,' he told her. 'But I will. A whole day, you'll see.'

Fizzy couldn't remember the last time she'd spent a whole day with Barry, just the two of them. Now she never would.

'Thanks, Dad,' she said, and firmed up her smile so he'd know she believed him.

Jeanette was on her knees with the brush and dustpan, determined to sweep the kitchen floor until it was crumb-free. Irritated, Kim watched her duck under the table just as the house phone rang. Jeanette caught her head under a corner and cried out. So did Kim, because the thud had made her spill her tea.

Kim reached the phone first. Jeanette stood waiting, one hand to her head.

'Yes?' Kim asked.

It was Barry's deep, dark voice, calling her Kimberlie and asking to speak to Jeanette.

'Have you heard from Fizzy?' she asked him. She didn't see why she should just pass over the phone as if she was some kind of extra on the set. She was his daughter after all, the only real one he had.

'Not exactly,' he said, and hesitated before he added, 'but she's with Braddock.'

Kim swore.

'If that's all you have to contribute, I've got nothing to say to you,' he said.

Kim pulled a face. 'I've got more words like that one. But I've got nothing to say to you either.'

She gave the phone to Jeanette, who waved a hand in her direction and put a finger to her mouth.

Kim could still hear the sound of Barry's voice, but not the words. Listening, Jeanette sighed, sat down and shook her head. Then all of a sudden she sat up very straight. Kim saw one hand making a fist on the table while the other held the phone and kept listening.

'What now?' asked Kim. No answer.

'I've no idea!' Jeanette told Barry. 'He may not know himself. He makes up stuff as he goes along.'

'What?' asked Kim.

Jeanette's face creased up at her. Then she positioned the phone close enough for Kim to hear the word 'police'.

'Yeah, call 'em!' shouted Kim into it. Not because Kris was dangerous, but because it would serve him right if they arrested him. Then Fizzy might wake up and see what kind of father she really had.

But would that be a good thing? And what had he done now anyway? Kim was sick of this, all of it.

Jeanette moved away. 'No, not yet,' she told Barry. 'Why?' she asked, getting up and walking towards the sink. 'He's not a child molester or an axe murderer. He's just stupid, that's all – not a thought for anything but his little-boy kicks. It's a fun day out to him!'

Kim swore, much louder this time. She knew what he'd done and no words were too bad for him. 'He's not stupid!' she cried. 'He's sick! He's a nasty, selfish, devious bastard! And he's not going to do to Fizzy what he did to you!'

Mouth open, Jeanette looked right through her. 'I've got it!' she told Barry. 'I know where he'll be taking her – Upton Park. Are the Hammers playing?'

'Not between seasons, no,' muttered Kim.

Jeanette's face scrunched into a disappointed frown. But not for long. She lifted one hand like a nervous child who wasn't sure she'd give the right answer. 'Peter Pan's Playground,' she said, 'if it still exists. They rebuilt the pier. Southend – it's where we met.'

Kim frowned. Wasn't that the seaside? Jeanette was repeating herself, as if she was sure, or determined to be sure.

'You'll keep in touch, Barry?' she continued. 'I know the place. I might be able to direct you, make suggestions.'

There was a pause while she listened, nodding. She added a 'thank you' but turned to Kim. 'He cut me off.'

'He would,' said Kim. 'Don't be too grateful.'

'Barry's going to Southend to look for them,' said Jeanette. She grimaced. 'He's taking some men from his church. What if I'm wrong?'

'What if you're right?' asked Kim. 'Kris Braddock's a loser. It doesn't take a mob of holy vigilantes to hunt him down.'

'They'll be wearing crosses, not guns! They'll find Fizzy and bring her home.'

Kim supposed it wasn't the right time to ask where home was, or whether there'd be a fight – and who would win. Barry had double the muscle and bulk, but Kris had been ducking and dodging all his life. And wore rings that could take out an eye.

Kim pictured Fizzy watching the two of them going at it without a ref, and crying as if she was the one getting battered. She'd hate it more than anything. But Kim couldn't see Kris handing her over with a smile and a handshake and Barry thanking him for his trouble.

It was impossible and she didn't want to talk about it. She went up to her room.

'For God's sake, Fizzy!' she muttered at her phone. 'Why don't you just answer your texts?'

She sent another: 'Where R U? On the train?'

But Kim didn't ask about Southend, because if Kris knew they were on to him he'd reroute.

She didn't bother to suggest that if they were somewhere on the Southend line, Fizzy might want to jump out at the next station and find a policeman, because of course there was no way sweet, innocent, manipulated Fizzy would do that to her poor misunderstood daddy.

It was enough to drive anyone mad. Why was everyone so stupid? Why could nobody find a solution – one that banned the fathers from being big, stupid boys who thought they made the rules?

A bad situation had been made a whole lot worse, and soon there'd be what the newsreaders called an escalation. It was hard to know who to hate more, Kidnapper Kris or Barry 'Call me the Avenger' Duvall.

Kris Braddock had never taken this kind of risk for her. So did he really adore his princess, or was there some other motive in his tiny mind? Apart from jellied eels and Bingo and Essex girls showing flesh all over, what else was in Southend?

Fizzy wasn't replying. She might be scared. She might be happy, but not for long.

Kim took a breath that was meant to be deep but ended up shallow and quick. She couldn't leave it. It was down to her.

CHAPTER TWENTY-ONE

The sun was hiding as they drove into Southend.
'Oi!' complained Kris, eyes upward. 'We want blue, not dingy!'

'I hope it doesn't rain,' said Fizzy.

He said that he supposed it must have rained on him sometimes as a boy but he didn't remember the bad things. 'It's what I call policy. No looking back if you want to move on.'

So far there had been no glimpse of sea. At a circular border of flowers in the road Kris said he had no time for pansies and laughed. Fizzy understood then, and wondered what he'd say if he knew Barry was against gay marriage too? So they agreed on something! But Fizzy was sure Kim had been right when she said, 'Jesus loved everyone, didn't he? Isn't that the point?'

As they drove towards an ugly boxed-in metal bridge over the road, covered in graffiti, he said, 'I did that, twenty years ago!' and laughed. 'You half believe me, don't you?' He shook his head. 'Sometimes I think that's all you ever do.'

'No, Dad!'

He smiled and told her to take no notice. Then they turned a corner where a fake plastic castle was missing a wall on one side. On the other stretched the KURSAAL, lined with Union Jacks and promising FUN.

'Fun's not the word for what I had in that place!' cried Kris, happily, as Fizzy saw they were on the sea front at last.

He took her past a sliced-off car park that was fraying, and a shiny blue Sea Life museum that he said was full of sharks.

'So close they could bite through the wall and take off your head!' he cried, grinning.

Fizzy hoped he wouldn't drag her inside to laugh at her being nervous, or take her bowling to find out she couldn't keep the ball under control. Hadn't they come for the sea?

Southend was the kind of place where Laura wouldn't want her to sit on the toilets. But as she looked out along the shore, the sun scattered light onto the water and made it shine. She was surprised by the darkness of the sand and the flatness of the land that just edged into water with no cliff drops, no drama and no views. It was only on the other side of the road that the land sloped up, to gardens with spiky Mediterranean plants and the funicular railway.

But if the sea, the breakwaters and the beach were all brown, everything else was day-glo, shiny and illuminated – unless it was closed down now and boarded up.

The tallest sights on view were brightly-painted rides snaking round and down, spinning like giant wheels or plummeting like lift shafts. Everything was on the move, writhing and racing, dodging and swaying, looping, twisting and diving. She saw a dragon's head big enough to swallow her, and an enormous tube carrying bodies like marbles in a rush on Damon's toy. The noise, as she wound down the window, was like a watery wall, thick with life. It gushed faintly through the juddery pulse of layered music.

If she let it all fill her, there would be no room for the scenes that were bound to come later. They cut in already, like trailers for something unsuitable.

'Adventure Island' said the sign rising above the plastic leaves that fringed it. Travelling funfairs suited daredevil Damon but she'd found out at an early age that she didn't like the smells: onion and ketchup spilling out of burgers, oil to keep the metal joints moving, and too much sugar in the air. She hoped she looked happier than she really felt – which was rather sick.

'The pier's been burnt down twice and sliced through by a tanker,' Kris told her, eyes all around. He asked if she fancied a train ride to the end of it, which she said she did. 'Longest in the world,' he said proudly, as if he'd laid the track himself.

Once they'd parked the car they walked back along what he called the prom. He sang, 'Oh I do like to be beside the seaside!' and pretended to take offence when she said that was a Victorian song they'd learned at school.

'Watch it!' he cried. 'How old do you think I am?'

She smiled and ventured, 'Ten?' because she thought he'd enjoy that.

He gave her a playful shove before he folded his arms in a fake sulk, pushing out his mouth and turning away from her in a wounded, 'I'm not talking to you' kind of way. Fizzy giggled, which brought out his biggest grin so far.

'Even your laugh is polite!' he said.

If he knew her better, he'd recognise the nerves in it. But sometimes she thought she wasn't herself anymore.

Then he looked serious and said she had to let go more because Barrington Duvall had inhibited her. Fizzy supposed Kris had no inhibitions himself, but was that always good?

They began with lunch at a café Barry would call a 'greasy spoon'. It was funny to see an adult order a large plate of chips, douse them in vinegar and dip each one in salt and ketchup. But Fizzy wasn't his mother so she didn't ask where the protein was, or comment on cholesterol.

She had tuna salad which, as he pointed out, cost three times as much. When Fizzy apologised he told her not to treat him like a skinflint. So she apologised again and he told her sorry was banned.

As they finished with the coffee he'd promised her hours earlier, she looked at the clock. She must speak to Barry and make him see there was no problem at all because they were having a lovely day together, the way a father and daughter should.

'I should let them know I'm all right,' she said, making herself say it after whole minutes of rehearsing it in her mind. Even though they couldn't hold it all against Kris after her lie, they'd be in a panic. Or a rage. Laura would be crying.

'Who is it you mean?' he asked. 'I'm your father, not Barry. It's not his business. But he's the kind who thinks everything's his business – and the world would be better if he ran it.'

Why did they have to hate each other? Fizzy had to call someone. 'Ro?' she suggested.

'She knows you're all right with me. She's all right herself, Ro, best of the bunch.'

Did that mean yes or no? 'I'll call her then?' she checked.

'If you must,' he said, and she could see that he wasn't

266

happy now, so she said she'd send a text instead. It was easier anyway.

Having a good time with Dad by the sea. Everything is fine so no need for anyone to worry. X

She passed it to him, thinking that the wording would please him, especially the 'Dad' part, but he'd angled his body away and only shrugged. Fizzy sent it and turned off the phone without opening another message from Kim that waited there.

As they stepped outside she told him to have a cigarette if he wanted, in case that put him in a better mood. He did, thoughtfully, without saying much, and while they walked he hardly looked at her, as if he'd forgotten she was there. Or was disappointed with her? Had she hurt his feelings?

Then he stubbed the butt out underfoot. She remembered the Buddha, and tried to smile like the statue had, even with ash in its belly button. She must follow her dad's policy, she told herself, and forget the bad things.

'Best not to tell them where we are,' he said.

'I didn't,' she said, because Britain was an island so the water wasn't much of a clue.

'I know.'

The sun broke out from behind clouds as they headed towards the pier, and Kris clapped it.

'See?' he said. 'I told you this was going to be a great day, the best!'

Kim heard the surprise in Brad's voice, but since she'd had to go along to Operation HQ at the Duvall house with Jeanette, and she was calling him from the bathroom – one of many – there was no time for a story.

'Brad, I need you to buy me a train ticket online, all right? From Liverpool Street to Southend, single will do, on your credit card.'

Kim heard him tapping away at once. She could picture him at his student desk, looking out on Sheffield. He was her hero!

'Can I ask why?'

'Yeah, but I can only give you a short version of the answer. Because Fizzy needs help. She's the damsel in distress and I get your role. It has to be me.'

There was a pause but only a short one. 'OK. It's up on screen. Time?'

'Now. I need to be on the two-fifteen from Liverpool Street.'

'Hang on.'

Kim ran the tap just in case anyone was outside on the landing. Brad was a techie but it didn't feel quite so instant at the other end, waiting, trying out a lame impression of a new recruit for MI6. He tried to ask her how she was but she said she couldn't talk because people might be listening.

'It's bought,' he said. 'Write down the reference number.'

Kim had an old bus ticket and a pen in her bag. She leaned on the window sill beside the bowl of scented paper roses, and wrote down the numbers. Then Brad made an 'Aagh,' kind of noise.

'I'm an idiot. You'd need my credit card with you too, to put in the ticket collection machine. I'm dumb, sorry. Late night, trying to finish an essay.'

Kim breathed out hard. Then it was hopeless. End of.

'Clear head, Kim,' he told her, as if he heard her thinking. 'Cool head.'

Kim said, 'Yeah, hard head! Thanks anyway,' and added, 'Bye, love you,' quickly, before he could tell her not to do what she had to do.

She had enough cash for the tube. After that she'd just have to use her initiative. First she needed to slip out unnoticed. Given the size of the Duvall house and the number of people in it, who included some random posh women from their church (with names like Haggar Washington) as well as Jeanette, Laura, Ro, Mike and Damon, it shouldn't be too hard.

Damon was on the landing when she came out of the bathroom. Kim cursed him inwardly. Then she felt sorry, because he looked lost in his own house.

'I feel… lousy,' she told him. That was close. A different word would have brought Laura hurrying up to talk to her about teaching her brother bad language. But maybe she wasn't so pure and prudish, once. Laura Glendenning was a bad girl with worse habits than swearing. Damon had no idea!

'Why?' he asked.

There was no answer to that. 'I'm lying down in Fizzy's room,' she said. 'She wouldn't mind.'

He shrugged. Kim thought he looked nearly as sour and hostile as she'd felt, before she thought up the plan. He was her brother after all.

'It'll be all right,' she said, and smiled because he was all right too, for a nine-year-old boy. 'And I'm not a bitch.'

She saw his shock, followed by an 'I'll tell Mum' expression. Then the church boy disappeared and he was in the playground.

'OK,' he said.

His grin was embarrassed so she winked. As soon as he'd gone into the bathroom himself she crept downstairs. She opened the front door centimetre by centimetre, as if there was some kind of unexploded bomb on the doormat. Slowly she closed it behind her. She knew the way. And if her phone rang, she'd only answer if it said 'Fizzy' or 'Brad' or possibly 'Ro'. Had she thought of everything? Because she knew she must.

Head high, knowing she looked old enough, she walked as fast as she could, and ran some of it, like anyone with a bus to catch. No delays. The traffic was only averagely bad and the bus driver only averagely insane. Then the tube came within a minute.

Sitting in the carriage, her phone screen blank in her hand, counting off the stops to Liverpool Street, Kim imagined HQ.

Prayers. Jeanette crying. Laura serving organic flapjacks. Everyone jumping when Big Barry rang. Had anyone taken a minute to check whether she was still on Fizzy's bed? They'd all think she was sulking, and if she'd been there, they'd be right. She'd barricade herself in with Bibles.

It seemed to Kim that everyone was out of order, not just Kris who was a total git with the brain of a Nursery child, but Barry who thought he was playing the lead in a Hollywood movie. Someone should tell him Fizzy wasn't his to rescue or snatch back.

They were like two stupid boys who both wanted the same Lego wheels from the tub in wet play. She couldn't understand why no one stood up to either of them. Or why Fizzy let them move her around like a counter in a stupid board game.

They were supposed to be friends, in this together. Did Fizzy care about Kris more than her? Maybe blood really was thicker than water. Because if that was the case, what did that leave her? Big Bad Barrington and Shapeshift Laura, and a brother she could like but never connect with, deep down, like she'd connected with Fizzy.

Kim felt as if Fizzy had run away from her, made a choice and shut her out. It had left her stuck in the middle, trying to bat away words like 'injunction' when Laura, aka Barry's mouthpiece, talked law and enforcement on the phone. And then, the next minute, trying to challenge Jeanette's theory that Kris was doing it to punish her and break her heart all over again.

'He's not thinking about you!' she'd told Jeanette. 'Don't kid yourself. He's thinking about the only person he's ever loved – Kris Braddock.'

'NEXT STOP LIVERPOOL STREET' showed above the ads that curved around the carriage wall. Kim stood. Kris had been Kris – knew no better – and Barry was hellbent on being Barry, but there was something else. Worst of all was feeling what she felt about Fizzy. It was her stupidity that had caused this crisis.

But at the same time, no one seemed to see that it was only a crisis – rather than a day out for two – if everyone at HQ (and on the motorway, where a small fleet of cars headed for Essex like an SAS unit with prayers instead of guns) called it one.

There was a different kind of crisis, a real one. Kim didn't know whether she trusted Fizzy anymore. Or whether she knew her at all.

The doors slid open and Kim stepped out onto the platform. Liverpool Street. As a signal came back with a breeze, a text came through from Brad: Don't get arrested. X

On the odd little train ride along the pier, Kris told Fizzy about her baby brother who died. In one eye she saw a tear that ran for the wind to lick dry.

At once Fizzy's eyes brimmed full for poor Jeanette. She told herself that what she was struggling with was nothing. And her father had suffered too. It was what she was there for, to listen, and let him know she loved him anyway.

'Happiest day of my life when she said she'd marry me. I thought I'd blown it with my coming and going. I'd let her down. But this was another chance. I was a big boy then, and I could see myself with a lad of my own, on the terraces at Upton Park, bit of fishing, all that stuff.'

Fizzy tried to find a smile that showed how sorry she was, but how glad that he was sharing his story and his pain. He was looking into the wind off the sea as the train rattled slowly along.

'We hoped The Bruiser would get used to me without headbutting me in the belly. I reckoned she needed some discipline.' He stopped. 'All right, I know she's your heroine. Keep it zipped, Kris.'

Fizzy looked out and murmured, 'Yes,' to the waves knocking the legs of the pier.

'When the bleeding started I knew. D'you ever get the feeling you're being punished? I don't believe like you but I felt it anyway. It was only a few centimetres long and I never saw it – thank Christ – but it was our new life down the pan. Flushed away.' He looked at Fizzy as the train stopped. 'I'm upsetting you. Of course I am. You're bleeding for us, aren't you?'

A windsurfer in black rocked on the swell. Fizzy followed his gaze as he watched. Gulls circled and screeched.

'They'll tell you I'm the rat who ran again. It was a kind of sinking ship. J wasn't staying afloat, that was for sure. I couldn't prop her up. No scaffolding skills, see. I didn't have the strength. I'd had the stuffing knocked out of me. It's not just the woman who feels the loss.'

His sigh seemed louder than the wind chopping the dark water. She leaned in close to him.

'Dad,' she said. 'I know you're sorry.'

'I tried to tell her that. J, on Good Friday. She's a lady, you know? But she hates me. I don't blame her for being right out of forgiveness as well as sugar.'

People were getting out of the carriage but Kris sat still, his hair windblown. Huddled, he looked cold. He was as thin as a boy. If the others could see him now, they couldn't hate him the way they did.

'I'll never let you down, Felicity. I swear. I'll be your dad, a proper one. You'd come to Upton Park, give it a go? I could get tickets.'

'All right,' she said. 'But I won't fish.'

'Course you won't. Wouldn't hurt anything or anyone, would you?'

They left the little train behind and walked back against a gusty wind that messed his hair. The sea was no bluer but from the land, the rhythm of the low, spreading waves was reassuring – even though he said they were weedy and should be ashamed of themselves.

273

Already it was nearly three o'clock, but he had plans that didn't seem to include driving back. He'd already talked about coaching her at ten-pin bowling but she must tell him Barry did enough of that and she never enjoyed it. She'd rather he talked, and let her love grow.

Now he said how much he liked the sound of Dragon's Claw. He made one of his own, the big black ring lumping out by his knuckles, and laughed.

'Dad,' she said, as they headed towards Adventure Playground, 'I'm not very good with rides that throw you about.'

'That's all right,' he said. 'I'll look after you and hold your hand. That's what dads are for.'

But at the playground there was a queue for Dragon's Claw and Vortex, and Kris said Ramba Zamba sounded girly. Then they came to some toilets and he said he'd 'only be a mo'. Fizzy said she needed the Ladies too.

Once inside the cubicle, she took out her phone, turned it on and paused. There was a text from Barry but it just told her: Stay strong, keep praying and trust in the Lord, not Kris Braddock. Fizzy's deep breath only heaved up and came out shaky. Why wouldn't he listen?

She didn't see why the Lord would mind her being in Southend with her father, even if the tangling in her stomach still felt like a knot. The messages from Kim would only pull and twist things tighter. She couldn't read them now. But one day, all three of them would come here together. One day, Kim would see what she saw, and Kris would laugh out loud at her impressions and love her too.

But not yet because her lie hadn't helped. Fizzy realised they hadn't believed her. She hadn't helped at all.

Looking for Kris outside, she found him some distance away with his back to her, talking on the phone. He hadn't seen her. She went back to the toilets. Ro, the mediator. She'd been on a course. She must know what to do.

The call was answered so quickly it almost made her jump with surprise. She heard Laura ask for the phone, and a gasp that might be from Jeanette, and Damon being hushed.

Fizzy was shocked. They were all there! Why did they have to make it such a big deal when everything was perfectly fine? Why couldn't they back off and give her room to breathe?

'Ro,' she said, 'please can you make it all right, with no trouble? No police or anything? It's not abduction. I want to be here, I do! I'll be home soon but I've got to go.'

As Laura asked a second time to speak to her, Jeanette said her name in a kind of gasp that was nearly a sob.

'Listen, Fizzy,' began Ro, but she couldn't.

Fizzy switched off. It was worse than she could have imagined. They'd have instructions, advice or orders, warnings, questions. It was too much to handle and Kris could turn round any minute and want to know what she was up to.

But when she emerged again Kris was still on the phone and laughing. He waved but kept on talking as he walked towards her, not really looking.

'Later!' he finished cheerily and put his phone away. 'You're spared Dragon's Claw. Change of plan. We're meeting a lady friend of mine and she's got a beach hut so you're going to get proper Southend, with salt and sand and bucket and spade.'

'Oh,' Fizzy said, taken aback. She could see her face wasn't the one he wanted. A lady friend? But it was a day for them to be together, the two of them.

'You know what?' he said. 'You make it hard to have a good time.'

Since 'sorry' was banned, Fizzy didn't know what else to reply. She felt sick again.

'I haven't got a costume,' she said instead. 'I thought…' But she stopped. The words would come out broken. She could feel the jagged edges already.

He rolled his eyes. 'Shell can sort you out. You'd probably fit one of hers – give it a bit of a stretch.' He lit a cigarette. 'Don't take offence, princess – she's petite, Shell. We were kids together. She got my name tattooed on her chest when she was about fifteen.'

She saw him grin as he blew smoke out towards the sea. Fizzy asked if it was far to the beach hut and he took it as a complaint.

'What's up now?' he asked. 'What's wrong with proper seaside? Or is it Shell? I don't suppose swanky Duvall types have tattoos or beach huts. Is that it? Has Barrington made you a snob?'

'No,' she managed. One word but it couldn't hold a note.

'Course you're not. You're just shy. But she's a diamond, Shell. She's keeping me straight. I've told her all about you. You two will get on great, trust me.'

She looked in his blue eyes. He was asking her to do what she needed most. But there were too many people already: too many on the end of her phone, too many people with ideas about her and Kim and their lives. And J, who'd loved him, might have given him another chance, once she saw how sorry he was and how much he'd changed.

But now he had someone else called Shell so her parents wouldn't fall in love again. It was another stupid idea that could only fool people who chose to believe in robins taking care of dead men's souls, and daisy chains strong enough to bind people together with love.

A crowd of seagulls lifted at once from the same roof and crossed flight paths over their heads. No formation, like swans or geese – just cries clashing and a near-collision of wings as they raced and chased. Or challenged. It was hard not to see them as bullies and Fizzy felt herself cower as she tried to tuck her head into her neck.

'Along came a seagull and pecked off her nose!' said Kris, and began to sing the nursery rhyme about the queen in her parlour and the maid hanging out the clothes. Then, as she straightened, he put out an elbow so they could link arms.

'I said I'd look after you, didn't I? That includes terrorist attacks from the air!'

But what about attacks from everyone, from all round and inside? He had no idea how they hated him. He had no idea how to make it stop.

Not the best day now, but the worst. Something even bigger than a promise felt broken like the daisy chain. Like the dream of marrying Michael. Like her friendship with Suranne. She'd thought she could find a place to stand – between Barry and Kim, between Kris and Jeanette, and between her real parents and the ones she'd always believed she loved – but where was it?

There would always be sides.

On her phone she saw three unopened texts from Suranne on her phone. No. Not now, not ever. Words she couldn't read, wouldn't read. Not angel but Judas. Princess. Liar. Felicity Kimberlie Braddock Duvall. The girl with no name.

Was it really all for nothing?

Approaching Platform Five, Kim saw the train waiting. In front of her were other passengers heading in the same direction, but the key difference was the tickets they all held as they went through the barrier. Tickets with today's date on them. Unlike the old ticket in Kim's pocket, dug up from the bottom of her bag, curling at one corner and cracking in the middle.

The man checking the tickets looked a bit like a soap actor with a Scottish voice Kim could do quite well, but a wink and an 'Och aye!' weren't going to cut it. Kim stood back, watching and waiting, keeping an eye on the time and the people. Maybe he'd get caught short and have to run to the loo. *Yeah, Kim, as if.*

Just behind her Kim saw a black woman who might have been Jeanette's big sister Lianna. As the woman passed, in heels that made her swivel like the headteacher's chair, Kim followed, as close as she dared, with her phone to her ear. Ahead, a short woman in a headscarf, long full skirt and sandals was asking questions in something not much like English, and getting distressed. Soapy started looking around for someone to help him out as the black woman stood waiting to go through, with Kim just on her shoulder.

The Lianna lookalike started looking at her watch.

While the headscarf woman lifted her arms helplessly and raised her voice as if she might sob, Soapy waved her on. Holding up her ticket, the black woman hurried through. Kim followed, the old ticket raised, calling, 'For God's sake! All *right!*' as if this was her mum and she was only a step or two behind because she was sulking.

Indignantly, the woman turned round and eyed her as they walked along the platform, but Kim pretended to be talking into her phone and laughing. She climbed into the carriage and walked along, glad to see that the seats weren't numbered. Anywhere would do. She sat down and took a breath. She'd done it. Kim looked at her reflection in the carriage window. Hair, check. Make-up, check. No one familiar running down the platform with a cop or two, check. She found an old sweet to suck, still wrapped at the bottom of her bag. Four minutes to go.

The whistle blew on time and the train pulled away. Triumph shone on the face she stared at in the glass, but it soon passed. Still no phone call! Did no one care that she was ill in Fizzy's room? Even if none of them believed that story, someone might have thought to take her a cup of tea. They were all too busy waiting by the phone to take orders from their Lord and Master.

So, thought Kim, she knew where she stood. Fizzy went off to Southend with her so-called but biological father and something called All Hell broke loose. Prayers were flying up to God in Heaven like birds from an African lake. *She* went off to Southend on her own, without a ticket, and nobody even noticed she'd gone.

It wasn't a game. She was a fare dodger, she was way out of her depth and even though none of it was her fault, it didn't mean she'd get away with it in the end. Kim looked at an old, glued-up slit in the upholstery opposite and imagined herself with a knife in her fist, slashing.

Fizzy tried to listen and smile as Kris talked about board games and toys. And a sandcastle he'd built once, that the big boys had clapped – until he'd been so proud he made a muscle man arm and put a foot on a turret!

It didn't matter how much she loved the boy when the man was Public Enemy Number One, still wrecking things without trying.

As they approached the row of beach huts Fizzy saw that they were mostly painted brown to match the sand, and white like the tips of the waves. Pretty and simple, like giant versions of kits to glue together, they seemed made for play and Let's Pretend. For boys like him. Sandy steps led up to the doors, some of which were open. Fizzy smelt coffee and hot, fatty food.

Sitting on the steps of the only striped hut in the whole row sat a woman in white shorts no longer than knickers, her bare legs crossed and wedge sandals tipping off the ends of her feet like seesaws. In her hands she held a mug as if it was warming her against the wind. Her short, spiky hair was a dark red, like Communion wine. Under the cardigan she pulled around her Fizzy glimpsed lilies outlined in gold, and the nails on her fingers and toes gleamed with five bright colours.

Through big sunglasses the woman stared, not waving or standing but her dark red mouth wobbling into various half-smiles.

'Welcome, stranger,' she said. 'I'm sixteen again.'

'You look sixteen,' Kris said.

'Yeah-yeah.'

Fizzy expected double cheek kisses, the kind her parents used when they greeted their dinner party friends, but Shell and Kris kissed mouth to mouth, leaning forward and puckering like children.

Shell, the lady friend. Had hers been the phone call in Mike's garden? The reason he'd disappeared from Mike's, and let her down that first Sunday when she'd waited and waited and he hadn't come?

As her cardigan opened in the breeze Fizzy saw a rounded tummy she hadn't expected.

'Good to meet you, darlin',' she told Fizzy. 'Kimberlie, isn't it?'

'Out of date information, Shell, remember?' said Kris. 'This is Felicity and she's a little lady so mind your language.'

Fizzy almost missed it but she thought she saw Shell give him a very discreet V-sign, not the kind that meant victory but the kind the boy character made on the cover of a book called *Kes* that Barry hadn't let her read in school when it was a set book.

'Come on up, Felicity,' said Shell. 'I know the score. I'm just bad with names – aren't I, Kevin?' She grinned. 'Maybe you can help us think of a nice one for your little brother.'

Kris put his hand on the tight tummy just for a moment and grinned. He turned to Fizzy. 'I wasn't counting my chickens – you know – early days. You like babies, don't you? You'll be a lovely big sister.'

'Half-sister,' she murmured. She didn't move at first. She loved babies but the words that told him so were stuck somewhere.

'Go on, then,' Kris told her.

Fizzy started up the steps.

Kim had never been out of London alone. Not because like Fizzy she was under a thumb that didn't know where it belonged, but because of money, and the space her life took up. Her world was bigger now but that didn't make it better.

For a while she'd been looking out of the train window on fields and hedges. Just because she was more familiar with graffiti than sheep and cows didn't mean she struggled to name them, or stared wide-eyed like a presenter in the rainforest. But what surprised her was nothing. It was all around them. Nothing and more nothing, as if people hadn't explored this far. They were all in Brick Lane! And she wished the dads were back there, both of them, settling it with knives, guns. With luck they could blow themselves away.

A text came through from Brad, worried. He knew her too well. Sorting it, she told him. Don't get your Y fronts in a twist. X

Kim had studied the diagram so she knew when she saw the name Prittlewell on the station platform that she was nearly there. Next stop. Then just as the train gathered speed again, she heard her phone. They'd woken up, had they? She saw 'Mum' on her screen, because she'd never changed it in her Contacts list and she wasn't intending to, either. But she couldn't face Jeanette crying, begging and wobbling. Kim clicked off, and swore under her breath.

Am just trying to help, she tapped. What was that phrase they used? Yes, that was it: Call it damage limitation. You know I can take care of myself. X Plus a smiley.

The train pulled in to Southend platform and Kim stepped out, holding her phone, making her way along with the rest of the crowd towards the Way Out.

A fat man in uniform was there, blocking it – just like she'd told herself he could be. No good the clear head getting fuzzy now. As she walked she rummaged. As she rummaged, the impression took over: flustered, a bit ditzy, law-abiding, close to panic but very polite. The impression was Fizzy, but at least sixteen – old enough to buy a ticket with a credit card but soft enough to lose it and feel guilty and scared.

'Ticket, love?'

'I can't find it,' Kim said quietly but precisely. 'I'm so sorry. It must be here.'

She looked in her pockets and tried her bag again, pulling out a bus ticket.

'Wrong ticket, love,' said the man, not accusing yet, not assuming. He almost smiled. A few impatient passengers passed through, holding out their tickets for him to glimpse.

'Yes, but this is my reference number,' Kim explained politely, talking as beautifully as Laura would love any daughter of hers to do, 'from the online booking.'

The guy squinted as he looked at the numbers, which were quite badly scribbled.

'I don't suppose it …' began Kim, and inspiration dawned, the way it often did when she was in role, 'constitutes any kind of evidence? I'm holding you up, I'm so sorry.' She knew Fizzy would be choking back a sob now and she called one up, just quivering under the words. 'I'll keep looking. It must be here, it has to be.'

The man shook his head and waved her through with a muttered, 'All right.'

'Oh, thank you so much,' she breathed, not quite acting now. She felt Fizzy's smile of relief as her shoulders sank. She almost added, 'God bless you!'

Twins after all, thought Kim, hurrying out of the station. She sent Brad a text: All under control. X As if!

She wanted to tell Fizzy too. She needed to hear her voice. If she sent her a message, would she announce it and give the game away? 'Dad, it's Kim, she's come to join us!' She couldn't risk him dragging her into a car or taxi and heading for the airport. Southend had one, and people too, plenty of them. Fizzy was one of thousands but Kim had to find her. In her bag she had a list of the places Jeanette had named, the Kris Braddock haunts. So she'd try them all.

Kim had set off in the direction of the seafront and walked some way, eyes open for the sea, trying to scent it, when her phone rang. Not Fizzy. Not Brad or Ro. She guessed, but until she heard his voice she hoped she was wrong.

'Kimberlie, listen, please,' said Barry, so loudly he might have been on a runway, underneath a plane taking off. She held the phone away.

'Jeanette is distraught. One missing daughter is one too many but two! It isn't helping – though I know that's what you want to do. Please tell me where you are so I can meet you. I'm guessing you're in Southend. I'm here myself. I'm asking you to trust me.'

'I can't.'

There was a pause. She'd winded him. Kim kept walking. She hadn't time for this.

'Kim, please. This has to stop. It's my duty to stop it.'

'You're making trouble for Fizzy, just like Kris. You're doing her head in. Just leave it! Leave her alone.'

'On the contrary, all I want is what's best for her, for you, for both of you.'

'God!' she muttered, not caring whether he heard. He was like a politician with a line he kept repeating, whatever anyone thought or felt. It was just a way of throwing his weight around and Fizzy would be beside herself, if she knew. It made Kim want to kick something.

'Southend's got a pier,' she told him, teeth almost clenched, shoulders tight.

'Yes?'

'If you want to help, Barry, go to the end and jump.'

End of. Kim was shaking. But if Kris had the nerve to ring her she'd give him the same advice.

CHAPTER TWENTY-TWO

Inside the hut there wasn't much room for furniture. A small table was littered with magazines and a six-can pack of Diet Coke, a couple of bananas joined at the stalk, and a bottle of sun cream with sand grains around the lid. A large flowery towel hung over one wooden chair and a costume in two pieces dangled over the back of the other.

Fizzy told herself she was used to a brother. When she held baby cousins in Jamaica, she loved the way they felt in her arms.

Remembering made no difference. Thinking never did – only love, and that was pretending after all. It was over: not just the day, but the future she'd longed for.

Fizzy could smell the sea in the wood, and the floor needed sweeping. She looked out. The view was almost completely filled by sand and water, breakwaters and sky – apart from a little strip of grey along the bottom edge of the frame where people walked past with their ice creams and dogs. It couldn't fill the space that grew inside her like the child inside Shell. Why hadn't he told her before, on the train, when he'd talked about the baby that died and Upton Park?

In the distance was a ship that might be huge enough to cut through the pier again, but it was miles out where the sea was darkest and edged into sky. Closer to shore a windsurfer in a black wetsuit brushed across the picture.

Maybe the same one, still there as if nothing had changed.

Kris and Shell were on the steps outside. She thought they might be kissing but she didn't want to see. Shell and the baby: his family now. Were they the reason he asked for the DNA test after all those years – a kind of trigger?

But fathers could love more than one child. Why would he make so much trouble just to see her, unless he wanted her too? The bump was small, like Shell. How long had he known?

She heard the wooden steps creak.

'Right,' said her father. 'Time for a swim.'

Fizzy hadn't noticed people in the water. Wouldn't the sea be freezing? But he was asking if she could borrow the costume on the back of the chair. Fizzy's mouth opened but before she could point out that it was in two pieces, Shell protested.

'What about me? I've got to bare my bits to the world, have I?'

'Don't see why not,' said Kris. 'There's no one out there.'

'Yeah, get me arrested. You've tried that before.' She turned to Fizzy. 'Go ahead, Felicity, love. I'll give it a miss this time. Your dad can keep you company.'

Kris said he hadn't got any trunks but Shell fetched a pair of long, full elasticated ones, one leg green and one leg yellow.

'No excuses,' she said. 'Show us what you're made of.'

There was a changing area at the back, like a big cubicle with a stable door.

'Little ladies first,' said Kris.

'It's a bikini,' said Fizzy, and looked up at him, begging him to understand.

'And?' he asked. 'You're a big girl, aren't you?'

Too big. There was too much of her. The bikini felt just slightly damp when he handed it over. It was stretchy and pretty and part of her wanted to believe she could look nice in it. But the fooling was finished now.

Behind the cut-off wooden wall she stepped into the bikini bottoms, which were so small that a great brown stretch of belly swelled over the edge. The top pinched and squeezed and pushed even though it also creased where she didn't fill it. There was no mirror but she knew she looked ridiculous. Her cheeks burned from inside.

'Let's have a look, then,' called Kris.

Fizzy stepped out with her arms across her chest. Shell winked, passed her the towel and helped to wrap her in it.

'I'll come down to the water, eh, and take that off you when you're ready to plunge in.'

Was she ready? She stood like a mannequin – but the wrong shape, not good for sales. She felt numb. Plunge? Kim would; she'd be like Damon and charge in with a roar. But had she ever plunged into anything?

'You can swim, can't you?' asked Kris.

It wasn't really a question. Fizzy didn't like lessons or races. But she remembered how much she enjoyed the feel of water on skin, the dreaminess of the float and flow. And feeling like a different species under the surface, where the world was a new place. She looked out to the horizon, a line that wasn't really there, a place no one could ever go. She didn't mind the idea of the salt water, even if it was cold at first. It didn't matter anyway. There was nowhere to stand and no one to be.

Following Shell down the steps and across to the sand,

she stumbled over the pebbles. Shell slipped out of her wedges and encouraged her to hurry with a quick, flappy hand.

The waves looked gentle enough, with their lacy edges and their see-through overlaps, and the wet sand underfoot was a relief. Shell stopped and reached for the towel. Smiling, she told her, 'You go, girl!'

Sudden gritty wind knocked her off balance and the sand gave way to pebbles that poked and tilted her as she faltered forward. Kris cheered from behind but his son would grow up braver, faster and much more fun. She lowered herself until her arms pushed forward in her first breast stroke pattern. The cold stabbed, seized and rattled her, but she kept on pushing. Never in her life, in the school pool, the Sports Centre, Barbados or Spain or Crete, had she felt such water. The smell and the taste were familiar, but the touch was as cruel as the colour. It felt as if all her softness turned to metal too.

So she told herself it was the shock and it was just a matter of time before her body got used to the cold. That unlike Shell, she had enough flesh on her to keep her warm, like seal blubber. But the salt stung her eyes as a gusty wave smacked her and her body felt stiff and heavy – but at the same time, tossed and bobbing like a straggle of seaweed. She knew she must look pathetic.

Kris shouted from the pebbles, 'No messing! Tough and strong! May the Force be with you!'

She turned, but he wasn't looking at her. Instead he seemed to be striking poses to amuse Shell. He was like a Mr Universe without the muscles, but hopping around in between shapes as if the pebbles under his feet had shot out of a volcano. Willing him to join her, Fizzy couldn't find the voice to ask. Besides, he wasn't listening.

Treading water now, she circled to keep everything moving, her feet springing from the seabed, and water slopping into her mouth, making her gulp and spit. But she was still icy-cold and there was no dreaminess and no peace. She didn't feel brave or tough, just scared and alone.

'Dad,' she murmured, but it was more of a breath than a cry.

Then he waved, and she tried to wave back without losing whatever control she had over her body and the water. While she watched, between bobs and splashes and strikes, he started to make his way towards her and the sea. Performing, shuddering and faltering, he pulled big-stretch, agonised faces as he tiptoed. He looked skinny and young.

Something inside Fizzy smiled but she had to keep moving. A wild, Damon voice told her to thrash, to beat the water down and fight it, but she almost lost herself in the swell and gush and foam.

Where was Kris? Coming to join her, to help her to feel something else, to be brave and playful and strong? For a moment she could see nothing but the head space above the surface. Then she glimpsed him between waves, scampering back to the hut. Clowning, but leaving her. Choosing Shell and their baby.

He'd decided. He didn't need her anymore. She was extra now, and she'd only be in the way. Never first. Just a part-time daughter, switch-on, switch-off. He didn't really love her, not enough.

As the seabed fell further and further away beneath her feet, Fizzy told herself she was getting used to the cold and the slapping. And the salt, and the sky that wouldn't hold still.

She kept swimming. She could plunge after all.

Walking faster, with her eyes left, then right, ahead then behind, Kim tried to regulate her breathing. Everything inside felt higher and tighter, but then she'd probably covered more ground in Southend now than she did over ninety minutes on a pitch. Her phone rang. The screen said 'Ro'.

'Don't let the mothers panic,' Kim told her. 'I'm fine. I'm listening. Where is she? Do you know?'

Ro's voice was level, steady. She didn't waste anyone's time. She just listed the places that had been crossed off the list, eliminated – by Barry or one of the others. Graham Washington? Wasn't that Suranne's dad? Hadn't he got better things to do? Even though Ro didn't call them a Hit Squad, she didn't argue when Kim did.

'You know why I want to find them first, Ro, don't you?'

'Yes, I do.'

'If Barry finds Kris, he won't buy him an ice cream. Fizzy won't be able to bear it.'

'I wish I was there, Kim. I should be.'

Kim wished the same. She told Ro about her cool head.

'I'm glad,' Ro said, and asked her to keep in touch and talk things through as they happened.

'Where should I go?' Kim asked her.

Ro said she'd pass her over to Jeanette.

'It'll do my head in if she cries!' Kim warned her.

But Jeanette didn't, even though she told Kim she loved her. She asked her which shops and amusement places she'd already passed by, and what she could see. Kim pulled a few names together, in more or less the right order, even though at that moment a lot of them were boarded up. Jeanette said she must be at the Thorpe Bay end.

'All right, there's a row of beach huts, Kim. Kris loves them. You might not be able to see them yet, but if you follow the road along the seafront and keep your eyes down on the beach, they're tucked in, against the wall. You should be able to get down some path or steps – I can't remember, it might have changed.'

Kim kept walking. The road curved round with the coastline. 'I can see them. Yeah. I love you too.' She was about to ring off, but she needed to ask. 'Have you told Barry this?'

'Yes.'

Of course, thought Kim, *he'd have the whole town covered.* 'Have you told him *everything*?'

There was a pause. 'Yes. I told Laura a while back.'

Laura? Since when were they bessies? Had Barry and Laura known before her about Kris and the lost baby? Kim didn't ask. She didn't care what Laura might have told Jeanette about rehab or rescue. Barry knew his enemy. The team would be moving in on their target any time.

Jeanette was still talking. but Kim's eyes were on the huts. She could see them now, from above, and the path that led along the beach to each of them. She didn't wait for Jeanette to finish, but shouted, 'Bye!' and hung up. She needed some peace to think.

Maybe someone should have broken the truth to Fizzy about her poor, lonely daddy. Better to have shot down the shadow before he turned up in the cheeky, smoky flesh

292

talking seaside and quality time and making it up to her.

If she could lean over the wall, she could see who was down there. But the road was busy, and there was no pavement on that side. Kim looked both ways and ran, pressing herself up against the wall, ignoring the hoots from the cars that passed. One after another they rushed alongside. A truck didn't so much pass as shave the air between them, but she had no time to shout.

Running, peering down and then running on, Kim had to shut out the traffic and hope the drivers didn't ignore her back. At last, as she looked along the row of huts for what felt like the tenth time, she saw a figure below that made her stop. A figure that could be Kris Braddock, stupid as ever, showing off, acting the fool. A small, red-haired woman was laughing at him from the steps of a hut.

But where was Fizzy?

There were kids on the beach, and balls scudding across the sand for a dog to chase. Most of the adults were wrapped up in winter jackets and keeping up a brisk pace, but an old couple sat together on a towel with a steaming flask. It wasn't Barbados. Further out, she saw boats and even ships, way out towards the horizon. Not too many swimmers, but a few who might be in wetsuits.

'Get off the road!' yelled someone from a car.

A head leaned out with a twisted face and a finger. Kim raised one back at him. If she didn't find those steps Jeanette half-remembered soon, she'd be flat as a ten pence piece.

The vehicles kept on coming, tugging and pushing the air. Kim's lungs felt full of fry-ups and saltwater. She ran on, her back to the traffic and her eye on the sea. Over the wall and out in the water, as far to her right as she could see, there was something, someone in the water – far out, tiny, bobbing.

'Fizzy!' she yelled, but the cars swallowed the sound. 'I'm coming,' she told herself, as she found the path down.

They were miles back. And who wore a suit on the beach? There was a Hit Squad agent ahead of her, with a grey pony tail and a hipster suit. Daddy Suranne? Whoever he was, he was closing in on Kris – wherever he was hiding himself – to put a stop to his laughing. She was too late.

And Fizzy was further out every time she looked. What did she think she was doing? Was there a drowning child to rescue or a burger tray to recycle, for God's sake? What was out there? What was she trying to prove?

Far behind her on the shore, Fizzy heard a dog bark. A child was crying. But the sea was louder, breaking up around her head. Fizzy wanted to cry too, to shout out, 'Daddy!' and tell him it wasn't fair. They were meant to be together, not apart. It was what the day was for, what the lie was for. Not this. Not grey sky and grey sea wrapping her round.

Treading water, her legs felt feeble. She could stop. She could swim back, pushed on by the tide, towards the sand and the towel. Back to the car to take her back – to a place that wasn't home. Parents that weren't hers. A life she'd liked, the only one she'd known. But she'd have to turn round and face it all again, and nothing would have changed. Kris was with Shell. Michael was with Suranne. There was nowhere to go.

Again she looked over her shoulder, back to the shore. Striding towards the beach hut was a man in a suit who didn't belong, with a phone to his ear. Fizzy swam, one stroke, another, out and away, but in her head she saw him still. It was a Sunday man, with the only grey pony tail in church, and the only suit with no tie. Graham Washington: not worrying about Suranne's soul but hers. He'd come for her, but that didn't mean he'd listen, even if she had anything to say. She'd rather be alone, left alone to the water and sky.

Fizzy swam on. But looking back, up above a wave that almost blinded her, she saw him advancing towards Kris. His right arm held a phone, but the left lifted and pointed, then spread out a hand like a warning or a 'stop'. Not to her but her father.

'Braddock!'

So loud it reached her. *No*, thought Fizzy. The name beat and swelled around her head and burst inside like saltwater. When would it stop?

She didn't want to see and she didn't want to hear. Fizzy turned back towards the ships and the cool glint of dark water as the sun struck it. No Barry yet, but Barry was there somewhere, on the phone, directing the operation. Maybe there were others too, obeying his orders, on the move. They would be all around, closing in, nothing she could say or do. Like Jesus in the Garden and the soldiers arriving. But no, that wasn't right. She was the Judas.

Forgive me, Father, she thought, and fell back down, arms pressing forward and legs circling behind. She got everything wrong. The lies felt heavy. Not a good Christian. Not a good friend. A coveter of kisses.

Swim, she told herself. *Keep swimming.*

Still tensing at the cold, she tried to find the rhythm she needed, telling herself to focus. *Force*, she thought, *May the*

Force be with you. No Barry yet, but no Ro to step in now. It was up to her. The water rearing around her must be deep enough to swallow Dragon's Claw, but she was safe here. She must find the float and flow because without it there was only anger and blame. Waywardness and darkness, too much to forgive, and no love left, not now.

Shouting into the wind, Kim ran down from the steps and along the path towards the men. One with a pony tail and one in a towel, they were squaring up, their voices striking first. All the while the sea and sky clashed too, way, way out of reach, and everything shook and pounded with her feet. With every step, she lost Fizzy to the grey, endless swell, and had to find her again. But every time she fixed her eye on the shape of her head, it was smaller, as if she was shrinking, as if the water was washing her away like soap…

'Kris!' she shouted. 'Fizzy! Help me!'

The words were snatched by the wind, lost! There were others, deep ones, clashing. Kris grabbed Hipster with one arm and threw a punch with the other.

'Stop it!' yelled Kim.

Kris turned but it wasn't her he needed to see. Pony Tail tried an arm lock. Kris kicked and wriggled, puffing and swearing. Kim went in low, head down, more rugby than soccer – right at their legs, all four. She broke it up and left them breathless. But their eyes were open now. Her fists beat Kris's chest. She pulled his wrist, dragging him down to the water behind her.

'There! Look! COME ON!'

Kim wasn't looking back at him or down at the pebbles.

As she pulled, she focused only at the speck that was Fizzy. Behind her Kris swore. Then he wasn't behind her anymore. Eyes on the sea, he shook her off and raced away.

With a cry Kim stumbled forward. As she fell, arms first, something poking out between the pebbles slashed her skin. Glass like shark's teeth. She felt the blood warm on her hands.

'Felicity!' Kris shouted – a new Kris, a stranger, a father now.

Kim stood a moment, her feet sliding on the pebbles, blood slipping from her cupped palm and splashing her jacket, her jeans. He'd need help. Into the water she ran, chest tight, salt burning where the blood leaked. Ahead of her, Kris met the waves and beat them down. But she couldn't trust him. She could do it too. She forced a way in.

Kim waded, her clothes heavy, a marbling curl of blood melting into the cold water.

'Fizzy!' she screamed.

Did she hear? Let her hear. Let her stop.

'It's me, Kim!'

Sounds knocked against Fizzy's head, blurred by water as she ducked beneath a wave. Voices she knew, hard but melting, with no mouths. Words floating like petals torn away. Her own name bursting inside her. Not hers. Not now. Counting, she moved out and on. There were rows of digits in her head, figures repeating and a pattern to cling to. The numbers kept the other sounds away, but her body was forgetting the strokes. Was the wind stealing the water or was she losing strength? It didn't matter. She was swimming on somehow. And she couldn't go back.

Ninety-seven. Ninety-eight. Was her body heavy or light? Had she left it behind? Time had lost its shape, and her mind couldn't hold the numbers. *Father, O my father, are you there?* The shapes were shifting, blending into sound. There was nothing to hear that wasn't thick and furry like a radio between stations, slipping away as she reached for it, soft but breaking through her fingers. *A hundred and six.*

No rainbows without sun. Somewhere outside her limbs and brain, the water rising up and knocking, Fizzy knew there were shouts spilling through the blur. They might have been a dream but they couldn't touch her. From somewhere far away her own voice lifted to God and filled her. Still now. A better kind of love. There was warmth inside her, and the light was full of colours. The Lord was with her.

Water rushed into Kim's mouth. Kicking, she spluttered. A man splashed behind her, reached out and dragged her back. As a wave knocked her into him, his pony tail swung through the spray, its grey tip a flick against her face. Her fists beat his chest once, twice, and shoved him forward.

'Let me go!' she managed, pushing him away towards the water. 'Not me – her!'

Rocking, she bent on the pebbles, hands pressing the pain away into her dark, soaked jeans. *Faster!* Blood dripped on the stones. Kim wiped her face with her sleeves and let her arms hang heavy with fire. *Faster!* The grey pony tail balled up and down in the water, but out towards the sky Fizzy was still so far away. She couldn't watch and wait. Kim stumbled on, back into the foam.

'I'm coming, Fizzy!'

Behind her the pebbles crunched like ice breaking. Barry,

big and pounding! Throwing off his jacket, he hurtled towards her, making the sand fly.

He held her to him, just for a moment, long enough to feel his heat pressing firm against her. It soaked in deep, stilling her as she shook. A towel wrapped her. In her ear she heard, 'Enough. You've done enough.'

Then he was gone, the Jamaican in the sprint. It would be all right now.

Kim sank to her knees.

CHAPTER TWENTY-THREE

The world darkened around her till it was gone. When she opened her eyes on it again there was a small woman giving her a mug of water to sip. Hair the colour of raspberries. A baby bump. Perfume. Kim sat up, her head filling with the wind blowing off the sea. Underneath her the pebbles jabbed. There was a hanky tightly around one hand, brighter red with blood, but the woman said it was stopping now, the bleeding.

'Fizzy?' she asked.

'He's got her.'

Kris was grey as the water, sand gritting his skinny legs as he stumbled onto the shore with Fizzy in his arms. Limbs hanging loose, eyes closed, she might have been sleeping. But something had gone from her and left emptiness behind. As if the sea had taken her away.

At Kris's shoulder, Barry was bigger, wider and more solid than ever. He reached out for the body slung across Kris's bare chest. Kris looked exhausted, but he didn't want to let go. For God's sake! Were they still fighting over her?

'See!' Kim yelled, the waves snatching at her ankles. 'See what you've done! Now make it stop!' It was for both of them. Nothing was enough unless it was over.

She scrambled over the pebbles. Fizzy's hand was hanging down, small and discoloured. Kim closed hers around it. Cold. Soft but stiff as a dead hamster in a cage.

'Fizzy,' Kim murmured, the words breaking. 'Live! Fizzy, live!'

'She's alive,' Barry told her. 'She's breathing.' Kim felt his firm hand warm on her shoulder.

Kris was spent now. He passed Fizzy over and doubled up on the pebbles, his scrawny chest rising and falling. Barry's jacket lay limp beside a fag end and the plastic rings from a six-pack. Kim picked it up.

'Fizzy,' whispered Barry, covering her with the jacket. 'Breathe, darling.'

Kim shrugged off the towel and laid it down. Time to stop shivering and bleeding. Barry lowered Fizzy onto it, with the jacket on top. Washington added his own, charcoal on beige, pony tail dripping.

'The paramedics are here!' called the raspberry-haired woman, pointing up to the road.

'Thank you, Father,' murmured Barry, kneeling.

Crouching on her haunches, Kim reached for Fizzy's hand and squeezed. Inside her fingers, Fizzy's squeezed back.

The relatives' room at the hospital was quiet and bare. Kim lay across two seats, her head on Jeanette's silvered scarf. Inside her wrapped hands the heat had cooled, but spots of blood kept the bandage tight. Stitches were nothing. Kim played on with injuries, always had. Now with her eyes closed she shut out all of it, and all of them. Just like Fizzy had tried to do.

It was late and people kept telling her to take a nap, to rest and recover from the shock. How many hours now? Outside twilight must have edged into darkness. Kim heard

Jeanette click the fastening of her bag. In the silence the sound of metal joining metal, and the slap of plastic, felt strangely big. Kim heard her take out a tissue, blow her nose, wipe it, sniff, wipe again. *You could have stopped this*, she thought, *with less crying and a few growls. Better taste and a lot more pride.*

Opening her eyes just a slit, Kim saw Barry opposite. With his big hands on his lap, he seemed to be praying, his back straight and his shoes shiny. The creased jacket that had wrapped Fizzy was specked with Kim's blood and just a trace of the beach.

It's your fault too, thought Kim. *Are you asking for forgiveness?*

Kris didn't even know there was anything to be forgiven. His fault most of all. He was smoking outside but he'd be back – unless, of course, he had his passport in his pocket and did another runner.

Kris Braddock: stupid, but not so useless or weedy. Not obvious casting for the hero role, but he'd better milk it while he could, because like a Facebook status it would change soon enough. In any case, who sent her out to sea in some slapper's bikini? Who dragged her off to Southend in the first place? Who was still a waste of space whatever else Fizzy wanted him to be?

Laura and Ro were taking their turn in the ward, but Kim was impatient for hers. There were things she wanted to know, but she wouldn't ask the questions, not now and maybe never – and not only because she knew the answers.

Part of her felt angry with Fizzy too. For not trusting her like they'd promised each other they would. But mostly for trying to die.

Kim heard the door. She sat up, slouching, eyes narrowed. Kris approached, face so straight he looked like a man at last, not a boy. The sea had sculpted him small and wrinkled, but now his clothes hung loose again. He'd got his slouch back. Barry kept his eyes closed, but Kim was sure he picked him up on his radar. His body bulked tall in the chair.

Jeanette shifted and Kris sat down.

'Daisies?' Kim asked. 'Don't tell me you forgot.'

He pulled them from his jacket pocket, warm and squashed and faintly smoky. Smoothing them a little, Kim began to make the slits and thread them together. He'd picked enough, just about. It was good to keep her eyes down, to concentrate on the trickiness of it, even if it spared him the third degree he deserved. Kris might have remembered his daughter at the very last minute, but only because she tackled him, stopped his fists like a teacher in the playground and shouted in his twisted little fight-face. It didn't mean he was off the hook. He deserved to dangle.

Damon walked back into the room after a trip to the Men's. Kim gave him a smile and looked at the seat next to hers. Barry wouldn't like him using it, but just at the moment her brother could talk to her about whatever the hell he wanted – Formula One, Spider-Man, even Moses or Solomon. He sat down.

'All right, bro?'

Damon nodded. 'There's a machine with crisps and chocolate,' he told his dad, but Barry didn't seem to hear. 'Is Fizzy all right?'

'She's doing well,' they heard, each one of them looking up as Laura and Ro emerged from the ward. Barry stood.

Laura's grey-whiteness had pinked a little and her mouth loosened. Ro gave Kim a thumbs-up.

'Heyyyyy,' said Kris. 'Cool.' He stood, nodding. 'Sure she is. I knew she'd be fine.'

'All she needed was rest, not fuss,' said Barry.

Kim looked from one to the other as they made and held eye contact. Were they going to argue again, about whether the paramedics were an overreaction? Kris, no match for Big Barrington, was suddenly interested in one of the medical posters on the wall.

Ro said the doctors made it perfectly clear that there was no question of wasting their time. 'All the obs are looking good now, but you don't take chances in situations like that,' she added, and the mothers both agreed. 'They're just waiting on a blood test, but it's only a precaution.'

Jeanette laid a hand on Laura's for a moment.

'If I can't see Fizzy, can I go to the snack machine?' asked Damon.

'Soon,' said Barry.

'Fizzy wants to see you, Damon, of course she does,' Laura told him, 'but she'd like Kimberlie to go next. After all, she saved her, in a way.'

Was that just a dig at Kris?

'I didn't,' said Kim.

Laura was giving her a grateful smile, but Kim couldn't smile back. She was too cold inside.

Barry rose. 'Let's go together, Kimberlie,' he said quietly, and for a moment she thought he'd try to take her hand.

Laura touched his arm. 'Fizzy wants a few minutes with Kim on her own,' she told him gently.

'Kim? That OK?' asked Ro.

Kim nodded and stood. She looked at Jeanette, who nodded too, and just said, 'Go on, honey.'

'Of course,' said Barry. 'Just a few minutes, then.'

Kim gave her blood father a look. Barrington Duvall was still too quick to give orders, and he needed to think about where they'd led.

'She'll be exhausted,' he added.

As if she hadn't worked that out!

'Snack then, Damon?' she heard Barry ask as the door closed behind her.

Walking into the ward, Kim realised she was feeling it again, her chest tensed, her breath catching. So when she found Fizzy sitting on the hospital bed, her back upright against the pillow and her legs straight, she felt silly. No tubes or monitors. Fizzy was fully dressed, down to the bare feet which were circling in the air as Kim approached.

Her shy smile reminded Kim of the first one at Trafalgar Square. Kim felt herself grinning, because for someone who was virtually kidnapped and nearly drowned, Fizzy looked well. She looked shaken, but whole and herself.

'All right?' Kim asked.

Fizzy looked at Kim in her pink jacket and pale, embroidered jeans. For a moment she heard the voice again, hers but not hers, swelling inside.

'You're wearing my clothes!'

'Yeah. Twins do,' Kim told her. 'Laura brought them, but don't panic, I've got no plans to nick them. Long story. Later, eh?'

'Oh, your hands!' cried Fizzy.

'Don't worry about them! Couldn't have you getting all

the medics' attention, could I? Anyway I asked first.' Kim could see Fizzy still looked anxious. 'This is about you, not me.'

'I'm fine. I just got cold and swallowed too much water. One of the nurses said hypothermia.'

Fizzy's smile felt difficult to lift and hold. The explanation was one she'd practised and only partly true. The other words she could have said, like 'nearly died', made her shiver again. 'Half way to Heaven' was better, warmer and beautiful. But too close to tears.

She wondered what Kim thought of her: stupid, pathetic, mad? Fizzy felt her eyes cloud.

'I didn't want to…' She stopped. There were no words. 'I just chose…'

'Yeah,' said Kim. 'Anybody would.'

'I've caused so much upset and all I wanted was to make it stop.'

Kim almost understood, but it was hard to imagine. Fizzy Duvall out of control.

'You have,' she told Fizzy. 'Made it stop, I mean.' Hoping it sounded convincing. Hoping the message would penetrate the thick, fair head and the thick, black one too.

'I knew the Lord was with me.'

'Least he could do!'

Fizzy had a fuzzy memory of Kris's head flashing in and out of sight like a signal, there and then not there, hidden by waves. Of his arms and a rush of new air, and float and flow at last.

'Dad saved my life,' she said quietly.

'Yeah,' said Kim, 'if you say so.'

The life was Fizzy's, so she supposed it was her call, her

say and her version.

'But he needed a tip-off,' she added. There was something called truth and Fizzy deserved it.

'I know. Ro told me. Thank you. You came to find me.'

'Don't get emotional on me,' Kim told her.

'My dad – Kris – he didn't mean…' Fizzy said, wishing her voice sounded firmer and her eyes wouldn't leak. 'He only tried to look after me.'

Kim stopped herself from saying he had a funny way of going about it. She supposed Barry had the same idea, with his own holy SAS squad scouring Southend with phones to their ears and God directing ops.

Well, they'd found her, and she was alive, and nothing was any worse than before. But it could have been. It nearly was. Kim wanted to understand.

'I'm sorry to cause so much fuss,' said Fizzy.

'Yeah, you troublemaker!' said Kim, but thought she'd better add, 'Nothing's your fault, all right? Don't forget it!'

'It was like a dream,' Fizzy said.

She was wondering how she could share it, but the best dreams never could be captured, and Kim wouldn't see what it meant anyway, not yet.

One day she'd tell her about dying: its light, its warmth and flow. There was a phrase she'd heard whispered between the doctors, and it shocked her to remember. But it couldn't have been 'attempted suicide'. She'd been in His hands.

'You can't give up, Fizzy,' Kim told her suddenly. 'You can't let go and fade away.'

Kim could picture the face, lights off, out of it. Old soap would have had more glow and shine than Fizzy, almost washed away by sea, limp and closed in, shut down.

The dead-hamster hand was on Fizzy's lap now, soft and warm again. Kim placed hers on it.

Kim knew Barry would be standing, looking at his watch. Jeanette might have insisted the sisters went first, but she'd be longing to see what she saw now, and it wasn't fair to keep her waiting. Kim remembered the chain around her wrist. She had to unthread two stalks before she could place it around Fizzy's and make a slow, awkward business of connecting them again.

'There!' said Kim, when it was done. 'It's a bit soft, like you, but it's a reminder.'

'I know.' Fizzy smiled. 'I haven't forgotten. I never did.'

Kim could have said, 'Yeah, right,', but she wanted to believe her. 'I got Kris to pick them while he was outside having a fag. He might be trainable after all.'

Kim glanced towards the waiting room, trying to detect the atmosphere through the glass and wall.

'Thanks,' said Fizzy, smiling to picture her dad rooting around for daisies among the concrete. 'Will it be all right now?'

'Yeah,' said Kim, wishing she could believe it herself. She gave the hand with the bracelet of daisies a quick squeeze. 'They can't have a punch-up in here.'

Suddenly she launched into a solo impression of a fight, the way she'd seen a dead old comedian do on ancient TV, with a hand grabbing at the throat. Fizzy's smile stretched big at last.

'They wouldn't fight over me, you know?' Kim told her. Even if it really was a fact, she didn't want Fizzy to feel awkward about it. 'I guess I'll have to wait for the vultures to do that,' she added cheerfully.

'Don't,' murmured Fizzy. She might have pointed out that by the time vultures land, the soul has left the body. But she didn't want the picture. She needed to remember the softness of the colours and the warm, glowing brightness that filled the water and sky and broke inside her.

One day she'd ask Ro whether people could have previews of being nothing but a soul, and on the way. But not just yet.

Kim saw her friend's expression change in a way that was hard to label.

'Don't let Barrington bully you,' Kim almost said. Fizzy would only deny that he ever did.

It didn't matter who thought what, in the end. They just had to live.

'See ya then, drama queen,' she said instead, and when Fizzy called, 'Thank you!' she turned her head just enough to give her a wink.

Returning to the relatives' room, she said Fizzy looked good. Her eyes made the point with Kris and Barry in turn: too good for them. Then she looked from Jeanette to Kris, in case they needed telling who they were and what their job was. Maybe they'd worked it out at last.

The two blood parents headed towards their daughter's bed, with Damon, who was half-way through a bag of crisps, tagging along. Kim stayed on her feet, disconcerted by Barry's smile.

Laura invited Kim to help her fetch coffees, and Barry said he'd love a latté. Kim walked just half a step behind her and supposed Laura couldn't help commenting on the paintings along the corridor. That was her way. Kim didn't bother with words, just sounds.

'Thank you, Kim,' Laura said in the café, as they loaded a tray. The way her blood mother looked at her meant she wasn't talking saucers or little plastic milk pots. 'I don't know how to thank you.'

'You don't have to,' Kim told her shrugging. 'Fizzy's…' She stopped.

What was she? Her sister? The other side of the coin? More like the other lung. It'd be hard to keep breathing without her. She never finished, but Laura said, 'I know,' so softly that Kim couldn't say, 'Yeah, right!' or 'Dunno how.'

'When you were in trouble,' Kim began as she collected plastic spoons, 'did Barry rescue you?'

Laura looked up from the tray. She smiled.

'Did he carry me out of the water? Yes. In a way he did. But we all have to save ourselves in the end.'

Had Fizzy tried? Kim didn't need to know. All coins had two sides. Kim knew she'd never break like Laura and her Jagged Edge. But she was a dancer's daughter, and she didn't really mind.

They had only just given out the coffee cups back in the relatives' room when Kris and Jeanette brought Fizzy out with them, one arm each. Like a row of smiles on a slot machine!

'Yay!' cried Damon.

'They say I can go.' She paused. 'Home.' She smiled at Kim, so she'd know the word couldn't make her cry.

Kim smiled too, but she waited and looked. No one put in a bid. No one asked the question.

Then people started talking, and there was an attempt

to sort out who was going in what Kim called the limo and who was going in what Damon called the dodgem car.

'Sweetheart?' said Kris.

Fizzy thought he seemed stranded between the two groups, murmuring together as if no one else would listen or had the right to know.

'I'm going to stay here in Southend with Shell and get myself some thinking space. Make it work this time, no foul-ups. Ro's got the address. You know I never meant to scare you. I'll never ever, I swear…'

Kim looked to Barry, but he must have read her mind, because whatever thoughts bubbled up in his own, he kept the lid on them.

'You didn't,' said Fizzy, because that wasn't it. She wasn't a child. Only Kim understood.

'I can do crazy stuff,' continued Kris.

Kim kept the 'Really?!' and the 'No kidding!' to herself.

'To state the bleedin' obvious,' Kris said, and looked at Barry before using a finger to zip his mouth. 'Sorry.' He paused and took one of Fizzy's hands. 'I don't mean for the swearing. Well, that too. Just sorry.'

Fizzy gripped his hand a moment so he'd know she meant what she told him. 'It's all right,' she said.

He held her to him, kissing her cheek, then her forehead and the top of her head where the curls had sprung back.

'Salt,' he said, licking his lips. 'But still the sweetest thing.' He sang a snatch of tune.

Ro stepped forward to shake the hand he offered. Fizzy hoped she'd measured him against the heart like she said.

'I'll keep in touch,' he said. 'If…?'

He looked around from Jeanette to Laura. Kim noticed

his appeal excluded Barry. Jeanette murmured agreement. Barry's nod was so low-key that Kim wasn't sure an auctioneer would notice it if he was bidding.

'Of course,' said Laura, 'but only…'

'In more appropriate fashion,' said Jeanette, the words enunciated with a Barbados slowness and clarity.

'Yeah,' said Kris, 'understood.'

As he pushed the door he looked back at Jeanette in her leopard skin blouse with a sudden grin.

'Dunno what you'd know about 'appropriate fashion', J!'

Then he raised a hand and headed down the corridor.

'I know more,' Jeanette called after him, 'than you'll ever know about manners!'

Or parenting, thought Kim. Jeanette lifted her dark, curvy eyebrows and sighed as if some little boy in the library had been naughty on the Elmer rug.

'He knows,' said Ro.

'I hope so,' Barry muttered crisply. 'Because next time…'

'There won't be a next time,' Ro assured him. 'He told me why and I believe him.'

'That,' said Barry, 'might not be wise.'

But Kim could see that Ro was brisk now and not to be interrupted.

'The rest of us may not have got there yet,' she said, 'but Fizzy's forgiven him completely. Unreservedly. And that's life-changing. It means he can forgive himself.'

Kim hoped Fizzy didn't notice the way Barry shook his head, because even a trainee auctioneer would spot that.

'There are precedents for that kind of forgiveness,' Ro told him, 'in your favourite book.'

One-nil, thought Kim. But she didn't know how far away she was, herself, from forgiving anyone. Except Fizzy.

Along the corridors Barry and Ro led the way. Fizzy linked arms with Jeanette, who talked about Southend and a gig in a pub where Kris had once played with the band.

Kim walked between Laura, who gave her a smile, and Damon, who was unnaturally silent until he offered her half his chocolate bar.

'Thanks, bro, but give it to Fizzy, eh?'

'She's getting the other half,' he said.

As she chewed, glad of the sweetness and even gladder not to talk, Kim heard Barry tell Ro behind, 'I've said it before, but you have a very romantic theology.'

'And it serves,' said Ro firmly. 'I choose it.'

'Southend does eels and crabs and mussels,' said Damon suddenly. 'Can we get some?' He looked round at Barry. 'What are mussels?'

The answer was detailed and led from one meaning to another – with jokes from Barry, who promised to let Damon feel his biceps, and spelling points from Laura, who didn't like the taste of seafood at all. Fizzy didn't join in; she didn't need to, not now. It felt like a different kind of float and flow.

At the door that led outside, Barry waited for her, and took her hand.

'Forgive me too,' he said, and even though she wasn't sure it was a question, she bit her lip and nodded, her hand warming in his. He was still waiting, and looked back at Kim. 'Both of you?'

Fizzy smiled at Kim and Kim smiled back, but not at Barry, not yet.

313

'I got it very wrong, Kimberlie. I'm ashamed.'

Kim hadn't been expecting that. He caught her off guard.

'Yeah, well,' she said. 'You got the bum deal – you thought you'd lost an angel and won The Crab.'

'You're a remarkable girl,' he said.

Kim was glad he'd noticed, but she hoped he didn't think that was all it took. Still, it was hard to know what to say. And Fizzy's smile was bigger now.

The moon was full and creamy, and across the darkness the car park was well lit. Kim had no idea of the time, but she saw Barry looking beyond the two of them, out into the hospital grounds. Kim followed his gaze. Not meerkat, not tiger, but sensing all the same.

Just a few yards away two men were face to face, and one of them had already been in a fight not so long ago. Kris Braddock – never gone for good.

Shell was covered up now, pulling him away and calling his name. But who was the other man? Not Hit Squad. They were all back in London cooling off, keeping their eyes on their own daughters. Middle-aged and scruffy, the guy wore a loose jacket and jeans over old trainers. Not a Sunday look. Kris gave him a shove and told him where to go. Not Sunday language.

Kim looked to Barry. Fizzy's look was asking too. As they emerged through the revolving doors, Kris saw them and put up a hand.

'Press!' he shouted. Not an instruction – a warning.

'Is that right?' said Barry.

It was action hero delivery to match the posture. Had he guessed? Did the guy look nervous? Because Kim thought

314

he should be. Barry couldn't have been scarier if he'd run at him with a gun.

The reporter stood his ground as Barry strode towards him, but he shrank into his collar all the same.

'Mr Duvall?' he asked. 'How's your daughter now? The daughter who isn't technically yours?'

'No comment,' said Barry. 'Not now and not later. If I were you, I wouldn't waste my time.'

He took Fizzy's hand and reached for Kim. His was such a big, smooth hand, so strong that Kim felt something pass from him to her, a kind of certainty. She didn't say, 'Let go of me!', not this time. He ushered them all like a shepherd, his body always in place – between them and the man with a camera round his neck.

'In the car,' Barry muttered, and clicked the doors open with his key.

As he gathered them outside the BMW, he nodded towards Laura, who seemed to understand. Hurrying towards the car Ro'd christened Edna, she called to Kris and Shell. They followed, though Kris kept looking back at the journalist, arms up, like a boxer who hadn't heard the bell.

Looking back, Fizzy saw that Ro didn't hurry to the driving seat. Instead she placed herself in the reporter's path, blocking it.

'Miss Glendenning? Reverend? Can I call you a spokesperson for the family?'

'You may call me what you like but I won't be doing any speaking, not to you.'

It was the last Fizzy heard as she stepped inside and sat on the back seat, Damon behind her and Kim last. Jeanette took the front seat. Barry closed the driver's door and the locks clicked down. He was fastening his seat belt now, and Ro was heading for Edna.

Following her, the man stopped suddenly at the sound of the BMW purring away, spun round and lifted his camera. A burst of light. Fizzy covered her face.

Not much of an image, thought Kim, picturing the shot. No starring role for anyone but the car.

No one spoke as the BMW glided out of the car park and the hospital grounds. Kim looked back and saw Ro's little car not too far behind. No sign of Kris or Shell, so they must be on the back seat. Laura's head almost touched the roof at the front.

'How, after all this time?' asked Jeanette. 'We told no one, except…'

'It wasn't Brad!' cried Kim.

'I know, Kim,' Barry told her. 'I spoke to Brad yesterday. He's a fine young man.'

His voice was level, clear as water. But when Kim stared at his face in the driver's mirror, his eyes were on the road. Ahead, behind, both sides.

'I can only think Mrs Vince-Jones,' he said. But then he shook his head. 'No. She's a curtain-twitcher but she knows nothing. How could she?'

'Dad,' said Damon, fidgeting next to Fizzy, 'what kind of writing does Billy's step-dad do?'

CHAPTER TWENTY-FOUR

There was no car chase, even though Damon kept looking behind as if he hoped there might be. But Kim thought James Bond would have a job to out drive Barry, with his eyes switching from the mirror to the speedometer and back again.

Fizzy slept right through, and Kim noticed that whenever Jeanette or Barry looked at her face, they did it with the same kind of smile: the sort they'd give a baby in an incubator. But maybe power came in all kinds of packaging. Fizzy had knocked heads together in her own helpless way – and she'd better not do it again.

Between them, Kim, Jeanette and Damon kept in phone contact with Ro and Laura, passed on tips from the Sat Nav via Barry and made sure neither car took the obvious route back to London. Had they lost the reporter that easily? Kim couldn't believe they'd let go of a story once they'd sniffed it out like rats in the garbage.

When Barry praised the Lord for darkness, Kim let it go, even though she didn't think God had arranged that just for them. She didn't feel like arguing, or talking at all, and she'd rather not think either, back or ahead. Now was more than enough.

She checked, but Fizzy was still asleep, lips slightly parted, head tilted to one side.

'You need your sleep too, Kim,' Barry told her in a

whisper.

'I'll never sleep again,' said Damon. He started pinching the flesh of his own thighs.

'Bro!' protested Kim quietly. 'Whatcha doing?'

'Billy's not my friend anymore.'

Kim would have felt the same. She could see he wasn't up to Fizzy's standard when it came to forgiving, but she didn't expect Barry to tell him so, almost word for word.

'Forgiveness is something we learn,' he said, 'but not always soon enough. No point in harbouring grievances.'

In the mirror Kim eyed him incredulously and saw him eyeing her back and nodding.

'Don't worry,' he told Jeanette, quiet but firm. He looked back at Fizzy, as she stirred in her sleep and breathed out – as if she was dreaming of robins and japonica. 'We'll be rock-solid. Without the human stuff they feed off, they've got nothing but a Homepage sentence.'

'They're trash,' Kim growled, but quietly for Fizzy's sake.

She remembered the vultures, but if they were back again in a different form, nobody was dying, and she hoped nobody would be showing them any flesh to peck.

'We'll have to be careful,' said Jeanette. 'They're hackers too.'

Even though Barry said he was sure journalists didn't all behave like that, he agreed they mustn't take chances.

'They'll want us to say how we feel,' continued Jeanette, 'and it's hard enough to find the words just in private.'

Kim reached forward and touched her shoulder.

'They don't need to know, and we won't be telling,' she said. 'You think Guy Fawkes was tough? They can stretch us on the rack and turn the thumbscrews! They can shower us in cash and offer us our own reality show!' Maybe it was a good thing Kris and Shell were coming with them, but not in the same car.

'Our lives, not theirs,' agreed Barry. 'There's nothing they can do if we put up a united front.'

Kim recognised Wimbledon now. She'd walked this street with her new family. Looking at the back of Barry's tightly curled, shiny black hair and then at his eyes, full on hers from the rear mirror, Kim decided to believe him. He seemed rock-solid already.

Waking next morning, Kim took a moment to process the clues. Duvall décor. Duvall space. Damon's voice, louder than an F1 commentator and her own body in Fizzy's pale pink rose PJs. On the landing she met Fizzy, looking as sleepy as she felt herself, in a lime green pair with big yellow daisies.

'Same body clock,' Kim said. 'We'll be having the same periods soon.'

A snore came from another spare bedroom. Kim grimaced at Fizzy. Kris? Or Shell?

It was odd, washing and dressing in the house that might have been so familiar but felt so strange. Eating and smiling took all the energy Kim had, so she was glad Damon's bacon and eggs kept his questions to a limit she could handle mainly with sounds rather than sentences. She did wonder whether he might be going to school, but it seemed no one was, not today.

'I was thinking,' she said to Fizzy, 'you could tell me about Mary M sometime.'

'She was a …' Damon stopped. 'It's rude.'

'She's the best character ever,' said Fizzy, smiling at Kim. 'I love her.'

'You love everyone,' said Kim.

Damon disappeared to his room early on in the story. Which Kim thought was just as well because Fizzy fetched her laptop, clicked off the headlines on the Homepage and found some paintings of her heroine, not always fully dressed. A sexy woman, often sad, but with light on her face. Did Barry know about this?

At the end of the story, Fizzy said that, according to Ro, Mary was really the leader of the church to begin with, but Barry didn't agree.

'All right,' said Kim. 'I'll do the play.'

'Yes!'

Fizzy's smile stretched right across her face. Kim had no idea it could. She hoped Fizzy understood it didn't mean she was buying into anything. She just wasn't kicking either, not today.

When Fizzy went up for a shower, Kim stayed in the kitchen and made more toast. Her hands still stung when she used them – and when she didn't – but she could manage. She'd never felt so hungry. Jeanette, Ro and Laura were in the lounge drinking coffee too far away to be heard, so Kim was all alone. She had no idea why it felt so good. But it was the softest, slowest morning she could remember for a long time, until Barry came back from his run.

Kim heard voices that made her sit up straight and turn to the door. Appearing in the kitchen, Barry Duvall was too cool to sweat or pant. The women gathered behind him in the hall.

'Good morning, Kimberlie. I hope you slept well.'

She smiled, one thumb up.

'I'm glad,' he said. 'Fizzy?'

'She's showering,' said Kim, and added, 'She's good.' That was something he needed to know.

He carried a folded newspaper, but she hadn't thought, not until he handed it to her at the table.

'Page seven,' he said. 'I didn't want you to see, but we've had enough secrets. We're together now.'

'But Fizzy may not be ready,' murmured Laura, sitting down opposite Kim. She said it like a question, as if Kim might know the answer.

Kim flicked the pages, her spare hand making a fist on the table. Laura's long, cool fingers closed lightly round it for a moment, pressed, then lifted. The piece was smallish really, and Kim might have turned straight past it. No faces, no names in big print. Just a photo of the ambulance, and a question: 'WHO DROVE HER TO IT?'

Kim swore and Barry laid a hand on her shoulder, softly, like Laura's touch. She closed up the paper. It was already damp and dark at the edges from the morning rain, but she'd like to see it burnt to soft black shreds.

'I don't need to read it.' She looked up at Barry. He'd take them to the cleaners, wouldn't he? Or pray for their souls?

'There was a note on the doormat when I stepped inside last night, and five messages on the answerphone. It's disconnected now.'

Kim could have sworn again. Every word she'd ever used for Kris felt way too lame for this. But she just about kept her growl behind her teeth.

'That's a follow-up to a story they ran in the late edition yesterday,' he said. There was growl in his voice too, but he was keeping the animal on a tight lead. 'I'm sure the Internet is carrying it too.'

'Yes!' cried Kim, because now she remembered it had been there on Fizzy's laptop: the same photo, same question, clicked away because among the celeb images it had meant nothing.

'No names but Felicity and Kimberlie, and the right hospital. Just about everything else is wrong. But I think we can expect visitors.'

'Lock Kris in the bedroom!' cried Kim.

'Don't worry about Kris,' said Barry. 'We've reached an understanding. Late in the day but timely now.'

Kim guessed all Kris understood was zeros on a cheque. Could Barry outbid the papers? Maybe Jeanette knew what she was thinking, because she gave her a small, quick shake of the head – as if she'd been wrong all along, not just at Brick Lane. And Fizzy had been right. But Mary M was a fallen woman as well as a saint. Maybe when it came to Kris, they were both wrong and both right too.

Kim knew she must keep up, because the adults were talking strategies and they hadn't been too hot on those up to now.

'If we all speak with one voice,' said Ro, 'find a line and just keep repeating it like a mantra, they'll give up in the end.'

Fizzy stepped into the kitchen so quietly she might have been a ghost.

'All we need is silence,' she said.

It was all they gave.

*

Half an hour later they stood in a chain by the window, looking out to face the journalists approaching down the drive. It was a line of nine, holding hands, semi-circling round to fit. Mouths closed, all of them. Kim didn't wink, even at Fizzy.

On the front door there were knocks and impatient rings, but they stood quite still.

A hand tapped on the glass, but no head turned.

In the hall words spilt through the letterbox like junk mail. Some were in-your-face and others smooth as syrup, just like Barry had said they'd be. But no one listened.

Cameras flashed in their faces, but they only blinked. Their faces were flat as waxworks, nothing to read. Whatever there was to see or hear, they only looked ahead at the clouds passing – Kim's performance tip, in the absence of the clock in the school hall. For the TV crew that emerged from the van, there was nothing but an image with no movement and no sound.

Kim and Fizzy repeated it in their heads, on a loop somewhere deeper than the thinking. One message filling nine minds, and nothing else: no fear or anger, no speeches, no footage. 'OUR STORY. OUR RIGHT TO SILENCE.'

End of, thought Kim.

Casting a quick glance sideways, she felt herself smile secretly inside. Fizzy shone. It wasn't really an end. More of a beginning.

The red leaves hung on, but it only took a light tug to send them spinning slowly down. Fizzy tried to catch them, but they melted into snowflakes under a Barbados sun, blazing through a spray of sea and sand. Like a holiday-maker on a Lilo, the worry doll gazed up blankly at unbroken blue.

Fizzy heard the sounds from the river before she saw the oars: double sculls keeping time, Kim first and Barry behind. The baby was crying, until Kris played pat-a-cake with a garden Buddha who laughed aloud and sniffed the flowers round his head. A long, thick blanket of rainbow wool wrapped them all on the sofa, Laura's needles clicking like drums, in time with Nelle's. 'Count the widgets, Damon,' Kim told him, waving a hammer over flatpack packaging. Brad floated down on a prayer mat. And Jeanette was dancing with Ro – was it jive?

Stretching, Fizzy woke. Sometimes it was hard to tell where she was, just at first, but once she'd put the clues together, it was always home. If she breathed in deeply enough, she'd smell Jeanette.

Outside, autumn was cooler than she'd dreamed it, the river darker, but the swans were whiter than any beach. If she waited patiently enough, they might take flight.

Orange and spices below meant a Saturday cake would soon be baking – Barry's favourite. So Kim was up already, probably stirring the bowl in her vest and shorts, planning to run along with him – and to beat him too, tomorrow if not today.

The best dreams were very nearly real.

THE LIARS' AND FIBBERS' ACADEMY
by Laura Foakes

Danny Quinn isn't exactly lying when he announces that his sister has been reincarnated as a dog.

No one believes him though, and he is quickly sent off to The Liars' and Fibbers' Academy – a special place for deceitful children only to learn how to tell whoppers more convincingly.

Aided and abetted by a girl who insists she's a mermaid named Derek, and Inigus Jowly, the school's mysterious caretaker, Danny is able to hoodwink his family until he finally learns the truth.

But this turns out to be more outrageous than any fib he could come up with...

ISBN: 978-0-9928607-3-8

Also available from Candy Jar Books

Tommy Parker: Destiny Will Find You
by Anthony Ormond

When Tommy Parker packs his bag and goes to his grandpa's house for the summer he has no idea that his life is about to change forever.

But that's exactly what happens when his grandpa lets him in on a fantastic secret. He has a pen that lets him travel through his own memories and alter the past. Imagine that! Being able to travel into your own past and re-write your future.

Tommy Parker: Destiny Will Find You! is an exhilarating adventure that redefines the time travel genre.

You'll never look at your memories in quite the same way again…

ISBN: 978-0-9928607-1-4

Also available from Candy Jar Books

SPACE, TIME, MACHINE, MONSTER
by Mark Brake

Of the fifty biggest-selling movies of all time, most are sci-fi films. Ten million viewers tune in each week to watch Doctor Who. And in the ever-expanding world of computer games, sci-fi titles rule.

Yet our futuristic world was imagined long ago. Dreamt up in the minds of movie directors and classic sci-fi stories. And now it's the world we live in. How did THAT happen?! As space tourism becomes a reality and the first human to live to 1000 has already been born, it's about time you found out!

Jam-packed with aliens and time machines, spaceships and cyborgs and the end of time. *Space, Time, Machine, Monster* tells you how sci-fi helped build the world in which we live.

ISBN: 978-0-9928607-7-6